Charity's Gift

❦ Hearts Reunited With Love ❦

a novel

by
Sherry Ann Miller

A sequel to *The Tyee's Gift*

To Karen,
Believe in miracles!
Sherry Ann Miller

Published and Distributed by:

Granite Publishing and Distribution, LLC
868 North 1430 West
Orem, Utah 84057
(801) 229-9023 • Toll Free (800) 574-5779
Fax (801) 229-1924

Cover Photo: FDM Enterprises
Cover Design by Tammie Ingram
Page Layout and Design by Myrna Varga

ISBN: 978-1-59936-009-6
& ISBN: 1-59936-008-X
Library of Congress Control Number: 2006924807

First Printing June 2006

10 9 8 7 6 5 4 3 2 1

Printed in the United States of America

Charity's Gift

❦ Hearts Reunited With Love ❦

a novel

by

Sherry Ann Miller

Dedication

❧

Charity's Gift is dedicated to Bill Morgan,
who sees beyond the grammatical errors
and cluttered syntax
in my writing and pulls miracles
out of the chaos.

May your conservative and caring nature
lead you into piles of lively commentaries.
You're the best!

Prologue

Juaniata listened carefully until she heard her daughter, Charity, fall asleep. The deep breathing sounds had not changed in the twenty-five years and three months since Charity was born. Silently, Juaniata slipped from her bed and knelt between her own and her daughter's twin beds.

"My Father in Heaven," she whispered. "It is only me, Juaniata Perez-Blake, troubling you again."

Tears seeped from Juaniata's closed eyes, but she ignored them as her heart trembled inside her chest. "It has been twenty-five years today since my Daniel went to America, still he has not come for us, as he promised. In his absence, I have raised our two children by myself. I have struggled, but I have also been richly blessed. My children are healthy and strong both in body and spirit.

"Yet, I am so lonely for my Daniel, Father. Sometimes my heart breaks inside me, and I cannot catch my breath when I think of the future and what it may hold for us. Where is Daniel, Father? Why have you allowed so many years to pass with no answer to this question?

"My mind returns to those first few months of our marriage. Remember when Daniel gave me that blessing? I had just learned I was pregnant with Charity. He promised me in that special prayer that I would give birth to five sons and daughters. Not just one son and one daughter. Many, many times I have felt the whispering of the Holy Spirit tell me that there are still more children across the veil, waiting to come into my home. Without Daniel, they cannot come. I fear, Father, that my unborn children will be sent to other parents.

"Please, Father please. Help me understand what I am to do. I am forty-three years old, and in a few short years, I will reach the age when women begin to stop their child-bearing. I cannot remarry while I am still married to my Daniel. Besides, I cannot marry another because my heart still aches for my husband. Where is my Daniel? Please send him to us, Father. If you cannot send him here, then send us to America so we can look for him there.

"I beg you, Heavenly Father, please answer the blessing Daniel gave me so long ago. I am still young and healthy enough to have more children, but how many more years I cannot say. I do not want to miss the smiling faces of my unborn children.

"Besides, it is not good for my grown children to agonize over that which they cannot control. Perry will not even consider dating anyone, he throws himself into his medical studies to the exclusion of all other pleasures in his life. And Charity told me today that she will never marry, that she hates Americans, especially the men. I know her feelings stem from Daniel's long absence. Charity could have married several times already, but fear holds her back. Please send her someone whom she can trust . . . and learn to love.

"Think not that I am ungrateful for all that you have done for me and my two children, Heavenly Father, for they are a choice blessing to me, and have brought me so much joy. But how can they move on with their lives if the question of Daniel's whereabouts hangs over their heads like a great, gray cloud?

"Daniel promised he would come for us. It has been twenty-five years since he made that promise. Forgive me, Father, for I am weary of waiting. My patience wanes like the summer sun in the evening sky. If you have taken Daniel home, it is time you should tell me. If he is still alive, I must go and find him. When we live on two different continents like this, how can I search for him? Show me the way, Father. Open up the windows of Heaven and pour upon me the answers for which I have pleaded these twenty-five years."

After closing her prayer, Juaniata remained on her knees and wept softly against the bed sheets, waiting for God's response.

After only a moment, she felt the Heavens gather close around her, comforting her, but Father's response remained the same: "*Not yet, my child . . .*"

Just when she thought she would hear the Lord's second echoing phrase, "*Not yet,*" as she always had until that very moment, she heard instead a still, small, whispering voice say, "*But soon, my daughter, soon.*"

Gulping great breaths of air in astonishment, Juaniata tucked God's answer gratefully into a safe corner of her heart.

Chapter One

"Shark!" yelled Tom from the swim platform, as he scrambled atop it and swung his legs out of the water.

Hans saw his companion's fins raise above the waterline moments before the sleek blue shark reached him. He didn't know whether to be grateful or fearful, for now the blank-eyed animal would turn its attention toward himself.

They had been filming dolphins moments before, but when the dolphins fled, Hans knew something was wrong. Unable to see the keel of the *Bridger*, Hans' Hallberg-Rassey sailing vessel, from his position underwater, he had just surfaced to watch a dorsal fin swishing quickly toward Tom, who had been tethered to the swim deck. Tom had used his powerful arms to pull himself forward and reach the stern deck in time to avoid a disaster.

As his eyes widened in horror, Hans saw the dorsal fin swing around, and slice through the water straight toward him. Hans was nearly five hundred feet from the *Bridger* and the only thing between him and the shark was the underwater camera held tightly in his hands. Hans would have to use this awkward piece of equipment as his only weapon. As the shark approached, Hans swung the camera forward with all his strength, banging the lense against the shark's snout as it charged him. Then, Hans swirled around so his back was toward the boat, and began kicking his way toward the stern's platform.

Hans swallowed a lump of fear that had risen in his throat, and finned his way backward toward the swim deck, a prayer in his heart that the Lord would help him keep the shark away long enough for Tom to snag him from danger. The shark circled three times, and each time Hans spun around, keeping his eyes on the shark at all times.

Charging Hans a second time, the shark came in for the kill, but Hans used the camera again to butt the shark sharply on its snout, which now started to seep blood. *Great! That's just what I need. Blood in the water. That will bring all the other sharks within a three-mile radius.* With bold determination, Hans thought, *I have to reach the boat, or it'll soon be over for me.*

Trying not to panic, Hans watched the shark as he continued to work his way back toward *Bridger.* Hans' eyes did not stray from the streamlined animal that obviously wanted Hans for supper.

With its snout now bleeding, the shark became angry. It darted straight for Hans several more times, trying to get between Hans and the camera, but Hans' reflexes were excellent. Adrenalin quickened Hans' reaction time. When he heard the slapping of the water behind him, he knew the swim platform was close. Tom was yelling, "Just a little farther! Hurry!"

The only way Hans could survive was to watch the blue shark unblinkingly, and use the camera as his shield. Hans dared not risk turning his back to the shark, for he instinctively knew if he did, that would be the moment the shark would attack him.

When the shark charged wrathfully, it managed to clamp its teeth around the camera lense, shaking its massive head like a mangy dog shaking water from its body. Hans could scarcely hold onto the camera, but intense fear tightened his grip.

Suddenly, Hans felt something brush against his back, and immediately realized that Tom had tried to grab him, but the shark's pull on the camera was too strong to permit Hans to stay close enough for Tom to drag him aboard. Fighting off frantic bumps from the shark, Hans chanced a quick glance at the swim deck and was shocked to see Tom had left it. Or had he fallen in? Hans did his best to keep his eye on the frenzied shark while looking around for his friend.

The struggle for the camera continued for several moments, but Hans was not going to let the shark have it, not because it contained valuable film footage inside, but because it was the only weapon he had to fend off the crazed, oozing animal.

Suddenly, a loud banging sound echoed in Hans' ears. The shark went limp almost immediately, its spinal column sliced in half by a bullet from Tom's Glock Forty. *That cowboy can shoot!*

Relief came in great steadying gulps as Hans felt his chest heave in and out and his heart steady itself once again. He grabbed the limp shark by the tail fins and turned it over onto its back, uncertain whether the shark was actually dead or only waiting an opportunity to bite. Hauling the six-foot fish to the stern, he handed the underwater camera up to Tom with a broad grin. "Thanks for that!"

Tom shrugged as though dismissing his marksmanship entirely. "You keepin' it?" Tom asked in amazement, putting the safety on his weapon, and setting the camera and weapon aside as Hans grabbed the gaffing hook and sank it into the shark's gills, getting a good hold on it.

"Blue shark is delicious," said Hans, laughing in giddy, almost delirious relief. "And this is one fellow I won't mind eating!"

"Dang! It's my turn to cook and I ain't never cooked shark before," grinned Tom.

"I'll teach you," said Hans, pulling himself up onto the swim platform. "But let's bleed it and clean it first, before its brothers arrive."

Tom helped Hans drag the shark aboard and retrieved a sharp knife for him.

"Watch it!" Hans yelled as the shark's open mouth snapped at Tom's foot, missing his toes by mere inches as Tom jumped backwards.

"He's still alive!" Tom bellowed.

"Not for long," said Hans, slicing straight through the shark behind its gills.

Blood splattered everywhere. Tom grabbed the deck's wash-down hose and turned it on, washing the swim platform and Hans' arms and hands as he severed the shark's head from the body and tossed it overboard.

"You ain't even shakin'!" exclaimed Tom admirably. "I almost lost my lunch trying to hold my gun steady enough to shoot, and you ain't even quiverin' a mite."

"I haven't had time," grinned Hans. "And I'll choose your steady aim anytime over a camera to fend off a shark attack." Hans removed the blue fins, keeping the dorsal and adipose for soup, then cut the shark into two huge filets. He skinned them, then removed the tough cartilage. It didn't take long, and soon the shark was packaged up into two-portion servings and cooling down in the freezer in the galley below deck.

In the interim, several new sharks had appeared, their dorsal fins slicing through the water around them as they fought one another for the discarded head and entrails. Once the swim deck was washed of all traces of blood, Hans turned on the engine and headed *Bridger* away from the new arrivals, avoiding the rest of their feeding frenzy.

Charity kissed her mother, Juaniata, goodbye as she threw her duffle bag over her shoulder, then stepped quickly down the street from her home in San Pedro, a suburb of San José, Costa Rica, where she caught the next bus headed toward Puntarenas on the Pacific Coast.

Although Charity loved her mother, Juaniata, with all her heart, she'd had to try extra hard to keep the bitterness out of her voice that morning when she awakened and went to eat breakfast with Juaniata in the kitchen of their small, two-bedroom apartment. Anger surged through her as she recalled her mother's prayer from the night before. *It's always the same*, she thought to herself. *For twenty-five years we've waited for Daniel to come find us. When will Mamá forget this foolishness? God has no control over Daniel's free will. Daniel's never coming. He's either dead or remarried. He never wanted me and Mamá from the start.*

Rich Americans had become the bane of Charity's life. A ball of bitterness welled up inside her chest and she fought back a thousand tears. She had spent her youth crying over the loss of her father, but now she was an adult, and she was just plain angry that Daniel had abandoned them. And he *had* abandoned them! Charity felt in her heart that this was the complete truth, regardless of Mamá's insistence that Papá had not done any such thing.

She settled herself against the windowpane and listened to the clatter of the old bus and the chatter of its occupants as she endured another three-hour ride to Puntarenas, where she would board the Park Ranger's boat for her long crossing to Cocos Island, where she would work for two weeks each month. During her time off, she often taught diving lessons at the local dive shop in San José to earn extra money for her brother, Perry's, medical education.

"Whoa!" yelled Tom from the foredeck as he grasped the flogging foresail moments before it could fling him overboard. He worked his gripping fingers down toward the clew, then tugged the sheet tightly, bringing the whipping sail back into control. With one hand clinging to the handrail for stability, he ran the sheet back through the traveler and took up the slack, making the foresail even more secure. After tying the end of the sheet into a stopper knot for safety, Tom returned with the knotted end to the cockpit.

They were two hundred miles west of the Pacific Coastline, sailing southward past Central America. At the outset of their voyage, Tom could do nothing more than hang his head over the gunwale and moan in misery. Apparently, those days were now far behind them. Tom had found his sea legs, and Hans sighed in relief. He no longer needed to concern himself over Tom's seamanship.

Fortunately, it wasn't too windy, a minor eight-knot breeze, but it kept Hans' boat, *Bridger*, lazing along at three to four nautical miles per hour. Two-foot swells lapped gently against the cutter as it sliced through the water with the grace of a sleek porpoise.

While wrapping the sheet back around the self-tailing winch, Tom mumbled, "Sorry 'bout that!"

Hans, still in awe of Tom's tenacity for change and adaptation, smiled from the helm. "It's all right, Tom. You're still learning."

"Yep, I am. But, we been at sea fer three weeks," Tom complained. "You'd think I'd remember somethin' as simple as a stopper knot by now."

"After yesterday's experience with that blue shark, you're allowed a minor slip now and then. Besides, it amazes me that you came at all," Hans admitted.

"I wasn't gonna' let you sail yer new ship by yer lonesome all the way to Cocos Island, was I?" he asked. "No self-respectin' cowpoke would!"

"That's precisely the point," agreed Hans. "You're a cowboy, yet you've learned sailing and seamanship remarkably well these past few weeks."

"I ain't had no choice," grinned Tom. "Once a fella' sets to sea, he either learns to sail, or he throws his useless self overboard. I'm still surprised at how fast my sick spell left once we were sailin' fer a spell.

I ain't had no inklin' of bein' sick since then, with exception of yesterday, but that was outa' pure fear."

Recalling the shark, Hans nodded. "To tell the truth, I thought I might lose my lunch, too, but I didn't have enough time to worry about it, did I? Remember that storm we sailed into with Abbot and the Admiral two summers ago? I almost lost it that night, too."

"God was testin' all of us that day. 'Cept fer His mighty miracles, I'd rather fergit about that experience. I vowed when the Admiral and I were aboard that spur-sized dinghy, waitin' to be hauled back to *Bridger's Child*, I was gonna' learn to swim or die tryin'."

"Then you've kept your promise to yourself. When we reach Cocos Island, we'll let you start off in the bay before you venture out among the hammerhead sharks."

Tom shuddered, apparently remembering yesterday's fiasco. "I ain't worried about me," he said bravely. "I'm learnin' to adapt well enough. 'Afore we left, all I cared about was whether yer new boat could handle the trip."

"This beauty can go anywhere in the world!" Hans said, pride filling his chest as he looked across the teak deck towards *Bridger's* bow. "She's exactly what I wanted, and I've got spare parts for nearly everything that might break down. The hardest task was telling the Admiral that I'd traded my other boat in on a Hallberg-Rassey 62 cutter. I didn't think he'd be too happy about it, since he gave me the ketch as a graduation gift a few years ago. I'm still surprised he took the news as well as he did."

"The Gospel has a tendency to mellow us," said Tom, "yer dad included. Besides, with the archaeological site finally operatin' in the green, the Admiral was probably glad to see you git away from there, regardless that you bought a bigger boat. I reckon he figures you ain't gonna' meet no women with yer face stuck in the ground lookin' fer artifacts."

"The Admiral doesn't hide his feelings as well as he did when I was younger," admitted Hans. "I suspect he'll only be truly happy with me when I announce that I am getting married. To be truthful, I'd like to marry and start a family, but every woman I've liked so far has been in love with one of you Sparklemans. Perhaps bringing you along on this voyage will be a disadvantage."

Tom laughed. "Naw, I don't think a good woman is in God's plan fer me. I reckon I'll be the only one of us not to marry."

"You're too hard on yourself," said Hans. "I've always had a feeling God is preparing someone special for you."

"Hey!" yelled Tom, "Look there!" He pointed way off to starboard.

At first, Hans thought Tom was just changing the subject, but then he saw it for himself, and his mouth dropped open. A huge, four-foot-tall fin sliced through the water, heading straight toward *Bridger*. Behind it, perhaps fifteen feet, came a taller fin, this one sticking above the waterline five to six feet. A lump swelled up in Hans' throat so quickly, he almost couldn't breathe.

"What kinda' shark is that?" Tom asked, his voice mixed with fear and wonder.

"It's a whale shark!" Hans exclaimed. Excitement bubbled up inside him like an oxygen tank's valve opened wide up under water. "The gentle giants of the entire fish species." He kept a steady watch on the whale shark as he swallowed the lump in his throat and yanked the mainsail sheet out of its self-tailing winch. Maintaining a gentle but steady pressure on the sheet, he flipped the automatic switch on the mast's roller furling. After the mainsail had rolled up tightly just aft of the mast, he slipped the sheet back into the self-tailing winch. Then, Hans pulled on the foresail's furling line until the foresail rolled back into its tidy cylindrical shape, leaving only the cutter's staysail up. As Hans reefed the staysail, he kept his eyes on the shark, which seemed content to scoop up krill as it made lazy circles around *Bridger*.

While Hans worked with the forward sails, Tom went below and brought out a rebreather tank with regulator, mask and fins for Hans.

"You're not going in with a tether?" Hans asked in surprise.

"Naw. I'll run the secondary camera from the boom." Tom didn't need to explain he was still a little leery of anything alive with shark attached to its name.

Within a few moments, all three sails were secured and the sixty-two-foot cutter slowed from four knots to crawling through the water at less than a half knot.

Tom dashed down to the work room one more time, where he grabbed two heavy cameras while Hans stripped off his shirt and deck shoes, then donned his scuba gear, including one of his new six-hour rebreathers.

They didn't need to rush about, Hans decided, as the whale shark swam right next to *Bridger,* apparently in a vain effort to get acquainted with it. Hans went aft to the swim step, adjusted his face mask and mouth gear, then stepped off backward into the comfortably warm water. As soon as Hans had himself acclimatized, Tom handed him an underwater digital camera.

"Watch out fer them other kinds of sharks," Tom teased.

"Keep your pistol handy," said Hans, swallowing the small lump of fear that had settled in his throat at Tom's words.

Tom patted the holster that Hans now saw was attached to his hip. Hans smiled in relief, then turned his focus on the whale shark nearby, forcing himself to forget the horror of the last shark with which he'd tangled.

Knowing whale sharks to be plankton and krill feeders from his research during his years of marine biology in San Diego, Hans could scarcely catch his breath. The lump of excitement he'd recently swallowed seemed to be constricting his lungs now. This was one of the great experiences for which he'd sailed over three thousand miles, braving sea, storm and man-eating sharks. He had always wanted to swim with and film whale sharks! He could hardly believe they'd found success so easily when they were still far from Cocos Island, where whale sharks were frequently seen swimming nearby.

Tom sank a camera overboard, slung from the boom with a purchase and line, utilizing the boom's preventer to stabilize the camera, and filmed all the underwater movements of the shark whenever it was within fifty feet of the boat. He watched the excitement below from a sixteen-inch plasma screen mounted near the helm.

The whale shark's sleek gray/brown body, nearly fifty feet in length, was freckled with white dots ranging in size from four to ten inches in diameter, but she had no claspers, so Hans was able to determine her sex right away. She was not afraid of Hans, quite the opposite was true, as she moved through the water with grace and skill, apparently aware of Hans' human fragility in comparison to her own massive strength. One swish of her tail in the wrong direction and Hans could have been killed instantly. But, she seemed aware of the potential for danger, and she kept herself in check, always staying just a few feet away from him.

The new rebreather was working perfectly, leaving no bubbles to scare the massive female away, but Hans still felt somewhat intimidated by her awesome size. As Hans swam nearer, still amazed at his good fortune, his camera filming the entire time, the whale shark soon allowed him to come alongside her cheek, as though they were the best of friends.

The shark swam with other companions, as well. A small school of pilot fish, their slender bodies bluish above and shading to white on their bellies, with prominent dark bars around their girth, accompanied her every movement. Some of the pilot fish were two feet long, many were smaller. They were apparently feeding on whatever sea creatures the whale shark missed while consuming its almost continuous meal. The whale shark swam with its mouth wide open, filtering krill, small schools of herring, hatchling squid, and other tiny fishes from the water. Its small teeth seemed to have no mandibular purpose, but a massive set of gill rakers strained the seafood, allowing the whale shark to swallow its meal while expelling the seawater out through its gills.

Hans' camera rolled non-stop as he filmed the whale shark circling him. He shot an entire roll of film as the whale played with him, swimming around him for over an hour not far from the boat. When the film ran out, Hans took the camera back to *Bridger* and hoisted it up to Tom, who was still filming underwater from the starboard side while grinning from ear to ear.

"Your film is probably finished, too," Hans managed to tell Tom. "Do you want to replace it?"

"I already did," Tom grinned. Then his eyes widened in alarm. "Look out!"

Before Hans could respond, he felt a gentle nudge and he turned around in the water to see that the whale shark had not finished playing. She'd come alongside Hans, apparently encouraging him to return. Hans grabbed onto her dorsal fin, and the whale shark towed Hans with her, swimming gracefully, slowly through the water, careful not to injure her new playmate. At one point, she dived straight down and Hans began to wonder if he would have to let go, as the automatic rebreather would only allow him to dive about a hundred feet deep without resetting the oxygen mix. The whale shark seemed to sense his rising panic, and made a sharp turn upward again, to a point only a few feet below the surface, where she allowed him to ride along her back for twenty minutes more. As he rode, Hans stroked the side of her body, amazed at how velvety she felt when he rubbed the skin backward, toward her tail. Rubbing the other direction, toward her head, her skin was coarse, like fine sandpaper. When the whale shark seemed to tire of pulling Hans around, Hans let go and swam toward the shark's face, staring in amazement into one of her small, dark eyes.

It seemed to him that they had connected somehow, in this watery world of blue silence, becoming forever friends.

Hans stroked her face just behind the eye, his own eyes filling up with moisture and amazement. The whale shark moved aside gently, lifted a pectoral fin as if to wave goodbye, then swam away into the deep, until she could no longer be seen, and Hans was left alone in the crystal blue sea. He waved for Tom to join him, surprised to see that the sailboat had drifted nearly half a mile away. Tom didn't notice him immediately, so Hans blew on the whistle attached to his shoulder strap.

When Tom waved back, Hans knew he'd been spotted. Tom fired up the engine and turned *Bridger* toward Hans. Within moments, Tom had shut the engine off, and Hans was climbing onto the wide swim step at the rear of the boat. Hans removed his mouthpiece and slipped out of the rebreather, handing the tank up to Tom.

"Sorry," he apologized. "After she dived with you, I watched fer her everywhere but couldn't find her. When you finally surfaced, I couldn't see you at all."

Hans nodded, "I figured that's what happened. I probably should have brought a flare gun with me, but in this bright sun, I doubt you would have seen that, either."

Relieved, Tom said, "I heard the whistle. I turned the boat toward the sound before I saw you waving your arms."

"You've got good hearing then."

"When you live in the mountains you gotta' listen. The slightest sound could mean a rattler, a bear or a stalkin' mountain lion."

When Hans was sitting on the swim step, his feet and fins dangling in the water, he grinned up at his friend and changed the subject. "Did you ever see such a magnificent creature before?"

"I ain't never seen nothin' like her before," Tom confessed. "You said they was gentle, but whoa! Dang, if that ain't the first time I've ever been speechless!"

"Me, too," agreed Hans. "I hoped she'd never leave us, but I guess she had other commitments today."

"Glad both cameras were ready and waitin'," said Tom. "Let's git the film exchanged so we kin film her again if she comes back. Maybe I'll stoke up enough courage to swim with her."

"Sorry I didn't trade places," apologized Hans. "I couldn't leave her."

"That's okay," Tom said, shaking his head. "Besides, I coulda' tethered on, like we planned earlier. To tell the truth, her size scared the polecat right outa' me."

"Intimidated me, too," said Hans. "It's amazing she seemed to know my limitations. She's an incredibly intelligent creature."

"Maybe she'll come back."

"I doubt it," said Hans. "Except for mating, whale sharks are thought to be solitary creatures. Our seeing her this time was a miracle."

"Maybe we'll see another'n," said Tom.

"Since they only get together when mating, I think we're lucky to have seen this one." Hans removed his fins and stood up.

It didn't take long for the two of them to exchange film in the second camera and recharge the rebreather down in the handy workshop Hans had designed into the forward section of the boat. Normally, the Hallberg-Rassey's bow held a v-berth, two heads and two small staterooms, one to port and one to starboard, just aft of the forward heads. Hans had eliminated one head, the v-berth and the starboard stateroom, and turned these into his workshop/ computer rooms, complete with workbench and all the tools and equipment he would need to research, film underwater, record sound, and analyze data.

Since it was Hans' day for galley duty, he quickly made some sandwiches while Tom turned the engine on and headed *Bridger* into the wind. Hans went topside long enough to help with the hoisting of the sails, though on this boat there was little need for the extra manpower. The mainsail had a top-of-the-line roller furling, and was released and wound with an electric winch. The foresail and staysail were both on roller furlings, and rigged for single handling. All sail lines and sheets were run aft, into the cockpit, to self-tailing winches, and Hans could have single-handed the boat all the way around the world, if he'd wanted. The truth was simpler . . . he enjoyed Tom's companionship. Of course, he would prefer to find a wife to sail with him, which would also please Hans' father, the Admiral, but until that day came, Tom was good company. Besides, Tom was an excellent cook!

Soon they were eating sandwiches made with homemade bread, sliced blue shark seasoned with a tangy citrus sauce and sprouts. Sitting in the cockpit, sailing southward again, a light wind on their starboard side, they headed southwest toward Cocos Island, which Hans judged was about another day away. At the beginning of their voyage, they'd had strong winds and made good time the first two weeks, eight to nine knots an hour. *Bridger* had covered over three thousand nautical miles of the voyage, with less than a hundred nautical miles to go. This last week had seemed to drag because they were nearing the equator and passing through the doldrums, a becalmed area cursed by sailors since the age of discovery. In the doldrums, many a man had to row more often than sail. A die-hard sailor, Hans refused to turn on the engine, even in the calmest weather, preferring to conserve their fuel in case they really had a need for it. However, a fresh breeze had come in early this morning, and they were making *Bridger* sail every useful moment of it, with exception of their brief encounter with the whale shark.

It had been Hans' lifelong dream to sail to the remote Cocos Island, ever since his youth, when he watched *600 Days to Cocos Island*, a documentary that had captured his young heart and endeared him to this kind of adventure. Actually called Isla del Coco, the island is owned by the government of Costa Rica. Cocos Island is designated as a National Park, and also a World Heritage site, so getting permission to visit for any length of time at all is a time-consuming and costly undertaking. Hans had submitted his application over a year ago, when he first commissioned *Bridger*.

Normally, visitors to Cocos Island are allowed eight days moorage in either Chatham or Wafer Bays. A maximum of twelve visitors are allowed in any eight-day period, with no more than four vessels moored in each bay. If camera equipment is brought in, the stay can be extended up to twelve days, but only during off-season, which began the end of May. Tourist season normally runs four months, beginning the first of February. Later in the year, it is considered too warm, and in the fall and winter, too risky due to the presence of frequent tropical storms. All visitors must arrive by boat or floatplane, because the tropical island is three hundred miles west of Costa Rica. There are no hotels or sleeping accommodations at Cocos island, and all tourists must live aboard their vessels. Tourist entry is extremely limited because there are no amenities, just a rugged, beautiful island that is inhabited only by the park rangers, the dense jungle plant life and a few wild animals. The only facilities ashore include cold water, rest rooms, and a couple of hiking trails. Still, the reservation requests keep pouring in and they are always fully booked nearly a year in advance.

The main tourist attraction of the island is the fantastic diving, though this is strictly regulated. Absolutely no marine life may be disturbed within a ten-mile radius of the island. To a fisherman, be he sailor or not, that meant ten nautical miles surrounding the island were off limits to anything but sight-seeing, with snorkeling and diving allowed only by special permit. Since *Bridger* was still more than eight times that far away from Isla del Coco, riding on the back of a whale shark had not been a big concern.

However, Hans was beginning to understand why tourists would not want to visit in June, July or August. The temperature was already a hundred-and-two degrees in the shade, and they had resorted to boat hats that covered their ears, necks and foreheads, as well as swimming trunks and t-shirts. Their skin had bronzed in the continual daylight sunshine, and Tom, who normally sported a 'farmer' tan had finally removed his t-shirt and permitted his lean body to tan, as well as his bare feet which, up until this voyage, had hidden deep inside cowboy boots nearly his entire life.

Wiping sweat from his brow, Hans took the helm after cleaning up the lunch dishes, while Tom went below to rest. Tom would be on the first evening watch, and he often took a long, afternoon nap. Hans enjoyed this time of day, which gave him a brief respite from company. Thirty-four years old, Hans had learned to enjoy his own space, his own time. Yet, he was infinitely lonely, especially since being introduced to the Gospel of Jesus Christ by his twin brother, Joshua. For the first time in his adult life, and to his utter amazement, Hans longed deeply for an eternal companion. He'd even put off going to the temple until the day he could take his bride with him. Still, he had his recommend in his wallet, just in case he met the woman he was meant to marry and wanted to take her to the temple right away. Sentimental though it was, Hans wanted to share the experience for the very first time with his fiancée, should he ever be blessed to find her.

Tom, on the other hand, though he qualified for a temple recommend, refused to request one from his bishop. He always said he'd get one when he felt he could forgive himself for his past mistakes. Apparently, it was going to take Tom a long, long time.

As for the directions his own life had taken, Hans realized that, although he had all the university education one man could probably stand in one lifetime, and job opportunities aplenty, his life had little meaning. He needed no money because his wealthy grandparents had left a third of their immense estate to him, which fostered within Hans no reason to seek employment. Hans' biggest problem was that he had no purpose, "no reason for being" (as Ed Sparkleman's wife, Alyssa, had pointed out to him once). Hans had no one to remind him why he should try to keep trudging on day after day. Hoping this trip, the fulfillment of a lifelong dream, might give him direction, Hans left San Diego the last week in May, taking Tom with him.

Having never completely understood the whisperings of the Holy Ghost, Hans didn't know what to make of the tingling sensations that had beset him when he'd sent his application to Cocos Island National Park headquarters a year ago, and finally heard back from them with the upcoming time slot. For whatever reason, the Lord wanted him to make this voyage. At least, Hans felt as though that was the message he had received. Listening for the prompting of the Spirit was all new to Hans, yet in his heart, he felt warmed and comforted. It wasn't the burning in the bosom that he had expected, rather it was more a comforting, tingling sensation that started in his chest and spread outward, accompanied by a feeling of contentment that all was right with his decision to go to Isla del Coco. Now, he wondered why the Lord was telling him this journey was so important.

Having Tom join him on the voyage was a bonus. Hans felt sorry for Tom, who'd been to the depths of despair and back again, and had a miserable time trying to find a woman who would trust him. Hans trusted Tom completely, but he felt there was more to Tom's story than even Tom knew. Tom had shared his feelings with Hans only once. During that discussion, Hans felt in his heart that something was not right with Tom's situation. How could a man do something so vile, yet have no recollection of it, even if he was inebriated at the time? Wasn't Tom's situation one that only played out in movies and on television, and not in real life? Hans certainly had his doubts.

However, Hans was the kind of man who thought things through clearly before voicing an opinion. Unless he was positive of what he was saying, he rarely said much. Tom, on the other hand, was a talker, which suited Hans well because Hans knew how to listen.

With the afternoon breeze dying, slowing the boat's progress even more, Hans felt a little discouraged. He wanted to arrive on time at Cocos Island more keenly than ever, and the doldrums would only hinder his progress.

Now that he had survived a brush with death in the form of a blue shark, and gone swimming with a whale shark, Hans was more impressed than ever with his decision to take this voyage to Cocos Island. The marine life that he knew from his youth while sailing and fishing aboard his grandfather's boat, *Bridger's Child,* instilled in Hans the desire he used to have about being a marine biologist.

Should Hans allow his dreams from his youth to become his reality? With the right woman by his side, he felt his answer could be yes. Hans loved the sea and its diverse assortment of creatures, whale sharks in particular. If he found a woman who wanted the same kinds of experiences as he did, Hans would consider himself the richest man on earth, even if he were poor.

The Lord had some purpose for sending Hans to Cocos Island and he felt ready to take on any challenge God prepared for him. Whatever reasons the Lord had in mind, Hans was anxious to reach his destination.

Chapter Two

Charity Perez Blake stepped out of the inflatable dinghy onto the beach at Chatham Bay on Cocos Island, a small tropical island, approximately four miles long and two miles wide, sitting almost entirely by itself three hundred miles off the western coast of Costa Rica, and a mere five-degrees thirty-three-minutes north of the equator.

The ocean's temperature at Cocos Island was around seventy-eight degrees warm, and Chatham Bay was a little warmer than that. The water was as still and reflective as glass surrounded on three sides by dense, heavily vegetated jungle dripping with morning dew. The boulder-strewn beach bordered the vegetation, and huge oysters clustered haphazardly all around the bay.

Warm seawater washed around her ankles and water socks as she helped the other three Costa Ricans pull their wieldy, heavily-loaded boat tender ashore. They were greeted by two rangers who were leaving for their two-week rotation in Costa Rica. Everyone spoke Spanish, although all of them could speak English equally well. The ability to speak both languages was a prerequisite in becoming a Park Ranger on Cocos Island. Charity's bachelor's degree in Ecology and her minor in Biology had helped, too, and the fact that she was a certified diving instructor. Now, Charity wished she'd gone into marine biology for her master's degree, but further schooling was out of the question for her. She was stuck working until her brother, Perry, finished medical school. Nearly all her wages were going toward helping him become a doctor, as were her mother's wages, and Perry had three years left. She shrugged off her discontentment. Working in a marine park was the next best thing to becoming a marine biologist. It would have to suffice. She felt extremely fortunate to have landed this job two years ago.

The park's administrator, José Ávila, and his wife, Teresa, were dedicated to preserving the integrity of the island and its marine life. With them, they brought their sixteen-year-old daughter, Árima, whom they were also home-schooling at their home in Zapote, San José, as well as on Cocos Island. Teresa and Árima were not employed by the Costa Rican Park Services, but José was devoted to his daughter, and in his chosen occupation, nearly anything was acceptable as long as the work on the island was completed properly. That he was now the administrator aided him in terms of what rules he could make and break. Bringing Teresa and Árima was José's most obvious rule broken.

Árima left the group and started searching the shoreline for snails. She had just been telling Charity, on the boat from Puntarenas, how delicious they were to eat, and how she had discovered them at a recent youth function.

"No, Ree-ma!" scolded Teresa, using the shortened version of Árima's name, when her sixteen-year-old daughter stood up with a live snail resting on the palm of her hand.

Árima pouted. "It's just a snail!"

"It's protected the same as the other sea animals," Teresa said.

José patted his daughter's shoulder. "Even we must follow the rules, Árima," he agreed. "If everyone who comes to this island eats our snails, soon there will be no snails left."

Árima straightened. "People all over the world eat snails. Even in Costa Rica. Here, we cannot."

"We can," insisted Teresa, "if we bring them from Costa Rica."

"And carry the shells back out with us," frowned Árima.

Charity smiled as she coiled the painter and laid it atop the inflatable dinghy. She hadn't minded Árima's antics two years ago, when she first started working here, but the past few months, Árima had changed from being an enchanting teenager to a rebellious one, and she hoped Árima would soon mellow. The problem was that Árima was moody. One day she would be happy and cheerful, the next day she would throw tantrums much like a spoiled child. *Aha! Teenagers!*

After exchanging greetings and reports with the departing rangers, the foursome gathered as much as they could carry with them and headed toward the park ranger's house at Chatham Bay. Another house at Wafer Bay would accommodate the other two rangers.

These two buildings weren't really houses at all, more like rudimentary cabins with tin roofs that echoed and pinged with every single raindrop that fell atop them. On Cocos Island, rainfall occurred nearly every day from June through January, which made sleeping under a tin roof almost a deafening experience.

Along the trail, Árima glanced back at Charity. "We've been given clearance to rid the island of its pigs," she announced.

"Great!" Charity responded. "It's about time. They've destroyed the root system of so many plants that the soil is beginning to erode badly in a few places."

"The men over at Wafer Bay are going to hunt them these two weeks. We're allowed to use one of the pigs they catch for a barbecue with the tourists, but the rest are supposed to be taken off the island to Puntarenas, where a butcher has volunteered to prepare them for distribution to the poor."

"And a worthy cause, too," said Charity. "I'm glad to hear it." A big concern for Cocos Island, in her mind, were the animal species on the island not endemic to it. Introduced by seafarers through the years, the animals that had established themselves on the island included pigs, goats, cats, rats and white-tailed deer. The rangers had been given permission to trap the rats and destroy them, but removing the pigs was another big step forward. The erosion caused by the pigs rooting about was especially evident on the slopes, where it rained nearly every day of the summer, fall and winter. Now, the rain had started to wash away the black soil where thick plants had once prevented such erosion. The runoff had already started to leave trails of slick mud in many places along the hillsides.

Within moments, José, Teresa, Charity and Árima reached the tin-roofed cabin and placed their duffle bags and gear inside. The inspection of the cabins was always done by José and Teresa. They quickly approved the condition in which their cabin had been left, then the couple took the trail over to Wafer Bay, a half mile away, to inspect the cabin there. During their absence, Árima and Charity returned to the beach. They found the two departing rangers had already left, after unloading the rangers' dinghy and leaving the new crew's groceries and gear well up on the beach for them. Charity and Árima gathered the groceries and gear, and carried as much as they could back up to the ranger's house. They made the transporting of food and equipment in three trips this time, which was a personal best for them both. By the time José and Teresa returned from Wafer Bay, all the groceries and supplies had been carried up and put away.

By evening, the foursome had eaten supper, cleaned the kitchen area, and were discussing the new arrivals for the week. Since it was the summer season, the hottest of the year, and perhaps the wettest, Charity had always hoped there would be fewer visitors to Cocos Island. She was not surprised to learn that the maximum capacity of twelve live-aboard boaters were still coming, but she was surprised when José announced the plans for the next twelve days at Chatham Bay.

"We only have one boat coming to Chatham Bay this week," said

José. "The owner has reserved the entire bay for twelve days, and he should be arriving sometime tomorrow. That will make it easy for us, but not so easy for the men at Wafer Bay. They have three boats that arrived today. And ten people. They will have their hands full."

"Why would someone reserve the whole of Chatham Bay just for themselves?" asked Árima.

"A rich American," explained José. "We must do our best to see that he enjoys his visit."

Rich American. The words sent tremors through Charity's heart. *That's just what this island needs!* It surprised her how possessive she'd become of Cocos Island since she'd started working there. It almost seemed like her very own island. And some rich American was coming to add his unwanted influence. It wasn't the rich in general that Charity disliked, it was the Americans . . . particularly the males.

"How many will be on the boat?" asked Teresa.

"Just two men."

"Both Americans?" asked Charity.

"Yes. And both single, I believe," said José, looking at the application carefully. "Yes, both single." He gave her a quick wink.

"Ooh," gushed Árima. "Maybe you'll find your mate, Cari."

Charity did not mind Árima calling her Cari. Nearly everyone of Costa Rican heritage did. Daniel Blake had named his daughter Charity, which in Spanish was pronounced Caridad. If only Charity could persuade her mother to call her Cari, as well. Since that would never happen, Charity smiled at Árima's fond usage, for it pleased her.

"I would never marry an American," Charity responded.

Árima pouted. "Why not, Cari?"

"They cannot be trusted."

"How would you know that?" asked Árima. "Have you had trouble with one before?"

"You might say that," agreed Charity, refusing to elaborate. "Since the Americans are staying twelve days, they'll likely be bringing cameras and diving gear?"

José nodded. "But only two men are coming, not enough to do all the filming themselves. Perhaps you'll need to help them, Cari. It will mean extra money for you."

"If they pay the highest price, I will," Charity agreed. "Otherwise, my services will be limited to giving them the tour and instructing them on our hands-off policy."

"Hands off *you*, too," said Árima, teasing.

"They'll find that out soon enough," agreed Charity.

Sleep found Charity late that night. She tossed and turned for nearly two hours before she could shut off the images in her mind. *Two rich American men!* How she hated them! It would take all her patience to remain civil to them.

Sighing in bewilderment, Charity knew why she loathed American men so much, but she would never admit it to anyone. Especially not her mother, Juaniata Perez-Blake. After all, Juaniata still believed that Daniel Blake loved her. *What a blind spot her mother had for Daniel Blake!* In Charity's opinion, Daniel Blake loved no one but himself. He was less committed than the typical American soldiers, with their "love them and leave them" mentalities. Tell a woman anything to get her in bed with you, that's what American men thought. It disgusted Charity! As though sex was the only ingredient in the mystical force called love. Of course, some Costa Rican men were the same, but having become dear friends with José and Teresa, Charity realized there could be more to marriage than she'd once thought. Now, she almost hoped that someday she would find a man who would love her, and want to marry her, who would never leave her, but would faithfully give his whole heart to her.

And if she did find such a man, she still would not marry him unless he could also win the hearts of her family. It was the custom in her country to respect the guidance of one's parents in matters of the heart, for they were older and wiser than the young.

In Charity's world, dreams of a man who could win her heart, and the heart of her mother, were exactly that. Dreams. Nothing more.

By four in the afternoon, Charity could see the sixty-two foot sailing vessel belonging to Mr. Hans Clark through her binoculars. She was standing atop Churches Hill, grateful the cloud cover had lifted and they would have, perhaps, a few more days without rainfall. Mr. Clark's Hallberg-Rassey could easily be seen from her perch, as well as the two men sitting in the cockpit, both of them drinking something from a can. Of course, it had to be beer, of that she was fairly certain. She'd never met a rich American yet who didn't spend half his money on liquor and the other half on toys.

Oh, Charity, control yourself, little one, she remembered her mother's voice in her heart. Feeling duly chastened, she realized she was acting childish. These men had paid good money to reserve the bay for twelve days, and their money was just as lucrative as anyone else's. If they were only from any other nationality, she wouldn't have minded.

The last Americans to visit Cocos Island had been a family of four, a father, mother, and two young sons. The father spent every moment he could get away from his wife's watchful eyes making passes at Charity, and this happened just last month. She'd finally had to threaten him with a confessional visit to his wife. Her rejection had only served to anger him, and he'd spent the remaining three days scuba-diving by daylight and drinking up a storm by night. The last night of his visit to Cocos Island, he became loud and obnoxious, and the other boat owners had complained. José had to go out in the dinghy at one in the morning and ask the American to restrain himself. The American refused to cooperate and was subsequently banned from the Island, while the two boat owners who'd endured the American's night of rampage were given three free days of extended stay at Cocos Island. In fairness, Charity had to admit that this one American was the exception to the amicable others who had visited Cocos.

Most of the Americans who came to Cocos did so by commercial dive boat, and those always anchored at Wafer Bay. Strong currents swept in and out of Wafer Bay, and the dive boats shuttled their divers around by dinghy to the various rock formations that surrounded the island, most of them south of Wafer. Chatham Bay, on the northern end of the island, was known for its more tranquil waters and rock-strewn, but beautiful, oyster-laden rocky areas interspersed with sandy beaches. Chatham Bay was usually reserved for those who also wanted to explore the island.

Looking through the binoculars one more time, Charity noticed the Hallberg-Rassey's name, *Bridger,* painted two-thirds aft along its starboard side. No doubt it would be the same on the port side, too. She wondered if *Bridger* was a clever play on words for a vessel that was bridging the gap between the mainland and other ports of call.

Bridger was an extraordinarily sleek vessel, a cutter with all three sails up, and a spinnaker as well, no doubt trying to coax every ounce of wind out of the skies. Judging by the four-knot breeze that was sweeping over the island, the vessel would probably arrive at Chatham Bay by sunset. Perhaps a little before that if Mr. Clark turned on the engine. Then Charity decided not; any man with a vessel like that would want to show off his conquering prowess by sail.

Charity was sorely disappointed two hours later when she heard an engine humming into the bay. They apparently picked up a mooring buoy, then turned the engine off. Mr. Clark would have to wait for José to dinghy out to the boat and check Mr. Clark's credentials.

For now, Charity would be content to prepare the evening meal with Teresa and Árima, which didn't take long. Before dark, José had returned, and they were sitting at the table eating a simple supper of sausage fried with black beans, rice, mango, papaya and spices.

"They will want a guide, Cari," said José as he spooned another helping of food onto his plate. "I told Mr. Hans Clark the rate you stated, and he didn't seem the least concerned. In fact, they would like both of us to guide them."

"Both of us?" she asked, surprised at this information. "Yes, one on one. It seems the younger man, Tom, is fairly new at diving. He will need a seasoned instructor."

"That leaves me with Hans Clark?" she asked.

"Yes," José grinned. "You should get along well with Mr. Clark. He is not such a cowboy as his companion."

"Tom Sparkleman is a cowboy?" Charity wondered.

"Let's see, how did he put it? Ah . . . Yep! Through and through!" he drawled in imitation of Tom's response to a similar question.

Árima pouted. "Why does Charity get to guide them? I know how to dive, too. I could act as cameraman."

"Yes," agreed José, "but with that impetuous frown, I doubt that you are ready. Besides, you have school work."

"It's June!" complained Árima.

"And school for you is year round. It has always been so, my pet."

"It's not fair!" she yelled, threw her napkin on the table and flounced from the room.

"Perhaps you should let her go with you, José," encouraged Teresa.

"In a day or two, when she has improved in her studies," agreed José, "and her temperament."

Charity smiled. Remembering days when her mother, Juaniata, had all she could handle with her own insolent daughter. Charity knew it would be a monumental task to get through the next twelve days without wanting to strangle Árima. For the first time, Charity felt sorry for Juaniata Perez-Blake.

Realizing that Charity's own attitude toward the two American men she hadn't even met was no less contemptuousthan Árima's attitude toward not diving tomorrow was a rude awakening, and Charity promised herself she wouldn't allow it to continue. The cheerful Charity she knew so well would have to return in the morning. She would have to bite her pride and do her best to make the Americans feel welcome and well-guided. Charity only hoped she could accomplish such a feat successfully.

Early the next morning, with her scuba gear, bag and fins at her side, Charity found her way aboard *Bridger* with José.

"Charity Blake, please welcome Hans Clark and Tom Sparkleman," José introduced her.

"Pleased to meet you," she said politely, holding out her hand and shaking Hans' and Tom's with as much enthusiasm as she could muster. "I understand I'll be guiding you, Mr. Clark."

As Charity spoke to Hans, their eyes locked and, to her dismay, she found herself noticing more of Hans' handsome features than she intended, including his chestnut hair, tall stature, broad shoulders and bold blue eyes. She felt an immediate attraction, almost a connection, or it would have been, if she had allowed it to surface. Stubbornly, she refused to acknowledge it.

"If that's all right," Hans agreed. "Tom will need a little more patience than I can manage today. I've wanted to dive Cocos for over a dozen years and now that I'm here, I don't want to wait another minute."

José went through the companionway and below deck with Tom to check out Tom's new rebreather, while Hans strapped one to his bronzed back. Then Hans helped Charity wrangle into her own outdated rebreather. Like computers, rebreathers were obsolete about three months after hitting the market, due to the incredible improvements in the newer models.

"I'm afraid mine is a dinosaur compared to yours," she said. "How many hours do you get?"

"Six when it's fully charged. Today about four." Hans answered. "We spotted some mantas en route and used up some air time just prior to arriving.

"Hmm. I'm lucky to get two with mine. Hope I won't crimp your style too much." She gave him what she hoped was a cheerful grin.

"No. Two hours is fine."

"Have you been diving long?"

Shrugging, Hans said, "A few years."

"Then I'm one up on you," she told him. "My mother started me out when I was eight. She used to love to dive. Of course, that was back in the caveman days when we had to use oxygen tanks. Thirty minutes. Tops."

"I started diving after rebreathers took over the market. I was too busy at the University before that."

"Really? What did you major in?" She asked, curious about his education.

"Archaeology, anthropology, marine biology, geo—"

"Don't git him started," interrupted Tom, coming up through the companionway after José. "He'll talk yer ear off."

"Really?" countered Hans. "I thought that was your area of expertise."

Tom blushed right down to his toes.

Charity forced the conversation back to the day's focus. "If you're ready, Hans, I'd like to spend about twenty minutes here in the bay, before I take you outside it. My job is to see that you'll be safe, and there are precautions."

"Of course," he said. "Did José show you my dive card?"

"Yes, and your hours are impressive. But I'd still like first-hand knowledge about who I'm up against." She held up a pack of underwater display cards for him to see.

"I have to pass off basic diving signals?" he asked, a hint of humor in his voice.

Charity nodded. "In the water, if you don't mind."

She passed him and took her position on the dive step, her back facing the open water.

"Ladies before gentlemen," he suggested, joining her on the six-foot wide, teak-inlaid step.

After preparing her gear, Charity quickly stepped backwards into the water, and sank immediately down to twenty feet, where she waited for him to join her. The water was remarkably clear and warm. Immediately, she spotted a pair of scissortail damsel fish she had apparently disturbed. They quickly swam past her, their dark tail fins resembling a pair of open scissors. A school of yellow butterfly fish, with their black-ringed mouths, flat, upright bodies and contrasting black band marking the base of their dorsal fins shimmied away, as well.

Diving came naturally to Charity. Breathing through her mouth was automatic, and she didn't even have to think about it anymore. She was completely comfortable in the warm, brackish bay water, into which two healthy rivers emptied. When she looked back, she found

Hans was almost beside her, floating vertically in the clear water, his hand signal indicating he was ready.

As they slowly sank to the bottom in forty feet of water, Charity held up a card that read, *I'm cold.*

Hans hugged himself in response.

Another card read *I'm out of air.*

Hans moved his open hand in a sweeping motion across his neck.

Charity tried another card: *Help. I need aid or assistance.*

Opening his left hand palm up, Hans' closed right fist slapped into the left palm, repeatedly.

After several more cards that read: *Go right. Go left. Danger. Stop. Let's surface. Let's buddy breathe. I'm okay. Are you okay? Something is wrong.* Charity signaled that they should go back up to the boat.

Hans touched her arm. *No,* he signaled. In sign language, he asked, *Don't you want me to pass off anything else?* His hands and arms moved fluidly in the aquamarine water. It was almost like a dance, the way he spoke to her in sign language, and Charity was surprised at how much she enjoyed it.

Charity gave him a thumbs up, then signed, *No, it looks like you've mastered everything just fine.*

You can sign, too! he signed in amazement.

My aunt was deaf, she answered. Once again, she gave him the sign for going up to the boat, and he followed her without further comment.

When they arrived, Charity climbed up the ladder and sat on the dive step where she removed her fins and dropped her mouthpiece to her shoulder. Hans lifted himself out of the water with his powerful arms and shoulders, then sat beside her. "First time I ever felt pressured during an exam," he said, giving her a smile. "Now, come topside with me. I'll show you on the chart what I hope to see at Cocos Island."

Nodding, Charity followed him to the cockpit, where he spread out a nautical chart of Cocos Island on the port settee. His skin glistened from the moisture and the sun, and she was impressed with his deep tan that set off the sky blue in his eyes.

She bent over and studied his chart. Hans had circled every outcropping and rock surrounding the entire island. Charity smiled to herself. He had planned everything out precisely, writing next to each outcropping what he wanted to see at each location, including the types of fish he might find there.

Hans stood back, allowing her more room to study his notations. When Charity felt his eyes upon her, she straightened and frowned at him.

The look on his face told her quite clearly that he had been studying her, not the chart. His smile indicated that he also enjoyed himself in the process.

This only served to irritate Charity. Her intense dislike of Americans surfaced before she could prevent it.

"Hop in the dinghy!" she snapped angrily. "Let's get started."

Chapter Three

Strike one, thought Hans as Charity stepped into the inflatable dinghy and started the engine. Hans' biggest concern right now was Charity. He had unintentionally offended her and he wasn't exactly sure how he'd managed it. Most women seemed to enjoy a man's open admiration of them, but not Charity, apparently. Hans did not know how to correct the situation.

Tom and José were already exploring the damselfish of Chatham Bay, and Hans felt his friend was in competent hands, so he did not worry about him.

Charity, on the other hand, became a major concern rather quickly. Hans sank onto the starboard gunwale of the inflatable dinghy, then looked away as Charity opened the throttle wide and headed the dinghy out toward what he suspected was Manuelita Island, the first major outcropping on their counter-clockwise circle around Cocos.

Admitting to Charity that he thought she was a beautiful woman would not make matters any better, but he couldn't prevent his admiration any more than he could prevent the sun from shining. Her ebony hair she had braided from the top of her head to her waist in one long, beautiful, silky strand, which was held together at the end with a red ribbon that matched the color of her swimming suit, rebreather jacket, and fins. She had emerald-green eyes, bronze skin, and a trim, goddess figure that he guessed at about five-foot six-inches tall. Hans was also pleased that she had worn a modest, one-piece swimming suit, rather than the bikini style many women wore. Surprised that she didn't have the Hispanic facial features of most Costa Ricans, Hans realized that her straight nose, high cheekbones, pouting lips, even her defiant chin all said Caucasian, at the least. But her bronze skin, and dark hair said Hispanic. Her emerald eyes gave another hint as to her true lineage. Hans remembered her surname, Blake. About as British or English as you get, Blake.

Perhaps her father would be a starting point in a new conversation. Internalizing every situation and conversation was a habit with Hans. He agonized over it, weighing the pros and cons, and finally decided that he might get away with asking about her surname.

As he turned his head back to ask her, his eyes were drawn to her left hand on the throttle and he noticed she was not wearing a wedding ring. Of course, that meant nothing to divers because they don't ordinarily wear rings on their fingers when they dive. It's too big an attraction to fish who like to bite shiny, sparkling things, and a ring will often hinder the movement of a diver's glove. Hans saw no white tell-tale ring of skin around her left ring finger, either, which could only mean that she was still single. That was difficult to believe. She was too beautiful not to have had several dozen suitors by now. Yet, she didn't wear a ring.

Encouraged, Hans said, "Charity Blake, a pretty name."

"It's Charity *Perez* Blake," she insisted, emphasizing the Perez crisply. "And I'd drop the Blake if I thought my mother wouldn't have a stroke."

Strike two. "So your mother lives in Costa Rica?" he asked, hoping to change the topic quickly from her surname to any other topic.

"In San Pedro, that's the equivalent of an American suburb. It's not far from downtown San José," she nodded and gave him a timid smile.

Whew! That was close! "I've never been to San José," he said. "What's it like?"

"Busy," she admitted. "Lots of people and lots of color. Open air markets, street bands on the weekends and dancing in the streets."

"Sounds tempting," he said. "Tom and I are headed for Puntarenas when we leave here. Perhaps you might make a list of all the tourist attractions not to miss in Costa Rica."

"There are plenty of brochures if you want to see what the tourists see. They usually miss the best parts of Cost Rica, though."

"Then, perhaps you might make a list of the attractions most tourists miss?" Hans gave her a tentative smile.

"I might," she nodded. "If I thought you were going to stick around a while."

"You don't think we will?" he asked, puzzled by how she might have arrived at this inference.

When she didn't answer, he wondered if he'd struck out entirely, until she said, "Can you grab the buoy beside you?"

Hans leaned over and tied the painter to the buoy quickly as the dinghy bobbed around at the surface. "You have moorings all around the island?" he asked, thinking that might be a safe topic.

"Certainly. Boats are not allowed to anchor within ten miles of the island except in emergency situations. We installed buoys at most of the dive sites, to protect the coral and the sea floor. Each one of them is capable of mooring up to fifty tons, and we check the links twice a month."

"Clever," he said. "I understand that I am to touch nothing but rocks while we're diving. Was that your next bit of advice?"

"No, but it is a good point. Fines for damaging coral or sea life can get pretty severe. The only reason you would touch the rocks, would be to protect yourself from a predator, usually a shark."

"Have you had any shark attacks at Cocos Island?"

"Only one that I know about," she said, "but it happened several years ago. As long as the divers use caution, they're relatively safe."

"This is Manuelita Island, isn't it?" Hans asked, indicating the small outcropping of rock, jungle and moss closest to them.

"Yes, home to a wide variety of sea life. We're going to stay on the east side of the island for this dive."

"Because. . . ?" he left the question open.

"It's closest, and I have only ninety minutes of air in my rebreather."

Hans nodded, though he was disappointed. Tomorrow, he would suggest that Charity use one of his spare rebreathers back aboard *Bridger.*

"We might see a few white tip and hammerhead sharks that circle Manuelita Island," she cautioned. "Give them a wide berth. We'll try to stay below them, near the bottom rocks which we can dart behind if the need arises. This is usually the safest way to dive these waters." Charity spit into her mask, smeared it around, rinsed it with seawater, and put the mask on her face. Then, she bit into her mouthpiece, giving Hans the thumbs up sign.

Following her example, Hans was soon sinking through the clear, turquoise waters toward the bottom. Circling around slowly, he saw no sign of sharks anywhere, but he did see a tremendous variety of fish. Silvery, Pacific crevalle jacks made a close pass to investigate them. Schools of grunts, some with silver bodies and yellow tails, others with yellow bodies and black and white stripes down their sides, surrounded them as though they were just another obstacle in their course around the island. Blue and yellow striped Mexican goatfish retreated slowly away from them as they approached. Occasionally, a small-toothed jobfish, with its large and slightly down-turned mouth frowned at them, as though disturbed at their presence. The solitary grayish-green puffer, with its white spots and dark rings around the dorsal fins inflated itself rapidly by drawing in water, apparently feeling threatened by their presence. Feeding on sponges, a small school of Moorish idols with their elongated dorsal fins that trailed behind them several inches caught Hans' attention as they competed with a sea urchin for space.

The sea floor was covered in shallow, orange plate corals that gently waved in the surging sea. Hans noticed a strong current, and found he had to work his legs much harder to stay in one place than he had to in Chatham Bay.

As they explored the corals and rocks, Hans felt his interest focusing more on Charity and less on the amazing diversity of marine life.

Watching Charity dive was like watching poetry in an underwater dance of splendor. She had the grace of a mermaid, the speed of a dolphin. After several moments of admiration, he noticed that her braid had started to unravel, but she swam anyway, as though she hadn't noticed. Hans caught the red ribbon and placed it inside his rebreather jacket. Occasionally, Charity would turn to ascertain that he was still nearby, and her long, beautiful hair would float out around her in delicate wisps, as though she was surrounded and protected by it. When she wasn't checking on him, she seemed to swim in a world of her own. Charity was born for the sea, Hans decided, as her lithe body moved in fluid motion within its gentle embrace. Once in a while, she would point to a fish that she wanted him to notice, but truthfully, he hadn't found the sea life nearly as enthralling as Charity. He could hardly take his eyes off her.

When she turned around to sign to him that she was low on air, he signed back, *Let's buddy breathe another hour. Use my octopus.* At first, Charity hesitated.

Please, he begged. *We haven't seen any sharks yet.*

Reconsidering, she took his secondary regulator and placed it in her mouth. To keep her from floating away from him, he took hold of her left hand with his left hand, and put his right arm around her back, bringing her near his side. This would prevent the secondary regulator from being yanked from her mouth if she drifted away from him.

Charity began to swim beside him, leading him in a large circle around the eastern edge of Manuelita Island, exploring holes where zebra-striped moray eels gawked at them, past living lavender octopi that crept along the sea floor while searching for food.

The diversity of marine life should have astounded Hans, but instead, he was caught in the current Charity had unwittingly used to ensnare him.

Hans rolled himself and Charity over, so they were floating with their faces toward the surface, their backs a few feet above the bottom, their fingers interlocking. Together, they danced through the deep turquoise waters as one, moving their legs and fins in unison. They swirled around together, as though on the world's largest ballroom floor, floating across center stage with such grace and perfect timing that even the fish seemed to understand and make room for the divers to perform. This was a moment set in time, a memory encased in Hans' heart forever... this graceful dance beneath the surface, their fins a few feet from the coral sea floor, their hearts melding as one in the ocean's realm.

When Charity signed that they should get behind a rock barrier, Hans obeyed immediately, keeping her close by his side.

From their protected boulders, they watched in amazement as a small school of scalloped hammerhead sharks passed far above them, circling the island in their search for a snack. They were followed by a large school of small, silvery jacks that formed into a bait ball, and were so thick they blotted out the sun for a few moments. In their place came silky, white-tip sharks that darted among the jack ball and ate whatever happened to find their way into the sharks sharp-toothed mouths.

Holding Charity by his side, hand in hand, Hans had no fear of sharks or ocean. When the sharks were gone, they left their protective barrier and swam again as one, their fins inches apart, their legs occasionally brushing each other in a continual underwater dance.

Hans wanted this moment of absolute serenity and peace to go on forever, but their hour together slipped past them far too quickly. When his beeper went off, Hans knew their special moment was over. He didn't want it to end, but knowing it must, he studied the shallower waters and saw no sharks to worry about at the moment. Then, he pulled Charity up from the depths of the sea, by his side, and helped her into the dinghy when they reached the surface.

"That was incredible!" he gasped, taking off his mask and tossing it over the gunwale. Using his powerful arms and shoulders, he pulled, then pushed himself up out of the water and into the dinghy in one easy move.

"They're beautiful, aren't they!" she exclaimed. It wasn't a question, more a statement of fact.

Smiling broadly, Hans brushed his hair back with his hands, then removed his fins. "Unbelievable!" he agreed.

Untying the painter after she'd started the engine, Hans gazed steadily into Charity's deep, green eyes as she headed the dinghy back toward Chatham Bay.

Her long, ebony hair was swept behind her by the rushing wind, the air so warm it felt like they'd stepped in front of a giant blow dryer. She didn't seem to mind his watching her this time. It was as though she, too, knew something tangible and real had happened between them while they were twelve fathoms down. Something wonderful, spiritual and pivotal.

A still, small voice, way down deep inside told Hans that Charity was the reason he'd come to Cocos Island, the only reason the Lord had brought him here. With his spiritual eyes, he saw Charity kneeling across from him at a holy altar in the House of the Lord. This vision only lasted for a brief moment, a mere flicker across his mind, but its power would linger in his heart forever.

The Lord had sent Hans to Cocos Island to find and to marry Charity Perez Blake. That thought, more than any other, brought him abruptly back to reality when the dinghy touched *Bridger's* stern and Charity said, "We're back."

"Well?" asked Tom, as he reached out and took Charity's hand, welcoming her back aboard.

"It was great!" Charity exclaimed.

Hans continued to fumble with the painter a moment. He stood and stepped aboard the Hallberg-Rassey.

"We saw a school of hammerheads the size of kayaks," agreed Hans. "Reef fish of nearly every variety, and white tips feasting on a jack ball."

"We were getting worried," said José. "How did you stay down so long without running out of air?"

"I used Hans' octopus," said Charity, taking hold of the secondary regulator at Hans' shoulder.

"I've heard of these," said José. "They work well?"

"Great," said Charity before Hans could answer. "Of course, Hans was *forced* to hang onto me, otherwise the current would have separated us, and I would have lost the regulator. But, other than that *one* inconvenience, we had a great dive."

Her words were enough to shock Hans back into reality completely. *Strike three! And I thought she'd enjoyed that part.*

They said their goodbyes, but Charity wouldn't even look at him when she shook his hand. José agreed to meet them again later that afternoon for a tour of Chatham Bay's famous beach. Hans watched in agony as their dinghy pulled away from the Hallberg-Rassey. Charity did not wave or look back at him, not once, not even when they beached the dinghy and headed off into the thick greenery towards the park rangers' house.

Devastated to learn that Charity had not particularly liked having him remain near her side during the last portion of their dive, Hans went below for a cold shower.

Later that afternoon, Hans and Tom walked along the beach with Teresa, José and Árima while Charity remained in seclusion back at the tin-roofed cabin in which the rangers lived. As Teresa pointed out the rock carvings left by early seafarers, Hans could scarcely comprehend what she said.

His mind and heart were in turmoil because he had misinterpreted an underwater buddy maneuver into something it was not.

In the background, he could hear Teresa say, "Chatham Bay has one of the most unique guest books in the world. Inscriptions by sailors from as early as the seventeenth century are chiseled into boulders all along the bay."

Hans looked and saw a boulder that had chiseled into it:

His. Brit. Maj. Schr.
LES DEUX AMIS — 1797

Although his eyes saw the inscription, it did not inscribe itself into Hans' mind, for his heart was heavily clouding his thoughts.

What was that feeling he'd had on the dinghy on the way back from the dive? If not from the Lord, then from who? Surely, he hadn't imagined it. The stillness and smallness of the voice he'd felt was overwhelmingly powerful. How could he deny a feeling such as that?

Envisioning himself and Charity kneeling at an altar, however brief it lasted, was too real to him. Hans felt much like the prophet, Joseph

Smith, must have felt nearly two centuries earlier. He had seen a vision. He knew it, and he knew that God knew it. Hans could never deny it.

As a general rule, visions come rarely into a man's life, and Hans knew it. He would not back down now. He'd come too far to find Charity! Besides, wasn't she a challenge? Hadn't he been known his whole life as the twin who wouldn't give up? Somehow, he would find a way to touch her heart, to reach into her soul and show her what manner of man he could be for her. It was easy to persuade himself that the Lord intended them to be together.

The difficult part would be convincing Charity. In her mind, he'd already struck out. *It's only the first inning, though,* he told himself. *There will be other times for this batter to step up to the plate.*

Long after he and Tom had motored in *Bridger's* tender back to the gently moored sailing vessel, Hans remained deep in thought. Coming up with one scenario after another for how he should proceed with this new challenge, he wondered how the Lord would make it play out. Hans couldn't make a decision on which of his ideas would work best, and which was doomed to failure, and he spent much of that night in prayer.

With the dinghy secured to the stern by the painter, and the two men sitting on the cockpit cushions in silence for a long time, Hans didn't notice his friend growing restless.

Finally, as the sun was setting beyond the horizon, Tom said, "You know, yer gonna' have to talk about it sometime. What happened out there on yer dive with Charity? What's got you all festered?"

Hans gave his best effort at smiling, but he just couldn't get the grim set of his lips to curl no matter how hard he tried. Finally, he said, "Festered? What a choice repertoire of words you have at your command, Tom."

"I reckon festered is about as good a word as any," Tom debated.

"Somethin's eating at you, and you might as well spit it out."

Hans shook his head in abject misery. "I'm overwhelmed, I suppose. All those hammerheads out there."

"Yer not mopin' over no shark," insisted Tom. "If I didn't know you better, I'd say yer lovesick as a young pup." Then, as if a bolt of lightning had just struck him, Tom swatted his thighs with his big hands and declared, "I'll be a one-eyed polecat!"

"What?"said Hans, not even remotely interested in Tom's ramble, but trying to be polite.

"It's that Charity gal. She's sittin' inside yer heart, festerin' yer soul from the inside out!" Tom put his head back and laughed aloud. "Why didn't I see it before?"

Hans could not disagree with his friend. He just shook his head and commiserated, "Festering, hmm? For all the good it will do me."

"Yer right about that," agreed Tom. "She seemed to take an instant dislike towards both of us. She hardly said two words to me, and she was sure shootin' you down left and right."

"She couldn't wait to get away from me when we got back from the dive, either," Hans remembered bitterly. "What did I do to irritate her so?"

"Well," Tom drawled, "this time you can't blame it on one of us Sparklemans 'cause she don't seem to like me no better'n she likes you."

That was one point on which they could both agree, Hans decided later as he slid into the master stateroom and headed, once again, toward the shower. As the warm water poured over him, he only briefly thought how luxurious it felt to have a commercial-size generator and water-maker aboard, two luxuries he'd missed in the forty-nine foot Hallberg-Rassey ketch that his father had given him for graduation. Moving up to the sixty-two had given him courage to put to sea, as well. *Bridger* was big enough to feel relatively safe, rigged so that one man could handle it alone, and it had enough storage space for all the equipment he brought along.

Living aboard *Bridger* was much like having a luxurious apartment on the water. Hans enjoyed this kind of living, but he knew his lifestyle was not complete. Until he married, until he started his own eternal family, the joys of life were just bubbles of happiness along the way. And bubbles burst.

Hans was not so well-educated that he'd lost sense of life's true purpose. The hope that man should have joy came straight from the Savior. And true joy came from the spiritual side of life. Hans could not buy joy with all the treasures his grandfather had left him. Hans could not sail into joy with the finest boat and equipment money could buy. He could not film it underwater, or percolate it in a test tube. True joy came from earning celestial glory with your chosen eternal companion, the person you loved more than life itself.

Hans knew that true joy could not be had without both partners wanting it and working for it together. Charity had made it clear that she wanted no association with Hans.

No matter how hard he reasoned with himself, how didactically he resolved to overcome the conflict between Charity and himself, whatever it was, he always came up empty. The way his relationship with Charity stood right now, true joy was hopeless. His situation seemed so elementary it was laughable. One plus zero equals one . . . alone.

Chapter Four

Charity sat at the water's edge on a boulder and watched the sunrise over Chatham Bay, with its brilliant shades of fuchsia, lavender, pink, peach and orange dancing across the shimmering, reflection of the water. The view became a sweet memory she would always treasure in a special corner of her heart.

José, Teresa and Árima were still sleeping back in the rangers' cabin, and Charity had taken these precious moments to steal away and enjoy the morning without disturbance.

Yesterday, when she'd left *Bridger* and gone back to the cabin for lunch, she'd felt completely overwhelmed by all the emotions running through her. Hans had broken down her carefully structured defenses during their dive, and they had shared something incredibly real and spiritual together, even as they stared at one another on the way back to Chatham Bay from Manuelita Island. She couldn't say exactly what it was that they'd shared, but something that could be wonderful, yet unsettling all at the same time. Where had her resolve, that she would never get involved with an American, gone?

Knowing that whatever they'd shared would only lead to heartache and heartbreak, she had refused to join José, Teresa and Árima, as they went with Hans and Tom yesterday afternoon on their walk around the bay. Instead, she had filled up several buckets of water, added some heavy-duty soap, and spent the entire afternoon washing walls, windows, floors, cupboards, and ceiling fans in the reception room, then in the living and kitchen areas and in her shared cabin bedroom.

The visitor's center was divided into three sections. The center was used for arriving guests, and had a wall map of Cocos Island along the back wall, and brochures below it. A reception desk and a chair stood off to one side, and several chairs were grouped casually along both the side walls. The front of the Center was made of glass that was particularly difficult to keep clean, especially since there was so much rainfall on the island.

To the left of the reception room, a single door opened onto a dining area, living room and kitchen. To the right, three doors entered into two bedrooms and a unisex bathroom. Between the two bedrooms, and behind the unisex bathroom there was a secondary bathroom with shower that adjoined both bedrooms, for use by the cabins' occupants only.

Cleaning and scrubbing walls and floors in all these areas had taken Charity long into the night, and she had finally gone to bed after midnight, exhausted.

She hadn't slept long, perhaps five hours. The lure of the sunrise was too much for Charity to resist because she loved this time of day more than any other. She could hear the Cocos Island Cuckoo chirping off in the distance, and the thumping sounds of a pair of red-footed boobies doing a mating dance somewhere in the dense green foliage along the water's edge. A flash of green across the ground startled Charity as she caught a quick glimpse of a gecko racing swiftly along.

Charity's attention strayed out to the sailboat, *Bridger,* moored in the bay making a perfect backdrop for the rising sun. It was a remarkably beautiful boat, and Hans had outfitted it with every amenity possible.

The companionway opened and, judging by the dusty blonde hair, it was probably Tom who came up into the cockpit. Charity turned the other way, pretending she hadn't noticed, and hoped that Hans would not come topside as well.

Today, she would have no choice but to face Hans again. He had asked that Árima and Charity accompany him to Pajara Islet where he wanted Árima to film, and Charity to guide him in a dive around the islet that sheltered the opening to Weston Bay, which otherwise would be fairly unprotected from the North.

At first, Charity was tempted to ask Teresa to take the job, but when José told her that Hans had offered to double her salary, she couldn't refuse. Even in her proud Costa Rican world, the lure of extra money for a new dress for her mother or a pair of new shoes for her brother always won out over stubborn pride.

Charity stood and inhaled the damp, morning air. It would be much warmer in an hour or two, and she had a lot of diving to do today. She would need her strength. Quickly, she headed back to the cabin. Upon arriving, she started breakfast for the others, pancakes with chunks of papaya in a sweet mango sauce, and fried sausages.

Árima was first to join Charity in the kitchen. "It smells so good, I couldn't sleep another minute," gushed the teenager, as she took down the plates and started to set the table. "Can you believe how much money we'll make today?" she asked with a cheerfulness Charity found contagious.

"Yes, it will really help out," agreed Charity. "Especially since my mother is wearing the same dress to church that she's worn for almost two years."

"You're going to spend it on your mother?" Árima wrinkled her nose. "I'm going to get my hair permed at a salon, and maybe I'll get acrylic nails, as well. If I have enough left over, I'll also buy me some eyelashes and eyeliner. Father won't like it, but he doesn't realize that I'm old enough to date now."

"Ooh, does this mean you have a boyfriend?"

"No, but you know what it does to a man to curl your hair and dress up a little." Árima looked appraisingly at Charity and pouted. "No, I guess you don't. Your hair is perfect the way it is, you don't need makeup to attract any man. And, your skin is flawless,"she complained.

Smiling, Charity left the pancakes for only a moment and gave Árima a hug. "When I was your age I had greasy skin and hair, and several times I broke out with pimples. I felt like an ugly duckling."

Árima laughed with Charity who went back to the stove. "You're just trying to make me feel better. But thanks, anyway. I overheard Mamá talking with your mother one time. It seems that she has had to beat the boys away from your door with a broom."

"She exaggerates," defended Charity. "It was only one boy, and we were way too young to date. Anyway, I was only fourteen then, and plagued with hormone swings." Charity laughed, remembering. "You'd better wake your parents. The pancakes are almost ready."

Árima hurried into her parents' bedroom, and soon they were eating breakfast with gusto.

Teresa gave Charity a knowing glance and said, "Nice of you to clean the cabin yesterday. That Mr. Clark, he got to you, no?"

"No," denied Charity. "I was just in a cleaning mood. Besides, someone is supposed to be nearby in case a boater arrives."

"In the old days," said José. "Now, no one arrives without a reservation, and the seal of approval from the government."

"Still, there are emergencies," Charity insisted.

"They usually occur during inclement weather." José pursed his lips together, trying to suppress his laughter.

Caught in a cover-up, Charity confessed, "Well, I may like Mr.

Clark, but I would never marry him."

"You marry who you date, Cari," reminded Teresa. It was like hearing her mother chastise her when she was ten years younger.

"He's an American!" Charity protested. "If we spend some time together, so what? In ten more days he'll sail away, and we'll never see each other again."

"What have you got against Americans, Cari?" asked Árima, perplexed. "They can offer a lot of advantages to a girl trapped in San Pedro."

"Name one," challenged Charity.

"U.S. citizenship, for one," said Árima. "And if they're wealthy enough to reserve the entire bay, then money won't be a problem anymore. What about a big house, the American dream, two kids and a swimming pool?"

Charity laughed. "They promise those things for your kisses, Árima, but don't forget that they'll want your body, too. When your heart is completely filled with them, it is at that moment that your romance will all come crashing down around you, for they *will* abandon you! And what are you left with? Two hungry kids to feed and clothe by yourself, with no help from the father, whatsoever. American men walk away, Árima. Learn that lesson well, and you will never know the unhappiness I've seen."

José interrupted. "Americans have not cornered the market on abandonment, Charity. Men abandon women in Costa Rica, too. That is why our daughters must look for men of God to love them. A man who follows God's ways will love his wife forever, no matter what nationality." He took Teresa's hand as if to emphasize his point. "There are men in this world who cannot understand why anyone would leave their spouse, why anyone would stray from a love as strong and connected as Teresa and I share."

"Do you know what the divorce rate is in America?" Charity asked.

"Three in five marriages end in divorce."

"Hmmpf!" José snorted. "And you think the Costa Rican divorce rate is any better? I imagine you would be better off marrying an American, if abandonment is your biggest concern."

Teresa stood. "This discussion is getting out of hand," she said quietly. "Perhaps it is because we neglected to pray together this morning."

José nodded and bowed his head. Charity followed his example, as did Árima. Teresa remained standing and offered a prayer of peace for the park rangers, and peace for Charity and Árima. She then pleaded with the Lord to send to both of them men who would be true and faithful, and to help each one recognize that man when he appeared.

The prayer was very touching for Charity, and when ended, everyone hugged one another. "I am sorry," said José. "I worry about you, Charity. You are like part of my family."

"I know," she said, unable to hide the moisture collecting in her eyes.

"You need to work through these feelings," José suggested. "You need to learn to trust someone, sometime."

"I'll try," she agreed. "It's just so hard to reconcile myself with all that my mother has suffered since Daniel left us."

"That was more than twenty-six years ago," Teresa said, cradling Charity against her chest, hugging her as a mother would love her own child. "Besides, your mother has never given up on Daniel Blake, and you must not, either."

"Then, why hasn't he found us?" Charity asked, tears filling her eyes and spilling over. "In twenty-six years, why hasn't he even tried?"

Teresa shook her head. "In time, you will know everything. In time, Caridad, in time."

José rubbed her shoulder. "The brethren believe that Daniel died in Nicaragua during the war, and that is why he never came for Juaniata."

"Then, where's his death certificate?" she asked. "Who sent back my mother's letters that she wrote to him after the war?"

Shaking his head slowly, José said, "You know, when the Bishop recommended you for this job, I had a special feeling. You were sent here for a reason, Cari. Please trust me when I say that the problems you are facing in your heart will one day be resolved."

Nodding, Charity said, "I know. Across the veil, then I will understand why my father abandoned us. But, that doesn't help me now."

"God works His miracles in His own timetable, Cari. We must trust that He knows what is best for us." José's counsel was exactly the same as Charity's Bishop's two weeks ago when she returned to San Pedro from Cocos Island.

She sniffed and dabbed at her eyes with her napkin. "You surely don't think that Hans Clark is my miracle?" she asked them all.

José shrugged, Árima gave her a mischievous grin, but Teresa gazed into her eyes and said, "Only you can answer that."

❦ ❦ ❦

On their second day of diving, Tom and José continued in Chatham Bay, with the idea that during the next day, they might take on Manuelita Island. Meanwhile, Hans, Charity and Árima headed toward Pajara Islet.

Charity was not surprised to see that Hans had come well-prepared for diving. He had spare rebreathers that he loaned, one to each girl, so that they could spend an entire four to six hours diving, should they so desire.

Hans seemed very patient teaching Árima how to run his digital camera, showing her how to record moving film, as well as still shots.

While he taught, Charity studied the procedures carefully so that she could assist in the filming, if needed. She found it difficult to keep her eyes on the camera because Hans distracted her with his rugged, good looks. She wasn't even certain the term *handsome* would do him justice, with his wavy, chestnut hair, aquamarine-blue eyes, wide, strong shoulders, copper-tanned skin and slim body. Regardless of her attraction to Hans, here was a side of him she had not seen, his ability to interact with children. Of course, Árima wasn't a child anymore, not really. But, in Hans' eyes she was, and that was important to Charity. Hans had recognized that just because Árima was blossoming in feminine ways, in her mind she was still a child, and she still needed an adult to guide her. Charity was impressed by Hans' patience with Árima.

After the filming instructions, Hans and Charity were ready to begin their dive. Pajara Islet sat at the mouth of Weston Bay, and they arrived safely in the dinghy and tied up to the mooring buoy. As soon as they'd fitted their mouthpieces and masks, they fell backward over the side of the dinghy. Charity knew that Hans was going to enjoy this area. It always looked as though an entire cupboard of orange plate corals had been dumped down the south slope, and Charity showed Hans many of the moray eels that fed amongst the coral.

Meanwhile, Árima filmed them the entire dive. Following Hans directions, Árima would release one hand from the camera and turn around to make sure there was nothing behind her to concern her, like a shark. Charity had not told Hans that Árima had been raised in these waters, and she had a special affinity with sharks that Charity had never seen in any other person. Árima knew no fear of them, whatsoever, and some of them seemed to have a fondness for her. In fact, she had named several of the white-tips, and always looked for them whenever she dived. Truth be told, Árima was in a diving class of her very own.

Circling around the islet, the three saw green and hawksbill turtles rotate around a pinnacle to the west. Continuing on, they soon approached an eighty-five foot wall on the north side. Here they found a fat, ugly orange frogfish with mottled brown spots sitting on a ledge along the wall at about fifty-five feet down. It dangled its illicium, an odd-tufted lure on a narrow appendage, in front of it to attract smaller fish near its mouth. Its skin had flaps and folds of filament hanging off it, and it looked more like a coral than a fish. When they approached the frogfish to observe more closely, it opened its mouth and slowly hopped away to another ledge.

Everything Charity showed Hans seemed to delight him, and he followed her everywhere she went, looking at blue-striped snappers, thin, yellow, pipe-shaped trumpetfish, bright red, blotchy hawkfish. Every few minutes, Hans would turn back to make sure that Árima was still with them, and several times bumped right into her, apparently unaware at how closely she was filming the fish that fascinated him so.

About two hours in, Hans turned to check on Árima and noticed a young white tip shark approaching her. He signaled *Danger* by holding his right hand out in a tightly closed fist.

Árima whirled around just in time to get some great film of the shark approaching her. Árima signaled for Charity to join her.

Charity signed to Hans, *She's okay. This one's her friend. See the tag on the dorsal fin? Wait here and watch.*

Hans held out his hands and shrugged, but did as he was told.

Charity swam over to Árima and took the camera from her, filming the dance Árima did with the shark she had affectionately named, Atrevido, meaning daring, because this shark liked to play with Árima.

Atrevido liked to rub its backside against Árima's hands, over and over again. It would dart away, and come back just as quickly, as though daring Árima to chase it. When she wouldn't, the shark came back to her and circled her lazily, bumping against her with its sides. Árima reached out and took hold of Atrevido's dorsal fin. The shark struggled for only a second, as if knowing what came next. Árima turned it over and rubbed its belly from the chin down, back and forth, back and forth. The look on Atrevido's face seemed to be a cross between complete stupor and sheer ecstasy. When Árima finally let him go, he sank nearly three feet before he realized she was no longer stroking his belly.

When he came back to play some more, Árima grabbed him by the snout, shaking it slightly. After she let go, Atrevido left, swimming into the dark shadows of the sea, and didn't return anymore.

The entire time, Charity had filmed Árima's encounter, and when she turned around to see if Hans had enjoyed the show, he was directly behind her, closer than she'd imagined.

Árima swam over to them and took the camera back from Charity, who signed to Hans, *Are you okay?*

He gave her the thumbs up, and they continued around Pajara Islet until they were back at the hillside of orange plate coral. Then, they surfaced and climbed into the dinghy.

Looking at her watch, Charity was surprised to see that they'd been five hours underwater. It was nearly three in the afternoon, and this was the first time she'd spent that much time diving. Her old rebreather was only capable of two-hour dives. Amazingly, she felt no light-headedness nor any tingling sensations, and she was secretly pleased that Hans' rebreathers were top of the line.

Hans squeegeed his hair with the palm of his hand, away from his face. "You had me going there, Árima!" he exclaimed. "I honestly thought for a few moments that your shark intended to eat you."

"Atrevido would never hurt me," she said. "Not deliberately."

"I guess I should have told you," Charity apologized. "Árima and Atrevido grew up together here. This is her favorite dive site because she and Atrevido are such good friends."

"She names the fish here, too," he said, raising an amused eyebrow.

Árima shrugged and grinned. "I get along well with all the fish in the sea," she said, "except the hammerheads. They don't trust me, yet."

"I notice you qualified that," Charity observed. "You think you'll eventually get them tamed, but you'll likely be disappointed."

"I know they're like any other predator," said Árima. "I don't trust them, either. Nor do I trust most of the other white-tipped sharks. But, Atrevido and I go way back."

"How far?" asked Hans.

"Over two years," said Árima. "He was wounded, probably by a hammerhead, judging from the teeth marks, and I found him in Chatham Bay, struggling to survive. I made a nursery for him in the bay with a net, and nursed him back to health. Then, I taught him to fish for himself over at Pajara Islet, where the shark population doesn't seem as concentrated."

"Of course, we don't know what he'll do to her when he matures another year or two. He's still quite young, and has presented no posturing toward her yet," Charity explained.

"What would you have done today if he'd tried to bite you?" asked Hans, voicing some concern.

"Rolled him onto his back. You saw how docile he got when I did that. Then, I'd have stroked his belly until you were both safely in the dinghy, brought him to the surface and handed his belly-rubbing over to Charity to keep him docile until I was safe aboard, too." Árima started the engine and headed the dinghy back toward Chatham Bay.

Seeing a hint of dismay in Hans' expression, Charity explained, "We've gone over the regulations for shark safety with her many times, Hans. Believe me. She had another pet shark when she was twelve. Once, José had to help her keep that one docile until they were both safe. We're not totally irresponsible where Árima is concerned. We always have an exit strategy."

"And if you're wrong?" Hans asked.

Charity smiled at his obvious distress. "We can always go to plan B," she suggested.

"What exactly is that?" he wondered.

"Sharks have very sensitive skin. It senses vibrations in the water through its skin, and when you interfere with those vibrations . . . Well, we always carry these," Charity said as she removed a small stun gun from her weight belt. "In addition to stunning a shark, they send out an electronic signal that totally confuses the vibrations the shark receives. It takes several minutes to recover. That's the one area where we spare no expense. One shot from a stun gun will immobilize a shark for up to five minutes, depending on its size. Perhaps this explains why there's never been a park ranger bitten by a shark before."

"Still," Hans persisted, "a stun gun that size wouldn't have much impact on a large hammerhead, would it?"

"We're careful with hammerheads," she agreed. "We've never had to use a stun gun on one because, unlike some divers, we know when to back off, and when to stay out of the water."

"I suspected that was your reason for doing daylight dives," Hans said. "Have you ever done a night dive?"

"No, and I wouldn't advise a night dive to anyone, not even an enemy," Charity affirmed. "It doesn't make any sense to go in the water when the sharks are actively feeding, especially when visibility is near zero. I believe Atrevido could easily mistake Árima for food at night. Sharks have very good eyesight, something most people don't realize, but at night their vision is more limited. They identify food by scent, but mostly by vibration. When a shark bites a diver, its not necessarily because of the vicious nature of a shark, it's usually misidentification. Most shark bites are a one-bite occurrence. They will taste a human, usually with a single bite, when they've failed to identify one of us correctly, then they leave their victim without eating it because, frankly, they don't like the way we taste."

Hans nodded. "Unfortunately, sometimes all it takes is one bite from a shark to kill a human."

Charity gave him an encouraging smile. "Hey," she said, "It's more likely that you'll be struck by lightning than bit by a shark, whether you get in the water or not."

"I know all this," he agreed. "It's just that this is my first real experience with sharks from a diver's standpoint. It's a little unnerving, to say the least, to watch a four-footer caressing a young girl as though preparing her for his personal feast."

"That's what you thought Atrevido was doing?" Árima asked as she nosed the dinghy into the bay.

Shrugging, Hans agreed, "At first, yes, but when I saw that Charity wasn't afraid for you, I realized that she'd seen you do this before, with this same shark."

"Lots of times," grinned Árima.

This time Charity nodded. "Each time we come, she has me take her out to Pajara Islet at least twice, sometimes more often. It's one of the perks of working here."

"So how does this work, Charity? Do you and the other park rangers stay on the island full time, or . . . ?" Hans left the question open.

"I stay on the island two weeks, then I go home for two weeks. Of course, two days and two nights are always taken up with getting here and going back again, so that really only gives me ten days at home. All the park rangers rotate this way," Charity explained.

"Where's your home?" Hans asked.

"Here," said Árima as the dinghy's nose touched the stern of *Bridger*. "At least for you."

Charity raised an eyebrow and nodded a brief thanks to Árima when Hans turned his back to them to tie the painter to the boat.

Soon they were sitting in the cockpit, eating sandwiches that Tom had ready for them on their return, and sipping cold sodas. Surprised that they hadn't offered them any beer, as did every other boater that moored in Chatham Bay, Charity was secretly pleased.

It turned out to be a very pleasant day. Charity's talk with José and Teresa that morning had helped her be a little more polite today, a little less guarded. Hans seemed a nice enough man . . . *for an American*. He was good with teenagers, he had a genuine concern for others' safety, and he had cornered the market on drop-dead gorgeous, so that left Charity trying to find something about him that she *didn't* like besides his nationality. She hated to reject him just because he was born in the wrong country. Perhaps in the next few days, if she allowed herself to get close enough, she would find whatever it was about him that would be justifiable means for refusing his attention.

Whenever she looked in Hans' eyes, Charity could see his interest in her. If she spoke, his ears perked up and he always listened attentively, almost as if he depended upon her every word.

Yet, that wasn't really a fair description, because he was just as attentive to the others whenever they added something to the conversation. He seemed to know when to laugh, when to frown, when to tease, when to remain quiet. It was as though his mind was working, always working, trying to sort out the conversation he was in, figure out if people were saying what they really meant, or if there were hidden meanings in their words. He didn't add much to the conversation, unless asked a direct question, or unless he seemed to think that what he said would add something interesting to the subject.

Very little about himself did he share with them that afternoon, Charity recalled later that evening.

When José asked him what he did, he said, "Right now, I sail and dive."

"What did you do when you were back in San Diego, then?" José had persisted.

Hans had shrugged. "I'm a long ways from San Diego," he had answered.

His answers were polite, but he never told them anything more than they already knew. Hans' evasion seemed to get under her skin and nettle her emotions.

Tomorrow, she promised herself. Tomorrow, she would have to be more direct.

Chapter Five

By ten the next morning, Charity had led the divers to an area half a mile off Cocos's northwest corner, where building-sized boulders sloped down the south side of a deep chasm, and a three-hundred-foot wide channel separated an even more monstrous rock from a forest of pinnacles. While José filmed, the other three watched white-spotted eagle rays soar between gorges, their great wings lifting and stroking the water gracefully, but they gave them a wide berth due to the spines at the base of their long whip-like tails. Valleys greeted them, formed by huge boulders, monolithic statues of the deep. Schools of young hawksbill turtles paddled past them several times, circling them curiously, and numerous young octopi bobbed around on the rocks. At the entrance to the chasm, they saw a young whale shark with claspers, indicating its masculinity. A mob of dark gray to black mantas with white-blotched bellies cruised the abysmal channel below them, some with a wing span of twenty feet.

Since this was Tom's first experience in open waters, Charity paid particular attention to him, and noticed that he was enjoying the beauty of the sea almost as much as Hans had that first day, although with an almost comical expression of controlled terror in his eyes.

Hans, she noticed, spent a good share of his time underwater watching her, and for some reason, today, this didn't bother Charity as much as she thought it would. Then, she realized that she was probably studying him as often, and she made a conscious effort to attend to her guide services a bit more professionally.

By the time they were back at *Bridger*, it was nearing three o'clock. They snacked on cheese and crackers, and drank sodas together. José announced that they had all been invited to a barbecue. The Wafer Bay rangers had caught one of the pigs residing on the island, and were roasting it in the ground for a special feast. They arranged to dinghy over to Wafer Bay together that evening, bringing with them the side dishes that Teresa, Árima and Tom had cooked. The boaters in Wafer Bay were also invited to participate, and it would be an evening for everyone visiting the island to get better acquainted.

While Tom led José in a conversation regarding all the sea life he'd seen that day, Hans took Charity by the hand and asked, "Come with me?"

Charity nodded, and let him lead her forward to the bow. Hans sat down on the starboard side, his legs dangling over the edge. She sank down to the teak deck beside him. When she was seated, he slipped her hand into his.

"It's been a great day," he said. "Thank you."

"I've enjoyed it, too," she admitted, surprised that she really had. "And Tom was as fascinated as you were."

"Judging by the expression on his face, I'd guess that he was actually more terrified than anything else." He gently rubbed the back of her hand with his thumb.

Laughing, Charity nodded. "Still, he seemed to observe all the marine life with a certain bravado."

"Well, almost," agreed Hans. "However, I don't think he observed you quite as much as I did."

She smiled. "I did my share of observing right back."

"I noticed that," said Hans. "Charity, you're a great diver, and a beautiful woman."

"Thanks. You're not so bad yourself."

"That first day we were here," said Hans. "You didn't seem to like me much. Or Tom, for that matter."

Charity inhaled sharply at this astute observation. Sighing, she expelled the air from her lungs, wondering how to explain. She felt so comfortable with Hans, could she dare trust him with her feelings? Deciding in the affirmative, she finally said, "I did treat you both poorly the first day, and I apologize. I'd had a bad experience last time an American was here at Chatham Bay . . . making passes at me whenever his wife wasn't looking. It annoyed me, and I was worried that you two might be the same."

"I'm holding your hand," he pointed out. "You don't think—"

He almost released it, but she squeezed his hand and responded, "Not at all. It's different. Besides, you're not married."

"Ah, so it's only the men who stray that worry you."

"It's not only the married men who flirt," she admitted. "Mostly, it's the men who leave."

"Leave as in . . . leave the island?" he asked.

"No, I mean—the truth is, my father left my mother before he knew that she was pregnant with my younger brother, Perry. I was less than a year old, so I don't remember him very well. I do, however, notice the sadness in my mother's eyes when she thinks about him. She used to cry her heart out at night when she thought I was asleep. It hasn't been easy for her. She's had to raise Perry and me by herself, working every day as a seamstress, trying to keep us clothed and fed. My father was an American like you. Since he left, I've not met many American men that I felt I could trust."

"The old 'one bad apple' theory, hmm?" he asked.

"I guess so, but you don't seem like the kind of man who . . . like the American men I've had pictured in my mind," she said. "Just yesterday, José and Teresa were able to help me realize that not all Americans are scoundrels." Charity gave him a wide smile. "I decided I should give you the benefit of the doubt."

"Thank you," he said, stroking her hand with his. "Charity, I'm not the kind of man who trifles with a woman's affection. I'm the kind of man who stays the course."

"You say that," she admitted, "and I want to believe you. It's just that, I've always been afraid of ending up like my mother. I want much more from a man than my father gave us."

"Have you seen your father much since they divorced?" Hans asked.

Charity laughed to cover up her surprise at his question. Then she responded, "They never divorced! My mother lived in Nicaragua during the rebellion of the seventies. My father, I call him Daniel to separate him from the father I wanted and the man who left us . . . when Daniel's military unit was withdrawn from Nicaragua in 1980, he never came back for us. As near as we know, he finished his tour of duty and moved back to his home in Chicago. At least, that's where his mother was living in 1980."

"You've never seen him since he left?"

"No. Right after Daniel left, my mother's brother persuaded her to come to Costa Rica to stay with him, because of all the fighting in Nicaragua. He offered to take care of us until Daniel finished his military service. At first my mother said no. She trusted that Daniel would return. When we didn't hear from my father for two months, she accepted my uncle's offer, but she left our forwarding address with the man who owned the apartment we lived in, so that Daniel would learn where we'd gone when he returned."

"But, he never did?"guessed Hans.

Charity blinked the moisture back that threatened to collect in her eyes and shook her head. "No. I used to lay awake and pray that he would come home so he could tuck me in my bed at night. Just once, I wanted to feel my father hold me, to touch my cheek, to tell me that he still cared about me." The tears refused her efforts to hold them back, so she brushed them away with her fingertips. "But enough about me. Tell me about you. Where do you live? What do you do for a living?"

"I live aboard *Bridger*," he answered. "This boat is my home. I'm single, so I've never given much thought to buying a house. I like the freedom that sailing gives me. I can go and come when I please. I have to admit that since I graduated, I've been lonely. I've been looking for the right woman."

When he didn't elaborate any further, Charity didn't know how to react. Finally, she decided to change the subject. "What do you do for a living?"

He hesitated quite a long time, and Charity was just beginning to think she'd asked the wrong question, when he said, "I'm unemployed at the moment. I hope that doesn't disappoint you. If I had to choose a vocation, I'd probably want to run a research ship, and document the migration and biology of the whale shark. The creature fascinates me."

"Me, too," she announced, surprised to learn it. "I'd love to be a marine biologist, but unfortunately, I got my bachelor's degree in Ecology and my minor in Biology. I didn't realize how much I love marine life until I started diving Cocos Island three summers ago."

"Why don't you go back to school?" he asked. "I've heard they have a great marine biology program at the University at San José."

"I can't," she admitted. "It was all I could manage getting through what I did. Now, my mother and I are putting my brother, Perry, through medical school. He still has four years to go. Until he's finished, I can't possibly afford it."

"It must be tough having to squeeze every penny," Hans observed. "When my grandfather died, he left a small fortune to my grandmother. When she died, that was divided between my mother, myself and my twin brother, Joshua. I have no clue what it would be like to live as you have."

"We aren't poverty-stricken, if that's what you think," she protested. "We have enough to get by."

"I'm sorry," he apologized. "I didn't mean to imply otherwise. I was just thinking that you're fortunate to have learned the value of money, and appreciate it."

"As opposed to . . . ?" Now, Charity left the question open.

"Me, I suppose. I could live the life of a wealthy king for the rest of my life, just off the interest I make, and never touch the principle that my grandfather left me. What does money mean to someone like me?"

It was an honest question, but Charity did not know how to answer. After thinking it through, she said, "Believe me, I would know how to manage your money."

"But, you would never marry for money?" he asked quietly.

His tone was so sincere, it caught her by surprise. "I'm not that greedy," she admitted. "*If* I every marry, it will be for love, or not at all."

"So a man's financial stability isn't all that important to you?"

"I don't mind struggling financially," she admitted. "It's not been easy, but we've had joy along the way. The worst thing for my mother has been not having someone to share the burden. She's had to do it all by herself, and I won't live that kind of life. I've seen what it's done to her, it's worn her down. She has devoted her entire life to Perry and me, and she has no life of her own. If Daniel had come back for us, my mother would have had an easier life. She would have had his strength and his shoulder to lean on when times were difficult. His presence alone would have sustained her. Because I've seen that life from a child's point of view, I've made up my mind that I won't marry, or bring children into the world, until I'm absolutely certain that I won't have to carry the burden alone. Besides, putting my needs aside, it's so unfair to the children."

Hans nodded agreeably. "They grow up wondering, did they do something wrong to make their father leave? Were they unlovable? What could they have done different to make their father stay?"

He had guessed her thoughts completely, and it unnerved Charity. "Yes," she agreed. "And that won't happen to any child of mine. Even if it means I never have children."

"How will you know for certain that the man you fall in love with will stay with you?" Hans asked. "How can anyone be one-hundred percent certain?"

"He'll have to prove himself, somehow," she answered. "I don't know how, but I do know that he won't stand a chance until he proves to me that he is totally committed to me."

"That's a pretty tall order," Hans observed quietly.

Charity stood up, and encouraged him to join her. When Hans did, she reached up and placed a hand upon his rugged cheek. "I'll settle for nothing less," she told him. "I want all his love, or none of it."

When Hans nodded as though he understood, Charity wondered if perhaps he felt that she was asking too much. She did not know. But, she had told him the truth, and if he couldn't handle the truth, then he certainly wasn't the man for her, regardless how attracted she was to him.

❦ ❦ ❦

Later that afternoon, Charity took Hans on a hike to Aqujes Point, the northernmost tip of Colnett Peninsula on Cocos Island, overlooking both Weston Bay to the west and Chatham Bay to the east. Tom stayed behind to do some cooking for the barbecue that night, as did José, Teresa and Árima. As they hiked, Charity told Hans some of the history of Cocos Island, which was discovered in 1526 by the Spanish navigator Johan Cabeccas, and didn't appear on any nautical charts until that same year. Cocos is the largest uninhabited island in the world, and is second only to the Galapago Islands in terms of abundant marine life. And to Charity, Cocos Island is the most beautiful place on earth.

They talked like old friends and Charity began to feel more at ease around Hans. From his attitude, she guessed that what she had explained earlier to him about her hopes for a man who would love her forever, had not discouraged him. He had told her that he was the kind of man who stayed the course, and she would have to believe that . . . *until he proves different.*

The view from Aqujes Point took their breath away. They could see Paraja Islet, guardian of Weston Bay, clearly, and beyond it, the wild, blue Pacific Ocean. Sunshine sparkled like diamonds off the water. Great frigate birds with their bulging throats cawed raucously as they stole food from nesting, red-footed boobies, while white terns dive-bombed straight down into a huge bait ball near the surface of the water a few hundred feet offshore, coming back up like rockets shooting toward the sky, silver mackerel scad wriggling from their beaks.

Charity and Hans sat on a large boulder and continued their conversation. "So if you don't need a job, but you have all these degrees, why did you bother with a college education at all?" she asked.

"I like challenges," Hans admitted. "Learning is a fundamental part of who I am. It doesn't seem to matter whether it's learning in a formal classroom setting, or out of books, or learning something basic, like riding a horse, roping a steer, branding cattle. I'm not afraid of work, I enjoy it. I've got to be doing something all the time."

"I hadn't noticed you fidgeting," she said, surprised at his confession.

"I don't usually fidget," he said with a broad smile. "But, even when I'm sitting or resting, I have to be reading or listening or thinking about what happened during the day, deciding how I could have made the day better, or worse, or commiserating on how poorly I managed it."

Charity laughed. "You do seem to think things through before you answer my questions. Or anyone's, for that matter."

"Spontaneity isn't my strong suit," he confessed.

"Do you know what makes you analyze everything?"

"Habit, I suppose. Growing up with the Admiral, I've had to be cautious."

"The Admiral?" she asked.

"My father. My brother and I always called him 'Sir,' or occasionally we'd get by with calling him 'Father.' It's only been in the last few years that we've occasionally felt it appropriate to call him Dad."

"Your father must be military," she suggested.

"Retired from the Navy, but it's still inbred deep within him. Everything he does is regimentally set in stone. Schedules and sticking to them is how he lives."

"And your mother?" Charity swept her long, sable hair to her right side so it wouldn't interfere with looking at Hans on her left.

"We've always called her 'Mother' or 'Mom.' She's a special woman, you'd get along well with her."

"Oh?" Charity wondered, "What makes you think so?"

"You're both adventurous," he confessed. "You both love the sea." Hans reached out and held a strand of her ebony hair in his hand. "Mom would give her right arm to have hair as beautiful as yours, and she's determined that her marriage will last forever. She and Dad work at it every day."

"Really? How do they manage it?"

"Dad never leaves the house without kissing Mom goodbye, and she never lets him return home without a hug from her. He's always worrying about what he can do next to surprise her, make her laugh or bring her pleasure. She's continually anxious over whether he's eaten well, or rested, or if he's working too hard. They like to tease one another, but they take their marriage very seriously. To be truthful, Dad's a little rough around the edges, and Mom's a little soft. They balance one another out." As he talked, Hans reached around behind her and pulled her close to him.

Charity found it strangely comforting to sit this close to Hans, and she rested her head against his chest. "How long have they been married?"

"Nearly forty years."

"And they had only you and your twin. Joshua, is it?"

Hans nodded. "They wanted more, but it just never happened. Now, it doesn't matter, because as far as they're concerned, they're the parents of Tom and his three brothers as well."

"How does that work out?"

"Tom's father died a few years ago, and the Sparklemans lived across the meadow from Kayla, Josh's wife. Anyway, the boys and Kayla grew up together, and they're as close as brothers and sisters. When Josh married Kayla, we inherited the Sparkleman clan as part of our family, too. So if you ever hear me refer to Tom, or his brothers, Ed, Will and Abbot, as my own brothers, it's because there are ties between people that go way beyond blood ties. I spent the entire summer and fall with Ed three years ago, helping him run their ranch. With a little help from Kayla and the man upstairs, I was instrumental in getting Ed and his wife, Alyssa, together. And the summer after that, I spent with Abbot and Tom on an archaeological dig site in Northwestern Washington State. Last summer, Tom and I spent several months together at diving school and lived aboard my other boat while we got this one ready for sailing this year. The Sparkleman clan and I are just as close as Josh and I. Even though I've known them less time than Josh, we're all just one big happy family."

"It sounds great to have friends that close," she admitted. "I had a few friends at college, but after I graduated, they went their way and I came to work here at Cocos. My schedule doesn't include making ties like you have, unless you count José and Teresa. They're like substitute parents to me, and we're very close."

"I'm glad," he said, "because I think they're great people. José is such a thoughtful father, firm yet gentle, and Teresa is a jewel of a mother. Árima and you are very lucky to have them."

Charity turned and looked up at him. "I know," she murmured, thinking to herself that right now, she was very lucky to have Hans holding her the way he was, and looking into her eyes as though he never wanted to stop.

When his lips drew nearer, Charity thrilled to their first kiss, tasting his mouth upon hers and loving it.

Yet, she didn't want their kiss to become passionate. Not yet. She wanted to take her relationship with Hans slowly, until she'd had a chance to get to know him really well. Forcing herself to withdraw, she put a gentle pressure against his chest with her right hand, and he released her immediately.

Instead of complaining, like she'd expected from past experience, Hans gave her a gorgeous smile that almost melted her resolve. As if sensing the turmoil of emotions within her, Hans said, "We'd better head back. The barbecue will be starting soon."

Hans stood and took her hand, helping her up. Then, he stepped aside and let her lead the way. To keep from dwelling on the kiss that was still warming her lips and sizzling her emotions, Charity talked about the island and some of its unique features on the hike back to Chatham Bay. Anything to prevent Hans from taking up permanent residence within her heart.

By the time they reached Chatham Bay, both Hans' and the rangers' dinghies were loaded with food, and ready to set off. Taking the journey to Wafer Bay by boat was the quickest way to make sure the food arrived hot. Taking the trail would have taken forty minutes, but in the dinghies, they arrived in fifteen.

They tied their dinghies off on the inside stretch of a small dock at the edge of Wafer Bay where the park's patrol boat with its tall flybridge was moored.

Introductions were made all around, and a buffet table was set up outside the rangers' cabin, loaded with every complimentary accompaniment imaginable, from fresh fruit salad loaded with papaya, mangoes, fresh coconut and grapes, to curried rice, creamed corn casserole, baked potatoes, brownies, cookies and cheesecake. Tom had even brought his specialty, baked beans, which was an American tradition Charity had not yet tried. She found them deliciously sweet and very filling.

Charity didn't spend as much time at the barbecue with Hans as she had hoped because he was diverted by an elderly gentleman and his wife who were both from Germany. The man spoke only broken English, the wife only German. Surprised to learn that Hans spoke German fluently, Charity tried to make friends with some of the other guests while Hans spent most of the evening conversing in German. Meanwhile, Tom, wearing his boots, western jeans and shirt, and a camel-colored Stetson, was the center of attention for two young men from Guam who'd never met a real American cowboy before. Charity and Árima sat next to a Hispanic couple and their teenage son from Puntarenas, while the other guests intermixed and chatted amicably throughout the evening. They talked long into the night, eventually coming together as a group and swapping shark tales.

By the time they were headed back to Chatham Bay, it was pitch black, and they had to use their lanterns to light their way. The sea was unusually calm, the air still and muggy, portending to unsettled weather tomorrow.

Hans dropped Tom off at *Bridger,* then took Charity to the beach where she would join José, Teresa and Árima. When they arrived, he beached the dinghy, then stepped out and helped Charity go ashore.

She handed the leftover rice dish to Árima and told her she would be along shortly. Árima gave her a lantern and left Charity standing alone with Hans on the beach.

"That was quite the feast," said Hans, taking her hand in his.

Charity's heart quickened. "We usually have an evening meal about once a week with the tourists," she said, shrugging. "Everyone seems to enjoy it. Though I must admit, the roast pig was an excellent addition to our meal."

Nodding, Hans said, "And the cheesecake. I didn't know you could make cheesecake from powdered milk. Tom will be experimenting with the recipes he traded for the next month or two."

"He likes to cook," she observed. "And his beans were to die for."

"Charity," said Hans, as he pulled her hand close and kissed the tip of her fingers, "I really enjoyed our afternoon together."

"So did I." She looked up at him and was surprised at the depth of emotion she could see in his glistening blue eyes.

"We don't need to dive every day," he suggested. "Perhaps you'd like to take Tom and me to see some of those waterfalls we've read about."

"I'm here to guide you," she said, a little disappointed with his line of conversation.

"Actually," he admitted, "as long as I can be with you, I don't much care where we go."

Now, that's better! she thought to herself, giving him a wide smile. "Me, too."

Hans pulled her close and she enjoyed the feeling of his hands on her waist. He bent and gave her a gentle, though sizzling kiss, then stood erect and said, "I'll wait here until you swing your light. That way, I'll know you've made it safely to the door."

She thought for a moment to ask him to walk her, it was all of a hundred feet or so, but then she realized that she would want him to kiss her goodnight again, and there were three pairs of eyes watching for her at the cabin. No doubt Hans had thought of that, too.

"Goodnight, Hans," Charity whispered. "I'll see you in the morning."

"Count on it," came his reply, his voice a bit huskier than normal.

It was just the response she needed to warm her all the way up to the cabin, where she swung the lamp and watched him swing his in return. Then, she turned down the wick until the light snuffed out, and went inside.

Chapter Six

"That ol' chip on Charity's shoulder tipped off after that first day," observed Tom as he played a game of Uno with Hans at the teak table down in the spacious salon.

They had returned from the barbecue, and neither were sleepy yet.

Hans smiled. He had been thinking along those lines himself. In the last two days, Charity had smiled at him often, allowed their eyes to lock, didn't turn away when he admired her trim figure several times, and took his hand willingly, anytime he wanted. She had also let him kiss her twice. To his surprise, and his great relief, Charity's stance against American males had mellowed. Hans couldn't be more pleased.

Placing a three-yellow card on top of Tom's two-yellow card, Hans recalled every feature of Charity's lovely face, and how her copper skin made his own sizzle just beneath the surface. He was falling in love with her the more time they spent together, and this fact seemed more apparent tonight as he recalled their day together.

Dare he hope that Charity was falling in love with him, too?

The Lord had already told him that she was the right woman to marry, but Hans hadn't realized he would fall in love with her so quickly. Hans had rationalized that love between them would grow gradually, out of their day to day contact and interaction, during daily conversations and situations that would endear them to one another. Not so. Hans didn't know if it was possible to love Charity any more than he did right now, and the depth of his feelings astounded him.

Three summers ago, Hans had thought for a while that he was falling in love with Alyssa, who had married Ed Sparkleman, Tom's brother, six months later. Hans' emotions then were nothing like he felt now toward Charity. A delicious surge of surprise filled his heart, as well as a deep and abiding gratefulness that the Lord had led him to Cocos Island.

Something had softened Charity's heart towards him. Three days ago, she had no fondness for American men. Perhaps she'd had time to consider the underwater dance they'd performed together three days ago, and decided he hadn't been so far out of step after all. Maybe the counsel she'd received from José and Teresa had assuaged her indifference towards him. Perhaps the Lord had reached into her heart and brought Hans to the foreground. Hans didn't know why she had changed so drastically from yesterday, but he was infinitely thrilled with how kind, cheerful and attentive Charity was towards him today.

Enraptured by the thoughts of being with Charity tomorrow, Hans was surprised to hear Tom chirp, "Uno! Yee-haw! Yer so easy to beat when yer mind is somewhere's else."

Although Hans had a draw-two card he could have used, he chose to let Tom win and placed a one-yellow card on Tom's eight-yellow, then looked up at him with what he thought might be a sheepish expression.

"Sorry, Tom. That woman's befuddled my mind."

"Ain't that the truth!" Tom guffawed, and threw a wild draw-four on top of the other cards on the table. "I thought about playin' that card when I said Uno, but I figured you wouldn't even notice. This way, you know I scalped you." He counted up Hans' losing score, then gathered up the cards gleefully and put them back in their little box.

"Guess I'll turn in," said Hans as he stood up and stretched. He didn't know if he'd really be able to sleep, his mind was saturated with Charity and she was the only one, indeed, the only thing he could think about.

When he heard the satellite telephone ring at the navigation station across from the galley, he headed there first. Pressing the talk button, he held the phone up to his ear and answered, "Hans Clark."

"It's Josh," came his twin's voice from the receiver. "How are you two doing down there at Cocos Island?"

"I forgot to call you, didn't I?" asked Hans. "Sorry."

"It's okay. I knew you were safe. I didn't have that awful feeling I get when something goes wrong," said Josh.

Hans remembered well his twin's uncanny ability to sense when someone he loved was in grave danger. "How's Kayla?" asked Hans.

"The twins are driving us both nuts," Josh answered, "but especially now that she's morning sick."

Hans immediately calculated Joshua's meaning. "The twins aren't even two years old yet," he said. "I hope you and your wife have another pair of twins as due punishment." He laughed, then said, "You do know what you're doing, don't you?"

"Kayla says she wants a whole meadow full of children. I guess we're off to a healthy start."

"Did you tell the Admiral?" Hans asked. "And Mom?"

"I called them first," Joshua told him. "I didn't want rumors flying around the Sparkleman clan before I had a chance to tell them. They're both doing just fine, and loving their life in the Northwest."

"Have you heard from Abbot?"

"His mission's going great. He'll be home September 20th. Dad says Bekah is planning an October wedding. You'll be back by then, won't you?"

"If we have to leave *Bridger* in a port marina and fly back, you know we'll be there."

"Abbot wants all of us Clarks and Sparklemans at the wedding, too, Hans. Do you think Tom will want to go to the temple by then?"

"That's up to him," said Hans. "But, you know I'll be there." For a moment, he remembered his hope to visit the temple first with his fiancée on their wedding day, then sighed with the realization that he still had three months to convince Charity to marry him before that, and he silently prayed it would be enough time.

"That's great! I'll let Tom know."

"There's some other good news, too," said Josh. "I was going to let Ed call you about it, but he's in the hospital."

The statement was made in such an offhanded way that Hans knew his brother had held off the worst until last. "That's good news?" questioned Hans, wondering how on earth Josh equated Ed being in the hospital as something happy. "What happened?"

"He was chasing a mountain lion that had killed a couple head of cattle. His stallion slipped on a rock and rolled down the mountain with Ed still in the saddle."

"Is he hurt bad?" asked Hans, a knot growing in his stomach. Ed Sparkleman might be Tom's brother by blood, but Tom couldn't care about Ed anymore than Hans did.

"Broke his leg in two places, and a couple of ribs. He's still unconscious, they've got him in ICU."

"Unconscious? Was he hit on the head?"

"They're not certain. The doctors say he's going to be fine, but . . . Well, he *is* unconscious. Kayla and I are flying up in the morning with the twins. I've got time off from the University until September."

"Give me a second to tell Tom," Hans said. He relayed the information to Tom immediately, who was already standing shoulder to shoulder with him, waiting to hear what had happened.

"Tell that polecat brother of mine I'll be there just as soon as I can," Tom said, the second he heard it was Ed who was hurt.

Hans handed Tom the phone, and Tom barked, "Who's mindin' the ranch?"

After a few minutes, Tom said, "Okay, then. Guess you three kin handle it until I git there. I'll make arrangements to git there as quick as I can. Did you think about puttin' Ed's name in the temple?" Tom nodded. "That's good. As soon as our plans are nailed down, I'll call you and let you know when I'll be gittin' into town. You, too." He handed the phone back to Hans.

"I'm still trying to understand how this is good news," said Hans back into the receiver.

He could hear Josh hesitate in the background. Finally, he said, "I forgot to tell you the good part. Ed's wife, Alyssa, is pregnant, too. She and Kayla are due about the same time, right around Christmas."

"Not twins, though, right?"asked Hans, overwhelmed at this news.

"No promises, yet," said Joshua, forcing a laugh that Hans knew was intended to ease Hans' concern over Ed. "Oh! Kayla said to keep your eye out for a pretty woman down there. She's got one of her funny feelings."

Hans laughed aloud, hoping to convey the same message to his twin. "Boy, she's good, isn't she! I just met her three days ago."

Waiting a moment while Josh relayed this news, he then heard his brother ask, "Is her name Faith, Hope or Charity?"

"What?"asked Hans, completely bewildered.

Suddenly, Kayla was speaking to him on the line. "Hans, I'm so happy for you! I was reading the scriptures today, Moroni 7, and I just had a feeling that it pertained to you. I think you're going to find your soul mate in someone named Faith, Hope or Charity."

"Her name's Charity, little sister," said Hans, shaking his head in wonder. Kayla had been like this ever since her dad and Tom's Pa died, the day of the first Sparkleman/Clark miracle. Kayla could sense things through the Spirit like no other woman he knew. But, he didn't want Kayla to get her hopes up, yet. "However," he added, "we're nowhere near where you're suggesting. Not yet. There will be obstacles, Kayla, because right now, I'm not quite certain how she feels about me."

"Nothing that you can't handle," Kayla encouraged. "Just remember, handle every situation with prayer and everything will work out."

"Will do," he promised.

"Now, put Tom on a minute so I can talk to him."

Hans handed the phone back to Tom, and went into the salon where he took the Book of Mormon from the shelf and opened it up to Moroni 7. The moment he read it, he knew the feeling Kayla had received because he felt it, too. His eyes fell upon verse forty-seven, which seemed to fill up every cell in his body with inspiration and hope:

But charity is the pure love of Christ,
and it endureth forever; and whoso
is found possessed of it at the last day,
it shall be well with him.

Hans blinked back the tears that threatened to gather in his eyes, and bowed his head in a silent prayer. Hans wanted with all his soul to believe that he had the pure love of Christ, because he knew at that moment that without that unselfish, unconditional and all-encompassing love, he would never be able to prove to Charity how steadfast he loved her.

When he finished his prayer, Hans noticed that Tom was busy in the galley, and the satellite phone had been put back in its holster at the nav station.

"I'll get a floatplane out here to pick us up at daybreak," Hans said.

"And hire a Captain to take *Bridger* into Puntarenas for me." Hans' heart ached with the conflicting emotions of wanting to stay and spend time with Charity, and wanting to hurry back to the Bar M ranch so he could be with his brothers during their hour of need. Hans knew that if he was to truly exercise the pure love of Christ in his life, he would have to do whatever the Savior would do. And he couldn't imagine the Savior staying to court a woman while his brother lay unconscious in the hospital.

"Thanks," said Tom, sniffing. "I was worryin' how I was gonna' git back in time to be of help to Ed."

"A floatplane's the only answer," said Hans. "Otherwise, it would take us three days to get into Puntarenas."

"You reckon you kin find a competent Captain to come git *Bridger*?" Again, Tom sniffed, but kept his back to Hans as he popped up some popcorn on the stove for a late-night snack, a common occurrence aboard.

"You know," added Tom, "yer twin thinks he kin handle the Bar M by himself. It's a good thing he's got Marcus there! And Will told his father-in-law he'd work at the ranch 'til I git there. Don't imagine that was an easy thing fer Will t'do with him bein' in the river runnin' business in the middle of summer."

One more sniffle and Hans suddenly realized his good friend, Tom, was actually trying not to cry. Hans stepped into the galley and touched Tom's elbow. When Tom turned around, he had tears running down his cheeks in rivulets.

"What?" Hans asked, completely dismayed. "The doctors said Ed was going to be fine, Tom."

"I know that, partner," growled Tom, apparently irritated that Hans had noticed his tears. He wiped his eyes with a paper towel before he said, "It's nothin' bad, Hans. It's just . . . well, Kayla reckons there's a miracle waitin' fer me back at the ranch. She didn't say what, but you know Kayla and her feelin's. She knew about Charity, didn't she?"

Hans laughed and gave Tom a bear hug, then stepped back and pounded him on the shoulder. "You sly old coon," he chuckled. "Are you chomping at the bit to get back for Ed's sake . . . or your own?"

"I reckon it's a little o' both," Tom admitted. Then, he burst into laughter. "I'm gonna' git my own little miracle!" He danced a snazzy jig right there in the galley.

It was so funny, Hans joined Tom in laughing. He had to hold his stomach and sit down on the settee before he fell over, he was laughing so hard.

Before Tom had devoured all the popcorn, Hans had telephoned Puntarenas for a flight plane and a Captain. Both would be arriving by eight tomorrow morning.

After reading all of Moroni from the Book of Mormon in bed that night, and concentrating a due amount of serious study to Moroni 7, Hans offered a prayer of thanksgiving and a prayer for healing.

He had so much to be grateful for, he hardly knew where to begin. First of all, he expressed his appreciation for having met Charity. He recognized her as one of God's chosen daughters. Even if nothing ever came of their budding relationship, Hans had already had the opportunity to spend time with her that he would never forget. For this great honor and blessing, he thanked the Lord from the bottom of his heart. But, he did not doubt that their relationship would eventually mean something far more divine than park ranger and tourist, and more eternal than a simple summer fling.

Hans expressed to the Lord his love for his family, for those who were legally family, and for those whom he claimed as his brothers, the four Sparkleman men who'd been raised across the meadow from Kayla Dawn, who'd married Hans' twin, Joshua Bridger Clark; for Josh's twin sons, Mont and Sparky, and for the unborn child of Josh and Kayla. He remembered Alyssa in his prayers, who was now Ed Sparkleman's wife, and her pregnancy, and asked the Lord to watch mightily over them all. Family meant more than anything to Hans right now, and as he prayed, he tackled the obstacles that were preventing his family from feeling pure joy.

Ed Sparkleman's health was Hans' first concern, and he dwelt on that with the Lord for a while before continuing, discussing with Him all the reasons why Ed could still be unconscious, how bad Ed's leg might be, and whether or not his lungs had been damaged when his ribs broke.

Next, he spoke to the Lord about Tom Sparkleman's heart. In Hans' point of view, and he felt the Lord already knew this, Tom had been punished enough for a crime which the poor man didn't even recall. In addition, Tom was lonely. Quite simply, Tom was starving for a good woman with whom he could share his life. Someone who wouldn't judge him, someone who could love him with her whole heart.

Then, turning his thoughts to Charity, Hans told the Lord he had decided to pursue a permanent relationship with her, to eventually propose to her, and marry her. He asked the Lord for confirmation that he had made the right decision.

Immediately, he felt enlightened and full of truth and knowledge. A warm, tingling sensation started in the center of his chest and spread outward through his whole body, to the top of his head and the tips of his fingers and toes.

Hans pleaded with the Lord, asking that He continue to soften Charity's heart so that he would stand a chance of kneeling across the altar from her. He may have to convert her to the Gospel first, but Abbot had converted his fiancée, Joshua and Kayla had converted Hans, and their father and mother. Charity's membership would have to be one of his many challenges, and Hans accepted the challenge willingly. The Lord knew Hans thrived on challenges, and converting Charity would just have to be one obstacle that he would have to overcome with time and patience and the pure love of Christ.

Next, Hans asked the Lord to bless Charity, that she would understand why he had to leave the island tomorrow. He had wanted it to be a day of discovery and joy and love between them. Hans wanted to leave a good impression with her so badly he could almost taste it. His heart ached at having to leave Cocos Island so soon. But, he also needed to do what the Savior would have him do. He wanted to be his brother's keeper, and show Tom and Ed how the pure love of Christ works in a man's life. Surely, the Lord would help Charity to understand that.

Finally, he asked that the Captain who was coming, would find a safe voyage from Cocos Island to Puntarenas, that he would have fair skies and a fresh breeze to get *Bridger* safely into port.

When he concluded his prayer, he climbed into bed and pulled the sheet over him. It was too hot for more than a thin covering. But, Hans did not sleep. His mind raced with thoughts of tomorrow, and what it might bring into his life: true joy or agonizing heartache.

Regardless of Charity's reaction or rejection when she learned they were leaving so soon, Hans promised himself that Charity was the one person on whom he would never give up. He would stay the course, no matter what obstacles were thrown into his path. He would meet every challenge head on, and one day, he would see that brief but glorious vision fulfilled when he knelt across the altar from Charity in the House of the Lord.

Tossing and turning for nearly an hour made him more tired than ever, but he couldn't sleep. He got out of bed and left the master stateroom. Tom was not in the salon. Quietly, Hans walked forward toward Tom's stateroom and knocked at the door. When there was no answer, and no snoring, he opened the door quickly, but Tom wasn't there, either. Both heads were empty, and Hans began to worry. He made a beeline for the companionway and found Tom up in the cockpit, gazing at the stars. It was pitch black out, except for the stars and the sliver of a pearly moon. Tom was leaning back on a cushion, staring off into space.

Hans sat opposite him.

"Couldn't sleep?" Tom asked.

"I could," Hans said, "if I could get Charity out of my mind."

"Yer in for some sleepless nights, then, partner," said Tom with a chuckle.

"How do you think she'll react?" Hans asked.

"If she can't accept that Ed's yer brother, and he needs his family with him right now, then maybe she ain't the girl fer you," said Tom.

"She has this issue," admitted Hans. "Her father apparently deserted his family when she was less than a year old, and he was an American soldier. She wants a man who won't leave her."

"You ain't leaving her. Yer goin' to be with yer brother. Where would she be if'n it was her brother?"

"Good point," said Hans. "Any rational person would understand, wouldn't they?"

"Who said love is rational?" asked Tom.

"She'll just have to trust me," Hans insisted. "I can't control the way God moves me around."

"You could stay here," offered Tom. "Ed would understand. He knows what its like to love a woman even when she's drivin' you crazy."

"That's out of the question. I won't abandon my family when they need me, anymore than you would."

Tom tipped back his Stetson. "I guess the only thing a man kin do now is to pray."

"I am praying," confessed Hans. "I haven't stopped praying in my heart since I heard the news about Ed."

"Yer a true friend, Hans.

"I'm not just your friend, Tom. I'm your brother just as much as Ed is."

"I know that. The feelin's mutual."

They were silent afterward, both of them lost in their thoughts. Tom, no doubt, was worrying about Kayla's inspirational conviction that a miracle was headed his way, as well Tom's concern for what trials may still be ahead for their brother, Ed. As for Hans, he worried about Ed as much as Tom. With all his heart, he prayed that Charity would understand.

Chapter Seven

Charity pulled the pillow over her head, dismayed at the pounding rain on the tin roof overhead. It was unusually loud this morning, meaning the deluge season had finally arrived. But as she listened, the sound didn't have the tinny ring to it with which she was so familiar. She lifted her head up and removed the pillow. It was only then that she realized someone was knocking on the reception room door.

Glancing at her watch, Charity saw that it was nearly seven-thirty in the morning. Her alarm clock would be going off in a few minutes. The knocking stopped and she heard male voices muffled in the background. Then, José knocked at hers and Árima's bedroom door.

"I'm up," said Charity, swinging her legs off the bed, and noticing that Árima hadn't even stirred.

"Hurry," said José, "Hans wants to talk to you before his plane arrives."

"What?"she asked, but José had evidently gone back to his bedroom right after delivering his message. *What plane?* she thought irritably, pulling on her ranger pants and t-shirt. She ran a brush quickly through her thick, black hair, slipped on a pair of sandals and hurried from the room, leaving her bed unmade and Árima still sound asleep.

In the reception room, Hans was pacing back and forth in front of the big map of Cocos Island along the back wall. He turned to face her when she arrived.

"Hi," he said. "Did you sleep well?"

"Yes, fine." Perplexed at why he should have come up to the cabin so early, and what plane he was waiting for, Charity furrowed her brow and asked, "What's wrong? Where are you going?"

"We got a call last night from my twin, Joshua. There's been an accident at the ranch. Tom's brother, Ed, was injured when his horse rolled over on him."

"Is he all right?" she asked, remembering Hans telling her that Ed was like a brother to him.

"His leg and two ribs are broken, but our biggest concern is that he's still unconscious." Hans held his hand out and she placed hers willingly into it.

"How terrible for your family," she said. "Oh, Hans, I'm so sorry."

"After Josh hung up, I must have made at least a dozen phone calls, but I was finally able to locate a floatplane to take us to Puntarenas, where we'll catch a cab to the airport. It'll take all of today and part of tomorrow, but we should reach Utah by tomorrow afternoon."

"Utah?" she asked. "Are you and Tom Mormons?"

Hans grimaced, but she squeezed his hand in encouragement, which seemed to help, and he nodded sheepishly.

"That's wonderful!" Charity exclaimed. "We are, too. José, Teresa, Árima, my mother and brother."

"You're a Latter-day Saint?" he asked, his voice almost squeaking.

"Yes, that was the only good thing Daniel left with us . . . he converted my mother shortly after he met her. I was baptized when I was eight years old," she admitted, smiling broadly.

Hans grinned right back. "No kidding! Here I thought one of my biggest obstacles would be converting you to the Gospel, and you've been a member longer than I have! Why didn't you tell me?"

"Why didn't you tell me?" she countered.

Hans shrugged. "Something to do with getting shot down at every turn, I suppose. Are you angry I didn't tell you?"

Charity punched him playfully in the shoulder. "How could I when I didn't tell you, either? But, just knowing you're LDS, that changes everything, you know!"

"It does?" he asked timidly.

"Yes," she insisted, nodding her head. "Now, you're an American *and* a Mormon, just like Daniel was when he met my mom." She bit her lip and hoped Hans knew that she was joking.

Apparently not, for he gulped and shook his head in dismay. His expression was so forlorn, Charity almost burst out laughing. "I'm teasing," she smiled. "There are some really good men in the Church who never leave their wives . . . the prophet, the twelve apostles . . . our Bishop!"

"I've only been a member for thirty months!" Hans protested. "I hope you don't expect apostleship or bishopric status out of me anytime soon."

Charity laughed. "You're off the hook for a little while. But Hans, how did you find a floatplane so quickly?"

"I told you about my money management skills, didn't I? You know, offer enough money and you can get a pilot and a captain to do just about anything."

She considered his response for only a moment, then said, "Thank you for coming to tell me you were leaving. That was very considerate." She couldn't tell him that his news devastated her emotions entirely.

"I will be back," he said quickly.

Almost too quickly, thought Charity. She didn't respond to this promise.

With desperation resounding in his voice, Hans added, "I know that you probably think I won't come back, Charity, but I will. May I have your address in San Pedro so I can come to see you? And your phone number?"

Charity shook her head. Was this really such a good idea?

"*Please,*" he begged.

She reasoned with herself that it wouldn't matter whether Hans knew her private information or not. With his money, he wasn't into stealing identities, and if he was serious about coming back to see her, then perhaps she should agree.

Apparently noticing the debate going on inside her, Hans said in a great rush, "We've only known each other for a few days, Charity, but I have a good feeling about you. I want to get to know you better. Obviously, I can't do that right now, but as soon as I know Ed will be all right, I'll come back. You know I will, my boat will be moored in Puntarenas while I'm gone."

"How will you manage that?" she wondered aloud.

"I hired a captain to take it there. He's coming this morning with the pilot."

"How do I know you didn't hire a captain to take your boat back to San Diego, or to one of those shipping boats?" she asked wearily, dismayed at this news. "You could have it shipped wherever you want it, like most of the rich do." Charity wondered if she should have given in long ago, but she couldn't help teasing him for a little while.

"Charity," he admonished, almost scolding her.

She had to keep the situation light-hearted. If she didn't, she feared her emotions would disintegrate.

Suddenly, Hans reached behind him and pulled something out of his back pocket. "I was worried that you would feel this way, so I brought this for you. Here."

He handed her a heavy piece of parchment that looked very much like a legal document. "What's this?" she asked, reading the paper quickly. "This is the title to your boat?"

Hans nodded. "You said you needed to know that a man had staying power. You had to be able to trust him. Well, I'm trusting you with my boat, Charity. That's over a million dollars if you sold it today. If I trust you that much, can you not trust me just a little bit? Because when I return, I want you to know that I'm not coming back for my boat, Charity," he pleaded. "I don't care about the boat. I care about you. I've been debating about this all night, so hear me out. I thought if you had the title . . . look, I've signed it over to you!"

Charity noticed that he had, indeed, put her name under new owner, and signed the bottom of it, turning it completely over to her ownership. Her mouth dropped open and her green eyes widened in surprise.

Interrupting her thoughts, Hans continued, "Then, you might believe me when I say I'm coming back. I plan to court you, Charity. I want to see you again and again and again. If you want to sell your boat, I don't care. It means nothing to me, but *you* do! You mean everything to me. The only thing that'll prevent me from returning to you is if God calls me home, because I am coming! I'm not leaving you. I promise. Now, will you give me your phone number and address so I can find you when I get back?"

"You can't buy my phone number, Hans. It's insulting," she announced.

He placed his hand upon her shoulder and squeezed it. "Just keep the title for me, if that's all you want. Take care of *Bridger* when you leave Cocos Island. Live aboard it if you'd like. Sail it or sell it, or just let it rot in Puntarenas, because you're the only reason I'm coming back."

It was at that moment that Charity knew she had to change the situation to laughter, otherwise she would burst out in tears. "You don't have to be this persuasive," she said with a mischievous grin. "You had me at *please*."

Hans grinned from ear to ear, then pulled her into his arms and kissed her soundly. "All right!" he exclaimed when he let her up for air.

Charity laughed aloud, hoping to show Hans a lighter side of herself. "You are too funny! But, I don't want the title to your boat, take it with you." She tried to give the title to him.

He pushed it back into her hands, then dug his satellite telephone and a piece of paper out of his shirt pocket, and gave them to her. "No, I want you to check up on the boat when you get back to Puntarenas. If you are the legal owner, you're authorized to move it, or do with it whatever the marina might want from you. I'll pay for the slip in advance when we arrive there this morning. And on this other paper, I've written my cell phone number, my parents' phone numbers, as well as all my brothers' and the Bar M Ranch . . . that's where I'm headed. I'll buy me another satellite phone as soon as I get near a store that sells them, then I'll call you with the number. I've also written down the security code to open the companionway lock. The keys are in the nav station's top drawer. And you'll also find the address to the ranch, in case you'd rather write, but I'm thinking I'll be back here before a letter would reach me."

"Hans, this is too much!" she insisted. "I don't want your boat."

"I know. I know," he said. "I'm rushing things, but I know how I feel, and I don't want to lose your trust, not without first being given a chance to prove I'm trustworthy. We both need to see where our feelings lead us."

"*Our* feelings?" she asked, dismayed that he did not even have an inkling of where her heart stood, somewhere between retreat and surrender.

Hans nodded, still with that silly grin of his. "I'm hoping that my leaving you this morning won't put you off dating me, Charity. I think that you might like me, a little. You do, don't you?"

Now, Charity laughed. "I am fond of you, Hans. You're a sweet man, but all this is just too much."

"No, it's not. It's something I need to do. You said when you gave your heart to a man, he would have to prove to you that he would never leave you. Right now, I have no choice but to go to Utah. My brother is injured and I have to be with my family. I'd take you with me, if I thought I could persuade you to go, but I have a feeling that would be pushing you too far. I hoped if you had the title to my boat, you would at least entertain the possibility that I *will* be coming back."

Charity wrapped her arms around his waist and he pulled her close, rubbing her back with his warm hands. "You're too much!" she declared. After a brief moment of silence between them, she acquiesced. "Okay, I will keep the title in a safe place until you get back. But, when you return, I'll give it back to you."

"Mmm," he moaned huskily, "I like the sound of that. *When you return*. See, you're already considering that it is possible for me to return."

Laughing, Charity released him and backed off to arm's length, afraid that her own emotions were too heavily invested. "This doesn't change anything. It will take time to win my trust, Hans Bridger Clark. You haven't done that, yet."

"You did say 'yet', and yet means up until now, and yet leaves the door open for later on, doesn't it?" he persisted, laughing with her and pulling her close to him once again.

In the distance, Charity heard the engine from a floatplane drawing nearer. Immediately, a knot rolled up in her flat abdomen and a lump arose in her throat. "You're plane is arriving, Hans. You'd better go."

"Come see me off," Hans said, taking her hand and leading her outside.

"I hate goodbyes," Charity responded, pulling back. "You know I do." To her dismay, she found her hands trembling and her heart racing.

Hans stopped just past the threshold. Gathering her into his strong arms, he kissed her once again, longingly, lovingly, like he could never get enough of her. When he released her, he said, "You're right, of course. I'll see you soon."

And with those words he left her standing on the trail at Cocos Island. He didn't even turn at the bottom of the path to wave goodbye, and Charity knew that he was doing his best not to let the word 'goodbye' enter into their relationship in any way.

She cared about him all the more for it, and hated herself for doing so. Her feelings were headed toward major heartbreak and she could not allow that to happen.

Turning around, she went back inside and rushed to the bathroom, where she locked herself in and turned the water on full blast in the shower so no one would hear her. Then, she sank onto the commode lid, where she cried until long after the water ran cold.

❦ ❦ ❦

The float plane arrived safely in Puntarenas, but it hadn't carried Hans' heart with it. Hans' heart was left behind on Cocos Island with Charity. He tucked his feelings away, into a deep recess inside himself, and got down to business.

After speaking with the marina authorities, where he made arrangements for *Bridger* to be moored on a six-month lease, he visited the manager of a local sign shop. Then, Hans and Tom took another small plane to the airport in San José, Costa Rica. By three that afternoon, they were able to depart on a commercial flight to Los

Angeles. Then, they took a commuter plane to San Diego, where they had a four-hour layover.

While in San Diego, Hans and Tom stopped by Josh and Kayla's condo, where they watered the plants, put out the garbage, and retrieved Sparky's "Wimby," a plush toy bear that his nephew slept with, and whose absence was going to drive Kayla and Josh into sleepless exhaustion if not retrieved. The gangly stuffed bear had been crouching upon the kitchen counter since before Josh and Kayla took the twins to the airport for their flight to Utah almost twenty hours earlier.

At a store on their way back to the airport, Hans was able to purchase another satellite phone. The first person he called was Charity. She didn't answer, so he left a message with his new number on it, and wondered if she would know how to pick the message up. He'd written the instructions on the note he'd given her, but would she read it?

Back at the airport, Hans telephoned a private investigator. He had a lot of instructions to give regarding Charity's father, the missing Daniel Blake. Meanwhile, Tom picked up some magazines to read.

From San Diego, they got a morning flight to Salt Lake City. Upon arrival, he called Charity, but there was still no answer, and Hans began to worry that she wasn't going to answer any of his calls. He left another message, then phoned Josh's cell phone to check on Ed's progress and to tell him that "Wimby" was en route. Josh said that Ed was beginning to regain consciousness.

Hans and Tom rented a car at the Salt Lake International Airport and drove the remainder of the way to Vernal, Utah, where they arrived late that afternoon at the hospital.

When they walked toward the front desk, Kayla and the twins saw them from down one of the halls. Squeals of delight swept over the boys faces as they realized who Hans and Tom were, and they came running toward them as fast as their little legs would carry them, squealing in delight, "Unk 'ans! Unk Tom!" almost in unison.

When Sparky spotted Wimby, he ran straight toward Hans. "Mine!" he squalled. "Mine Wimby!" Hans quickly gave his nephew the bear, and Sparky hugged him ferociously for it.

Then, the twins were all over them in a matter of seconds! Hans was surprised to find that young Mont and Sparky still remembered them, and missed them, too. Of course, Hans did look remarkably like their father, so it was easy to understand their affection for their Uncle Hans. Tom, however, seemed to be their personal favorite, perhaps because he got down on all fours and played with them often while they were in San Diego commissioning *Bridger,* before they sailed to Cocos Island. Tom had endeared himself to the twins quickly.

When the boys were cradled, one against each of their uncles' shoulders, with Wimby secure under Sparky's arm, and Tom had released Kayla from a whopping big hug, Hans managed to ask, "How's Ed doing?"

"He's much better this evening. They're moving him from ICU to a regular room, so I told the boys I'd take them to the gift shop. They want to get Uncle Ed a present."

"And Josh?"

"He stayed with Alyssa in the waiting room. She's a little more relaxed than she was yesterday. Those first twenty-four hours were hard on her, even though Will and Morning Sun were here with her."

"How are you holding up?" asked Hans.

Kayla nodded, but before she could answer, Mont started yelping for a bathroom, and that kindled Sparky's interest, too. Kayla took Sparky from Hans, and said, "You two go on up. I'm used to handling these two wranglers on my own."

Tom put Mont down and they left Kayla with the boys, then went down the hall toward the waiting room. When Hans saw Alyssa, an entire flood of memories came back to him, as she stood and rushed over to him, throwing her arms around him. "Oh, Hans," she gushed. "I'm so glad you came." That, alone, made the trip worthwhile. Alyssa and Hans had a bond of friendship that went way back, and her words affirmed that she still needed his strength to get through the rough spots in her life. They were as close as a brother and sister could get, yet they were not truly related in any way.

Alyssa withdrew and gave Tom a hug. "And you!" she exclaimed. "Josh tells me you're lassoing sharks now."

"A slight exaggeration," drawled Tom. "But, you kin believe anythin' you want about me."

Hans embraced his brother, Josh, then stood back, while Tom shook Josh's hand. Josh pulled Tom close for a quick hug. "You think we Clarks will settle for a handshake from a brother, do you?" asked Josh.

"Guess not," said Tom. "How's our eldest cowpoke?"

"He's going to be all right," said Josh. "This morning when we first got here, he was opening his eyes a little, but by late afternoon, he had turned irritable and the nurses threatened to strap him down. They finally decided to move him, when he insisted he didn't need the care they provide in ICU. There's a lot of fight left in him, that's for sure."

"Ed doesn't make a very good patient," admitted Alyssa with a weak smile. "But, I think the worst is over. Now, if he'll just mind the doctor and rest a few more days here, I think they'll let him go home."

"Why was he unconscious so long?" asked Hans.

"If you saw the lump on the back of his head, you wouldn't need to ask that," said Josh.

"They didn't realize the lump was so bad until he started to wake up. His biggest complaint is that the back of his head is too sore to rest on a pillow," Alyssa explained.

"Sounds like he plumb knocked himself out," said Tom. "He's a hard-headed one, that's for sure."

Alyssa laughed. "You can say that again!"

A nurse came in and announced, "Mrs. Sparkleman?"

"Yes," said Alyssa, turning toward her.

"You can go in now."

"May we all go in, or do we need to limit his visitors to two at a time, still?"

"You can all go in," smiled the nurse. "He could use some cheering."

Alyssa put her hand on Hans' arm. "Why don't you men go in first? I'm going to freshen up."

Josh said, "I'm going to go rescue Kayla. I'll be back shortly."

Tom shrugged. "Let's go," he said to Hans. "Did someone tell him we were comin'?"

"No," answered Josh. "He's been too ornery to chit chat much."

Hans laughed. "Then, I know he's getting better. Sounds like he's back to his normal self."

They left Kayla and Josh and went down the hall to Ed's room. Ed's left leg was in a brace from his hip to his toes, and he had a little swelling across the bridge of his nose, but other than that, he looked good. His sand-colored hair and gray-green eyes were as troubled as always. Otherwise, Ed was looking good.

"Hey!" said Ed. "I thought you two were sailing around the world, or something like that."

Hans bent over the bed and gave Ed a good glare. "Where would you be if I was in that bed, brother?"

"Or me?" echoed Tom, shaking Ed's hand.

Ed looked up at both of them and a sheepish grin stole across his face. "You know, I really just wanted to spend more time with my wife, and I figured this way she'd have to give me plenty of attention."

"From the sounds of things," said Tom, "you'll be waitin' on her from yer crutches. Pregnant women kin get downright ornery sometimes."

"I haven't seen any of that yet," Ed assured him, "but thanks for the warning. Sit down, both of you, and tell me all about Cocos Island. I looked it up on a map, you know. You'd never get me out in the middle of the ocean in a big-boy's toy."

"We weren't in the middle of the ocean," assured Hans.

"Could you see land from your boat on the way down there?"

"Nope," grinned Tom.

"That's the middle of the ocean in my book," said Ed. "But, what I really want to know about is Charity. Hans?"

"Kayla told you about Charity?" Hans asked in surprise.

"Kayla tells Alyssa everything, and Alyssa tells me. I've got a nifty grapevine," Ed confessed.

"This here polecat fell in love with Charity in three days," whispered Tom conspiratorially. "He even gave her the title to his boat!"

"What?!?" roared Ed. "Are you nuts? You sank a million bucks into that boat!"

"How much is a woman's love worth?" Hans asked with a sheepish grin.

"Danged if I know," answered Tom.

When Ed got over the initial shock of Hans' irrational behavior, they talked freely about love and women, and how much men depended on them for their very lives.

By the time visiting hours were over, Hans had greeted Ed's brother, Will; Marcus, the ranch's second in command; Luke and Sidekick, two of the eight ranch hands; Morning Sun, the ranch's housekeeper, and her son, Matthew, who spent the better part of the evening entertaining the twins with coloring books and crayons.

After they left the hospital, they all met together at the Golden Corral, where they ate a late supper, then Tom went back to the ranch with Josh and Kayla, while Hans stayed in a motel room down in Vernal, his excuse being that he wanted to be nearby in case there was anything he could do for Ed. However, he suspected that everyone knew he didn't want to get out of cell phone range, in case Charity called him. Hans didn't know if she had received his message telling her what his new satellite phone number was, and for all he knew, she might not even know how to access the message.

Hans dialed Charity's satellite phone number again, the moment he got to his room, but there was still no answer. Since it was ten at night in Vernal, he knew it would only be nine at Cocos Island. Hans couldn't imagine why she wasn't answering. Hoping that her reason for not answering was that she had thrown herself into her work on the island in order to keep her mind off him, he stretched out on the bed. After saying his prayer, Hans expected to remain awake until dawn, worrying about Charity, but he was so exhausted from being up for almost forty hours straight, he fell into a deep and dreamless sleep.

Chapter Eight

For an entire week, Charity kept Hans' boat title, satellite phone and slip of paper beneath her bed in a small box of memorabilia she had collected from various tourists over the past two years. Right after Hans left, she had turned the satellite phone off, and put it away so that it wouldn't be a temptation to her if she heard it ring. Besides, this way she would conserve the battery.

Hans left a gaping hole in her heart when he departed, and she knew that calling him would only make the wound wider and deeper, something she dared not do. Not yet. Not until her heart had a little time to heal. She understood why Hans had to leave, but she did not really believe that he would return to her. That she had made such a show of laughing with him, and letting him kiss her, only proved the fragile state in which he'd left her.

To Charity's dismay, she was beginning to feel more than fondness for Hans, and this knowledge scared her more than anything else. A wise woman admits defeat, but Charity knew that if Hans failed to return to Costa Rica, she would never trust another man.

In the meantime, José had contacted the park service and told them that Chatham Bay had been vacated, and within two days, two boats with four tourists from Puntarenas had arrived at Cocos Island to keep her busy. The tourists, two couples who spoke not a word of English, wanted to tour the island first. After reading her Sunday School lesson and the accompanying scriptures, and saying her prayer, Charity took the two couples that Sunday morning on an eight-mile hike around Church Hill loop, showed them the overgrown wreck of a B24 airplane that had gone down years earlier, and two waterfalls, one along the trail above Wafer Bay, and one at Church Bay. She also took them into the tunnel which was dug by treasure-seekers on Cocos island more than a hundred years earlier. Working three Sundays in row was not Charity's idea of a spiritually healthy work environment, but José always insisted that after park ranger duties on the Sabbath day, that the women study Relief Society lessons together, while he studied his Priesthood manual, and then they would get together to discuss the things they'd learned, and eat fresh mangoes for dessert. It wasn't quite the same as attending church services, but it was the best they could do.

After the Sabbath evening prayer, Charity sought the quiet of her room and read from her scriptures a while longer. When she finished, she said her own prayer, then pulled Hans' note and satellite phone from the box below her bed. She read the note over carefully, making certain that she knew how to use the phone should she ever decide to call him.

All day long, she'd had doubts in her mind about whether or not she could trust Hans to return to Costa Rica. Shuddering, she feared that no matter how hard she wanted to, trust had to be earned, and Hans had not proven himself. Not yet. He thought giving her the title to his boat would appease her mind about his trustworthiness. But, so what if he'd given her the title to his boat!? That only proved that he now had *no* reason to return to Costa Rica. She didn't doubt that giving her full title was his idea of giving a gift to her, and that the boat would be at the Puntarenas marina when she arrived there, as he said it would.

Otherwise, why would he give her the title? But, Hans didn't own *Bridger*, not anymore. Apparently, he thought the title would make her trust him, but it had the opposite affect.

Sighing, Charity put the phone and the paper back in the box below her bed, then fell into a restless sleep, where she had a terrible nightmare about sailing into a raging storm with waves fifty feet tall. She was all alone and afraid for her life aboard *Bridger*.

The following day, the tourist couples wanted to dive at Two Friends, and had asked José to guide them, so Charity took the opportunity to do some cleaning, and when she was finished with that, she continued the opening of a trail to Point Ulloa that the rangers had been working on periodically for a year now. The vegetation was so thick, she needed a machete to get through it, but the trail was nearly finished. Charity didn't have more than a few days' work left to complete it.

There were four trails on the island, one that led from the Chatham Bay ranger station to Wafer Bay, and from there it made a loop up to Church Hill, the highest point on the island. There were also two narrow trails, one from each ranger station, going out to the tips of Colnett and Presidio Peninsulas. This last trail, the final one authorized by the park service, went from Chatham Bay ranger station to Point Ulloa, the northeastern tip of the island that overlooked Lobster Rock. These trails gave the island two half-mile trails, a one-mile trail and an eight-mile trail (or six-miles if starting from Wafer Bay), which offered plenty of choice depending on the diverse capabilities of the tourist trade, but still kept a healthy balance of undisturbed vegetation and tropical rain forest on the island.

By late in the evening of the sixth day, Charity had returned to the cabin weary, and she wasn't certain whether it was due to exhaustion or emotional anxiety. All day long, in her swing of the machete along the trail to Ulloa Point, she kept thinking about Hans, wondering how he was, what he was doing, whether or not his brother was all right. He must think her terribly insensitive not to call him when he'd given her a phone for that very purpose. Then, she worried how much the call would cost him. Satellite phones were not only expensive to purchase, they were very expensive to use. In her world of pinching every coin until it literally squealed, she didn't want to put an extra burden on him.

It was difficult to equate Hans' wealth to her own meager circumstances, for she had nothing with which to compare it. Charity shared a two-bedroom apartment with her mother, and slept in a twin bed in the same room with Juaniata. Perry had his own bedroom, but Charity had never *not* shared a bedroom with someone. When they first moved to San Pedro, in her uncle's home, near where he taught at the university, she and her mother had shared a room with her cousins, Lucita and Pepita, who were both older than Charity by three and five years.

After nearly six years at Uncle Rafael's home, they were able to rent the apartment they had now. It was a two-bedroom unit upstairs from a designer clothing store, where Charity's mother worked. Juaniata Perez-Blake was an exceedingly fine dress designer, as well as a seamstress, and she made all the alterations for the clothing they sold, and sewed all the fabulous dresses the owner required. It was a very upscale store in the front, but a sweatshop for Juaniata at the rear, where she worked from sunup to sunset, designing and sewing the creations that made the store owner famous and wealthy. Upstairs, via a staircase that came off the back alley, their two-bedroom apartment also had a small kitchen, front room and one bathroom. The front room looked over the main street, just above the clothing store entrance, and had a little balcony where Juaniata kept plaster urns filled with blossoming plants of all varieties, while baskets of flowers hung over the wrought-iron banister.

Sometimes Charity missed the sweet, spicy smell of petunias and the bright, coral colors of the camellias, but mostly she missed her mother's dark, sparkling eyes as she sat on the edge of the second twin bed and said, "Goodnight, sweet Charity. Your father used to call you that, did you know?"

"You've told me a thousand times," Charity would smile, watching her mother go back, if only in her mind, to a happier time.

Juaniata would always sing *I Am a Child of God*, and kiss Charity's forehead, then sink into her own bed while Charity would drift off into a sweet, and peaceful sleep.

Although Charity missed her mother during her eighteen-day absences from San Pedro, right now Charity missed Hans even more. She thought it fairly ridiculous that she could know a man only three days and feel so overwhelmingly attached to him. But, she would never tell him how she felt until he truly could prove his loyalty to her. And in his absence, she had seriously begun to doubt that would ever happen. He'd once said that he could live the life of a wealthy king, and never touch the principle of his inheritance. If that meant that he could give away million-dollar boats to every girl he met in port, he must truly be a wealthy man.

As far as she knew, coming to Cocos Island had been Hans' first ocean voyage, with exception of some runs from the California coastline to Catalina or the Channel Islands. So, he couldn't have met too many girls in ports around the world. Still, Charity's doubts had prevented her from calling Hans all week long.

Charity slipped between the bed sheets, but by one in the morning, she had tossed and turned in bed without sleeping. Perhaps she should attempt to call Hans at least once from the island, but glancing at her watch, she wondered if he might be asleep. It would be two hours later in Utah, so tonight would not be a good time.

Later that morning, before the sun was completely up, she awakened with a start. She'd been dreaming about the storm again, and she was just about to pitch-pole *Bridger* when she had heard a distinct voice say, "Charity, wake up!" And, she did.

Quietly, she removed the satellite phone and the paper from beneath her bed, slipped into her day clothes, and left the cabin, then walked briskly down to the beach. It was nearly a full moon, and she glanced at her watch to note that it was almost five o'clock. The sun would be rising within the next half hour.

Would Hans be awake this early? Probably not, but she couldn't wait any longer. Although her mood seemed rather odd to her, she realized that she just needed to hear his voice. She said a quick prayer and asked the Lord to let him wake up in a pleasant mood, then she dialed his cell phone number and pressed the send button.

She didn't even hear a phone ring when the call was answered with a harried male voice, saying, "Charity?"

"Yes, Hans," she answered, smiling at how good it felt to hear him say her name, and to hear his obvious distress. "Did I wake you?"

"No, I haven't been sleeping much. You finally got my messages?" he asked.

"No. Did you call earlier?"

"Of course I called earlier. I've been calling every day."

"I'm so sorry," she responded, feeling truly apologetic. "I had turned the phone off and put it away. I didn't want to run the battery down."

"It has a two-week battery in it. I just assumed you'd leave it on so that I could call you."

"And here I thought you'd left it with me so that I could call you."

Hans laughed and the sound of his voice gave her such a thrill that she giggled aloud.

When they stopped laughing, Hans asked, "Would you mind leaving it turned on?"

"All right," she agreed. "I guess you now have two weeks of battery left."

"I'll be with you by then," he responded, "and won't need to phone you."

"Your brother is getting better?" Did she dare hope that he was telling her the truth?

"They're sending him home from the hospital today. I'm flying to San Diego tomorrow, with Josh, Kayla and the twins. They want me to stay through the weekend and go to church with them. My flight to San José leaves from Los Angeles early Monday morning. When will you get home from Cocos Island?"

"I leave Saturday, but it takes until Sunday night to get to Puntarenas. I have to take the last bus to San José and a transfer to San Pedro. I usually arrive home around midnight."

"Why don't you spend Sunday night aboard *Bridger,* and rent a car in Puntarenas? You can pick me up at the airport when my flight gets in at four in the afternoon."

"I'd have to call my mother so she won't worry. Is that all right?"

Hans laughed again. "Talk to her all you want. What? You're worried how much it will cost me?"

"Well, yes, actually."

"I bought the satellite plan with unlimited minutes. Talk all day if you want, just save a little battery time to talk to me."

"All right, I will. What have you been doing all week?"

"I've been playing card games with Ed, keeping him entertained so he doesn't go stir-crazy in the hospital."

"He's doing well, then?"

"Yes, the doctor says he has to be off his leg all summer, and in physical therapy all fall and winter, but he should be back to normal by spring."

"I'm so glad to hear it. Will Tom be coming with you?"

"No, Ed needs him to take over as ranch foreman until after the cattle are moved to the winter range."

"How long will you be staying?" she asked.

"However long you'll let me," he answered.

"Oh, then I guess you won't be leaving anytime soon."

"Well, I have a wedding to attend in October. Our brother, Abbot, gets home from his mission September 20th, and he's getting married in the Seattle Temple the following month. Do you want to go with me?"

"To your brother's wedding?"

"Yes."

"Let's see what October brings," she insisted, unwilling to make such a long-distance commitment just yet.

"I won't take that as a definite no, then."

Charity laughed at the surprise in his voice. "Hans, we need to take this relationship a little slow. I'm already worried about it moving too fast. I need time."

"Only because you don't know me," he insisted. "But soon, you will. I want you to plan out the entire time you're off work so we can spend every day together. And will you reserve a room for me in a hotel near your home?"

"Yes, anything else?"

"Plan to bring your mother along some of the time, and Perry, if they'd like to come."

Smiling at his generosity, Charity teased, "Hmm, how about my bishop and his family?"

"That would be great," agreed Hans, "As long as we get some time alone together. "And if you have any ward activities, I hope you'll include me in them."

"Hans, I don't think I can stay overnight in your boat. I'd be all alone."

"It's no different than staying in an apartment of your own. The marina has full security, my boat has an alarm system, and an interior lock on the companionway. I left instructions on how to run everything on the galley counter top."

"What I meant to say was, I may still have to go home first. I didn't bring any dress-up clothes to work with me. I can't meet you at the airport in my park ranger clothes."

"I left a line of credit for you at the marina's grocery and chandlery. They have some women's clothing there, as well as toiletries and food. The selection is a little limited, but you should be able to find something."

"It sounds like you thought of everything."

"I tried."

"Listen, Hans. I'm sorry I turned the phone off. Will you forgive me?"

"You don't even need to ask," he said.

"The sun's starting to come up, and José will be getting up pretty soon."

"Then, I'll let you get back to work. But Charity, I plan to call you this evening around nine your time. Will you please answer the phone?"

"If I hear it," she agreed.

"I'll call back every hour afterward until you do," he insisted. "You don't know how worried I've been the entire week."

"Well, stop worrying. I've made my way around for twenty-six years, Hans. I'm fine."

"But, I'm not. I think of all the sharks you dive around and the tourists who might make passes at you, and I worry."

"You don't need to worry about these two couples. They seem pretty devoted to each other."

"Like I am to you, hmm. That's good."

"Hans! I know you care about me, but slow down!"

She could hear him inhale sharply, then exhale, on the end of line.

"Charity, if it takes the rest of our lives, I'm going to prove to you that I have staying power."

"That's exactly how long it will take," she teased. "I'll see you Monday, Hans."

"Monday, then."

They didn't say goodby. Charity couldn't have taken that. It was too much to ask of her right now. She sat on the beach and looked at the two trawlers sitting in the bay, the water mirroring their reflection as the sun started to rise on the horizon.

For a moment she saw the curling of a spotted eagle ray's wing raise gracefully out of the water and sink back down again, without leaving more than a tiny ripple.

After telephoning her mother, to tell her she would be arriving Monday evening, and bringing a guest for dinner, she left the beach and went to work.

Later that morning, José asked Charity to take Árima out to Pajara Islet. She knew it was his way of rewarding Charity for all her hard work on the trail to Point Ulloa. The tourists planned to relax today before heading back to Puntarenas tomorrow, and José planned to trap a few more of the island pigs to take off the island with them Saturday morning.

Other than that one idyllic dive with Árima, in which Charity saw memories of Hans everywhere, the rest of her work week was taken up with finishing the trail to Point Ulloa, and cleaning the Chatham

Bay cabin for tomorrow's arrivals, while José and all the others wrestled pigs.

She spoke with Hans briefly Thursday night, ascertained that he was now safely in San Diego at Josh and Kayla's condo, and wrote down his flight number, time of arrival, and marina instructions.

On Friday, she was so busy getting the cabin readied and her clothes packed that she didn't have much time for chit chat, so she told him she would give him her undivided attention on Monday.

If Charity had been truthful with herself, she would admit that she was beginning to have hope for Hans and herself, and that scared her more than anything. She didn't know how to assuage her fear that he would never arrive at the airport on the flight he told her to meet. In her state of mistrust and doubt, she fully expected the airport authorities to have her committed to a mental hospital when they found her weeks later wandering around the airport in a daze, unable to reconcile herself to her disappointment.

By the time they were ready to leave on Saturday, they had loaded nine pigs into cages, three pigs to a cage, all near the stern of the park services boat. In addition to the rolling swells and the howling wind, a summer storm had approached, and washed waves over the bow, down the decks to the stern where the water swept the pigs off their feet in their cages. The rangers tried to amuse themselves with card games and magazines, but eventually everyone was seasick, including Charity. They raced one another to the gunwale and lost breakfast, lunch and supper. By dark, their bodies were too weary to care anymore, and they curled up in their berths, too sick to sleep, and waited with prayer for the waves and the wind to ease. By morning, although a blustery wind still whistled past them, their prayers were, at least partially, answered. It was probably the worst crossing Charity had experienced, and one she would not soon want to repeat. If Hans had telephoned Saturday, she would not have heard the phone ring because the roar of the wind and the squealing of the pigs deafened all other sound.

By Sunday afternoon, the seas were relatively calm and the wind had been replaced with the blazing sun. Charity helped José replace fresh water for the pigs in their cages and mop up the decks from all the salt crystals that had formed in the heat. It wasn't until nearly dusk that the boat pulled into Puntarenas, and Charity was immediately relieved that she had Hans' boat to shelter her for the night, as their boat had been driven so far back in the storm that they had missed the last bus.

Charity offered to let José and his family stay aboard with her, but they said they preferred to sleep in the bunks on the park service boat that night, and catch the early morning bus. She promised to see them again in ten days, picked up her heavy duffle bag and headed toward the gated marina where *Bridger* awaited her.

Walking inside the brightly painted marina office, she was greeted by an elderly man who said, "You are Charity Perez Blake, no?"

Surprised that he had been expecting her, she said, "Yes."

"Mr. Clark telephoned and asked me to give you your key to the gate, and to tell you that *Charity's Bridge* is in slip number C7." He handed her a key, and added, "And this package arrived Friday for you."

"Thank you," she said, taking the small box from him, impressed to see Hans' neat handwriting. "Excuse me, did you say *Charity's Bridge?*"

"Si, Senorita, the painter finished it on Friday, before the big storm."

"I see," she replied, surprised and anxious to see what Hans' had done to *Bridger.* "Thanks."

She walked out the door and down to the landing, then inserted the big key into the lock of the gate that secured the marina from casual intruders. The lock clicked and she pushed the gate open, stepped past it and waited for it to swing shut and lock again before she turned and hurried down the ramp. At the bottom, she turned to her right, her passage lighted by the electric posts that headed each slip, and street lights that were mounted in each main corner. Turning left, she walked out to dock C and turned left again, then hurried over to slip 7. These slips were much larger than those on docks A and B, and they faced the Bay of Puntarenas.

Charity's Bridge was moored stern in at slip 7, and she easily stepped from the dock to the swim step, then up into the cockpit. After placing her duffle bag and the package onto one of the benches, she left the boat and stepped around the dock to look at the name on its port side.

This gesture, more than any other, brought tears to her eyes. Hans had gone beyond thoughtful. Surely, this proved he cared about her, and gave her hope that he had staying power. Charity laughed aloud, jumped quickly back, and twirled around giggling. She owned a million-dollar boat that meant nothing to her, nothing whatsoever. In fact, she would be returning the title to him tomorrow. But the name Hans' had chosen for it meant everything.

When she stopped twirling and had caught her breath, she read the name once again. *Charity's Bridge.* There was a curly design fore and aft of the name and she noticed at the very beginning of *Charity's*, a little anchor dipped off the swirl, followed by two tiny hearts linked together.

Charity went over to the other side of the dock and looked across at Hans' boat. The same name had been put on the starboard side as well, only the anchor and hearts came after the swirl that followed *Bridge*. She clasped her hands together and danced her way back aboard *Charity's Bridge*. Hans' thoughtfulness knew no boundaries.

She was so excited, she fumbled with the keypad, trying to remember the code to get inside. When it finally came to her, she found her fingers trembling with happiness, her heart singing.

It was then that she noticed the roses. It was so dark she'd had trouble seeing the keypad, but when she went to slide the companionway hatch open, the roses seemed to jump out at her. *Two dozen roses* in a huge crystal vase were waiting on the hatch for her.

Charity lifted them off and realized they couldn't have been delivered more than ten minutes before she arrived, as the base was still cool to the touch. After inhaling their sweet fragrance, she set them down on the bench beside her duffle bag and slid the companionway open, stepped inside to find a light already on over the stove, and another note on the counter top.

> *Dear Charity;*
>
> *At the nav station you'll find a list of all the components and how to operate them. The air conditioner switch for the master bedroom is beside the bed, on the starboard side.*
>
> *I'll see you soon.*
>
> *Affectionately yours,*
> *Hans*

Hans had trusted that Charity would come aboard sometime in his absence. He had trusted her, and now she would have to start trusting him.

Charity smiled. In all her life, she'd never slept in an air-conditioned room before. She was about to get her chance. Quickly, she carried the vase of roses, her duffle bag and the package down to the galley. She placed the roses on the salon table, stood back to admire them, then spent several moments sniffing each blossom, trying to determine which of the two dozen smelled best.

The entire cabin was spotless, and she guessed that Hans had hired a cleaning service so that she wouldn't have to worry about anything tonight. Charity closed the companionway and locked it from the inside, then followed Hans instructions to arm and disarm the alarm, several times so that she would know how. Leaving it armed, she went into the galley, opened the refrigerator box, and found a quart of fresh milk, a large freshly made spinach salad with chicken chunks, a container of creamy Italian dressing, and a bowl of fresh fruit.

She removed the fruit and put it on the counter, then located the master bedroom suite aft, where she slipped into a warm shower and ran it until the water was cold.

When she finished dressing in her nightgown, she returned to the galley and pulled out the milk, spinach salad and dressing. In a cupboard, she found a box of crackers, and ate a healthy meal before doing what few dishes needed cleaning.

Before going to bed, Charity remembered the package Hans had sent, and she opened it quickly. Inside she found two credit cards with her name on them, a Visa and an American Express, and a gift-wrapped barrette made of polished silver with her name carved into the bow. Charity pulled her hair over her shoulder and admired the barrette's color compared to her ebony-shaded strands. Hans was definitely spoiling her, and she was loving every delicious moment of it.

Turning the air conditioner on, Charity let the air blow over her body and cool her down. She had never slept in a bedroom without a companion anytime in her life that she could remember, nor on a sailboat. Feeling supremely blessed, she rolled off the side of the bed and said her prayers.

Chapter Nine

Hans settled into his seat on the small, commuter plane. He wanted to make a phone call from the plane, but it was way too early. Exercising patience, Hans decided to wait until after he'd switched planes in Los Angeles, before making the call. The flight to LAX was incredibly short, and he soon boarded his flight to San José, Costa Rica, where he sank into a luxurious first-class seat and stretched out his legs to relax, then asked the flight attendant to let him know when he could use one of the plane's phones.

Troubled because the private investigator he'd hired had found absolutely nothing about Daniel Blake or his family in Chicago in over a week's worth of searching, Hans had asked Josh's bishop, yesterday, if it would be possible to locate Daniel Blake through his church membership. The Bishop agreed to see what he could do, and Hans agreed to call him and remind him a little later this morning. Since his flight from Los Angeles to San José would take a little over eight hours, he would have plenty of time to phone while en route.

While Hans had enjoyed being home in the United States, his focus for the first five days had been on Ed in the hospital at Vernal, Utah. Keeping Ed's mind occupied so he didn't have to think so much about his leg, or the ranch, had not been an easy assignment. But now, Ed was home at the Bar M with Alyssa, and Tom had taken over the reins of the ranch. Meanwhile, Will was back at work running river rafting trips on the Green River.

Hans spent the weekend in San Diego with Josh and Kayla, who were settled back into their condo. They were considering buying a house near the University of California at San Diego, where Josh could work on his teaching assignment at the University for eight months a year. He also learned that they would be staying at the Bar M ranch for the better part of their summers, after their next child was born, at least. At the rate they were going, they would soon have too many children to spend all summer aboard Josh's boat, *Bridger's Child.* They still moored the sailing vessel up at their dock in Friday Harbor, Washington, where the Admiral occasionally used it, and where Josh and Kayla would 'steal away' whenever the grandparents offered to babysit. But, they were thinking about trading Kayla's Ericson 38 on something a little bigger that the whole family could use in the spring, winter and fall. The *Lady Dawn* had been Kayla's boat before she married Josh. Now, it seemed she was ready to move up, and they were considering one of the largest sailing vessels available, so that when the children got a little older, they could do some serious cruising with all of them aboard.

All in all, it had been a good trip from Cocos Island to Utah, to California and back toward Costa Rica, except for missing Charity.

Hans closed his eyes. Immediately, his memory filled with sweet recollections of his first dive with Charity at Manuelita Island. Other 'firsts' came to mind: the first time they held hands at *Bridge's* bow; their first kiss at Aqujes Point on Colnett Peninsula; the way she smiled when she said, "You had me at *please*."

Learning that Charity was also a Latter-day Saint had been an important highlight . . . for both of them, Hans recalled.

His disappointment when she didn't answer his calls that first week, and his anxiety that perhaps he'd pushed her too far by giving her the boat, had certainly disturbed him. Making the boat a gift to Charity was a major chunk out of his nest egg, but not enough to worry him. Hans smiled to himself when he remembered Ed's reaction. The whole family, including the Admiral, considered committing him. Hans did not know whether Josh had deliberately let that point slip to their father, or not.

At first, Hans felt a little disappointed that Josh seemed to be developing such a good rapport with their father. But, as he thought about it, he grew happier by the moment. Hans had been the apple of his father's eye to start with, only because Josh had such a rebellious streak about earning his own way in the world, while Hans willingly accepted any gift the Admiral cared to give him. The Admiral didn't understand Josh's hesitation, not at first. But, Josh had finally earned their father's admiration. If Josh and the Admiral were drawing closer to one another, it was the best thing that could happen to the Clark family.

Hans did not feel the least bit remorseful about signing over his boat to Charity. If nothing happened between them, he would still be glad that she had the boat. She could sell it and put herself and her brother through school. She wouldn't be forced into hard manual labor for the rest of her life, and she could become the marine biologist she hoped to become.

In his heart, Hans dared to hope that Charity was beginning to like him. At least, she'd been kind and attentive on the telephone, even though she did not answer Saturday night. Hans had deliberately not called her last night, he wanted her to have some time to herself, to enjoy the surprises that he had arranged for her upon her arrival at *Charity's Bridge.* If he'd been able to find musicians in Puntarenas, he'd have sent them there to serenade her, but that was something no one, not even with his vast resources, could locate on such short notice.

After takeoff, Hans was served a delicious breakfast of French toast, fruit and juices. He read from his scriptures for a while after the flight attendant took his tray away, then dozed off to sleep.

When he awoke, he was surprised to find his scriptures still open on his lap, and the sun almost coming into his port-side window. The flight attendant, seeing that he was awake, walked down the aisle toward him and said, "I didn't want to wake you, sir, but you asked to use the plane's phone, and it's in service now."

Hans glanced at his watch and was surprised to see that he'd slept through most of his flight. It was nearly two in the afternoon.

He picked up the phone and dialed the international codes, then the telephone number for Josh's bishop. After two short rings, a woman answered, "Carlton residence."

"Hi, this is Brother Hans Clark. Is the Bishop at home?"

"He just left, Brother Clark, but he left a message for you. Just a minute, I'll get it." The rustling of papers sounded nearby, then the woman said, "Yes, here it is. The Chicago Stake President's number."

"Thank you," said Hans, writing the number down. "Tell him I appreciate it very much!"

They said their goodbyes. Hans dialed the country code and the number he'd been given for the Chicago Stake President, but there was no answer. He would have to try again later. Hans slipped the telephone number into his wallet, and picked up his scriptures to read from Moroni 7. He certainly hoped Charity had seen the Book of Mormon. He had left it on the bed aboard *Charity's Bridge*, and he hoped the cleaning crew did not move it.

Anticipating their meeting at the airport, Hans was so excited, he could hardly stand the waiting. Whatever hold it was that Charity had on his heart, it certainly wasn't the same with Alyssa or Kayla, or any of dozens of women he'd met in his university years. That he was fond of Alyssa had been evident within moments of meeting her, before he knew that she was sent to the earth for Ed Sparkleman. Infatuated, yes, but in love, no . . . Hans now keenly understood the difference between the two emotions.

Hans played over in his mind their upcoming meeting at the airport: the excitement in her sea-green eyes when Charity saw him again; the quickening of her footsteps as she moved toward him; the gentle bounce of her waist-length, shimmering hair as she hurried along, picking up speed, then running ever faster to be with him again; Hans taking her in his arms and kissing her right there in public, in front of everyone; swinging her around and listening to her delicious laughter!

Hans absolutely couldn't wait. Anticipation welled up within him, making it difficult for him to breathe. His heart quickened and his palms were sweating. He felt light-headed and giddy as a school boy, almost euphoric, which he realized at once meant that his heart was in serious trouble if Charity did not or could not return his affection.

Charity waited impatiently at the airport. She had twirled her hair up into a sophisticated twist and secured it with the silver barrette Hans had sent her. Using her own credit card, knowing full well that she should have spent the extra income she had earned dive-guiding for Hans on her mother and her brother, and feeling totally selfish, she'd bought a shimmering, sea-blue dress with silver threads that complimented the barrette, and a pair of silver staccato heels, with a small silver purse that matched.

She wanted Hans to realize what a beautiful woman she could be when she actually dressed up. The only way he'd seen her so far was in her ranger khakis and t-shirt, hiking boots, or in her bathing suit surrounded by an assortment of diving gear.

In her purse, waiting to be given back to Hans shortly after he arrived, were two credit cards and the title to his boat. She was keeping the barrette and the flowers, although she knew the roses were already beginning to wilt in the car she'd rented for Hans. Perhaps she could save them if she cut the stems and gave them fresh water the moment they arrived at her apartment, which she shared with her mother and brother in San Pedro.

When she saw Hans come up the airport tunnel, a lump formed quickly in her throat, her pulse raced, and she felt faint and frustrated that he should have such an overwhelming affect on her. Like a statue, completely still, her eyes searching his, she waited patiently for him to approach. She dared not approach him, for fear she would start running straight into his arms and knock him over in the process since it was so like her to develop an irrational clumsiness when she got excited.

Hans stopped the moment he saw her, as though he, too, were waiting for her to approach. It wasn't so much that she refused. It seemed more like her feet were glued to the floor. Charity tried several times to lift one foot up and put it in front of the other, but she couldn't budge. Fear held her cemented in place.

Finally, Hans nodded, smiled, waved at her, and came hurrying toward her, his bold blue eyes alight with apparent happiness. Hans was running now, watching her completely. Fearing Hans might develop his own clumsiness and bowl her over in his path, she stepped backward and to the side. In doing so, she stepped on the toe of a young man with a surfboard bagged up on his shoulder, wearing a t-shirt and a low-slung pair of baggy pants, probably a tourist who'd come to surf the Pacific swells off Costa Rican beaches. As the surfer turned to see who had stepped on his foot, the board swung around and caught Hans square in the face. In his haste to reach her, Hans' forward momentum added to the punch and he was knocked backward where he fell onto the concrete floor, banging the back of his head in the process.

Charity gasped and sank beside Hans, whose nose was bleeding and swelling at a rapid rate. His eyes rolled around a bit before trying to focus on her and failing. "Hans," she cried. "Are you all right?"

"Hey, sorry dude," said the young man. "I didn't see you coming."

When Hans did not respond, Charity's fear consumed her and she started crying in earnest. "Help us!" she called, gathering Hans into her arms. "Someone help us!"

The young man grimaced and set his surfboard down. "Hey, I'm really sorry. It was an accident! He came out of nowhere. You saw it, didn't you?" he asked Charity.

After that it was total chaos. Policemen came rushing over, talking on radios and commanding calls. Medics rushed in, checked the pupils of Hans' eyes, which were still unresponsive, and put Hans on a stretcher. Charity didn't know where the young man had sidled off to, her total focus was on Hans.

Within minutes, Charity was carrying Hans' overnight bag, trying to follow the stretcher to the front doors of the airport. An ambulance rushed Hans to the nearest hospital. Meanwhile Charity had to locate the rental car which, at the moment, she couldn't remember where she'd left it. When she finally found it, she was certain that Hans had died on his way to the hospital. How on earth could Hans' returning to her have changed into such a terrible event?

By the time she reached the hospital, Hans had already been there at least an hour. Charity parked the car in the hospital garage, found a nurse who knew where they'd taken Hans, and set out to locate him.

Knowing she was reaching a genuine panic, she stepped behind a curtain in the emergency room where a doctor was examining Hans. Relieved to see that he was now awake, she rushed to his side.

"Mrs. Clark," said the doctor when he saw her, "your husband will be all right. He's much improved over when he first arrived."

"He's not permanently injured?" she asked, ignoring the doctor's mistaking her for Hans' wife. Let them think what they wanted as long as she got to stay near Hans.

"No," he smiled kindly. "But, he will have a headache for a few days. The medication I'm giving will be strong, and you'll need to watch him closely for signs of concussion: slurred speech, one pupil or the other that doesn't dilate properly when exposed to light, extreme sleepiness. If he has any of these problems, bring him back and we'll examine him further." He nodded, turned to leave and put his hand on the curtain.

"He can go?" she asked, completely bewildered. "That's all you're going to do?"

"There is not much we can do for a broken nose and a bump on the head. Just give him cold compresses for the swelling, and his medication for the pain."

"But, he was unconscious," she persisted, turning toward the doctor, her voice accelerating in volume.

Hans reached out and squeezed her hand. "I'b all right," he whispered. "I'b bid through buch worse thad this."

Charity whirled about and stared down at Hans. "Oh, you look terrible!" she exclaimed.

And, he truly did. His eyes had black and blue streaks beneath them and his nose resembled a great, purple snowball snugged against his swollen face.

"Thadks," he muttered, sitting up. "Shall we go, Bissus Clark?"

"You're so swollen you can't even talk clearly," she complained. "Oh, Hans, I am so sorry."

"I'b dot. This way I'll get your ud-divided attedshud." Hans tried to give her a smile, but it apparently hurt to do so and he winced, instead.

"Put your arm around my shoulder," she said with determination.

"I hadn't planned on bringing you home to meet my mother this way, but it seems we have no choice. I'll make a bed for you on the sofa."

'Thadks," he said.

"Don't talk," she implored. "It's probably too painful for you. Just let me get you home."

Hans didn't talk after that, and she could only imagine what he must be thinking. If her nerves had held out, she wouldn't have stepped back onto that young man's foot, and he wouldn't have— But, all the "if only" phrases in the world wouldn't heal Hans now. Charity would be his guardian for the next ten days, at least. This certainly wasn't how she envisioned spending his first day back with her.

Within the hour, Charity had driven to her apartment and parked the rental car in the back alley. The swelling in Hans' eyes had increased to where he only had slits to see through now. Furious with the hospital for not helping Hans more, she led him up the stairs and unlocked the kitchen door. Her mother would still be working in the shop below them, and not wanting to worry her, Charity retrieved a pillow and bed sheet for Hans, and made a resting place for him on the sofa.

When Charity had Hans comfortable and heavily medicated, with a bag of ice over the bridge of his nose and across both his eyes, now completely closed, she sat in a chair beside him and held his hand.

"I know you can't see our apartment clearly just yet," she said in what she hoped was a steady, assured tone, "but it's really quite comfortable . . . about the size of your boat, Hans. We have two bedrooms. Mamá and I share one, and my brother, Perry, sleeps in the other."

"Where are dey?" he enunciated slowly.

"Mamá is at work and Perry is at the medical center. He's studying to be a cardiologist. He has two more years of residency there, and two years in Boston at some special cardiology unit. We are now saving up for his trip to the United States."

"Souds like a bright bad," said Hans.

"He is a bright man," Charity agreed, smiling to herself at Hans' pronunciation. "Hans, I would have insisted they keep you at the hospital if I didn't have Perry's expertise to rely upon. He'll be home around midnight, and he can tell me if we need to worry about your injuries or not."

"My ow-d live-id doctor," nodded Hans. Wincing with the pain this apparently caused, he remained quite still after that.

"I'll get you something to drink," she suggested. "I know that in this heat you should keep your fluids up."

"Thadks," he offered.

"No, don't talk," she insisted. "It must be terribly painful to even move. I'll do the talking for a little while."

Charity brought Hans a glass of grape juice with a straw, then resumed her position in the chair beside him. Leading the straw to Hans' mouth, she helped him sip the juice, and when he'd finished, she began talking to him almost non-stop about Costa Rica and all the places she wanted to take him when he felt better. It wasn't until an hour later that she realized he was sleeping.

Quietly, Charity left the front room and retired to her bedroom where she removed her blood-stained dress and underclothes, and soaked them in cold water in the bathroom sink. She took a quick shower, then dressed in a comfortably thin cotton blouse and gauzy fuchsia skirt.

By this time of day, the apartment started to cool down slightly from the sun setting behind the first row of apartment buildings behind them, which were four stories taller than the one in which they lived. After sorting her laundry and putting a load in the washing machine next to the kitchen counter, she debated whether or not to run it, and decided she should wait for Hans to wake up first.

In the meantime, she carefully washed the silken threads of her new dress until she finally got all the blood out, then rinsed it thoroughly and hung it on a clothes line that stretched from the kitchen window, overlooking the alley, to a building across from theirs where it wrapped around a pulley at both ends. Her more personal items she hung across the shower curtain rod in the bathroom. By the remarkably short time it took for her new dress to dry, Charity had tidied the apartment, swept the floors and mopped them, too.

Still, Hans slept, and Charity began to worry if this was normal. It was almost ten at night when she heard her mother's footsteps on the back stairs.

Hurrying to the kitchen door, she opened it for her mother and gave her a quick hug.

Her mother, looking over Charity's shoulder to the sofa, exclaimed, "Mamá-mia!" Glimpsing Hans for the first time, she asked. "Is this Mr. Clark?"

Charity nodded.

"What happened to him?" Juaniata asked next.

"Shhh," Charity whispered. "There was an accident at the airport."

"Perry will look at him in two hours," said Juaniata. "I suppose this means you didn't have the candlelight supper I prepared for you."

"No," said Charity, stepping back into the kitchen while her mother paced toward Hans. "Hans drank some juice and fell asleep."

"Let me look," said Juaniata. "He shouldn't sleep so much if his head is hurting."

Charity grimaced as her mother removed the ice pack. "Mamá-mia! Was he hit by a truck?!"

Hans jerked awake as Charity rushed over and took the pack to fill it with fresh ice. The swelling seemed a little less pronounced and Hans could almost blink his eyelids.

"Hello," he said weakly.

Juaniata put her nose inches away from Hans' face and studied his blue eyes for a moment. Then, she turned to Charity. "His eyes look good for an injury like this. Perry will be happy to see it."

"I suppose you're Charity's bother?" Hans asked.

Smiling, Juaniata patted Hans' hand. "Yes. You must call me Mamá. Charity has never brought a man home before now. You will stay here with us, yes?"

"Since he's in no condition to refuse," Charity answered for Hans, "he will have to accept your generous offer."

"You like my daughter?" Juaniata asked, and the interrogation began.

Hans nodded. "Vedy buch," he said.

"You're an American?"

"Yes."

"You're a Latter-day Saint?"

"Yes."

"You have a temple recommend?"

"Yes."

She noticed the thinness of his white shirt and said, "You have not been through the temple, though."

"I was waiteed to go through wid by fabily."

Juaniata nodded briefly, then her eyes narrowed. "You have sufficient means to care for my daughter?"

"Mamá!" Charity protested.

"Hmmpf!" Juaniata made her way back to the kitchen where she opened the refrigerator and pulled out a pan of spicy pork with cooked cabbage, hot peppers and tangy mango slices, a meal she had previously prepared for Charity to heat up for Hans. "A mother needs to ask these questions, Cari. If Daniel were here, he would ask."

Hans chuckled, then winced and said, "Baybe adother paid pill. But, they dock be out, you dow."

Charity got him a pain pill and a slice of toast. "Try to eat something with it, perhaps it won't make you so drowsy." She looked deep into his blue eyes, glad that she could now see them a little more clearly. The pupils were the same size and seemed to move in unison with each other.

Smiling, apparently at her concern, Hans said, "I'b feeling buch better." He ate the toast and took another pain pill with the juice.

Juaniata now had the stove lit and was heating up the supper she'd prepared. "I am waiting," she said impatiently from the kitchen.

Charity moaned. "Mamá, you cannot expect Hans to answer you when we've only known each other a short time and—"

"Yes," Hans interrupted, apparently quite willing to answer Juaniata's earlier question. "I have suffished beads, yes."

"Then you may court her," said Juaniata. "But, only if her heart permits it. Also, she is a good Latter-day Saint. You must respect her at all times."

"Thadk you," said Hans. "That's what I plad to do."

Charity placed the fresh ice pack back over Hans eyes and sat down wearily upon the chair. He reached out for her hand and she placed it willingly in his.

For a moment Charity allowed that her heart might permit Hans to capture it, if that is what he really wanted. Then she tried to ignore the thought with a gentle reminder: any courting to be done would have to survive her mother!

Chapter Ten

With Perry's reassurance that Hans would survive the accident at the airport, and that his nose would heal back into its normal shape and size, Hans rested easily Monday night. Charity got up every four hours that night to make sure Hans had his pain medication, but he assured her by Wednesday morning that he shouldn't need much more medicine. One tablet before bedtime seemed to help most, as did plenty of fluids and bed rest.

When Hans' began to return to normal around Wednesday, Hans and Charity spent long hours conversing and sharing their life stories with one another. Hans was surprised at how easy Charity was to talk with, and the time they spent together that day was priceless.

By Thursday evening, Hans was feeling much better, although his face still looked discolored and slightly misshapened. He and Charity went for a walk as soon as the sun sank behind the apartment buildings across the alley from them. They had only walked about four blocks when Charity turned onto a street where vendors were selling their wares from brightly colored booths. Red, green, yellow and blue lanterns made from crinkly paper were strung around a garden plaza.

Shopping at the market was an exciting event. There was pottery in every form and size, jewelry, skirts, blouses, sombreros, ponchos, chili peppers, fruits and vegetables in all varieties. Vendors spoke in rapid Spanish, extolling their wares from their booths to every passerby that ventured within twenty feet of them. Musicians with concertinas, marimbas and bongo drums played for castanet dancers wearing brilliant shades of scarlet, royal blue and sea green. Their skirts were full, and they wore matching peasant blouses. A dancing spider monkey, wearing a red, purple and white-striped costume performed to music from a fipple flute played by a man dressed in a costume that matched the monkey's.

Between the musicians, dancers and vendors, a cacophony of sound swelled around them everywhere they walked, and there was no escaping it. In the center of the plaza, where a multi-colored, lighted fountain of water shot skyward, the noise surrounding it drowned out whatever noise the fountain made.

"Is it always this loud?" asked Hans, as he and Charity sank onto a bench that encircled the fountain.

"Yes, but this way, it's more difficult to overhear conversations between people."

"I suppose this is the Costa Rica that the tourists usually miss?"

Charity nodded. "The noise is the reason I brought you here," she added. "I didn't want my family to hear what I have to say to you tonight."

Hans gulped nervously. "What is that?" he asked, almost afraid to hear her response.

She opened up her handbag and withdrew two credit cards and the title to *Charity's Bridge,* then placed them into his hand. "I must return these," she said. "I know you meant well by giving them to me, Hans. But, I cannot accept them."

"Why not?" he asked.

"Because I cannot be bought," she suggested, giving him an odd smile. "Besides, a sea-faring gypsy like yourself will need a boat."

"My intention wasn't to buy you," Hans replied, hurt that she would think such a thing. "I only wanted to make life easier for you."

"I cannot accept such expensive gifts, Hans." Charity insisted. "You need to understand, I'm not unhappy living in the lower class. Quite the opposite, actually. Mamá has always been my rock in the storm, and my brother is the brave defender of us both. You cannot come along and expect me to change who I am simply because you have money."

"I'm not trying to change you, Cari," said Hans, using Perry's affectionate name for her. "What is wrong with life being a little easier for you and your family?"

"There's nothing wrong with it. But, when it arrives in a golden chalice, it leaves no room for dignity. We earn what we receive in life, it has always been so for us, Hans." She turned and placed her forehead against the front of his shoulder. "Please try to understand. Our family would love an easier life, but we also like to go to bed at night believing that we have earned it."

"What would you have me do? Sell the boat to you and expect you to make payments to me?" Hans asked.

Charity pulled her head back and smiled broadly. "I don't need a boat right now," she insisted. "Besides, I would never buy a boat like yours, unless I had the means to pay for it. If you want to help us, your generosity should go toward something that will make us more capable of providing for ourselves. And we will insist on repaying you."

Hans thought he understood her intentions, but he did not comprehend the fierce pride she had regarding the repayment of expensive gifts. Josh had the same kind of pride, and it always surprised him that his twin did not accept the Admiral's gifts more graciously. Hans calculated in his mind what he hoped would help her, and said, "Perhaps I could loan you and Perry enough money to finish your education. When you receive your degrees and enter the workforce, you could repay the loans. Would that be something that might interest you?"

"It would depend on whether or not Mamá approved."

"You cannot make your decisions without her approval?"

Charity nodded, then explained, "Certainly, I can. But, I choose not to because she has never been wrong. All my life, she has had to take the role of my father and my mother, and she has prayed earnestly for the Lord to lead her in her parenthood responsibilities. Because we share the same bedroom, I have heard many of her prayers. The Lord listens to her and answers her. In all my life, she has never counseled me contrary to what is best for me. If I disrespect her by not listening to her advice, I would lose the blessings that her counsel would have given me, and I fear that I would also lose my honor."

"So, in order for me to offer anything to your family of value, I would first have to get past Mamá?" Hans asked, making himself use the name Juaniata had requested from him when she first met him.

"You will have to get past Mamá for anything that would change my life, for better or for worse," Charity insisted.

"If I wanted to marry you—" Hans began, feeling as though he had to find out how Charity was truly feeling toward him.

Charity gasped and said, "Hans! You must not speak to me of marriage unless you have approval from my mother!"

"You mean to say that you would let your mother decide whom you should marry, regardless of your feelings toward the man she chooses?" Hans asked, incredulous at the suggestion.

"I would seriously consider her advice," agreed Charity. "Do you not remember that on Cocos Island I told you that *if* I every marry, it will be for love, or not at all."

"Yes, but now you're saying that your mother will make the final decision. If I—" Hans hesitated. He didn't want to cross that barrier again. "If a man should ask your mother for your hand in marriage, and she agreed to the arrangement not because she felt that you loved one another, but because it would benefit your family financially, would you consider marrying the man she chose?"

Charity turned away. "How can I answer hypothetical questions for which I have no experience?"

Hans' blood began to boil just beneath the surface, making his temperament moody and reckless. He put his hand on her shoulder and turned her back around "Tell me the truth," he demanded. "If I, or someone wealthy like me, wanted to marry you, and your mother said to you, 'He is a good match for you,' but you didn't love him, even though you agreed with your mother that marriage would benefit your family, would you marry him?"

"I would prayerfully consider her advice. Do you think Mamá is so shallow that she would ask me to marry someone who I was not already fond of?" Frowning, Charity glared at him.

"Charity, there is a world of difference between fondness and love," insisted Hans, completely bewildered at how little she really cared for him in the manner he had wanted.

"But, fondness can grow into love, can it not?" she asked, her lower lip quivering slightly.

Hans sighed in defeat. "Yes, I suppose it can," he admitted. *And, fondness will have to be enough for now*, he told himself.

❦ ❦ ❦

Last week certainly didn't turn out the way I'd planned, Hans worried as he sat on a balcony chair at the Blake apartment. The two women were in the kitchen doing the dishes. They'd refused Hans' offer to help from day one of his staying with them, regardless that Hans' face had nearly healed, except for the brown and yellow blotches across his nose and under his eyes.

They had just finished eating a wholesome meal of spicy chicken and avocado slices wrapped in homemade pita bread and red lettuce wedges smothered in a tangy fresh salsa. Juaniata Perez-Blake, a superb chef, made exotic dishes as her specialty.

Although Hans enjoyed attending Sunday services in Charity's ward, he felt much more comfortable sitting here on her balcony, hiding behind bright coral and peach-colored camellias, surrounded by fuchsia, lavender and white petunias that hung from baskets around the perimeter of a black, wrought iron bannister. The fragrant blossoms reminded him of honeysuckle and cinnamon. While at church, Hans had felt out of place because the members seemed to stare at his discolored face as though they thought he'd been in a brawl. It was probably his imagination, but he hoped his normal skin tone would return soon.

Through the past week, Hans had spent a good share of his time stretched out on the sofa, resting or visiting with Charity as they played a game of canasta. He blamed his inability to concentrate on his headache.

A kind, attentive and beautiful woman, Charity won his heart over and over again during their past week together. Very domestic, she kept the apartment clean and tidy, taking over the major portion of the housekeeping and meal preparation while her mother worked downstairs.

Dismayed to learn how many long hours Juaniata had to work to keep her boss in designer dresses, Hans vowed to himself that Mamá's slavery was one thing he would put a stop to as quickly as possible. He knew of a building in Mission Beach, near San Diego that was for sale. Perhaps he could persuade Juaniata to move her family to California, where Hans could sponsor their U.S. citizenship, and set Juaniata up in her own designer clothing business. The apartment that he could have the builders create for her and her family above that store would be three times the size of this one. And, if Juaniata insisted on repaying him for the costs involved in setting her family up in business, Hans could negotiate a personal, interest-free loan that would help Juaniata retain her sense of independence and dignity.

Whether or not Charity could learn to care about Hans the way he loved her remained to be seen. Hans did not have an inkling as to Charity's true feelings toward him, as she had not yet expressed them. He recalled with clarity her departing words to him at Cocos Island: *It will take time to win my trust, Hans Bridger Clark. You haven't done that, yet.* She had said *yet,* and Hans hung onto that one word with all the hope he could find in his heart.

Regardless of Charity's trust . . . or love, or the lack of it toward Hans, he could make a beneficial and rewarding life for all three of the Blakes. Their store and apartment would not be far away from both a medical school for Perry and the Marine Biology Center for Charity. The University Medical Center of Southern California had a world-renowned residency program that would be great for Perry to finish his education. If they, too, wanted to retain their dignity, he could grant them interest-free loans, also.

Once he put his plans into action, Charity would have the opportunity to earn her degree in marine biology. While she was attending school, she could get to know Hans better. Perhaps she would learn to love him in time. Although he wanted to remain with Charity in Costa Rica for as long as she required it, he prayed that she would soon want to accompany him back to San Diego.

Josh and Kayla had already offered to sell Hans the condo they owned once they bought their family home. This would give Hans the first permanent, land-based residence he'd had since leaving his father's home for college seventeen years ago. It might persuade Charity that he wasn't a sea-faring gypsy, as she'd accused him of being on Thursday night.

Before long, Perry had returned from the hospital, and Hans spent the evening in an informal Family Home Evening. Sunday was the only evening Perry could occasionally be home. It was a great experience for Hans, sitting in on an evening of religious instruction, family games and refreshments. Josh and Kayla often invited him over for Family Home Evening, but Hans had never formally done one when he was by himself. Rather than prepare a lesson to teach himself, Hans spent time each evening with his scriptures. Glancing over at Charity, Hans dared to hope they would one day participate in their own Family Home Evening together.

Looking a lot like Juaniata, Perry had black, cropped hair and copper skin, but he had emerald-green eyes, like Charity's. Both her children had Daniel's eyes, Juaniata had told Hans. Perry was about six-foot-five inches tall, a height not often seen among Costa Ricans. Perry's real name was Daniel Perez Blake, but Charity had started calling him Perry when she was around eight years of age, and could not be persuaded to call him anything else. Her mother had allowed this change, probably because she could not deal with breaking Charity's heart a second time. Hans guessed that the name change came about the time that Charity truly gave up on her father ever finding the Blake family.

Juaniata usually talked about how her husband, Daniel, would have been proud to know that Perry was in medical school, or that Charity had a lucrative position as a park ranger at Cocos Island.

All Perry could talk about was his anticipation of going to Boston in two more years. Apparently, Perry had been wanting to go to America for a long, long time.

Because Hans had spent the week resting and recuperating, he had not telephoned the Stake President in Chicago. Besides, he didn't want Charity to overhear the conversation. Hans hadn't approached Charity regarding finding her father, and doubted that he should until he knew more about the elusive Daniel Blake.

Early Monday morning, Hans and Charity went to the airfield where Hans had reserved a private plane tour of Costa Rica. It was Charity's first airplane ride, and she let out a little whoop of exhilaration as the wheels lifted off the ground. It took less than an hour for the plane to reach the Caribbean Sea, where the pilot flew over the colorful village of Tortuguero, with its yellow and turquoise painted houses, some with thatched roofs, then on over Tortuguero National Park with its lush vegetation and spectacular waterfalls. They landed and lunched at the Caribbean Clipper, a ship snugged into the harbor that gave gunwale-side table service. Soon, they were back aboard the plane once more, but by this time, the clouds had moved in and they headed toward the airport in San José, their flight cut short by inclement weather.

"At last," Charity announced when the plane slipped beneath the clouds and rain started to pelt the windows.

"What?" asked Hans.

"The rainy season has arrived. Normally, we would have had rain nonstop since around the beginning of June, but this year it's a month late."

"You mean it's going to rain the rest of the summer?"

"We have only two seasons here, Hans," Charity told him. "Wet or dry. It looks like dry is over."

"So you don't have a cooler season, or a hotter season?"

"Hot is the only temperature we have," she said, smiling.

"Whether wet or dry, it's always hot?" he asked.

"Yes, but I love the rain, so this I can live with."

Hans gave her a weak smile. "Doesn't that make it difficult to get out to Cocos Island?"

"Our storms are not the kind you're thinking about," she answered. "Most of the time, the air is pretty calm. We usually only get high winds in October and November. Ocean travelers can expect wind the same time of day as the rain. We have lots of clouds June through December, and lots of rain, but our rain falls in the late afternoon or evening, with the mornings dewy and still. Actually, one of the worst days for wind and wave we've had was at my last crossing. That was rough."

"I tried to call you that Saturday night. Was that your reason for not answering?" he wondered.

"I didn't hear the phone ring. The wind was so loud we couldn't hear ourselves think. Add to that the crashing waves and the squealing pigs, and you'll have a small glimpse of what our crossing was like."

"I'd forgotten you were taking the pigs to Puntarenas."

"We ended up with nine of them, and the poor things were just as seasick as we were. The Captain was the only one aboard who didn't get sick."

"And, I suppose, you'll have to go back to Cocos Island on Friday?"

"Of course. I would be dismissed if I didn't show up, even if I called in sick. The men on the island depend upon us replacing them. Right now, they are waiting their turn to go home to their families. If I don't go, one of them would have to stay an extra two weeks. That would not go over well with José."

"What if I hire a float plane to fly you in Saturday morning? That would give us one extra day together."

"No. The trip over is very important. That briefing and planning day is always a part of our crossing, in which José gives us our personal assignments."

"What about the trip home?" Hans persisted.

Charity gave him a delicious smile. "Now, that I could do," she agreed. "It would give us Saturday together, and we could go to church on Sunday."

"Very well, that's what we'll do."

It seemed impossible that Charity would be willing to face another three-hundred-mile crossing and two more weeks on the island, particularly during the rainy season, when Hans could offer her a way out, but he sensed that she wasn't ready to give up her job just yet. She had to trust him first, and for some reason, he hadn't sensed that she did.

Hans prayed Charity would miss him so much while she was on the island this trip that she would be more than willing to give up her job by the time she came home. He hoped to have a few surprises for her by then. If Hans had anything to say about it, a lot of things were going to change before Charity left Cocos Island again. Some of the changes he hoped to discuss with her on Friday. Others would have to come more as a surprise. With all his heart, Hans prayed that Charity would be willing to discuss some permanent alterations in her lifestyle, with the blessing and approval of her mother.

By the time the pilot dipped the plane below the clouds and landed at the airport, they had discussed their itinerary for the next three days. Hans wanted to tour a tropical rain forest on Tuesday, have Charity take him on a guided tour of the city of San José, including three museums on Wednesday, and visit the Irazu Volcano on Thursday, but Hans didn't want those days to begin, for that meant they would also end.

On Friday, Hans and Charity would drive back to Puntarenas, where she would board the park service boat for two nights and a day at sea, and begin her fourteen days laboring on the island.

If there was nothing else Hans was sure of, Charity would not be taking the park boat back to the mainland. Since she had agreed that Hans could hire a float plane for Saturday morning, he knew that she would be home two days earlier than normal.

Hans would miss Charity terribly, and hoped that she would miss him as much. Perhaps not, he realized. She had not said she was anything more than fond of him. This discouraged him, but he would never give up. Hopeful that during her absence he would be able to win her mother's heart, and change their meager existence into something special in which the entire family could take pride, Hans set his mind to other matters and tried not to think about how much he was going to miss Charity the next two weeks.

He didn't think that convincing Charity to move to the United States would be difficult, nor Perry for that matter. But, Juaniata would be the challenge. Unless Charity's mother trusted Hans, there was no way on earth he would be able to convince her to take such a mighty leap forward.

Chapter Eleven

Friday came too soon for Charity, who didn't want to admit, even to herself, that she was dreading the separation from Hans as she went back to work on Cocos Island. He was capturing her heart, piece by tiny piece, and she worried that he would soon fill up the entire empty space within her that she had guarded ferociously all her adult years.

The only consoling factor was that she now sensed that Hans was serious in his pursuit of her. Still, conflicting emotions forced her heart to sway back and forth in her decision about how she really felt toward him. Titillating as the prospect of his affection might seem, she had not come to completely trust him, and she worried if she ever would.

The skies were boisterous and dripping overhead as Hans drove through San José on the road toward Puntarenas. He'd been unusually quiet, and Charity couldn't help feeling that he was about to tell her something of great importance. She'd learned to know Hans well enough to realize that when he was about to say something startling or of great importance, he dwelt on it a long time beforehand. This seemed to be one of those times.

Around one, they stopped at a quaint little restaurant called La Cocina de Lena in San José, which Charity had recommended because of their specializing in Costa Rican style dishes, and no Americanization at all.

After ordering the glazed pork for both of them, Hans turned his attention to Charity by taking her hand across the table and caressing the back of it with his thumb.

"Charity, I hardly know where to begin. I've been debating all day how to start, and I find that one way is no better than another," he said, his bold blue eyes searching hers.

The discoloration of his face had diminished almost completely, except for a faint hint of yellow right over the bridge of his nose. The smile he gave her seemed more timid than usual, but it lit up her heart all the same.

"Take the bull by the horns," she encouraged. "That's what Mamá always taught us."

"She's a wise woman, your mother," he said. "While you're away, Charity, I will ask your mother for permission to marry you."

Charity fought down the lump that had arisen in her throat and tried to do the same to the tears now forming in her eyes, to no avail. She hoped he wouldn't misinterpret her reaction. To her own amazement, she suddenly realized that she wanted this proposal almost more than life itself. Hans pulled a handkerchief from his coat pocket and gave it to her. Taking the crisp cotton from him, she dabbed at her eyes and hung onto it, in case she still needed it. Folding her hands in her lap, she waited for him to continue.

"Whether she'll approve or not, I have no idea," he admitted. "But, I can provide for you and your family, Charity. I want to do everything I can to make your life, and their lives, more comfortable, while allowing all of you to maintain your dignity." Hans waited, as though expecting her to respond.

Nodding, Charity said quietly, "Go on."

"I'd like to take your mother away from the sweat shop she works in, and move her to San Diego, where I can set her up in her own dress shop, where she will get credit for the fabulous designer dresses she makes. Once the shop is doing well, and I know that it will, she will be able to repay me for whatever it costs to get her business going. I'd like to make Perry a student loan, so that he can attend medical school in San Diego. They have a great program at Southern Cal University. I know because I considered medicine once, and investigated the school thoroughly at that time. When he finishes there, if he still wants to go to Cambridge for cardiac training, his loan can cover those expenses, as well. When he's set up in medical practice, he can begin repaying the loan."

Charity nodded. She had expected nothing less from Hans, and had known from his expression when she'd given him the title to his boat and his credit cards at the Plaza over a week ago, that he would probably come up with a plan like this. It did not surprise her, although she wondered whether or not her mother would accept such a plan. Juaniata Perez-Blake was not so proud that she would deny her children the opportunities Hans was offering. But could Juaniata leave Costa Rica? She had been forced to flee from Nicaragua in 1979, and had blamed Daniel's inability to find her upon this action. At that time, the Sandinistas were bearing down hard on the villagers, and it was only a matter of time before they were all slaughtered. In leaving, Juaniata had probably saved their lives. Leaving word with three neighbors and the landlord where she would be staying in Costa Rica, Juaniata had fled the village carrying Charity in her arms and Perry in her womb. Along the route, she had met others who were also fleeing, some from much farther than Nicaragua as Juaniata had. Charity's mother had walked over two hundred miles before reaching the border, where her brother, Rafael, had picked her up in a dusty old truck and took her to his home in Costa Rica.

"Mamá may not agree to leaving Costa Rica, Hans," she responded.

"I will convince her," he insisted.

"Your total confidence surprises me, but you don't know Mamá. She is certain that the only reason why Daniel has not come home is because he cannot find us. She left her brother's address with four people when we left Nicaragua. If we leave Costa Rica, she will be forced to give up hope that he will ever find us."

"But, she will want to do what is best for her children," Hans persisted. "Mamá is not so in love with Daniel that she would sacrifice her children's happiness for him, especially in a place where he has never found her."

Charity reconsidered. "No, you're probably right. She has always denied herself in order to provide for us."

"If Mamá approves our marriage, where will your heart be, Charity?"

"I will prayerfully consider where my heart stands, Hans," she promised. "For I am fond of you."

"Then, we are still worlds apart, for I am in love with you," he confessed, and she noticed moisture welling up in his eyes, as well.

Handing him back his own handkerchief, she waited while he wiped his eyes, then held her hand out to him. "There is still room in my heart for love, Hans. But, fear gets in the way. You are still an American."

"So are you," he argued. "You live in the Americas the same as I do."

Smiling at this sly approach, Charity nodded. "Yes, you're right, of course. And you have proven that you know how to return. But, Daniel proved this, too, for the first year of Mamá's marriage to him."

"Perhaps you'll be able to allow me more room in your heart as we celebrate each anniversary through the next fifty or sixty years." Hans lifted his hand to her cheek. "If fondness is all that you can offer right now, I will take what I can get."

"If Mamá agrees to our marriage, I would like a long engagement. At least a year," she suggested.

Hans nodded, although she could see that it disappointed him to agree to her suggestion. He was quiet after that, and they ate their lunch in silence. When they had started on dessert of rice pudding mixed with coconut and papaya chunks, Hans asked, "Today, I would like you to give José notice that you won't be returning to the island after this trip. I know you love your job, but I would love the opportunity to help you get your marine biology degree."

Charity grimaced and he raised his eyebrows, his eyes widening in alarm.

"You don't want to leave your job?" he guessed.

"I'm conflicted," she admitted. "For two years, I have dreamed of the day when Perry would get out of medical school so that I can return to the academic life. But, I also love my job. Cocos Island is my second home. José, Teresa and Árima have been my family away from home. It will be difficult to leave them all behind me."

"We can take a voyage to Cocos Island every summer break while you are back at school. And, when you graduate, we can go there more often, if that is what you want. I can start filling out the applications now, so that we will have an annual entrance card."

Her green eyes filled with tears, and Hans gave her the handkerchief a second time. "You are so thoughtful, Hans," she sniffed and wiped at her eyes and her nose. "I had no idea that someone with so much empathy could come into my life and disrupt it so selflessly. What will you get out of all your sacrifices?"

"Your happiness," he whispered. "That's all most men really want, Charity, to fill the women they love with happiness and joy. To provide for them and make them comfortable with their lives. Men want to know that they put a smile on their wives' faces."

"It hardly seems fair," she complained. "We fill your stomachs, but you fill our hearts."

"It's a trade-off," he agreed. "Tom's father, Sparky, once told him that if husbands and wives would spend their lives filling the needs and wants of their spouses, marriages would never fail. Both parties' needs and wants would be met, and both would be happy. I believe the prophet calls this unconditional love."

"The pure love of Christ," she amended.

"Like Charity . . . from Moroni 7:47."

"*But charity is the pure love of Christ, and it endureth forever; and whoso is found possessed of it at the last day, it shall be well with him*," she quoted.

"You've memorized it!" Hans said in amazement.

"How could I not?" she asked. "It's the scripture from which my name came. Mamá recited it often to me when I was growing up. I know it as well as I know my own thoughts."

"I've read Moroni 7 perhaps a dozen times in the past two weeks. In helping your family, that's what I'm trying to do," Hans confessed.

"You are trying to show us that you have the pure love of Christ?" she asked.

Hans shook his head. "Show the Lord that I am striving for the pure love of Christ," he amended. "I am not so foolish, nor so well educated, that I cannot recognize my failings. To presume that I already have such a gift would be ludicrous, at best. The pure love of Christ involves stepping outside yourself and allowing His love to work through you. It takes a greater man than I to succeed at such a feat. You forget that I am relatively new to the Gospel. My baptism was less than three years ago. I've only had a short time to put the Savior's precepts into my life, and I am far from perfect."

"You're getting close," she told him. "Which is one of the reasons why I am so fond of you."

"There's that word again," he complained. "Fond. Someday, I hope your fondness for me will grow into love, Charity."

"It will take time," she reiterated. "I see no reason to rush my feelings." Shaking her head, she could see the disappointment on Hans' handsome face.

Charity wanted to change the look in his eyes to happiness, and a warm and wonderful feeling seeped into her heart, filling her up with comfort and peace, as though the Spirit were whispering to her that she already loved Hans. She wanted to tell him that she loved him, but she couldn't do it. A coldness wrapped around her heart, almost unbidden, dampening the inspirational feelings she'd just had for Hans. Dare she give Hans that much power to hurt her, as Daniel had hurt her mother? *No! Not yet!* Not until she felt she could trust him completely.

So far Hans had proven his staying power, but he'd had little choice once he arrived. He'd had to stay in order to be nursed back to health. After he began to heal, her mother wouldn't hear of his going to a hotel. And Hans hadn't argued the point, either. Of course, it would take quite a man to win a disagreement with Juaniata Perez-Blake.

After leaving the restaurant, Hans drove the rental car back to Puntarenas, where they checked on his Hallberg-Rassey 62, *Charity's Bridge*. Just seeing her name upon the starboard and port sides of the boat brought new joy to Charity. Hans surveyed the new artwork with a keen eye, and when it seemed that he was completely satisfied, he turned to her and asked, "Do you like it?"

"It was very thoughtful of you," she agreed, nodding her head. "Thank you."

"She seems to be secure here. The security is adequate, and the captain managed to bring her in without damaging her."

He stepped aboard and unlocked the companionway, then went below to check the bulge pumps and other security checks. Charity waited for him on a cockpit bench. When he put his head out of the companionway, she said, "Is everything okay?"

"Yes. But, the cleaning service put my scriptures away. That's why you never mentioned them after you arrived."

"Your scriptures?" she asked.

Hans handed her a quadruple set bound in a handsome brown leather. The zipper was open, and an envelope was inserted in a particular passage. Charity opened the book where the envelope had been placed and saw that Hans had highlighted Moroni 7:42—47. Since they had just discussed one of these verses during dessert, she was surprised.

Noticing that the envelope was addressed to her, Charity lifted the flap and slid out a card that had a sailing vessel much like *Charity's Bridge* embossed on the front of it. Opening the card, she read:

> *Dear Charity;*
> *I was reading from Moroni 7 tonight, knowing that in the morning I will have to leave you to look after the needs of my brother in Utah. This family obligation could never have come at a more inopportune moment, not because I have to leave the island, but because we have not had sufficient time to learn to trust one another. I first wanted to prove to you that I have no intention of ever leaving you now that I've found you. You are the spring in my step, the twinkle in my eyes, the hope in my heart.*
>
> *I hope that you will read Moroni 7 while you stay aboard "Charity's Bridge," and that it will come to mean as much to you as it does to me.*
>
> *All my love,*
> *Hans*

"You wrote this before you left the island?" she asked, knowing the question had already been answered.

Hans came out through the companionway and sat beside her, his arm going around her shoulders as he snuggled up against her. "Charity, I've loved you from that very first day we spent together, when we shared my rebreather and swam above the coral watching the marine life swim around us. To me, it was like an intoxicating dance. Since that day, I've never been the same."

Charity gave him a broad smile. "I was well paid for that dance, Hans. And I hated you that day. You represented everything in my life that I feared." She said it in a teasing manner, so that he wouldn't be insulted.

"I know that," he admitted. "But, somehow José and Teresa convinced you to give me the benefit of the doubt, and you did. Is it any wonder that I love you so? You can look beyond your fears, beyond what you expect of American men. To be able to overcome such a deep-seated fear takes great character and determination. It's just one of a dozen reasons why you captured my heart."

"Hmm," she mused aloud. "Then, you understand that the only way you can conquer my heart is if I set my mind to it?"

"I understand," he admitted. "And, I'm not giving up. I happen to think you're worth the effort."

"My mind is still whirling from all the changes you want to make in my life, Hans. But, if you plan to spend your life pleasing me, I suppose that I can strive to step outside myself and try to do the same for you." She focused on his blue eyes as he studied hers, and his gaze went far beyond fondness.

Hans bent his head toward hers, and captured her lips in a tender and gentle kiss. When he withdrew, he said, "I'm not going to rush you, Charity. If it will take time for you to trust me, I will give you all the time you need."

He stood and led her aft of the cockpit and down the stern steps to the dock. Holding her hand as they walked the rest of the way to the park services dock, Hans admonished, "I trust you'll be careful while you're at Cocos Island. I don't want some shark mistaking you for supper."

"I probably won't get to dive much this trip," she confessed. "It's my turn to run the patrol boat."

"What does that assignment include?" he asked.

"Every morning and evening I circumnavigate the island. Sometimes Árima joins me, sometimes Teresa."

"Do you ever go alone?" He raised an eyebrow of disapproval.

"Sometimes." Charity tried to keep the impatience out of her voice, but she couldn't help it. "Hans, I've been working at Cocos Island for two years. Just because you've entered my life, that doesn't mean I have suddenly become inept or incompetent."

"Sorry," he said quickly. "I didn't mean to imply that you have. What if our roles were reversed, and you were going to stay here while I was going to Cocos Island for two weeks?"

"I wouldn't worry about you," she insisted. "You're a competent diver. You must be a decent sailor or you'd have never found Cocos Island in the first place." Charity shrugged. "I would ask the Lord to watch over you in our absence and trust Him to do just that."

"Aha!" he teased. "So that's why women are privy to so much inspiration. They have a child-like faith that God will protect the people they care about."

Charity shook her head in disagreement. "Sometimes, bad things happen to good people. It doesn't mean God isn't watching over them. If they are wise, they will use the experience to build some additional strength to their character. Perhaps God will teach them an eternal truth they didn't understand before."

"So, except for men you don't trust, you're an optimist," guessed Hans.

"I try," she admitted. "Although, you do seem to set off warnings whenever I'm around you. I want to be optimistic about you, but I keep seeing these red flashing signs that read *Danger! Danger! Danger!*"

"Thanks a lot," Hans grumbled. "That was a real boost to my ego."

"I apologize," she said, "but you don't want me to lie and say that my signs are reading *Trust Hans!* or *Fall in love with Hans!* do you?"

Hans seemed to consider her response. "No, I wouldn't want you to lie about a thing like that. But, if your warnings ever do change to read something complimentary about me, you will let me know, right?" he asked.

"I will," she agreed as they headed down the dock toward the park ranger's boat. "Here's one already." Charity smiled, and she hoped with all her heart that what she was about to do would never come back to haunt her.

José greeted her with a bright, "Hola, Caridad. Our friend made it back safely, I see. Welcome back, Mr. Clark."

Hans shook José's offered hand. "Call me Hans," he insisted.

"José, it's so good to see you. Where is Teresa and Árima?"

"They went to get a few more groceries, Cari," said José. "They shouldn't be much longer."

Charity didn't know quite how to begin, so she just plunged right in, giving Hans a hopeful smile. "José, I'm afraid this is my last two weeks at Cocos Island. My mother and brother will be moving to San Diego soon, and I will be going with them."

For a moment, José didn't seem to know how to answer. Finally, he said, "This is not good news for us, Cari. Why are you moving?"

"I will explain it all to you when Teresa and Árima arrive. That way I won't have to tell the story twice."

"I suspect Mr. Clark has been a major influence in your change of plans?" José guessed.

While Hans grinned, Charity nodded. Then, Hans pulled Charity closer to him and put his arm about her waist, tucking her gently beside him, and she allowed it, which spoke volumes to José without her having to tell him anything.

"Your brother, Ed, he is all right?" José asked Hans, changing the subject.

"Yes. In fact, I spoke to him last night, and he is doing much better."

"And Tom?" asked José.

"He stayed in Utah at the ranch."

"In Utah. Your family, they are members of the Church of Jesus Christ of Latter-day Saints?" A broad grin spread across José's face, and a hopeful glance at Charity told her that this news was, perhaps, better than the fact that she and Hans had grown so fond of one another.

"We are,"admitted Hans. "I'm surprised Charity didn't tell you so after we left the island."

"Ah," said José, "As you will learn, Charity is a private person who also respects the privacy of others."

"Yes, I am learning that."

"Well, come Cari, let's get your gear aboard. I'm very happy for you and Cari," said José, shaking Hans' hand once more. "Very happy!"

Charity looked up into Hans' face and saw the pleasure it had given him for her to give José her two weeks' notice, and she was pleased. Standing on tiptoe, she put a hand upon his shoulder and he lowered his head enough to kiss her soundly.

"Call me every night?" Hans asked. "I won't sleep, otherwise."

Smiling at this confession, Charity acquiesced. "All right."

"I love you," he said. "Don't lose sight of that these next two weeks."

"I won't," she promised. "Take good care of Mamá and Perry."

"Don't worry," he advised. "That's my next order of business."

"That's precisely why I *will* worry," she laughed.

Hans kissed her once more, then stepped back and waved goodbye. When he turned to walk away, Charity watched him go until she could no longer see the top of his head over the cabin tops of main boats in the harbor. Then, she turned to José and handed him her first duffle bag.

Chapter Twelve

Except that Charity had not fallen madly in love with Hans yet, Hans felt their discussion before seeing her safely aboard the Park Service's boat, went rather well. In fact, Charity seemed to have anticipated his wanting to move her family to San Diego. She hadn't been surprised, and this only meant that, contrary to what he considered himself, Hans was too predictable.

Before heading toward Juaniata's apartment in San Pedro that evening, Hans stopped at a fast-food taco stand near the airport in San José, and went through the drive-up for a light supper, which he scarfed down quickly in his parked rental car.

After he finished eating, Hans telephoned the Chicago Stake President's home phone number from his satellite phone. Within a few moments, a woman's voice answered.

"Is President Ely at home?" Hans asked, and was relieved to hear the woman calling the president to the phone.

"This is President Ely," came a deep, husky voice.

"President Ely, my name is Hans Clark. I wonder if Bishop Charles Dalton spoke with you a couple of weeks ago?"

"Why, yes, Brother Clark. Though I must say, I had expected you to call before now."

"I had a little accident at the airport," Hans explained.

"Oh? I hope it wasn't anything serious?"

Quickly, Hans explained about the surfboarder and Hans' first week at Charity's home, adding, "I'm afraid her mother wouldn't allow me to leave after that. Something about Costa Rican hospitality."

"I'm certainly glad you're feeling better, Brother Clark. Now, what may I do for you?"

"I'm looking for a man named Daniel Blake. His parents lived in the Chicago area at one time, and he may have returned to their home after he was released from the military."

"Why are you looking for him?" asked the President warily.

Hans gave a rather long explanation, while President Ely took down all the information that Hans could provide.

Then, President Ely said, "I'm not sure we can locate him, Brother Clark. It's been twenty-six years, and he could be anywhere by now. But, I'll give the name to my clerk, and have him distribute it to the ward clerks. We could also send his name out to the two other stakes in the Chicago area. I just want you to understand, though, that with the time that's passed, and the size of the USA, you realize that you're looking for a needle in a haystack?"

"Yes, President, I do. I've even hired a private investigator, but I'm afraid that he's not had much luck, either. So, anything that your people might be able to find for me, I'd really appreciate it."

"If Daniel Blake is still alive . . . and if he still lives in this area . . . but even if we can connect all the dots, Daniel Blake may not want his past dredged up. He could have remarried and have another family," reminded the Stake President.

"Believe me, President, I've considered nearly every possible explanation for his failure to return to his wife, Juaniata, in Nicaragua. The brethren in San Pedro have counseled her that Daniel was very likely killed during the Nicaraguan conflict," Hans confided.

"We will do what we can, Brother Clark. For the family's sake, it is time that they get some kind of closure regarding Brother Blake's disappearance."

"Thank you," said Hans. "If you can't reach me, feel free to telephone Colton Wright." Hans gave him the private investigator's number. "We'll look forward to hearing from you."

After he hung up, he turned the key in the ignition, drove back out into traffic and found his way through the dark streets of San José back to San Pedro and Juaniata Perez-Blake's apartment.

Hans was not surprised to see Juaniata still awake, when she greeted him eagerly. "Ah, Hans, you are home!" She gave him an affectionate pat on his cheek. "Charity, she arrived safe at Puntarenas?" asked Juaniata.

"Yes, Mamá. Did Perry get home, yet?" he asked.

"No, he was going over to the church for an interview with the Bishop. I think they want to give him a calling, but he is so busy at the hospital, with his internship. They know this already, so perhaps it will be a small assignment, yes?"

"He won't be long?" Hans asked.

"I thought that it might be him, when I heard your car pull in, then I remembered that Perry's car has a squeak in the brake. That's how I knew it was you before I even looked." She gave him a broad smile, then sat across from him at the kitchen table, placing a plate filled with empanadas before him.

"So, Hans," she began, and Hans knew by her astute expression that the great inquisition was about to begin. "Tell me what you think of my daughter?"

Deliberating how to respond would not work with Juaniata, and Hans knew it. Charity's mother liked the answers you gave her to come direct and from the heart. "I'm in love with your daughter," Hans answered. "I would like your permission to marry her."

"Does she love you?" Juaniata asked.

"Charity says that she's fond of me. I'm hoping that fondness will grow into love." He folded his hands politely in his lap.

Apparently disregarding the fact that Charity had not said she loved Hans, Juaniata reminded him, "You said that you have sufficient means to care for my daughter. Now, you must be specific. Will you live in an apartment, or can you buy a house? Will you live in Costa Rica, or move to San Diego? How many children can you afford to raise together? All these questions and more, you must answer to my satisfaction. Her father is not here, and I must take his place. I must act as her father in this regard."

"I understand," said Hans. "About my finances . . . my grandfather was a very wealthy man. When he died, he left everything to my mother and my grandmother. A little over two years ago, my grandmother died, and she left everything to my mother, myself, and my twin brother."

"So, you got twelve and one-half percent of your grandfather's original estate," Juaniata said quickly. "What does that amount to exactly?"

"It's usually best that specific amounts be kept private," Hans told her, "but I earn enough in interest to buy about six sailboats a year, just like the one I own in Puntarenas . . . after I pay my tithing and taxes, of course."

Juaniata's mouth gaped open for a moment, then she snapped it shut. "But, Charity told me that your sailboat is worth more than a million American dollars," she gasped.

"Yes, that's correct," said Hans. "To answer your questions as specifically as I can, we will probably live in a condo for the first little while, until Charity can get her master's degree in marine biology. We will first live in San Diego. After that, we'll live wherever Charity wishes. When the children start arriving, we can afford to raise as many as the Lord chooses to send into our home. Is there anything else I can tell you to assure you that my intentions are honorable?"

Juaniata, flustered and surprised, broke apart an empanada and crumbled it upon the table, eating only a nibble or two. "I see," she finally responded, not answering his question. "So, you would take Charity away from her family until she has finished school?"

"No," said Hans, shaking his head, and reaching across the table to take Juaniata's hands in his. She was very much like Charity in her slender build, her black hair. Her eyes were a rich, brown-black. Juaniata's Hispanic facial features were distinctly, yet beautifully, different from Charity's. "Mamá," he comforted, "I would take you and Perry with us, to live near us in California."

Gasping as though she could not catch her breath, Juaniata finally squeaked out a surprised, "What?"

"I would like to make a business proposal," Hans explained quickly. "With my financial backing, and your skill and expertise, I would like to open a designer dress shop near San Diego. I even know of a building that is currently for sale. It is a two-story building, so if you would like, we can remodel the upstairs into a grand apartment for you and Perry to share while he finishes medical school, or find you a condo nearby, if you preferred. In the meantime, you could design clothing to your heart's desire, hire seamstresses to sew your creations, and become wealthy like the owner for whom you now work."

"No," Juaniata shook her head. "No, Hans. I will not do this thing."

Hans swallowed the lump that had risen in his throat. He had hoped she would at least be willing to consider his offer.

Still shaking her head, Juaniata said, "I could never be like Mr. Julio. He is a slave driver. If I hired seamstresses, they would only work eight hours a day, with weekends off, and paid holidays, vacations and sick leave. And, I would install air conditioning in the entire building so that we could all work in comfort. Do you know that I have not had a full one-week paid vacation in all the years I have worked for Mr. Julio? When Perry won a football championship, and the loser slammed Perry's face into a wall in revenge. Mr. Julio let me have three days off to take care of Perry. Charity had to take two days off school to watch him while I went back to work the rest of that week."

Relieved that Juaniata had considered his offer seriously, Hans said, "You will be in charge of everything. My only involvement will be to put up the money. In return, I will take thirty percent of the profits."

"Twenty-five," she bargained.

Giving a wince, and hoping she didn't see right through him, Hans said, "You drive a hard bargain."

"Twenty-five," she nodded, "and I will design all of my grandchildren's clothes for free."

"Sold," said Hans, shaking her hands, both of them, vigorously.

"Now, about Perry," she changed the subject swiftly. "If I make a good living from this dress shop, I will be able to pay for his education. But—"

Interrupting her, Hans said, "Perry will receive a student loan from the Hans Bridger Clark Foundation, as much as he needs to meet his expenses and get his doctorate in cardiology. When he graduates, the loan will cover the expenses he'll need to open up his own practice, and once it is established, he can start repaying the loan."

"He'll want a low interest," she demanded, a firm set to her jaw.

Hans hesitated. "I hadn't planned on making him pay interest," he admitted with a sheepish grin.

"Two percent," she insisted, nodding her head. "It is very low, but it is honorable."

"Two percent," Hans agreed. "Simple interest. Not compounded."

"Agreed," she said, patting his hands with hers. "Now, when will we go look at this building you want to buy?"

"Is Monday too soon?" Hans asked.

"No. I will give Mr. Julio my notice first thing in the morning." She gave him a conspiratorial smile. "Now, about our United States citizenship?"

"We'll go over to the INS while we're in San Diego."

"You will sponsor all three of us?" she asked warily, as though expecting him to say no.

"Of course I will, Mamá. What kind of loving son would not?"

Juaniata stood gracefully, proudly, her shoulders squared. "If my daughter is inclined to marry you, she will have my blessing."

Hans stood and stepped around the table. He gave his future mother-in-law a quick hug, then said, "I hear a brake squeaking down in the alley. It must be Perry."

"Wait until he hears," Juaniata gushed. "He will not believe this!"

Perry, apparently anxious to get on with his life's upward swing, paced back and forth at the Los Angeles Airport, waiting for their smaller plane to San Diego to arrive. He had his transcripts in a briefcase held tightly in his hand.

They had flown eight hours today, and Hans couldn't help smiling, recalling all that had transpired in the past two days.

First, Juaniata had told Perry about her discussion with Hans. He welcomed Hans into their family, and thanked him vociferously for the student loans.

Next, Juaniata spoke to Charity on the phone. She told Charity of Hans' proposals, and gave Charity her blessing and permission to marry Hans if that is what Charity wanted to do. She'd also counseled her daughter that Hans was a good man, but she should do whatever her heart told her to do. Hans guaranteed Juaniata that, regardless of Charity's decision, the dress shop and student loan would go ahead.

Feeling as though he had squeezed Charity into a very tight spot, Hans was a little nervous, too. Allowing Juaniata to tell Charity all that had transpired that evening was Hans' most difficult task, but it was their custom, and Hans would not overstep his limitations. Besides, Juaniata would have had it no other way. She told Charity that she should be prepared to give Hans an answer when he picked her up in two weeks' time.

Early Saturday morning, Juaniata had given her boss a written notice of her immediate intent to quit her job. In the letter, she stated that she would no longer work for him, and she would be out of the apartment within two weeks.

To Hans' dismay, Mr. Julio fired Juaniata on the spot, then told her she had until Monday to vacate the apartment. To Hans' amazement, Mamá remained undaunted.

That left a lot of scrambling for boxes, all of which they shipped by UPS to Josh's condo. Josh had agreed to rent a small storage unit and haul the boxes there until the Blake family was ready for them. There wasn't that much to pack. The Blakes had lived like paupers the past twenty years, and the only things they took with them were their clothing and a few collectibles they'd made over the years: a box of Christmas decorations, including a nativity set, a few school photos and drawings, some dainty hand-crocheted doilies, several handmade quilts and crocheted afghans, certificates of graduations, and a few legal documents. Most of the dishes, pans, kitchen utensils and linens they left behind because it would be less expensive to buy new ones than to ship them all the way from San José. Hans tried to persuade Juaniata that he didn't mind the shipping bill, so long as she was able to take with her whatever she wanted, but she insisted that it would be "good money wasted."

Hans had been surprised that all three Blakes had current passports, with visas to leave the country. Juaniata had insisted that Daniel would come for them, and so, these papers she had always kept up to date and in order.

When Hans had talked to Charity on Friday, Saturday and Sunday nights, he had sensed no alarm in her voice at all regarding the changes in her life and the lives of her family, and he supposed because she hadn't once objected that she approved his plans. He hoped with all his heart that she would eventually learn to love him, because he was so deeply in love with her he almost couldn't think straight.

On Saturday, Hans returned in his rental car to Puntarenas, and hired the same Captain and two crewmen the Captain had recommended to sail *Charity's Bridge* back to San Diego. It would take more than a month because the Captain would be sailing to weather, and he would have to tack back and forth all the way to California. Hans also left a new satellite phone with the captain so he would have a more reliable means of communication. Then, Hans drove back to San Pedro.

On Sunday, Hans attended church services with Juaniata and Perry, who were asked to speak in Sacrament meeting to say goodbye to everyone. That afternoon, ward members arrived in droves at the Blake apartment, bringing together a potluck supper like no other. They all shook Hans' hand, and wished him well, telling him to let them know when his wedding date was set.

It had all seemed a little overwhelming, almost surreal. So much had happened so quickly. Hans was responsible for uprooting an entire family from another culture and transplanting them on U.S. soil. Had he thought a month ago that this would be his life a few weeks later, he would have considered himself delusional.

The flight to San Diego was announced over the airport intercom, and he followed Perry and Juaniata out to the plane. Within the hour, they touched down in San Diego, where Josh and Kayla greeted them at the airport.

Josh and Kayla had driven two cars over, theirs and Hans'. They gave Hans the keys, welcomed his new family to America, and invited them over for supper the next evening. Hans wasn't certain that he wanted the title 'new family' applied to the Blakes until Charity gave him an answer. Juaniata seemed to think that Charity's response could be nothing but affirmative, and this alone gave Hans a nugget of hope. He hadn't mentioned the proposal to Charity since Juaniata was the liaison between them on that issue, but he certainly hoped she would give him some indication when he picked her up a week from this coming Saturday.

Hans told Josh the real estate agent was scheduled to pick Hans and Juaniata up on Tuesday morning, while Perry would take a taxi over to the University to have his papers submitted and his registration forms filled out. They agreed to meet at Josh and Kayla's condo tomorrow around six in the evening.

In the meantime, Josh had signed a six-month lease on a three-bedroom, furnished condo for them at Greenbriar in downtown San Diego, and this was where Hans headed his Cadillac SUV after they picked up their luggage at the baggage claim area. Hans would be staying with the Blake family at the condo, until he could arrange something more permanent for them. Besides, Juaniata had insisted that Hans was family, and would not hear of him renting a hotel room somewhere else.

At their Greenbriar condo, they put their clothing away. One of the three bedrooms had two double beds, while the other two had queen-sized beds. Perry acquiesced quite readily to share the room with double beds with Hans, after Hans suggested that Charity would want to have her own bedroom, perhaps for the first time in her life. After unpacking, they went to dinner at a restaurant just down the street. Hans enjoyed being a silent observer as Juaniata and Perry kept up a constant dialogue regarding how much bigger San Diego was than they'd thought it would be, how busy the traffic, the amount of new cars (as opposed to older models) on the roads, and the size of the condo where they were staying with all its fine amenities, including swimming pool, hot tub, sauna, exercise room and game room. Juaniata also mentioned, perhaps ten times, that she would enjoy the dishwasher and microwave in the kitchen, something she'd never had back in San Pedro, Costa Rica.

Seeing San Diego through someone else's eyes enchanted Hans, and he could only hope and pray that Charity would see it the same way, that she would say yes, and that, with time, she would learn to love him.

❦ ❦ ❦

When Hans viewed the list of telephone messages for himself, he found an urgent one from Colton Wright, the private investigator he'd hired. Seeking privacy in his shared bedroom, he dialed Wright's number. The phone was picked up almost instantly and an out-of-breath male voice answered, "Wright here."

"Hans Clark, Mr. Wright. Is this a bad time to call?"

"No, I'm just coming in from my five-mile run."

"Have you found out anything?" asked Hans. Although Hans was calling from a cell phone, he didn't want to say anything too revealing to someone listening into his side of the conversation.

Wright answered, "Wait a minute while I get to my room."

Hans heard footsteps, the rustling of papers, the squeaking of a chair, and then Colton Wright said, "I got a call from that Stake President you told me about. His tip panned out. Daniel's family is still living in Chicago. I located Daniel Blake's birth certificate, his parents' birth certificates, and his sister's. I've got his Social Security number, and he must still be living because I found no death payment through SSA. His discharge papers from the army came yesterday, and he was discharged in February, 1980. Did you know he had an engineering degree? I saw his grades from his college years, and he's a very intelligent man. After his discharge, he worked at his father's manufacturing plant in Chicago until his father died, which was only just a few months later. After the distribution of his father's estate, Blake seems to have vanished off the face of the earth. His sister married in 1990 to a Robert Cragonne, he's French, I think. I don't know what became of Blake's mother, but his sister will probably know. Do you want me to speak with the sister personally?"

"No," said Hans. "You know where she lives?"

"Sure. She lives in Chicago Heights with their three children. Her husband is a dentist there, has a booming practice. Everything about them seems all right."

"I'd like to speak with her myself," said Hans.

"Do you want me to stay here in Chicago and continue searching for Blake?" Wright asked.

"Absolutely," agreed Hans. "He's got to be somewhere. Besides, I'll need you to follow the sister for a while, and check her phone records after my visit to her, in case she tries to warn Daniel that I'm looking for him."

"When will you get here?" asked Wright.

"Sometime next week. I'll call you when I know for sure."

"You're the boss," said Wright.

"Anything else?" asked Hans.

"I'm still waiting for several Illinois counties to fax me on marriages from 1975 to the present for any Daniel Blake. Next, I'll start pulling Illinois court records to determine if he was ever involved in any civil matters."

"Thank you," said Hans. "I'll be in touch."

Chapter Thirteen

"He's gone out of town on business, I think, to Chicago," Mamá said cheerfully.

As soon as the words reached her ears, Charity knew what Hans had done, and her heart sank. To make certain that she hadn't mistaken the statement, she asked her mother, "What did you say?"

A moment's hesitation on the other end of the line told her that Juaniata was debating whether or not she should have said anything to Charity. Finally, her mother said, "Forget about it, Charity. It's nothing."

"Mamá, it *is* something! Why did Hans go to Chicago this week?"

"We were finished with all the contracts and negotiations, and he wants me to design how I want the apartment upstairs. I'm meeting with the architect tomorrow. Don't worry, Charity. Hans will fly from wherever he is to San José. He will pick you up at Cocos Island early on Saturday morning. He is renting a small plane that will take you back to the mainland, then you will both leave Costa Rica and come home to San Diego."

"I'm not worried about him picking me up, Mamá, and you know it! How could you let him do this?"

"What has he done?" Juaniata asked her simply. "He told us that he had a business trip that he needed to take this week, and he would be gone until he brought you home with him late Saturday night. You and Hans will be so tired, both of you. When you get home, I will cook for you. But first, you must both sleep. It is a long journey from San José."

"You know why he's going to Chicago," Charity accused. "He's looking for Daniel."

"I do not know that. No, I do not," Juaniata insisted. "But, if he has gone to Chicago, I am not upset. Charity, we need closure about Daniel. Perhaps I have been wrong to hope all these years. It has not been good for you children to be raised without a father figure. Perhaps I should have divorced Daniel and remarried another man. If Hans is planning to offer us closure, he is a very wise man."

"I am so angry," Charity said with gritted teeth, "that I may refuse to come back to San Diego with him when he comes. Goodnight, Mamá."

She pressed the talk button, then turned the satellite phone completely off, and watched with widened eyes as the little red button faded to black.

Charity would never sleep now. Hans had gone to Chicago to find Daniel so that he could present Charity with closure. She didn't want closure. She didn't know what she wanted, but closure wasn't even on the list.

Dragging a piece of paper from her pants pocket, she unfolded it and studied it by the light of her flashlight.

WHY I SHOULD MARRY HANS	*WHY I SHOULD NOT MARRY HANS*
He loves me	*Do I love him?*
He makes me laugh	*He makes me cry*
He can provide for me	*I can provide for myself*

He's LDS
He can take me to the temple
He loves the Lord
He's kind
He's thoughtful
He's devoted to me
He loves my family
My family loves him
He is a marine biologist
I want to be a marine biologist
He can help me become a marine biologist
He is helping my family become more self-sustaining
He loves diving and I love diving
He wants to study whale sharks and so do I

Pulling a pen from her pants pocket, she spread the paper out upon her knee and, in bold letters under the heading ***Why I should NOT marry Hans***, she wrote:

He wants closure for me!
He has no clue what I want!
He is manipulating my entire life!

Then, crushing the paper in her hand, Charity wept.

Hans found his hand trembling when he pressed the doorbell, so he folded it into his other hand behind his back to stop it. He couldn't remember when he'd been so nervous before, with exception of when he had arrived in San José to see Charity after Ed's accident.

The home of Robert and Angela Blake Cragonne was impressive, a red-brick, two-story with white, ornamental pillars, a circle drive and wide front steps in an upper-crust neighborhood in Chicago Heights.

"Is this working?" he asked no one in particular.

In his ear he heard Colton Wright say, "Loud and clear."

Wearing a miniature ear phone and transmitter, Hans wondered if all the cloak and dagger stuff was really necessary. Then, knowing he was too anxious about what might be said, he concluded that the only way he could be certain to retain the information he gathered here was to record it.

Suddenly, the front door opened and a tall, slender woman with surprisingly blonde hair dressed casually in capri pants and a cotton blouse looked up at him curiously. "May I help you?" she asked.

"I'm looking for Angela Blake Cragonne," Hans told her quickly, recovering his wits.

"It's Cray-gawn," the woman said with the emphasis on the *gawn*. "How may I help you?"

"I'm Hans Bridger Clark," Hans told her. "I'm looking for your brother, Daniel Blake."

"Why?" she responded. "He hasn't done anything wrong?"

"I'm not a police officer," Hans assured her. "Some *friends* of his from Nicaragua were wondering how to locate him, and I volunteered to help them."

"Come in," she said. "But, I don't know what I can tell you. Mother and I have been searching for Daniel for almost twenty years."

She led him through a massive entry hall to a swank living room, and called out, "Mother, someone's here about Daniel."

As Hans sat down on the chair she indicated, an elderly woman, perhaps in her seventies, entered from beyond the entry hall, wiping her hands on a dishcloth. "You're inquiring about Daniel?" she asked.

She was frail and gaunt, with a waxy look to her wrinkled skin, but her green eyes were bright, their expression inquisitive. Hans realized at once where Charity got her beautiful emerald eyes.

"Yes, Ma'am," said Hans, standing up. He shook her hand. "Hans Bridger Clark." Returning to his chair after they had both been seated, he asked, "Are you Daniel's mother, Anna Blake?"

"I am. Why are you inquiring about Daniel?" asked Anna, her tone sharp, accusatory.

"I know some friends of his who once lived in Nicaragua," Hans answered, wondering how much information he should give them. "They have been wondering about him for many years."

"Daniel is no longer with us," she said, her voice cracking.

"Mother!"

"It's true," she insisted. "Ever since—"

"We're looking for Daniel, too," interrupted Angela, scowling at her mother as she said it. "He's been missing since the year our father died."

Suddenly, Anna paled and her bottom lip quavered. For a moment Hans wondered if she was going to faint. Shakily, she stood up. "I'm going to lie down for a while, dear. Will you see Mr. Clark out?"

"I will when I've finished talking to him," said Angela. "Would you like me to check in on you when he goes?"

"That won't be necessary." Anna walked from the room and up the spiraling staircase to the second floor.

"Forgive my mother's rudeness," Angela apologized. "She and Perry were once very close. He vanished shortly after they quarreled, and I fear she's never quite gotten over it."

"You've never heard from him since then?" he asked.

"Daniel calls me on my birthday every year," she admitted. "But, I have not shared this information with my mother the past few years.

Her hearing is going, and her mind, too, I'm afraid."

"So, Daniel's still alive?" asked Hans, wondering whether to be relieved or worried.

Angela nodded her head. "When he first left, we thought there might have been foul play. The police sent out state-wide bulletins, our friends and neighbors walked the woods around his apartment looking for him, but he was never found. About four months later, he called me and asked me to call off the search. He said to tell our mother that he would never forgive her. I asked him why he was angry with her, but he started crying and wouldn't answer. I asked him to come home, but he said he would never come home. Whenever I've confronted Mother, she has refused to tell me what the quarrel was all about. I was too young to help him back then. Since then, he calls me once a year. He always says that he's fine, that he loves me, and that I shouldn't worry about him."

"When is your birthday?" Hans asked, although he already knew the date.

"In May," she answered. "He called me this year. His message was the same."

"Did you know that he had married while he was in Nicaragua?" Hans asked, hoping he could trust her with this information.

Angela's eyes widened and filled with moisture. "No," she answered. "When he was released from the military, I was ten. My parents were very private about Daniel. He didn't live with us then, but he had an apartment in town, somewhere. Daniel worked for my father in his manufacturing business, but when Dad died, Daniel remained here only long enough to sell the firm and all of Dad's holdings except Mother's house, and to divide Dad's estate between the three of us. Mother was very angry that Daniel sold nearly everything. She had wanted him to keep the business going and build it even larger, as our father's legacy. Because Dad had made Daniel the executor, Mother was cut out of the loop. I don't know when I've seen her so furious. They had this big quarrel and Daniel left. I always thought that Daniel's selling the business was the reason for their quarrel, but over time, I've begun to think it's even more involved than that."

"He's never returned home?" asked Hans, completely perplexed by Angela's story.

She shook her head. "I've hired detectives, I've had the phone call traced every year. Once he called from a pay phone here in Chicago, other times from Oklahoma City, Miami, Seattle. It's never from the same place, and it's always from a phone booth with cash so that his location cannot be traced."

"I know this is probably too personal," Hans said, "but from the income of your father's estate, would there be enough money for Daniel to live without working?"

Angela nodded. "It pays our house payment and groceries," she explained. "We've never needed to touch the principle, thank goodness."

"So he could be living anywhere?"

"I've had his Social Security accessed. Daniel hasn't paid a penny to the IRS since the settlement of Dad's estate," she confessed. "I hoped I'd find out where he's living because I miss him so. My three children don't even know their uncle."

"You would think he'd have to pay some taxes on the interest he draws from his portion of the estate," Hans wondered aloud, thinking how much his own taxes cost him each year.

"And something else is odd," Angela told him. "Mother has never mentioned that he had a wife."

"The operative word is *has*," Hans corrected. Angela Blake Cragonne had diligently searched for her brother, Daniel. She deserved to know as much as Hans did. "He has a wife, a daughter and a son he doesn't even know about."

"How can that be?" she asked, tears welling up in her eyes and spilling over. "Are they still in Nicaragua?"

"They're in San Diego," Hans answered. "And they've been waiting over twenty-six years for Daniel to find them. In your conversation with Daniel each May, has he ever mentioned a wife, or children?"

"No. I've told him about my husband, my children, hoping he would tell me whether or not he had someone in his life. Once, I asked him if he'd married, if he had a family. He said to ask my mother."

"Did you?" Hans wondered.

"I asked her, but she refused to answer and went to her room. She's lived with us since we married."

"Perhaps it's time to confront her with the evidence," said Hans, giving Angela a copy of the marriage certificate, and the birth certificates of Juaniata's two children.

Indignation arose on her face as she read them. "I can hardly believe that she's kept all this a secret these many years. You may rest assured, Mr. Clark, that I will discuss these with my mother. She should have said something to me." Then, as though it mattered very much to her, Angela asked, "Are they Hispanic?"

Hans nodded, "The children are also half Caucasian," he reminded gently, hoping he wouldn't have to elaborate. "Charity is exceptionally beautiful. I hope to marry Daniel's daughter, Charity."

"So that's why you're looking for them," she surmised. "She wants her father around to walk her down the aisle."

Grimacing, Hans said, "I haven't told Charity that I'm looking for Daniel. I hoped to find her father before telling her. I wanted to give her some kind of closure before we marry. Their Bishop counseled them that if Daniel loved Juaniata as much as he claimed, he would have to be dead not to have returned for her. They had surmised that he had been killed during the Nicaraguan conflict, before his unit left the area. Now, at least I know that he survived the war and is still alive."

"Bishop?" she questioned. "Are they Catholic?"

"They're Latter-day Saints," Hans answered, "just like you. Daniel converted Juaniata during their marriage. He was transported from Nicaragua by the military before either realized she was pregnant with their son, Perry."

Angela smiled at this news, and tapped her fingers on the armrest of the sofa. "I won't be able to tell Daniel about them until May," she moaned. "That's too far away!"

"Not unless he calls before then." Hans handed her a card with Colton Wright's cell phone number, as well as Hans' phone number. "I hope you'll let Daniel know we're looking for him. If he has no interest in seeing his family again, when you tell him about them, I think you'll know it. Please let us know one way or the other."

"I will," she promised. "And if you find him before I do, would you return the favor?"

"Of course." Hans stood and walked toward the door.

When he was back inside the gray sedan that Colton Wright was driving, he removed the wires from beneath his clothes. "Did you get all that?"

"Yes. Odd, isn't it?" said Wright. "Why did he go into hiding? And why won't he surface other than to wish his sister happy birthday?"

"I have no idea," Hans admitted. "But, I'm glad I won't be there when Angela tells her mother about Daniel Blake's family. If her temperament is as volatile as her daughter indicates, I would not want to be sitting in Angela's shoes right now."

"The mother has to know about Mrs. Blake, Hans. It sounded like the daughter was fearful they were Hispanic. Perhaps she's prejudiced."

"Enough to quarrel with her son?" Hans wondered.

"Enough for him to distance himself from her all these years," Colton Wright nodded in agreement.

❦ ❦ ❦

Charity walked the beach around Chatham Bay as dawn ascended across the sky with tiny slivers of silver and gold against the gray backdrop of never-ending clouds. Hans would be arriving early this morning, and she was worried how to broach the subject of Daniel and Chicago with him. Her mother had finally confessed, only last night, that she had overheard Hans say something about Chicago in a telephone conversation he'd had with someone, and when Hans later said he was taking a business trip, she had assumed it would be to Chicago. Did Hans go to Chicago, or didn't he? If so, why? If it was to search for Daniel, how could he possibly think that was something that she wanted? And where did that leave Charity?

In her mind, there could be nothing worse for a girl than having her father abandon her, unless it was learning that after a twenty-six year absence, her father *still* didn't want her. And this was not just about Charity. Perry's feelings had to be just as vulnerable as hers. Why expose themselves to further anguish?

What if Daniel was dead? If Hans found that Daniel died back in 1979 or 1980, she could live with that news. But, if Daniel died after his military service ended, after he had time to collect some money together and come find them, that information would just be another slap in the face. Hadn't they had enough?

Yet, if Charity said anything to Hans about her suspicions, and he was innocent, she could offend him terribly. If she said nothing and Hans sprang any information about Daniel upon her, like so many other of his surprises, Charity didn't know how she would react. Right now, she felt like she'd probably come out with her stun gun blasting.

Last night, when she'd talked with Hans on the phone, he'd sounded weary. He wasn't even upset with her for turning off the satellite phone. Her pretext that she had talked a lot to her mother and wanted to save the batteries so she would be able to know that he'd arrived in San José safely, had apparently worked.

The most crucial question, *Did she love him?* had yet to be answered in her heart. But, could she tell him that? Did she have enough courage to place her hand in his forever, not knowing if she truly loved him? Like her mother, she would never divorce once she married. In her eyes, her marriage would have to be eternal. Was gratitude the forerunner of love?

❦ ❦ ❦

Charity heard a faint hum in the air around her, and watched the skies closely as the sound magnified, until she saw a plane coming in for a landing just outside the mouth of the bay. It touched down on the glassy water beautifully, and she jumped up and down and waved at the same time, hoping Hans saw her.

Had she missed him? *Oh!* How she'd missed him! Would she tell him? Not yet. They still had several kinks in their relationship and she wanted to iron them out before she made any long-range planning.

She raced along the water's edge back to the park service dinghy and threw her two duffle bags inside it. José was waiting to take her to the plane. Having said goodbye to Teresa and Árima last night, she did not want to wake them this early in the morning. Pushing off, she hopped inside while José started the engine, then he taxied toward the plane as it turned about and headed its nose northward, then settled into the trough it made in the water.

The door swung open, and Hans stepped out onto the pontoon, wearing a pair of tan pants, white oxford shirt and a blue blazer. His chestnut hair had been freshly cut, his rugged face cleanly shaven. He held a bouquet of red roses in one hand and a box of expensive Costa Rican chocolates in the other. She was just beginning to think that everything he'd planned was absolutely perfect, until his foot slipped, he lost his balance and fell ungraciously into the water.

Turning off the engine, José let the dinghy glide over to him, laughing heartily.

Charity leaned over and gave Hans what she hoped was a vivacious smile. "Good morning, Hans!"

He grimaced first, then grinned and exclaimed, "We've got to stop meeting like this!"

Laughing with Hans and José, she took the wet roses and dripping candy box from him and tossed them into the bottom of the dinghy. Hans pulled himself into the raft and unceremoniously sank onto the opposite gunwale from her.

"I do hope you brought a change of clothes," she giggled.

"The ones I wore yesterday," he announced, arching an amused eyebrow at her. "You're looking lovely."

"For a woman wearing park ranger clothes for the last time," she agreed. "I didn't think to bring anything else to wear home. I didn't know that I wouldn't have a home to go home to!"

As they neared the starboard side of the plane, Charity gave José a quick kiss on the cheek. "I'll miss you," she told him. "Tell Teresa and Árima to write to me."

"I will, Cari. Remember to follow the Lord's path, always, and you will find true joy."

"Yes, you will," Hans said, as he grabbed hold of the plane's cross bar and held the dinghy steady while she boarded the plane.

"I will always live the Gospel," she told him. "Now, about Mamá's new apartment. Do you know she's never had her own bedroom in her entire life."

"Neither have you, I hear," he commented, handing her the duffle bags, saltwater roses and ruined chocolates.

Hans turned to José and shook his hand. "Thank you for everything, José. You've been a great friend, to both of us."

"Take good care of my Cari," José said. "We will miss her."

Turning back to the plane, Hans stepped up onto the pontoon. Charity had a moment of panic when she thought he might fall in once again, but he surprised her.

"I'm very proud of you," she said as he took his seat on the plane beside her.

"For what?"

"For allowing Mamá and Perry to keep their dignity. It was very kind."

"She talked me down to twenty-five percent of the profits, you know," he teased. "That woman could dicker a walrus out of his ivory tusks."

"And make him feel sorry he didn't give her a better deal," she agreed, laughing.

When they were buckled in, had their earphones and mouthpieces on, and had waved goodbye to José, the pilot explained emergency evacuation and their flotation devices.

Charity asked, "Is there any chance we can circle the island before we leave it?"

Hans nodded to the pilot, who said, "It's your money, Mr. Clark."

"Thank you." Charity slipped her hand into Hans. "I guess we'll have to go shopping before we catch our next plane."

"Agreed," said Hans.

"Ooh, look!" she exclaimed as the plane slid through the water before a quick ascent, and rose gently northeasterly, where they passed Lobster Rock and Silver Cove, then around the southeasterly part of the island, zooming near Church's waterfall, and Tea Cup Island.

Out to sea, Hans spotted a shadow and asked the pilot to fly over it.

To Charity's astonishment, he'd spotted a huge whale shark bigger than the small plane they were flying. "It's amazing!" she gushed as the pilot swooped lower for a better look. "Oh, Hans, promise you'll bring me back here, someday. I have to come back as a tourist, and dive all the hot spots with you."

"I promise," he said, a smile curling the corners of his mouth as he looked over at her.

The pilot headed the plane toward Two Friends Rocks, and past Punta Maria, where a dive boat had just arrived. One of its crewman was attaching a line to the buoy floating there. This particular dive boat had almost unrestricted access because of the many donations it had made in terms of underwater filming and marine conservation.

As they passed Dirty Rock and Wafer Bay, heading northeast toward Puntarenas, Charity felt a great pull on her emotions. It would be a long time before she returned to her beloved Cocos Island. Tears slipped down her cheeks as Hans put his arm around her and let her cry softly against his chest. When she felt she could cry no longer, he released her and said, "I'd offer you a handkerchief, but I'm afraid mine is a little soggy right now."

Remembering how Hans had looked coming up out of the water at Chatham Bay, Charity started to laugh.

When she finished, he said, "That's twice now that I've made a fool of myself upon greeting you after a short separation. Perhaps we should plan not to separate anymore. I may not live through another meeting like this."

Chapter Fourteen

Since Charity had never flown over the water before, the pilot kept the plane just under the cloud cover so that she could see the Pacific Ocean from the air. Turbulence made the flight a bit bumpy, but she didn't seem to mind, and Hans enjoyed seeing her excitement over passing the park service boat en route to pick up José, Teresa and Árima.

After landing at Puntarenas, they went shopping at the only tourist trap open that early, where they bought Hans a new pair of cargo pants and a sail-boat printed cotton shirt. Charity chose a simple summer dress that complemented the colors of his shirt, and a pair of sandals. They changed clothes in the restrooms of a local restaurant where they ate breakfast, then headed east toward the airport with Hans' jacket, pants and shirt flapping from three of the four car windows that she had snugged up to keep the clothing from flying away.

They dropped the rental car off at the airport office, went through customs and caught the one o'clock flight to Los Angeles. Charity seemed to enjoy sitting in first class, having lunch brought to her on a silver tray, and receiving unlimited access to all the lemon-lime soda she wanted, but she expressed having a difficult time understanding why their plane had to fly into Los Angeles when San Diego was so much closer. Other than that one culture shock, Hans thought, she seemed to be handling their flight arrangements quite well.

While Charity had not said anything about whether or not she planned to marry Hans, she had asked him to bring her back to Cocos Island someday, and that certainly indicated that she planned to be friendly enough with him to keep up a diving relationship, at the least. Besides, Hans was certain that Charity would follow Costa Rican custom and tell her mother her decision first. Hans would have to wait until Juaniata told Hans, he supposed. If Daniel had been in the picture, Hans would have had to go through him, and for a brief moment, he felt relieved that Daniel had chosen not to enter back into his family's life. As uncommunicative as Daniel seemed to be, it could be years before he got around to making his daughter's marriage arrangements.

As Hans thought about Charity's father, he wondered what Daniel and Anna had quarreled about their last day together, twenty-five years ago. What horrible situation could have created a chasm so deep between a son and his mother that the son would refuse, for the rest of his life, to have anything to do with the family again?

To turn his back on his own sister, when she was, apparently, innocent in the entire situation, was wrong. Dead wrong. Hans could not fathom the mystery. Except for Charity, Hans had thought of little else since his visit with Daniel's sister, Angela Cragonne.

"Are you tired?" asked Charity from the seat beside him.

Nodding, Hans said, "I slept perhaps two hours last night, and before that it was probably three nights' sleep that I missed."

"You must be exhausted. What have you been up to that would keep you away from your bed so long?"

She stacked her empty lunch tray on top of his, then pressed the flight attendant button. Immediately, the flight attendant removed both trays, and they secured the tray tables into the back of the seats in front of them.

Turning in her seat, she said, "Turn your back to me."

Hans complied, and Charity rubbed his shoulders and neck repetitively, kneading the stiff muscles with finesse. "That feels good," he said. "If this is what I have to look forward to, don't plan on my leaving you until forever."

"I won't," she agreed. "This is how I worked my way through college. It only takes six months to certify as a masseuse, and I used to go around with my collapsible massage table to the richer neighborhoods and give deep, pressure point massages. It paid my tuition and books."

"You are just full of surprises," said Hans, feeling the tenseness in his shoulders begin to ease.

"So are you," she suggested. "Mamá says you went on a business trip."

Hans had expected that, so he turned to face her, interrupting the massage, to give her the explanation he had rehearsed. "I went to *Tiffany's* in New York." Reaching into his pocket, he pulled out a long velvet box. "They are renown around the world for designing exquisite jewelry exactly the way their customers want." As he opened the box, he noticed the widening of Charity's eyes, the pooling of fluid around the lower eyelashes. He had to admit that the bracelet was superbly re-crafted.

"Oh!" Charity exclaimed as diamonds sparkled at her. "This is the most beautiful bracelet I have ever seen!"

"It was originally my grandmother's, and had only two diamonds set into it, between those three gold heart-shaped links in the center," said Hans, removing it from the case and fastening it around her delicate wrist. "My grandparents were both born in April. My grandfather had it made for her at Tiffany's over sixty years ago. When my mother married the Admiral, Grandma took it back to Tiffany's for an update, and added two more hearts and these two stones." As he pointed to each one, he explained, "The ruby is my mother's birthstone, she was born in July, the garnet for the Admiral, in August. When Josh and I were born in September, the Admiral took it back to New York, where he had two more hearts and two sapphires set in it for us, and had a second bracelet, identical to this one, made also for Josh. Since I was born eight minutes before Josh, I got the original. When I learned that your birthday is in March, I wanted you to have the most beautiful aquamarine birthstone set in it before I gave it to you."

"That is the sweetest thing!" she said, giving him a long hug that Hans savored. "You went all the way to New York to have this made?"

"Actually, I had it delivered to them by courier almost a month ago, so they could begin the design work and insert the extra heart before setting the final stone. I wanted to pick the stone out myself because the aquamarine comes in varying shades, and I wanted it to be perfect." He shrugged. "I hope you like it."

"I love it," she gushed, holding it up to the light filtering through the plane's window and watching the varying birthstones glint in the sunshine.

Hans had not lied to Charity, he simply had not told her about his two-day layover in Chicago. Surely, the Lord would understand this omission. How could he tell the woman he loved that her father, who had abandoned her before she was a year old, was still running from the life he'd created, and that he had, unexplainably, gone into hiding? He couldn't. Not until he found Daniel Blake and confronted him about his past.

Seeing Charity's smile over the bracelet had made the trip to New York more than worth his effort, and the sleepless nights trying to get back to San José in a timely manner. He had become a regular jet-setter the past week, and he was exhausted. But, the glitter in Charity's eyes told him that his time had been well spent.

When she had settled back in her seat and rested her head against his left arm, he said, "So, tell me what you did at Cocos Island while you were there."

"Only if you promise to tell me everything you did while we were apart," she bartered.

"You first," he insisted, then listened attentively while she told him.

"I had patrol duty most of the time. I would take the big boat out—"

"The old Tolly they keep moored at Wafer Bay?"

"The one with the flybridge, yes. But, whoever is on patrol keeps it in the bay where they stay their two weeks. It was moored at Chatham most of the past two weeks, so I wouldn't have to go so far to retrieve it every day. Anyway, I would take *Poppy* out around seven in the morning, and circumnavigate the island in a five-mile radius, looking for poachers, illegal divers, boats in distress. *Poppy* cruises well at about fifteen knots, so it takes me about four hours a loop. I stop back at Chatham for lunch, then head out again around two in the afternoon. I always make two loops a day, but most of the time it's just water and the boat."

"I'll bet that eats up a lot of gas," Hans observed.

"Diesel, about thirty gallons a day. We have fuel shipped in at our ranger trade-offs, every two weeks. It's offloaded at the dock you saw at Wafer Bay the night of the barbecued pig."

"Did you find any poachers or other problems?" Hans asked.

"Someone always finds poachers," she said. "But, this time they were taking sharks. I knew I couldn't outrun them, so I notified the mainland. They sent a helicopter out to delay them, and I boarded their boat and put them in handcuffs attached to the port and starboard handrails until the big boys arrived."

"I didn't know that your job was more risky out of the water," Hans confessed. "And I'm not sorry, now that I've learned this, that you won't have to work there anymore. What if they'd had weapons and fired upon you?"

"The helicopter guys carry machine guns and deck-blasters."

"Deck blasters?"

"Guns with bullets as big around as a lemon that will blow a melon-sized hole through both the ship's deck and hull. They also carry grenades. When a poacher's boat is approached, the occupants are notified of the government's intent to sink them should they resist. As near as I know, they've only had to fire on one boat before, and they were able to subdue the crew before having to resort to more drastic measures."

"What would happen if the boat's crewmen started firing upon the helicopter?"

"That's easy. The helicopter stands down until the boat reaches well beyond the demarcation zone, then the helicopter is given clearance to fire at will. I mean, where are the poachers going to go? They're surrounded by three hundred miles of ocean. Any escape route will be cut off before they reach any land mass. They have to leave the protected area sometime." Charity shrugged. "It's not as dangerous as you might think."

"What if the boat travels faster than the helicopter?"

"At over a hundred miles an hour, that isn't going to happen."

Hans smiled. She seemed to have everything under control when she worked at Cocos Island, he was simply glad that she wouldn't have to work there any longer.

"You had a boat with poachers, and secured them until a police boat arrived. What else did you do?"

"I had to go back and tell Árima that Atrevido was one of the sharks the poachers had killed," she told him.

Shaking his head, Hans said, "How did she take that?"

"Not as badly as I would have thought. I think she felt that Atrevido was getting a little more aggressive than he should have, she mentioned this after our dive together, when you filmed her. She didn't cry, like I had expected."

"Perhaps she's wiser about marine life than I had considered," said Hans. He thought that Atrevido's death would have devastated Árima, but not so.

"She just said, *tough break* and went on with her studies."

"Anything else exciting happen?"

"José had no trouble replacing me."

"That quick? Who?"

"Árima."

"But, she's only sixteen," he protested. "And her education?"

"Árima turns seventeen the end of August, which makes her the legal age to work for the park service. But, she had to promise she would not throw any more tantrums, that she would spend no less than six hours every day studying, in addition to the ten-hour days required on the job, and she would save half of her income for her education. Oh, and she will only be allowed to work until she can pass the entrance exam into college."

"Sounds like it's been a productive week," Hans smiled.

"It's been very rewarding, but enough about me, what about you?"

"I would have thought your mother told you everything."

"I want to hear it from your perspective," she encouraged. "Tell me about the building you purchased."

"The main floor is about four thousand square feet, with sixteen foot ceilings. It is being divided off into a three-thousand square foot showroom, and a thousand square foot workroom filled with sewing tables and machines. But, the upstairs is going to be your mother's pride and joy. A quarter of the floor will be used for storage, supplies, and the like, but the rest is being built into a four- bedroom, three-bathroom apartment, with a gourmet kitchen, and a huge front room with sliding glass doors that open onto a balcony that takes up the entire store front, making a rain-stop for customers. She's having a peach-glazed firestone brick front installed, and the balcony will have a black wrought iron bannister and hanging baskets of flowers all around it. White shutters and window boxes will be installed around the large display windows, with an elegant sign that reads "Blake's Boutique" that will be hung directly over the main entrance. She's already working in the storage room with three seamstresses and an entire collection of her own designer label dresses."

"It sounds wonderful," said Charity. "She hasn't said much about the apartment or the store, only that the architect had finished, and the builders would start working this Monday."

"She's wants to open the store before the Christmas rush. Her goal is for November 15th."

"Will it be ready by then?"

Hans smiled, "If I have any influence on the workers, yes."

They spent the rest of the afternoon talking about Charity's childhood, and how much her family struggled. Actually, Charity did most of the talking because Hans was such a good listener. Besides, Hans did not want to compare stories; his childhood was so completely opposite hers. Hans feared that she would be offended to learn that he and Josh grew up in a capacious French-style villa on a twelve-acre estate overlooking the Pacific Ocean north of La Jolla, California. While Charity survived by sharing a room with her cousins for the first seven years of her life, Hans had ambled around in a mansion with six guest bedrooms, not including Josh's and Hans' separate bedroom suites, and more space than two small boys could explore in a month. Nor did Hans think it advantageous to tell Charity that he and Josh had their own valets and private tutors. His parents also employed a full-time gardener, chef, three housekeepers, a butler and a chauffeur.

Fortunately, Charity would never see inside Hans' boyhood home, for his parents had sold it two summers ago, and moved to northwestern Washington where they built another ocean view property, this one less than a third the size of the one they sold, and both parents were heavily invested, both monetarily and physically, in an archaeological dig site world renowned as COSAT.

When the plane touched down in Los Angeles, the sun was just beginning to set in the western sky. From LAX, Hans had chartered a private plane to whisk them off to San Diego, where the pilot had been previously instructed to bring them in from the west, so that Charity could see the city lights from the harbor. Hans had to get special clearance since the military base protects the western entrance, but Josh had arranged for a military escort, and soon two helicopters were directing them toward the military runway at San Diego.

Hans felt the extra effort was worthwhile when he watched the delight on Charity's face, her green eyes glistened as she stared, enthralled, at the city's night skyline. He couldn't wait to introduce her to all the places he enjoyed about the city, and its surrounding attractions.

When Hans and Charity stepped off the plane, they were greeted by Hans' brother, Joshua, and his wife Kayla. Their toddler sons were both sound asleep, one on each parent's shoulder. Charity was amazed at how much Joshua and Hans looked alike. She hadn't realized they were identical twins until she met Josh that night on the tarmac. Kayla, a vivacious blonde, with deep brown eyes and a beautiful smile, was also a patient mother, as Charity found out when young Mont and Sparky woke up the moment they heard Uncle Hans' voice as he introduced Charity to them.

"We're so glad to finally meet you, Charity," said Kayla. "You're all Juaniata talks about . . . you and Hans."

Josh added, "Or you and Perry."

"I am happy to meet you, too," said Charity, sweeping her long dark hair off her shoulder.

"Unk Hans?" asked Mont sleepily from his father's shoulder.

"Unk Hans?" echoed Sparky as he lifted his head and pushed himself out of his mother's arms.

Hans took Sparky quickly, "Hey, Sparky, I missed you."

Mont reached for Hans, too, and his uncle complied, holding both boys, one in each arm.

"Love you!" said Mont, then Sparky echoed, "Love you, too!" It was a game the two boys played, seeing who could say something new first, the other following suit.

"I love you, Mont. I love you, Sparky," said Hans. "This is Charity."

"Chair-ee—" began Sparky, looking at her shyly.

"Tee!" added Mont, who suddenly left Hans' arm and fell into Charity's. "Like Mamá 'ata." He gave her a big hug.

"Yes," she smiled. "Mamá Juaniata is my mommy."

As though Sparky could now see the resemblance, too, he threw himself from Hans' other arm into hers, and Hans helped steady her. Sparky hugged her, too, then shoved against Mont. "My Chair-ee-tee!"

"You may call me Cari, if that's easier," she said. "Car-ee."

"My Car-ee!" squealed Mont, pushing Sparky away.

"Boys!" Kayla scolded. "You must share Charity, or we will have to take you away from her.

Both boys wrapped their arms around Charity's neck, making her top-heavy. Hans stepped behind her and said, "Lean on me."

She was grateful for his strength. "Thanks," she said, leaning back until Mont released his grip on her. "What do?" he asked with an endearing curiosity.

"Why don't we take Uncle Hans and Aunt Charity to their car?"

said Kayla, clapping to Mont until he gave in and went to her. Josh took Sparky from Charity, as well.

Hans picked up their duffle bags in one hand, and took Charity's hand with the other. "Good idea."

"Now, remember," warned Kayla, "you're all coming over to the condo tomorrow for supper."

"It'll have to be after six," said Charity. "Mamá already has an appointment with our new bishop."

"That's right," agreed Hans. "I think he already has a calling for her."

"Shall we say six-thirty?" she asked, as they walked to the parking lot, while Mont started reaching for Josh, and Sparky started reaching for Kayla.

"Great," said Hans. "We'll tell the others."

Charity watched as the parents exchanged children three times before Kayla said, "That's enough, boys. Pick one of us, and stay there, or you'll have to walk."

Immediately, Sparky snuggled up to Josh and Mont grabbed Kayla's shoulder, hugging her fiercely.

"That's a first," said Josh. "How did you manage that?"

"Your guess is as good as mine," laughed Kayla. "I think that's the first threat that's ever really worked."

Charity laughed, "I guess you use whatever works with your children."

Hans nodded as he put the three bags down, released her hand, and took the car keys from Josh.

They hugged one another, and waved goodbye to Josh, Kayla and the twins, who headed toward another vehicle farther down the parking lot.

Charity turned away from the family to see that they now stood behind a silver-gray Cadillac SUV. Hans opened the back door and put the duffle bags inside, then closed the door and brought her around to the front passenger door.

"I didn't realize you and Josh were identical twins," she observed. "He's really quite handsome." She gave Hans a teasing smile.

"Thank you," he said, opening the door and helping her up onto the seat. "I've always thought so," he bantered back.

Hans closed her door, then hurried around to the driver's side and slid onto the seat. "Buckle up," he said. "It's the law in most states here."

Charity complied, and soon Hans had the car headed south, off the military base past a squat row of military buildings that resembled a fat, yellow, segmented caterpillar stretched across the desert sand.

"This center building is where Josh and Kayla used to work. It's where they met before they married. Josh now teaches oceanography and climatology at the University. Those are pre-requisite classes for the San Diego Marine Science Institute. With your bachelor's degree in biology, you could easily take those two classes from Josh, and qualify yourself for acceptance to the SDMC. That's where I got my first doctorate in marine biology.

"Why did you go to the University of Utah, then?" she asked, a bit confused.

"I couldn't decide which I liked more, archaeology or marine biology, so I determined I should also get a doctorate in archaeology, which would help me decide," he explained.

"Did you?" she asked.

"For the most part," he agreed. "I enjoyed working with COSAT at the archaeological dig site we discovered two summers ago."

"You were in on that discovery?" she asked. "I thought some little boy found that."

"Yes, Cody Owen Stevens," Hans agreed. "Abbot, Tom and I were all with him, as was Abbot's fiancée, her brother Ryan, and his wife, Gail."

As he drove, Hans explained about the COSAT center, regarding the many buried houses, dating back several thousand years, that COSAT had already unearthed in the Northwest. By the time they reached Greenbriar, where her mother and brother were living, Charity began to feel the exhaustion settle upon her from not sleeping well for the past several nights, plus the long trip today, from Cocos Island to Puntarenas to San José, to Los Angeles to San Diego, which was soon to become Charity's home.

After greeting her mother and brother, and noticing how terribly exhausted Hans looked, Charity said, "Mamá, I think I'll go to bed now. We can talk tomorrow, when we've rested."

"Church is at one o'clock, Charity," reminded Juaniata. "I will let you sleep in, if you want."

"And miss church? Mamá!"

"We shall see how late you want to sleep in tomorrow," said Juaniata sagely. "For I have never seen you look so tired, Charity."

"I'm going to turn in, too," said Hans. He took Charity's hand and walked her to her bedroom door. "You're safe with me," he told her, in a loud enough voice that Juaniata could hear him. "I promised your mother, and besides, I'm still hoping for a temple wedding."

Charity smiled at his thoughtfulness. Of course, she would never want their relationship to turn in any different direction. They kissed goodnight briefly, under Charity's mother's watchful eyes, and said goodnight.

After closing the door, Charity locked it, not because she could not trust Hans, but because this was San Diego. She was a stranger in a strange city, in an entirely new environment, Charity was not ready to trust anyone outside her family's safe shelter. She changed quickly into a nightgown, knelt by the bed for a ditto-like prayer, too tired to really focus on anything but the sleep that she desperately needed. Then, she climbed into the luxuriously big bed and pulled the sheet and comforter over her.

Her mind whirled with thoughts of her mother, and how happy Juaniata seemed. Juaniata had never exhibited such a delightful sense of purpose and commitment, and Charity hoped that Hans' generosity, while allowing them all to maintain their dignity, would be the catalyst that led each of them into vocations which would give them a sense of self-worth and accomplishment.

Rolling onto her side, Charity focused her thoughts upon Hans, and what a truly delightful sensation of peace and happiness she had whenever they were together. *Is this love?* she asked herself. *Is this how Mamá and Daniel felt when they were together?*

She remembered the anxious knot in her chest and her concern over the past few days about whether or not Hans had gone to Chicago, when he told her he went to New York for her heirloom bracelet.

Looking at the bracelet upon her wrist in the moonlight as it filtered through the window and spread onto her bed, she watched the gemstones sparkle. Hans had certainly proven he loved her, beyond all doubt.

In the deepest recesses of her heart, a place where no one had entered but herself, she asked again, *Is this love?* Her eyes closed as the question rolled lazily around in her mind. *Is this love?*

Before she could answer the question, Charity fell into a deep and peaceful sleep.

Chapter Fifteen

Sunday came too soon for Charity. Hearing a knock at her door, she rolled over, blinked, glanced at her watch, then sat bolt upright in bed. It was already three in the afternoon. She had slept through church, though that had not been her intention when her head hit the pillow last night.

"What?" she asked.

"It's Hans," came his concerned male voice behind the door. "Are you all right?"

"I overslept." Taking her robe from her duffle, she slid her arms into the sleeves, wrapped the front across her chest both ways, and knotted it at her waist.

After unlocking the door, she peeked out at Hans. His rugged good looks had charmed her more than once, but this morning he looked particularly handsome in his pin-striped navy suit. His bright blue eyes reflected his deep concern over her welfare.

Stepping into the hall, she said, "I'm fine. Really. I was so tired."

"Perry had to wake me," he responded. "I attended Sacrament meeting, but I was worried about you, so I came back to check on you. I've been out here pacing for half an hour, deliberating on whether or not to knock. You didn't respond when your mother knocked around noon."

"I didn't hear her."

Hans nodded. "She said that she usually lets you sleep in on your first day home, back in San Pedro."

"Of course, I don't sleep well on the boat crossings. It takes thirty-six hours, you remember." She went up on her tiptoes and gave him a kiss on his cheek. "Mmm, you smell good."

"It's a new aftershave," he admitted. "Kayla suggested it, said it drives women wild."

"You want to drive women wild?" she asked with a crooked smile.

"Just you," Hans admitted. "I still don't know what your answer is, and I've about reached the end of my rope while waiting. Have you said anything to your mother yet? Because if you have, she hasn't shared it."

Charity stretched and yawned, then wandered around the kitchen bar toward the refrigerator. "But, Mamá told me it is no longer between me and her. She told me to make my decision and tell you directly when I decide."

"That's a switch," he admitted, a fair amount of surprise in his voice. "What changed her mind?"

"We now live in the United States. Mamá told me we must follow their customs." Charity pursed her lips together, and gave him a crooked smile.

"What have you decided?" he asked, concern gathering in his eyes.

"I haven't decided," she confessed. "I made up a list of pros and cons, and so far the pros are winning. But, we do have some obstacles to overcome."

"Such as?" he asked, slumping onto a barstool at the kitchen counter while she poured them both a glass of apple juice.

"I like the Greenbriar. Josh did a good job picking this condo out for us. I'll bet Mamá feels completely lost here. It's three times the size of our old apartment. But, I like it."

"You're evading the question," he said, raising an eyebrow about the same time as he raised the glass of juice to his lips.

Charity cringed, but knew she must begin somewhere. Finally, she said, "First off, you're wealthy and I'm poor. I'm having a hard time getting used to all your money, Hans. I know that you don't think this should cause any problem, but how can you live like this?"

"Like what?" he challenged.

"Never having to worry about whether there will be enough money for a few stalks of celery to go into the stew you want to make this week," Charity tried to explain. "You can run off to New York to choose the perfect shade gemstone in an heirloom bracelet that you intend to give away, while I'm worrying over being able to pay for the ingredients in a pot of stew, spaghetti, or soup. In my family, we often cook one large pan full of soup because it will last over half the week. Sometimes, we cannot afford juice or toothpaste, so we settle for water or a little sodium bicarbonate on our toothbrushes. I don't know how to spend money without calculating which bill I will be robbing from in order to spend it. When I need a new nightgown, I must ask myself if I should I resort to wearing long t-shirts because they are less money and wear longer? All my life, Hans, I've had to think through every single purchase, evaluate it, consider it from every angle. I don't even ask if it is a want or a need, I ask is it a need or a desperate need? The dress I wore to the airport, is a perfect example of my anxiety. Here you were, bleeding and unconscious on the floor, and I couldn't decide what upset me more, the fact that I had caused your injury, that you may never recover, that I had damaged you for the rest of your life, or the fact that I may never be able to clean the dress I had just charged to my credit card! I don't think I can change twenty-six years of financial anxiety overnight, Hans, no matter how much you want me to try."

"You didn't cause my accident," Hans began.

"I did," she confessed. "I am such a klutz! I stayed in one spot so that I wouldn't knock you over if I ran toward you and flung myself at you when you arrived. Then, you started running toward me, and I thought you were going to pull a Charity and bowl me over. So, I stepped back and to the side and accidentally landed on that young man's foot. You probably didn't notice that. He was only wearing sandals. He turned around to see who had stepped on him, and you know the rest."

Hans laughed aloud. "So that's why you didn't come toward me. I waited, hoping you would, and when you didn't, I wanted you to see how eager I was to see you." He shrugged and gave her a sheepish expression. "I guess there's no hiding how I feel about you."

"No," she grinned. "You've made that perfectly clear."

Coming around the counter, Hans pulled Charity into his arms. "There are ways to solve the emotional chaos you go through over money, Sweetheart."

It was the first time he had called her sweetheart, and she found she liked the sound of it. "How?" she asked, looking up at his handsome face.

"Let's see," he began, "my father used to handle the money, but he always gave my mother allowances. So much for clothing, so much for food. Suppose I set you up on an allowance."

"For what?" she asked. "That won't augment any dignity, Hans. Besides, we're not married, yet."

"You always add that little word, *yet*," he allowed. "That leaves room for the other word, *when*."

"Why don't you understand?" Charity complained. "Mamá has a way to repay you for what you are doing, and Perry has a contract with you to repay his loan for his education. You still want to *give* everything to me, and I am not a gracious recipient. I feel like you're trying to buy my affection, and I can't be bought, Hans. It leaves no room for dignity."

"If we can resolve this conflict, will you be any closer to making your mind up about marrying me?" he asked.

Charity inclined her head toward him and agreed, "A little bit. Yes."

"Then what else is standing in our way?"

"Do I love you?" she asked. "And if I do, how will I know?"

"You don't know?" His forehead knitted into a deep frown of sorrow.

Turning her back to him, but keeping his arms wrapped around her, Charity leaned against his chest. "Hold me," she said. "Just for a little while, hold me. I think I love you, Hans, but how can I know for sure?"

"How do you feel when we're apart?"

Could Charity tell him the truth without getting his hopes up too much? She doubted it, but she knew that he needed to know. "Let me get out of my nightgown and into some Sunday clothes. Perhaps you can take me over to a park where we can walk."

"How would you like to walk upon the San Diego Temple grounds? They're really quite beautiful." said Hans. "Perhaps you'd like to share your feelings there."

"I'll go change," Charity answered, slipping from his arms and heading toward her bedroom.

"I'll leave a note for Mamá telling her where we've gone."

Within a few minutes, Charity had changed into her silver and blue dress, the one she'd worn at the airport the day Hans had been knocked unconscious, along with her silver staccato heels and her silver purse. She brushed her long, silky hair and coiled it into a coif at the crown of her head, then secured it with the silver barrette Hans had given her. Standing back to study herself in the mirror, she hoped she looked like a grownup. In her heart, she sometimes felt as though she was still a little child, and she wanted to talk with Hans from a more mature point of view.

"You had to wear that?" he asked, stepping immediately towards her when she left the bedroom.

"You don't like it?" Charity pouted playfully.

"I do! That's the problem," he admitted. "I promised your mother I would respect you, but in that dress, it's going to be difficult!"

"Good," she said. "You deserve to feel what it's like to be tested."

Within a few minutes, they were headed north on Interstate Five. As they came up over a hill, Charity saw the San Diego Temple for the first time. The sight took her breath away. Six tall, white spires greeted her, with the tallest pinnacle topped by the angel Moroni and his golden trumpet.

"The photos don't do it justice," she murmured, a lump arising in her throat.

"This is where I'd like to be married," Hans said, reaching across the space between them and taking her hand in his. "Unless you prefer the San José Temple."

He turned the SUV off of the Interstate and drove through a residential area back toward the temple.

"I've seen the San José Temple," she announced. "I went through at the Open House, when I was twenty-one. We all did. Mamá received her endowments a short while later. During that time, while I was working as a masseuse, and attending college, I worked in the Primary. When I took my job at Cocos Island, I had to give up my calling. It was my one big disappointment, but José and Teresa always made certain that we had some sort of services on Sunday evening."

"You never received your own endowments?" he asked as he parked the car in the parking lot.

"No. I am waiting for my wedding day. I want it to be perfect."

Hans smiled at her as he helped her out of the Cadillac. "I have my temple recommend," he admitted. "I haven't used it yet, but I suppose I'll have to use it in October when Abbot marries Bekah."

"Don't you want to go to the temple?" she asked.

Hans took her by the hand and led her to a bench that overlooked the gardens with the temple in the backdrop. "I've been praying for the Lord to help me find the right woman. I wanted to use my recommend for the first time when we are sealed together."

"You want to marry before October?" Charity was not surprised, not really. For Hans, everything had to be done right now.

"I want to marry you before October," he clarified. "But, if you're not ready before then, I'll wait until you are. In the meantime, I can't disappoint Abbot. He's depending on me to attend his wedding ceremony, especially since I've agreed to be his best man."

Nodding, Charity considered their notion that they should marry when they first attend the temple. "Do you suppose that we should attend the temple together for the first time, perhaps early next month, even if we're not getting married then? Perhaps we could attend a few more times together, until October. That would prepare us for when we attend Abbot's sealing."

Hans seemed to consider her suggestion, then he smiled and nodded. "It's a good idea. We'll both need escorts. I plan to ask Josh."

"Mamá will be my escort, of course. In San José, she always attended the temple on the third Thursday of every month. That was the afternoon that the biggest shipment of new fabrics, threads and adornments would arrive at the dress shop in San Pedro. Her boss did not like her to go, but she always returned to her job immediately after attending the temple, and stayed until she finished putting away the new supplies, and catching up on what she left behind."

"That shows a great dedication to her work," said Hans. "Which means she'll also be a devoted store owner."

"I expect that with Mamá's expertise, it will only take her a few years to repay you for the startup money you've invested, then you'll start seeing a profit. I cannot tell you how happy it makes me to see Mamá so involved in this project. You've given her life new meaning, and I shall always be grateful, Hans."

"Grateful is not the emotion I want to elicit within you, Charity," Hans hinted. "You were going to tell me about how you feel when we're apart, and whether or not you're beginning to care about me."

Charity gulped quickly, her hands began to sweat. Gathering courage, she said, "When we're apart, I miss you for hours before we separate. I don't want to leave you. I don't want you to leave me. I'm angry that we have to go our separate ways for a while. This last time, it was all that I could do to board the park ranger's boat and say goodbye."

"That's good," Hans said, smiling.

"What does it mean?" she asked. "Does it mean that I love you? Because I thought that I would know when I fell in love."

"How do you feel when we're together?" Hans asked.

She snuggled up to answer him, and was grateful when he put his arm around her and held her close against his side. "Hans, I feel safe, secure. I'm not afraid to face life with you by my side. You've more than proven that you have what you call staying power. I don't think you're anything like Daniel, because you've shown me that my family and I will have a permanent place in your life. You cannot know how much I appreciate that."

"When I kiss you?" he asked, brushing her forehead with his lips. "How do you feel then?"

Pulling away for a moment, Charity ignored the question, but looked deeply into his blue eyes and said, "I could get lost in your eyes, Hans. When you hold me, it is not enough. I want more, but I know the limitations of our relationship, and I try to distance myself from those feelings."

"And when I kiss you?" he persisted, bending his mouth to hers, kissing her gently, persuasively.

Suddenly, Charity pulled back. "I want you, Hans. There is no denying that. But, we must have respect for one another, so I force myself to focus on something else."

"If we were married, could you let your feelings meld with mine? Could you let go and give yourself to me completely?" he asked.

From his expression, Charity could see that kissing especially brought out the desire in his eyes, and she knew that they were very close to merging hearts. "Yes, Hans," she admitted. "I could." Then, Charity stood up and stepped back from him. "But, until we marry, we must be cautious, and exercise good judgment."

He stood up beside her and gently took her hand in his. With his other hand, he tilted her chin up so that she had no choice but to look at him. "You just said *until we marry*, Charity. Does that mean that you've made up your mind?"

Tears filled her eyes and dripped down her cheeks as she studied his expression. The love that she saw in his eyes, the care and concern, his tender regard for what she wanted, overwhelmed her. Charity blinked and, ever so slightly, nodded her head.

To her amazement, tears filled his eyes, as well. Suddenly, he pulled her close and held her against him, weeping, "Charity, my sweet Charity. I love you. I love you."

At first, Charity could not say the words. And yet, she loved him! She was so overwhelmed by this knowledge that her lips failed to respond to her urgent request. As he held her tight, she prayed, asking God to loosen her tongue, so that she could assure him her feelings were the same. As she prayed, she told the Lord she loved Hans with all her might, mind, heart and strength, and asked if her feelings were in keeping with God's will. Charity felt an undeniable sensation of warmth, the sweet testimony of the Spirit within her breast, and the still, small voice within her heart, telling her that the Lord had consecrated their love. Finally, Charity knew that she could, indeed she did, love this man.

She felt his chest shudder as he tried to gain control of his emotions. When she sensed that he had done so, she stepped back and he led her back to the bench, where she sank upon it, her legs trembling.

Hans bent upon one knee, and withdrew from his pocket a burgundy velvet ring box. "Will you marry me?" he asked, his voice trembling, tears streaking his face and dripping from his chin. He opened the case and revealed the most beautiful diamond ring she had ever seen.

Charity smiled broadly. "I will, Hans."

"Even though I'm rich and spoiled?" he asked.

"In sickness, in health, in poverty, in wealth."

"For time and for all eternity?"

"Yes, my love, I will."

His eyes widened, and he laughed aloud, still crying, yet laughing at the same time. "You just said the 'L' word," he reminded.

"I know, Hans. I do love you. Even if you are too rich."

A grin crossed Hans face from ear to ear. The dimples in his cheeks deepened, and his moist blue eyes sparkled. Removing the ring from the box, he placed it upon her left ring finger and said, "If you want a long engagement, I will understand. But consider this . . . if we marry soon, I won't have to listen to Perry's snoring anymore."

"Will we have our own home?" she asked.

"If you want," he agreed.

"A real home, with grass and trees?"

"Wherever you want."

"May I design our home?"

"Anyway you want."

"Will we have children?"

"As many or as few as you want."

"Will you ever leave me?"

"Never."

"Will you love me forever?"

"Longer than that."

Then, Hans leaned forward and kissed her again. How she loved his lips upon hers, and how he made her want more!

Charity pulled back and gave Hans what she hoped was an endearing smile, and said a small, silent prayer of *Thank you!* to the Lord. She never knew that love could feel so powerful.

Standing up, Hans pulled Charity to her feet. They hugged and cried, and hugged some more. When their tears were spent, they sat back down on the bench, both of them trembling.

As they held hands and gazed upon the temple, they talked for most of the afternoon. Hans told her that after they married, they would move into Josh and Kayla Clark's condo, since Josh and Kayla had already bought a home and were planning to move into it the middle of August when the renovations were finished.

Shelter View Condominiums overlooked Shelter Island, with San Diego in the background. Hans and Charity's condo was on the top floor in the southeast corner, and had three bedrooms, two bathrooms, and an open living area with kitchen, living room and dining area. Shelter View Condominiums were housed in a white stucco building framed handsomely with sandstone red tile roof, giving a definite Spanish flavor. Fringed palms and red ginger plants lined every pathway, and the gardens were well-maintained. An underground parking garage added security to the building, and each condominium was allotted two parking spaces.

Charity could remodel the entire condo the way she wanted, while she and Hans searched for the perfect place to build or buy their house later on, after the addition of children forced them into larger accommodations.

In the meantime, he explained that he wanted her to enroll at the University of California at San Diego, to fill the requirements for entrance to the Marine Science Center, which was not far from Scripps Oceanographic Institute.

Hans confessed that his trip to Cocos Island had made him realize how much he wanted to research whale sharks, and that he would need her aboard to help him. They agreed that he should contact the Marine Science Center to determine if they had any openings for a researcher with a doctorate in marine biology, who could teach marine biology while doing research in his chosen field. It would be the best of both worlds. Hans would finally have a viable career, and he would be helping others gain the skills and knowledge they would need in their own career goals. It may mean buying a bigger boat . . . a long-range power boat, but Charity assured him she would help in the dickering. And if they needed to boost their income to pay for the research, they could always make underwater films of the marine life they studied.

More important to Charity, she would become one of Hans' students, as well as his wife. Life could be perfect between them. She would have to learn how to refrain from agonizing over money so easily, and he would have to learn not to spend it so readily.

Hans even encouraged Charity to take over his finances, so that he wouldn't have to pay an accountant. His suggestion meant a lot to Charity, in terms of his trust and confidence. She decided she would also take some classes in accounting. Investing in a good computer of her own, and buying a few accounting programs, would also help her. It had been two years since she left school, but she had excelled in computer literacy in college, and she was buoyed up by Hans encouragement. This was an area of their union that she felt she could tackle and succeed. Since Hans was already paying his accountant over eighteen hundred dollars a month, Charity considered Hans' financial proposition a viable way to earn her keep.

By the time they had worked out many of the kinks and obstacles they might face as a couple, it was nearing five o'clock, and Hans suggested that they should pick up her mother and brother, and go on over to Josh and Kayla's place, where supper was waiting.

Everyone at the supper party expressed their delight and congratulations as Charity showed them her engagement ring, and Hans formally announced their plans for a fall wedding. They would get married on September 28th in the San Diego Temple, in exactly two months.

Chapter Sixteen

By mid August, Hans' brother and sister-in-law, Josh and Kayla, had moved into a large, well-appointed home that looked over Tecolote Canyon National Park at the northern end, in a neighborhood of seven-figure estates. Their house stood on two acres of fenced land, but more importantly, it had six bedrooms, and a cottage above the four-car garage for guests. The renovations had barely been completed on time, and they had moved in a week ago, leaving their condo empty for Hans and Charity.

Wedding plans were well under way with invitations ordered, photos taken, dresses designed and tuxedos purchased, flowers ordered and catering services reserved. The wedding would take place in the San Diego Temple, and the reception would be held at Josh and Kayla's new home. It was large enough to move indoors in inclement weather, but had a beautiful patio and huge back yard, where the wedding planner could set up a massive dining and dancing tent. Hans had spared no expense in helping Charity order every conceivable amenity for their upcoming wedding.

En route to Shelter View Condominiums one day in late August, Hans received a telephone call from Colton Wright. Because he was driving the SUV with Charity beside him, Hans told him he'd have to call him back. Charity was seated beside Hans on their way over to the condo to do some more painting.

The condo carpets had been removed, and new carpet ordered, but it would not be installed until they finished the walls. Charity had wanted to do most of the work themselves, and Hans had agreed to please her. To be truthful, he liked physical labor, and sometimes wondered why he'd bothered with ten extra years of college. He should have started his career when he earned his first doctorate in marine biology, since that seemed to retain his interest best.

"Who was that on the phone?" Charity asked as Hans turned the car into the underground parking garage.

"Colton Wright," Hans answered truthfully, pulling into one of their two parking stalls. "He's a man I met a month or two ago."

"What did he want?"she asked.

Hans cringed inwardly, but tried not to show any emotion on his face. "I don't know. I couldn't very well talk to him while I'm driving."

Charity didn't say anymore as he set the brake and turned off the ignition. Hauling bags of cleaning and painting supplies to the elevator, she apparently forgot about the phone call, because she said no more about it.

However, Hans could not get the call out of his mind, and wondered how he would ever get away from Charity long enough to call Colton Wright back. With Hans living in the same condo with her mother and brother, they were rarely ever apart, not that he minded. Being with Charity had been the answer to many prayers, and he was looking forward to their marriage and their life together with more anticipation than any prior event.

The more time they spent together, the more Hans loved Charity, although he didn't realize that was possible until he calculated that each day he had twenty-four hours more *to* love her, which mathematically meant that he loved her more. But, his feelings went way beyond simple calculations. She had become his reason for being, his purpose, his life's desire.

By the time they had loaded all the painting and cleaning supplies into the apartment, Hans had let the phone call slip from his mind. While he prepared the second and third bedrooms for painting, Charity painted around the woodwork in the kitchen. Soon, Hans had installed a new bathroom sink, and had the plumbing working right. He hoped.

Looking for his fiancée, he found Charity painting the walls in the third bedroom, where Hans set to work rehanging the closet door, after adjusting the roller, and noticed that yesterday's paint inside the closet still felt slightly tacky.

It was almost dusk when Hans remembered the call from Colton Wright and tried to figure out a way to call him back without raising Charity's suspicion.

"I'm starving," he said. "How about you?"

Paint roller in hand, Charity nodded. A stray lock of her sable hair came loose from the ribbon with which she had it tied. "Your hands are cleaner than mine. Come tuck my hair back for me, will you?"

Smiling at her simple request, Hans walked over to her and pulled the stray lock back, untied the ribbon, tucked the hair in with the rest of the braid, and retied the ribbon tightly. "Not such a great job, but thanks for trusting me with it," he said, giving her a kiss on the forehead, the only spot on her face where the paint spackles looked dry.

"Thanks," she said. "You know, we're almost finished. Perhaps we should call the carpet people tomorrow."

"We have to wait for the walls to dry completely," he said. "It's too muggy in here this time of year to dry properly. The kitchen paint is still wet, and so is the closet. After supper we should go over to the hardware store and get one of those dehydrators we saw last week."

"How about you go buy the dehydrator and bring supper back?"

Charity suggested with a flirtatious grin. "I don't want to leave off painting this room until it's through. It's our last room."

"How about I help you, then we can go—" he pretended, hoping she would insist on his going without her. He was not disappointed.

"You're not the only one who's starving," she interrupted. "How about tacos from that place I like?"

"I'll be right back, future-Mrs. Clark."

"Hurry, future-husband. I can't call you future-Mr. Clark because you're already Mr. Clark. Don't you think it's unfair that men get to keep Mister and women have to change from Miss to Mrs.?"

"This is the twenty-first century, Sweetheart. You don't even have to use my surname if you don't want. However, I was sort of hoping that you would."

He gave her another kiss, this time on the top of her head, as she said, "Tell them not to put so much onion on my taco. Maybe we could call me Ms. Clark?"

"It's up to you," he agreed, but I think Ms. only applies to a woman whose marital status is unknown."

"Or irrelevant," she disagreed. "I heard a woman at the store say that Ms. is used when a woman doesn't want anyone to know whether she's married or not."

That deflated his ego a little. "Which is it for you? Do you want people to know you're married, or will your marriage be irrelevant?"

Charity smiled up at him. "I think I'll stick with Mrs. Clark."

"It works for me," he said, heading toward the door. "Two taco grandes, light on the onion, coming up."

"Don't forget the dehydrator."

"I won't," he promised, leaving the condo and going down to the garage.

Soon, Hans parked the SUV at the hardware store and had the

cell phone cradled in his hand. It only took three rings for Colton Wright to answer.

"Hans Clark here. Sorry I couldn't call sooner, I needed to find a place where I could talk privately."

"I figured something like that," said Wright.

"What's up?" Hans asked.

"I found something interesting down at a little courthouse in Naperville, Illinois. They have a document showing a Daniel John Blake legally changing his name to Juan Perez about the same time your Daniel disappeared from Chicago. The birth dates are a match."

"Perez is Juaniata's maiden name," said Hans, calculating. "And Juan! Isn't that a male version of Juaniata?"

"Actually, I think it's the other way around. Juan is usually translated to John in English."

"Did you find anything else with Juan Perez's name on it in Naperville, other than the name change?"

"No, but online there's about six hundred listings for Juan Perez in a country-wide search."

"Contact everyone with that listing that you can," said Hans. "See how old they are. Daniel would be forty-six by now. And go back through Chicago records to see if Juan Perez still lives in that area."

"He married young, didn't he?" said Wright.

"Young and broke," admitted Hans. "Call me as soon as you find anything."

"As long as you're paying the tab," said Wright. "Not that I don't like Chicago, but I hope this job is over before winter. The locals say it's freezing around here at Christmas."

"I hope so, too," said Hans, thinking that Charity would start taking over the finances by the end of next month, and he didn't know how he was going to explain Colton Wright's bills to her. "Thanks, Colton. I hope you find him."

"Don't worry, I will," encouraged Wright. "But, I don't understand why he would change his name to Juan Perez."

"Maybe his family in Nicaragua meant more to him than I thought," Hans suggested. "For Charity's sake, I hope so."

After hanging up, Hans picked up the dehydrator, tacos and sodas and returned to the condo. Charity was washing up at the kitchen sink. She looked startlingly beautiful with her unkempt hair, jeans and t-shirt, and little splatters of pale green paint on her clothes, arms and shoes.

"Supper's here," Hans told her as he placed the food on the counter, then removed the dehydrator from its box, plugged it in and turned it on. Then he sank onto a barstool next to it.

"I'm starved," she said. "We should have brought more than apples and water."

"Agreed," said Hans, opening the bag and placing her taco next to his. "Thank goodness we don't have to do any more painting. Now, we can get down to buying furniture and decorating."

"We only have a month," she said, drying her hands and sitting beside him on another stool. She opened the taco eagerly, spread out the paper, then said, "It must be my turn for prayer."

Hans smiled. Charity always remembered to pray over their food, and they had worked out an arrangement that when they were away from her mother and brother, he would ask the blessing on the food on odd-numbered days, and she would do it on even-numbered days. He bowed his head and waited. Charity gave such beautiful prayers, it was easy to tell that she had a personal relationship with the Lord by the casual way she talked to Him.

After the prayer, Hans and Charity ate in silence. They were both so hungry they didn't take any time to converse during eating. When they were full, and sipping on sodas, Hans said, "As soon as the carpet is laid, and the master bedroom furniture arrives, I'm going to move out of your mother's condo and into ours."

"Don't you like sharing a bedroom with Perry?" she asked.

"He snores," admitted Hans. "Perry should have had his tonsils and adenoids removed when he was young. But, that's not the only reason why I want to move out of your mother's condo."

"Why?" she asked.

"The more we're together, the harder it is for me not to sneak into your room at night," he confided.

"I lock the door every night."

"I know that. But, the temptation is still there,"

"Mamá would never forgive you if you came into my room," she insisted.

"Nor would I. Charity, I love you with everything I have. But, I've found myself staring at the ceiling at night, sometimes for hours, wishing I could elope to the temple with you right now. It's only when I realize that we always elope to the temple in my fantasies that I shake myself out of it. I see the temple in my mind, and I think of our first visit to the temple grounds, and I remember my promise to take you there. It's like getting hit with a tub full of ice water. Our being together all the time like this is too hard for me. I'm finding it more and more difficult to resist. There's a reason why the Lord wants perspective newlyweds to spend some time apart, and I'm sorely learning why."

She rubbed his shoulder. "You're right," she agreed. "Mamá won't like your moving here, but when we explain about our honor, she will understand."

"You'll explain," he said. "I'm not sharing this with your mother."

"I will explain," she agreed, looking over at him with a curious smile. "You really want to come into my bedroom?"

Hans turned and stared at her incredulously. Clueless Charity was sipping her soda, her lips caressing the straw like he wanted them to caress him. He wanted to loosen the ribbon from her hair and run his fingers through it, to pull her close and hold her completely. Their condo might be the right place, but today was not the right time.

"Come on," he said. "The sooner we get the carpet installed and the bedroom furniture . . . on second thought, maybe I'll move in before the bedroom furniture arrives."

Charity giggled, "It's that bad, hmm?"

"You have no idea."

"You think women don't have needs, too?" she asked. "You think I haven't thought about leaving my door unlocked, and letting you know it is?"

Hans took her by the hand, leaving the sodas on the kitchen counter. "Don't even start," he said. "I don't need any encouragement."

He grabbed his keys from the counter and headed for the door, taking Charity with him. Soon, they were back at her mother's condo, playing a game of canasta with Juaniata and Perry, while Juaniata entertained them with an account of what had been accomplished at the store and its upstairs apartment that day.

The workers had laid the kitchen floor and were ready to install the cupboards tomorrow. The plumbers were still working on the bathrooms, while the balcony was almost finished. The upstairs apartment would be heated with radiant wall heaters built into the decor of each room.

Downstairs in the store, the plumbing for the two restrooms and the radiant-heated floors was completely installed, and the floors throughout the main level of the store would be poured tomorrow. The big boiler used to heat the main level was expensive, but in the long run, far more cost-efficient than forced air furnaces. Hans had assured them that they wouldn't need heat for more than a few months each year, as San Diego was entirely too warm most of the year to need it. The ducts for the air conditioning had already been boxed in, and would be finished after the floor's concrete was laid.

Perry had been accepted at the Southern Cal Medical Center for his internship, and would start Monday on his first rotation. He was so excited, he could hardly contain himself until after Mamá had given her report, but Hans was pleased to notice that Perry would not do anything to trump his mother's joy.

After Juaniata and Perry had shared their day's news, Hans and Charity gave a full report on how the apartment was coming, and Charity announced that they would call the carpet layers tomorrow.

Hans' cell phone rang and he stepped away from the card game to answer it. "Hans Clark."

"Captain Fernandez," said a weary voice. "We're outside San Diego harbor, where we plan to stay for the night. Do you want to meet us at your dock in the morning around ten? We should be arriving around that time."

"That's great!" Hans said. "Any trouble with her?"

"No, sir. She handled sweet . . . all the way."

"It's been six weeks, then," Hans calculated. "Did you run into any rough weather?"

"A little, but nothing she couldn't handle. A storm hit us around Mexico City, and we had to heave-to for a few days. We found a cotter pin on deck one morning, but soon found that it had come out of the back stay. It wasn't too difficult to replace it, but it delayed us one full afternoon. Other than that, we didn't have any problems."

"Great!" exclaimed Hans. "I'll see you in the morning, then."

"Slip D19, at the Bay Club Marina."

"I'll watch for you."

Hans could not express his relief when he hung up the phone. "I'll need to run down to the marina in the morning," he announced. "Want to go with me?" he asked Charity.

"She's home?" Charity asked, a smile on her face.

Nodding, Hans said, "Very few problems, and almost home. They're staying outside the harbor tonight, rather than bring her into the dock in the dark. It's unfamiliar territory for them."

"Mamá and Perry should come, too," said Charity. "I suppose this means you'll want to go back to living aboard until we marry?" She winked at him, and he understood her message.

"Yes," he agreed, "that would be nice."

"Mamá-mia!" Juaniata exclaimed. "You are always welcome here, Hans."

"I know that, but right now my boat is like home to me," he insisted. "I've missed *Charity's Bridge*, Mamá."

"What did you call it?" she asked, her focus changing directions.

"*Charity's Bridge*," he answered. "That's been her name ever since I fell in love with your daughter."

Juaniata gave him a broad, approving smile. "We shall all go! I do not need to see how they pour a floor! Charity!" she scolded. "You did not tell me Hans named his boat after you!"

"Sorry, Mamá. It was a private ceremony." She gave Hans a sheepish smile.

Had it been a ceremony for her? Had she been pleased with the name? He recalled her thanking him for it, telling him it was a thoughtful thing to do, but had he pleased her? Hans decided he should ask her tonight.

When they finally tired from canasta, Hans said, "Mamá, do you mind if I walk with Charity down by the pool for a little while?"

"Go," said Juaniata. "Enjoy yourselves."

Hans turned to Charity. "Do you want to go with me?"

"Of course," she said, taking his offered hand.

He couldn't believe how much it thrilled him to hold her hand in his, to walk side by side together. Every time. They had known each other for almost eleven weeks, and he still thrilled to hold her hand. In his heart, he knew it would always be so. Charity had become a part of him in the short time they'd known one another. Hans could not imagine his life without her now. It seemed as though he had existed on two levels: *before* he met Charity and *after*. The short weeks he'd lived after meeting Charity were far more important to him than all the years that passed before she came diving into his life.

They took the elevator down to the pool area and walked around the indoor atrium across from it. Muted lights shone around them, softening the darkness. "Tell me how you felt when you saw I'd changed the name of our boat."

She turned and smiled at him. "Thrilled, Hans. I even did a little dance right there on the dock."

"So that was the private celebration you mentioned to your mother?"

Charity nodded, giving him a wide, dimpled smile.

Really?" he asked. "Because, you never told me until now. I thought that when you saw your name on the boat, it might convince you to keep it."

"No," she laughed. "I never wanted your boat, but the name you chose meant everything to me."

"I'd like to see you dance," he confessed.

"We could dance at our wedding reception. Mamá mentioned the other day that she would really like that."

"With a live band?" Hans asked.

Charity smiled, her emerald eyes mirroring the pool's reflection. "I'd like that, too," she said. "Only it would be nice to have Central

American music. Do you think anyone in San Diego plays that?"

"I'll find someone," he promised. "Even if I have to ship them in from Costa Rica."

"Oh, Hans," she said, leaning against him. "You spoil me so. I haven't done anything for you."

Wrapping his arms around her waist, he pulled her close. "You *are* everything to me."

"But, I haven't *done* anything," she complained. "I don't even have a job now, so I can't even get you a wedding ring."

"Is that what's bothering you?" he asked.

"Yes." She looked up at him, and pressed her hands against both his cheeks. "I want to be able to pay for your wedding ring myself, but I don't have any money left. Everything I brought with me is gone, and I'm almost penniless."

Hans stepped back and opened his wallet, putting two credit cards in her hand. "I never canceled these cards you returned. If you want to get me something, use these. If you want to pay me back, consider your charges a loan. I can wait for repayment until you get your degree, or anytime you choose to pay me back. But marriage, Charity, means that my money is your money, and your money is mine. There is no give and take. Everything we have we share equally."

"But, I have nothing to share," she complained. "Nothing."

"You have your smile, your personality, your intelligence," he persuaded, "not to mention your sweet spirit, your mothering instincts. And after we marry, we will share the physical side of the marriage covenant, as well. Do you know what it does to me just to hold your hand? To know that your hand is soon going to take my hand forever?"

"That has no monetary value," she murmured.

"It does to me," he whispered, his voice growing husky, his wants trying to supercede his will. "I would give everything I own just to hold your hand for one moment, Charity. If you're so upset about my money, I will give it all away, every penny to the Church. I will become a penniless man, but I will love you no less. Money, or the lack of it, does not define who we are . . . it's how well we love one another, it's how we spend our lives caring about and sharing with one another, proving to the Lord that we have the pure love of Christ in our hearts."

"You would give everything you own to the Church just to comfort my bruised ego?" she asked, her lower lip trembling.

"Yes, but I hope you won't ask me," he teased, giving her what he hoped was an irresistible smile.

"If I said I really wanted you to," she persisted.

"Fine," Hans said, wanting nothing more out of life than to make Charity happy. "I will give everything I own to the Church. Right now. Come along, we'll go upstairs and I'll write out a check to the Bishop."

Charity laughed and cried all at once. "You must really love me," she said. "How could give everything you have away for me?"

"If our roles were reversed," Hans suggested. "What would you do with all that money?"

When Charity winked, he knew he had been reeled in hook, line and sinker. "I would not be so foolish as you," she teased, then she went up on tiptoe and kissed him.

That was all Hans needed to persuade him. He gathered her into his arms and returned her kiss with a passion from deep within him, and she responded with more fire than he expected.

Quickly, Hans withdrew. "You'd better lock your bedroom door tonight," he whispered huskily. "I think I'll go stand in a cold shower for a while."

Hans turned and took her by the hand, leading her back to the elevator, where he had a few moments to reconsider his position. When they reached the condo door, he turned the key into the lock and opened the door for Charity to enter, but he remained outside it.

"Hans?" she questioned, turning about to face him.

But, Hans shook his head. "Not tonight," he said. "I'm going to a hotel."

"But, all we did was kiss one another," she teased.

He arched an eyebrow and gave her a crooked grin. "I love you, Charity, so I'll pick you up at nine-thirty tomorrow morning."

Without looking back, Hans turned around and went to the elevator. His hand shook as he pressed the button marked *down*.

Finding a hotel was no problem compared to what he would have faced if he'd stayed at the Blake family's condo that night.

Tomorrow night, *Charity's Bridge* would be home, and Hans would live aboard her until the day he knelt across the altar from the woman he loved and they became an eternal family unit.

Chapter Seventeen

"It's time to concede that we need to hire a plumber," agreed Hans, as he saw the pool of water that had collected beneath the bathroom sink he had installed a few days ago.

They were standing in the main bathroom, and Charity threw a stack of cleaning towels over the water to sop it up. "I guess so," she giggled, "Plumbing is not going to be one of those areas we should try to save money on."

"Apparently not," he admitted with dismay. "Thank goodness it's only a small leak. It could have seeped out into the hall and ruined the new carpet."

Charity saw the defeat in his sad blue eyes and tried to encourage him. "But, the closet door works great!"

"What about the dishwasher?" he asked. "Does it leak?"

"I haven't run it yet," she answered. "Perhaps we should have the plumber check it, too."

"Good idea. Do you mind calling a plumber?"

"You're not staying at the condo with me?" she asked, somewhat confused.

"I have to meet the rigger at *Charity's Bridge* this morning."

"I thought you said nothing was wrong with her," Charity asked.

She and Hans had inspected *Charity's Bridge* thoroughly when it arrived, and it had passed their careful scrutiny.

"I'm not going aloft," he announced. "In an emergency at sea, I would. But, I have a wedding coming up in two weeks, and I don't want to be laid up in the hospital with a broken leg on that day."

"What needs to be done aloft?" she asked.

"When you lose one cotter pin, that doesn't mean that you assume all of the rest of them are still intact. It's just a precaution before I take you and your family out sailing on Monday. When the rigger gives me the thumbs up to move her, I'll need to fill up with diesel, and empty the holding tanks."

"Oh," said Charity, finally understanding his anxiety to get the rigging inspected. He was worried for her safety, and that of her mother and brother. "I guess I'll stay here for the drapery lady."

"Exactly," he agreed. "Do you mind?"

"Not at all. And, I think I'm capable of finding a plumber." She went up on tiptoes so she could kiss him on the cheek.

"Will you be back in time for when the furniture arrives?"

"I'll try," he agreed. "It will depend on how long the rigger takes. But, I'll call you when I have an ETA."

Hans kissed her back, and left her standing at the bathroom door. Charity shrugged. It was just like Hans to think of safety issues with his boat. The day after *Charity's Bridge* arrived, she and Hans spent four hours going over every inch of the Hallberg-Rassey to make certain she wasn't damaged anywhere. He had even donned his diving gear and taken an underwater light with him to examine the hull, propeller, shaft and rudder, and to brush off any marine growth that may have accumulated while he was away from it.

For the first half hour, Charity worked in the bathroom, sopping up the water, moving the dehydrator to the bathroom, and locating a large bucket to put beneath the dripping pipe.

When the doorbell rang, Charity looked through the peep hole and was relieved to see the woman who owned the drapery store. She was dressed in a working jumpsuit, and had a male assistant with her.

Opening the door, Charity said, "Come in. We're ready for you."

Soon, the draperies were hung in the living room and all three bedrooms, as well as in the kitchen and master bathroom. It only took them two hours, and as soon as they'd left, Charity had some time to stand back and look at the place she would call home for the next few years. The carpets had been laid earlier that week, and the drapes complemented the flooring quite nicely. Charity was beginning to feel that she might have her mother's eye for color.

The condo was about sixteen hundred square feet, with a large, open kitchen, dining area, and a living room that extended across one end of the condo. At the other end there were three bedrooms and two bathrooms. The main bathroom opened off the hall's archway, with the master bedroom and bathroom suite to the left, and the two smaller bedrooms to the right. The condo was about twice the size of the one Charity had grown up in, and would remain their domain until they outgrew it.

They had chosen soft, muted colors for the living room, dining room and kitchen, with bolder shades for the sofa and love seat that would be arriving this afternoon. The dining table and chairs were made of rich oak to match the new kitchen cupboards. In the master bedroom, they'd chosen forest green bedding with navy blue and a touch of mauve and cream to go with the deep cherrywood four-poster frame and matching dressers.

Right after she'd eaten a tuna sandwich, Charity checked on the bucket beneath the bathroom sink, but it had only a small amount of water in the bottom of it. The furniture started arriving before Charity had a chance to call for a plumber. It took quite a while for the movers to load the sofa, love seat, end tables, lamps, bookshelves and two bedrooms full of furniture into the elevator, and up to the condo, and they had to make several trips. After the bedroom furniture was set into position in the master suite, the movers from the furniture store were finished. She thanked them, signed the delivery receipts, and bid them goodbye. The only furniture remaining undelivered was the computer desk, which had an evening delivery schedule.

Now, Charity would have time to locate a plumber. It was already four in the afternoon, and she doubted she could find one to come out that evening, but she had to try. Briefly, she wondered if Hans had eaten, but dismissed her concerns and sank onto a stool at the kitchen counter, in front of the telephone and yellow pages.

Charity opened the telephone book, thumbing backwards, as was her nature. Psychologist, Psychiatrist, Promotions, Prom Dresses, Private Investigators. The telephone rang, and Charity paused in her search, leaving the book open on the counter.

"Clark residence," she answered. Just saying the name gave her a thrill, even though she wasn't a Clark yet.

"Sweetheart, it's Hans."

"Hi!" she exclaimed, happy to hear his voice. "You should see how our condo is shaping up."

"Did the furniture and drapes arrive then?" Hans asked.

"Yes. I'm just waiting for the desk and chairs for the den," she answered.

"And the plumber?"

"I've been busy. I'm just now looking for one. Besides, the bucket isn't full yet, there's only a little bit in the bottom of it, so it's not a major leak."

"The rigging on the boat is fine, and I'm headed back. Do you want me to pick up a pizza or something?"

"I'd suggest we go out for supper," she said, "but we need to wait for the desk."

"I'll pick up a pizza," he suggested again.

"I really feel like a salad, do you mind?"

"No, they make salads at the pizza place."

It was Hans' way of saying they could both have whatever they wanted. She could not fault him for his affinity towards pizza. "That would be great. Italian dressing. I don't care much for that blue cheese stuff you like."

"Italian it is. See you soon."

After they hung up, Charity resumed her position on the barstool at the kitchen counter. The page of the phone book was open to Private Investigators. *There must be a thousand of them in San Diego!*

Charity picked up the page, still going backwards to the previous entry, to continue her search for Plumbers, but a name she recognized was spread across the top in a half-page advertisement. The name prevented her from proceeding further. Indeed, the name took her breath away. The top portion of the boldly printed ad read:

COLTON WRIGHT
PRIVATE INVESTIGATOR
MISSING PERSONS ARE MY SPECIALTY!

Immediately, she started searching her memory for when she had heard the name, Colton Wright. She remembered the telephone call Hans had received two weeks ago, and his response to her inquiry came burning into her mind, "*He's a man I met a month or two ago.*" Charity's anger sizzled.

How could Hans have met Colton Wright a month or two before if he'd been in Costa Rica? More importantly, why had Colton Wright telephoned Hans that day?

Then, Charity remembered Hans' trip to Utah. He had a layover in San Diego on his flight to Utah, and on returning to Costa Rica, he had stayed several days at Josh and Kayla's condo. At this condo. Hans would have had easy access to Colton Wright in San Diego. Suddenly, she knew in her heart what Hans had done. He had hired a private investigator to find a missing person. And she had no doubt who Hans wanted to find. Daniel Blake.

Anger didn't even begin to describe Charity's feelings. Furious and bewildered, she felt hot tears sting her eyes. Her stomach lurched and she raced to the bathroom, where she lost what remained of her lunch. She washed her face, and her hands trembled.

How could the kind and thoughtful Hans she loved hire a private investigator to search for Daniel when he knew how Charity felt about her father?

Reading the half-page ad thoroughly, Charity picked up the phone and dialed the number. A male voice on an automated answering service said, "You've reached Colton Wright. I'm temporarily out of the office, but I can be reached at . . ." and he gave the number. Charity wrote it down next to his name on the yellow page.

Her hands shaking, she dialed the number, but it only rang twice when a gruff male voice answered, "Colton Wright here."

Suddenly, Charity couldn't find her own voice. Instead, a large lump arose in her throat, and she almost gagged on it. Replacing the receiver, she went back into the bathroom and waited for a momentary feeling of nausea to subside.

Returning to the telephone directory, she ripped the page out with Colton Wright's ad, and the secondary number that she had written next to his name, and crumpled it up in her hand. At first, she thought she should throw it away and never mention to Hans what she had discovered that day. But, as she analyzed the situation, she realized she hadn't discovered anything. Hans knew a man named Colton Wright, a man he'd met a month or two ago. And there was a private investigator named Colton Wright who specialized in missing persons, whose office was in San Diego. It couldn't be a mere coincidence, could it?

One thing Charity knew about Hans, he would not lie to her if she asked him directly. He had always told her the truth, hadn't he?

She recalled her fear when her mother mentioned Hans may have gone to Chicago right before Charity left Cocos Island for the last time. But, she'd asked Hans where he'd gone, and the bracelet on her wrist proved that he'd been in New York. His sincerity about the bracelet had overwhelmed her, and she'd felt guilty for even thinking that he'd gone to Chicago.

Now, she feared that she was too much like her mother, and had jumped to the wrong conclusion without finding out for certain. No, Hans would tell her honestly, if she questioned him. Charity resolved there was nothing left to do but to ask Hans if he'd hired Colton Wright to find Daniel Blake.

Trembling, Charity went into the bedroom where she sank onto the plastic-covered mattress on their new bed, curled up into a fetal position, and wept.

❦ ❦ ❦

Hans pushed the door open with the toe of his shoe, his hands full of pizza, salad and drinks. "I'm back," he called, but he did not get an answer. The condo was silent. Painfully silent.

He put the boxes and cups on the kitchen counter, maneuvering past the dining table and chairs. Then ignoring the new furniture, Hans went toward the hall to find his fiancée. She wasn't in the main bathroom, as the door was wide open and it was empty.

Turning to his left, he heard a faint whimper and hurried into the master bedroom, where Charity was curled up on the bed, her back toward him. Her shoulders were shaking, and he could tell that she had been crying for quite some time, as great sobs of anguish washed over her.

Rushing to sit beside her on the bed, Hans said, "Charity, what is it? What's wrong?"

She seemed to ignore his questions, so he persisted. "Is it your mother? Is something wrong with Perry?"

He attempted to turn her over and pull her into his arms. He wanted to cradle her, to comfort her, but he was dismayed to feel her stiffen and refuse his gesture. Immediately, Hans backed off but he remained sitting on the edge of the bed waiting, wondering. Finally, he asked, "What have I done that you're so upset with me?"

This seemed to invoke a whole new wave of tears in Charity, and Hans felt compelled to stretch out beside her and hold her against him, to assuage her suffering, to console her. But once again, Charity stiffened and scooted farther away from him.

Hans sat up, returned to the edge of the bed, and said wearily, "You're going to have to tell me sometime, Sweetheart. We can't even begin to resolve a problem until we both know what it is."

Resigned to waiting until she was ready to talk to him, Hans remained in position, hoping she would, eventually, share with him the reason for her tears. After what seemed like hours, but was in reality only a few minutes, Charity lifted her hand and dropped a wadded piece of yellow paper on the bed behind her back. It fell beside Hans, and he scooped it up, noticing that Charity still refused to roll over, or to face him.

Hans opened the paper, recognized that it had been torn from a telephone book, and gulped as he read the half-page ad at the top. *Colton Wright*. He needed to read no further. Analyzing the situation from every angle, Hans knew that Charity had guessed what he'd been up to, and she knew that Colton Wright had telephoned Hans a couple of weeks ago. Charity had assumed correctly that he had hired Colton

Wright to find her father. Shuddering, Hans sighed deeply.

Placing his hand upon Charity's arm, he rubbed it for a few minutes, allowing his mind to clear as he tried to decide exactly how much to tell her, without alienating her any further.

Finally, he decided that the truth couldn't be as painful as her fears. Gulping, he whispered, "I'm sorry for hurting you, Charity. It was never my intention to cause you any pain. But, you've guessed right. I hired Colton Wright to locate Daniel Blake. I hadn't planned to tell you anything unless there was good news. I wanted to spare you this anguish, and here you are suffering in my absence. I should have told you sooner, so that this wouldn't have come as such a shock to you. I am truly sorry."

Waiting was not something in Hans' repertoire of character traits, and he didn't allow much time to pass before he said, "I can only say I'm sorry so many times before you either forgive me or. . . ?" He left the sentence open, knowing she could fill in the blanks.

Charity sniffed and he gave her his handkerchief. She dabbed at her eyes, and wiped her nose, then sat up and leaned back against the headboard, pulling her knees up to her chest and wrapping her arms around them. Her eyes were now a sad gray-green, her eyelids puffy and red, and he could see that she'd been crying for quite a while.

Hans guessed, "You found this when you started looking for a plumber?"

Charity nodded and took the yellow page away from him. She smoothed the wrinkles out, folded it neatly and put it beside her on the bed. Hans assumed it was her way of saying no matter what he told her, she would telephone Colton Wright and find everything out for herself.

Knowing the moment of truth had come, Hans said, "We found Daniel's mother and sister living in Chicago. I went to visit them before I went to New York to get your bracelet."

Her eyes flitted from her knees, and she glared at him angrily. Hans had never seen Charity so indignant, not even that first day at Cocos Island, when she thought he was the same as all American males, a "love them and leave them" guy, as she had later confessed. The rage that he saw in her eyes appeared wild, raw and unquenchable.

"Is he dead?" she demanded, her voice harsh and brittle.

Hans shook his head. How much should he tell her? It would only hurt her more if he told her everything that he'd learned thus far.

Charity nodded briefly. "You said you wanted to spare me. That you hadn't planned to tell me anything unless there was good news. By your keeping all this from me, it means that you've only found bad news?"

Hans didn't have enough information to tell her about Daniel's name change. If he knew why Daniel had changed his name, he would have more to offer. But, right now, it was probably in her best interest if she didn't know everything . . . until he had a chance to find Daniel and confront him. Nodding, Hans agreed, "So far, I don't have anything good to tell you."

"Except that Daniel is alive?" New tears streamed from her eyes. "He's alive?" she asked a second time, choking on a sob.

The only thing Hans could do was to nod in the affirmative.

"Take me home," she insisted. "Right now." She scooted past him, taking the yellow page with her, and jumped off the bed. Then, she grabbed her handbag from the kitchen counter and stuffed the yellow page into it.

Before Hans could protest, she had opened the condo door and stepped down the hall to the elevator. Hans quickly locked the condo behind them. His heart sinking, Hans followed Charity down to the parking garage and opened the SUV door for her. Taking his place in the driver's seat, Hans put the key into the ignition, then turned it on. The Cadillac's engine roared into life, and Hans backed out of the parking stall, then put the gear shift into the drive position, and quietly drove out of the parking garage, heading eastward.

Charity was silent the entire time, and Hans certainly didn't know what to say to break the spell of doom that had settled over them. He never dreamed his finding her father could wound her so deeply. Indeed, he'd hoped that closure would be a good thing for Charity. But, she couldn't get closure with her father still alive because it meant that he didn't go back to Nicaragua. He didn't try to find his family. This painful information only added insult to injury. Hans had no choice but to accept the blame for the condition in which Charity now found herself. And to his great dismay, she refused to let him comfort or console her.

As they approached the building where Juaniata's condo was housed, Hans reached across the empty space to take Charity's hand in his. She pulled it away.

"There's more to Daniel's story than meets the eye," Hans began. "I will tell you the rest, if you'll listen."

"I don't want to hear it!" she yelled. "Haven't you done enough, Hans? When does it end? When my heart is so broken it cannot mend anymore?"

"I'm sorry, Charity," Hans pleaded. "Please, forgive me. It was never my intention to hurt you. You must know that somewhere deep inside your heart."

Charity turned her head to the right, so that he could not see her face. He could only wonder at her expression and pray that, somehow, she could forgive him for what he'd done.

"Please, Sweetheart. I love you," he begged. "Forgive me."

Hans parked the SUV out in front of the tall building, sensing that Charity would not invite him into her home right now. And he was correct in this assumption.

Stubbornly, Charity pushed the SUV door open, not waiting for him to come around and open it for her. Just as stubbornly, Hans left the driver's seat and walked quickly beside her to the front door.

As she placed her hand upon the glass door's silver handle, he took her by the elbow, hoping to turn her back to face him.

Regret filled his heart as she complied. He could see no love in her beautiful eyes today, no sparkle . . . no hope that he had ever really earned her heart or her love.

"Charity, please?" he asked, one more time.

Her eyes narrowed and she looked up at him as though the only emotion she had ever felt for him was unadulterated hatred. "I will *never* forgive you for this!" she snapped. "*Never!*"

Then, she turned on her heel and entered the building without him. She didn't even look back, she just kept right on walking, past the elevator to the stairwell.

Hans realized she would be taking her anger out on an eleven-story jaunt upstairs. He stood there on the sidewalk, listening to the Cadillac still running, the honking of a horn, the squeal of a car's tires, the evening traffic in the background.

But, the only sound that echoed around in his mind was Charity's voice, and the only vision he could see was the look of hatred on her beautiful face, as she claimed she would never forgive him.

Somehow, Hans forced his feet to take him back to the SUV, where he sank onto the driver's seat and dug the cell phone from its holder on his belt. After dialing the number, Hans listened as Colton Wright answered.

"Hans Clark here," said Hans.

"Did you call me earlier?" he asked, "Because when I picked up the phone, it was your new apartment number, but no one was on the line."

"Charity called you," Hans admitted. "I expect she'll try again. Wright, I want you to tell her everything if she calls."

"Everything?" he asked. "She found out, hmm?"

"Yes, so tell her everything."

"You sure you want me to do that? It should come from you, Hans."

"I know, but right now she won't speak to me."

The hesitation on the line told Hans that Wright was assessing the situation. Finally, Wright said, "You're the boss. What about her family? You want me to tell them, too?"

"If they call you," agreed Hans. "I'm not holding anything back from them."

"You want me to tell you where we are now?"

"Yes. Any progress?"

"I'm down to seventeen men about Daniel's age, all named Juan Perez, several of them are in Southern California. You want to look them up? I'm still tracking down the ones on the East Coast."

"Sure. Where are they?"

"One lives near Los Angeles, two near Long Beach, and one owns an almond farm in Diamond Valley."

Hans laughed. "I doubt Daniel went into almond farming, Colton. He had an engineering degree, or did I remember that wrong?"

"No, you remembered right. I was just thinking that if he didn't want his family to find him, becoming an almond farmer would be a vocation they would never suspect."

"No, I can't buy that. Daniel was an electrical engineer." Hans grinned to himself. If there was anything Hans did know, it was what a man would give up for a good education. But, no educated man would squander his degree by becoming an almond farmer. "Give me the information, I'll see what I can dig up." Cradling the phone with his shoulder, Hans wrote down the addresses and phone numbers. After the Juan Perez address in Diamond Valley, Hans put a big question mark, knowing he would leave it until the very last.

"I'll check in with you later on," said Hans.

After hanging up, Hans sat in the Cadillac, the engine running, his vision blurred from moisture, until his hands stopped shaking.

Hours later, Hans didn't know how he had driven back to the Bay Club Marina on Shelter Island in San Diego. When he found himself stretched out on the bed in the master stateroom of *Charity's Bridge*, he wondered how long he had been there, and why the pillow beneath him was drenched and cold.

Chapter Eighteen

Charity went to bed immediately upon returning to her mother's condo, telling Juaniata and Perry that she had a headache. Stretching out on her bed and waiting, Charity listened quietly until she heard Perry and her mother retire for the night. It wouldn't be long before Perry was asleep, and only then would she seek the solitude of her mother's bedroom, the gentleness of her mother's arms, and Juaniata's patient and listening heart. When she heard Perry's deep, resonating snore muffled from the third bedroom, she slipped out of bed and put on her bathrobe.

After tapping softly on the door to Juaniata's bedroom, she heard her mother say, "Come in, Charity. I am awake."

"How did you know it was me?" Charity asked, knowing that Perry's snoring couldn't be heard this far away.

"You were crying this evening when you returned. And you did not bring Hans up with you. It was a simple deduction, Charity. You have had a lovers' spat. I knew you would come to me when your heart whispered you were ready."

"Oh, Mamá!" Charity burst into tears and sank onto the bed. "How can Hans truly love me? You do not know what he has done!"

"Tell me, Cari," said Juaniata, folding her arms around Charity, holding her close, and stroking Charity's cheek. Charity knew she had only used the informal Spanish of her name to please her, to gain her confidence. Charity loved her mother all the more for trying.

"He hired a private investigator to find Daniel," Charity complained, tears streaking down her cheeks. "How can he think that's what I want? Didn't he know how badly this would hurt me?"

"Why?" Juaniata asked. "Did he find your father?"

Charity nodded. "Yes, Daniel is still alive."

"And?" asked her mother, clearly expecting more information.

"You are not shocked, Mamá?"

"Hans is a good man, Charity. He does this thing out of his love for you and your family. If he had not looked for Daniel, then I would have been disappointed in him."

"How can he love me when he hurts me so?" Charity asked.

"What else did Hans find out about Daniel?" asked Juaniata, apparently unwilling to be put off any longer.

"He said that he had decided if he found only bad news about Daniel, he would not tell me. I suppose that means that if he had good news, he would have told me before now. I had to learn of his deception by myself! He said he met Daniel's mother and sister in Chicago."

"What did Hans mean, Charity?" Juaniata demanded. "How can learning that Daniel is still alive mean something bad?"

"I refused to listen to anymore," Charity whimpered. "It is one thing to think that the only reason why your father would abandon you is because he is dead. It is quite another to know he is still alive, but he did not come for you."

"But, you have always been the one to say that he was still alive, Cari," her mother clarified. "You are the one who always gave me hope that Daniel could still be alive."

"I only said that because it was too painful to think that my father died without getting to say goodbye," Charity confessed.

"You contradict yourself," admitted Juaniata. "All your life, you refuse to believe that your father is dead. Now, you are upset because he isn't!"

"Oh, Mamá! How can you be so blind? If Daniel is still alive, it means that he chose not to come find us. It means that Daniel didn't want us, either of us."

To her amazement, Juaniata stiffened and withdrew from their embrace. "That is not true, Charity. Your father would never make such a choice."

"Perhaps not the Daniel you knew," Charity admitted. "But, he must have changed when he returned to Chicago. He lived with us for nearly a year, in an under-developed country where his parents and his peers had no influence on him. Can you imagine what it must have been like to return to America, to freedom and money and power? He didn't need to acknowledge that you and I existed. In the eyes of the United States, he was a free and single man! Free to choose another woman as his wife!"

Charity had pushed her mother too far, and she knew it the moment her mother stood up. "I will not listen to my own daughter speak such things about her father! Go to your room!"

"Mamá! I am too old to be sent to my room. You and I must face the truth now! Hans told me that he hadn't intended to tell me anything about Daniel unless there was good news to tell. Only I found out too soon! When I confronted him, I asked him if Daniel still being alive meant that there was only bad news, and he said yes. What other bad news can there be, except that Daniel found someone else?"

"I will not listen to you speak such things about your father, Charity. You must trust that there is another explanation," Juaniata insisted. "Did you ask Hans to explain how he found Daniel. Has he seen

Daniel? There could be other reasons for why he did not return to Nicaragua. Perhaps Daniel was injured, perhaps paralyzed. Perhaps Daniel's disability was too great for him to come for us."

Charity was not surprised at this rationale, it was one Juaniata had used many times to comfort Charity in her youth. Her mother's irrational hope and unswerving faith in Daniel's love had always been the catalyst that drove Juaniata onward, that helped her embrace the toil and tears left in the wake of Daniel's desertion. But, Charity would accept no more excuses. Daniel was alive, and he had abandoned them. Regardless how her mother saw his absence, Charity could never forgive Daniel for his betrayal . . . nor could she forgive Hans for his. Her fiancée should have let Daniel remain dead to them. Now, Charity would always be faced with the question, *Why?* She was only an infant when Daniel deserted them, but why had he? Did she cry too much? Was she too fussy? Was she not pretty enough or was she flawed in some way she hadn't noticed? In her heart, she knew that Daniel would have found no reason to leave Juaniata, who was the perfect woman. Beautiful, shrewd, smart, loving, kind, generous and thoughtful. No one in their right mind would abandon Juaniata. That left only two schools of thought: Daniel was never in his right mind, which Juaniata denied; or Charity must have driven him from the nest.

Before Hans had pursued an answer to Daniel's disappearance in their family's life, he should have made certain that the answers would cause no harm. Her fiancé had certainly blundered in this situation, and this was not something that Charity could just laugh off. Heartbreak was something to which she thought she had adapted, growing up in a fatherless home. But, she had never known sorrow like this before. Now, her heart had been trampled by two men, and she doubted she would ever recover from it.

Silently, Charity stood and left her mother's bedroom.

Sinking down onto her own bed, Charity knew she would not sleep.

She pulled the scriptures from the night stand and allowed it to fall open to Moroni 7, which she had read quite often with Hans. It seemed to be one of his favorite passages.

So much had happened to Charity since Hans sailed into her world. He had been the driving force behind everything good that had come to her and her family. She wanted to hate Hans for searching for her father, but she could not. In her mind, his words echoed and resonated back and forth, up and down, and she could not escape them: *It was never my intention to hurt you. You must know that somewhere deep inside your heart.*

Her eyes wandered over Moroni 7, grabbing fragmented pieces of scripture, here a line, there a line, until all she could see was:

> *"But behold, that which is of God inviteth and*
> *enticeth to do good continually; wherefore,*
> *every thing which inviteth and enticeth to do*
> *good, and to love God, and to serve Him,*
> *is inspired of God . . . Wherefore, my*
> *beloved brethren, if ye have not charity,*
> *ye are nothing, for charity never faileth*
> *Wherefore, cleave unto charity,*
> [which is] *the pure love of Christ . . ."*

Charity was not so blind that she did not see the double meaning Hans read into his favorite scriptures, but until that moment, she did not realize that the Lord was speaking to her, also . . . about Hans.

God had invited Hans to do good, to love God, and to serve Him, and Hans had gone the extra mile in all things regarding her family and their welfare. Because Hans had done all that he had for Charity, Juaniata and Perry, he had to be inspired by God, as the scripture read.

If any man upon the earth exhibited the pure love of Christ, it was Hans. His generosity knew no bounds, not even where Daniel was concerned. Didn't that prove that Hans was striving to live his life as though the Savior walked beside him? Wouldn't the Savior want Charity to know what happened to her father? Wouldn't He want Juaniata to know where her husband was, regardless whether the information be happy or sad? As Charity sought understanding from the scriptures, a sweet and abiding peace fell upon her. Anger diminished as she realized that Hans might have been acting upon God's inspiration in trying to locate Daniel. Dare she hope that, eventually, something good would come from Hans' efforts?

Hans attended his own ward on Sunday because he dared not step foot near Charity, nor had he made any effort to contact her. His last impression of her anger and hostility towards him burned deep inside his chest. No matter how much Hans loved Charity, and notwithstanding all his efforts in her behalf, he had lost her trust and her love, and he knew it.

The first two days after he confessed to Charity about Colton Wright's assignment, Hans had spent most of his time in prayer or reading from the scriptures. After Sunday's services, he had returned to his boat where he continued in fasting and in prayer.

At the onset of this experience, he questioned his actions. How had he failed so miserably? Why hadn't he discussed his plans with Charity before contacting Colton Wright? If he'd known that she would be so upset, would he have gone ahead with it? But, after the questions came heartfelt prayers. When he asked the Lord for confirmation that he had done the right thing, he believed that the answer was *Yes*.

The sweet prompting of the Spirit had been with him in Chicago. Although there were many puzzles, the Lord had sent Hans there. Hans knew it. He also knew that if Charity asked him to stop looking, even now when she was so upset with him, Hans could not be compelled to call off the search. In his heart, he knew that the Lord had a better plan . . . and Hans was following that plan, regardless of the outcome.

He could only pray that Charity would forgive him, eventually. And that she would, one day, have a good reason to love him again.

Early Monday morning, Hans dressed quickly and telephoned Colton Wright. This gave Charity three days' time to call the private investigator herself. Since Colton Wright had Hans' permission to tell Charity everything in regards to the investigation, should she ever call to ask him about it, Hans had no doubt that she had already done so.

"Colton Wright," came the gruff voice.

"Hans Clark."

"Did you get the faxes I sent?" came Wright's first question.

"Yes, thanks."

"Did you check out those three names I gave you?" Wright asked.

"Not yet. How are you coming?"

"I'm down to two names in Florida, and six in the middle states."

"And you're coming up empty?" Hans asked.

"Yes. Every single one of these guys is Hispanic."

"But, you've talked to them, in case they've changed their appearance, as well as their identities?" asked Hans.

"That's why it's taken me three days," Wright assured. "But, my bet is on one of these Juans in California."

"Why?"

"If I were Daniel, I'd want to get as far away from Chicago as I could."

"That would be Alaska or Hawaii," reminded Hans.

"My search did turn up one guy in Honolulu, but he was twenty years older than Daniel Blake. Process of elimination."

"How near the birth year have you kept in tracking these men down?" Hans wanted to know.

"Within ten years. Trust me, anymore than ten years and they'd look either too young or too old to fit the Social Security data."

"Or, he could have changed his name again, from Juan Perez to John Smith."

"Don't get too discouraged," suggested Wright. "There's only one missing person I've never found, that wasn't already dead, that is."

"We've got to find Daniel Perez alive," insisted Hans. "He just spoke to his sister four months ago."

"Speaking of the sister," Wright said, "she called the other day. Wanted to know if we'd found anything."

"What did you tell her?" Hans asked.

"Nothing," said Wright. "You haven't authorized me to tell her anything, only to gather information."

"Did she say whether or not she had spoken to her mother about Daniel's marriage to Juaniata?"

"She did, but she said the old gal clammed up and went to her room."

"All right. Thanks, Colton."

"Yeah, don't thank me until you see the bill."

They said their goodbyes and Hans went out into the galley to prepare to break his fast. Bacon was sizzling in the pan when he heard a tapping sound on the exterior of *Charity's Bridge*. He turned the stove off, unlocked the companionway and slid it open. To his surprise, Juaniata was standing on the dock, her hands folded firmly around the handle of her red handbag.

"Mamá," he said, wondering why she had come to see him. Surely, Charity had told her everything, and she had just as much reason to hate him as did his beloved.

"We must have the talk," she said, stepping aboard. "You are alone?"

"Yes, I was just fixing breakfast. Are you hungry?" He wanted to ask about Charity, but decided he should wait and see what Juaniata wanted before he tackled a monumental task like his fiancée.

"Toast," she said, "and orange juice, if you have it."

Hans nodded. "Welcome aboard." He turned back to the galley while Juaniata stepped through the companionway and down the stairs. She sat at the salon table, propped her purse up next to a decorative pillow, and waited for him.

Hustling around the galley, Hans dug out dishes and silverware, juice and milk, and made some toast to go with his bacon and eggs, after making certain that Juaniata's toast was cooked to perfection.

Taking a seat opposite her, Hans unfolded a napkin and placed it in his lap. "Shall I say the prayer?" he asked.

Juaniata nodded. Hans bowed his head and offered a quick blessing on the food. He was pleased to hear her say, "Amen," and wondered if she had taken the news about Daniel a little better than Charity had.

As he dug into the eggs with his fork, he said, "What brings you here, Mamá? Everyone is well, I hope."

"No," she said boldly. "Charity is not well. Not at all. I cannot persuade her to contact you, and this makes my heart very heavy."

"She's not sick?" asked Hans, hoping with all his soul that Charity was all right.

"Sick in the heart," Juaniata nodded. "But, before we speak more of Charity, I must first ask you about my Daniel. Where is he?" She gave Hans a penetrating look that spoke more than her words could.

Shaking his head, Hans said, "I don't know."

"But, Charity said that you had searched for him. That he is alive."

"He was alive in May of this year. I know that much."

"Tell me everything you have learned," Juaniata insisted.

"He returned to the United States in November of 1980," Hans offered.

"This much I have guessed," she added. "What else?"

"His father died in 1980."

"This is not so good."

"Daniel and his mother had some sort of quarrel after the elder Blake died. It may have been over Daniel selling his father's business, but this is pure speculation. His mother was, from all indications, upset about it, but she couldn't do anything because she was not made the executor of the estate. After Daniel left, he never returned. His sister and mother have not seen him since then."

"But, you said he was alive in May," she persisted.

"It seems he telephones his sister on her birthday, which is in May, every year."

She sighed in relief. "He telephoned Angela in May?"

"You knew about Angela?" Hans asked, surprised.

"Daniel and me . . . we spent a year together and we had no secrets. We knew that his mother, Anna, would probably not approve of Daniel marrying outside of his culture. Even before I met Daniel, his father was sickly, and had not wanted him to join the military."

"This information could have saved me some effort," Hans scolded, raising an eyebrow.

"How else was I to know that Daniel had told me the truth?" she asked. "I have had so many questions since the day he left. Now, continue."

"It seems that Angela and her mother have been searching for Daniel ever since he disappeared, though unsuccessfully. By a sheer stroke of luck, my private investigator discovered that Daniel changed his name shortly after selling off and settling his father's estate."

"Mamá-mia!" Juaniata exclaimed. "How can this be?"

"In the United States, all it takes is a good attorney and six hundred dollars. At least, that's how much a name change cost Daniel." Hans sopped the leftover yolk from his plate with a piece of toast, amazed at how well Juaniata was handling the news regarding her husband.

"His new name, what is it?" she asked, almost hopefully, Hans thought.

"Juan Perez."

Juaniata clapped her hands together gleefully, and giggled, "I knew it! I just knew it!"

"You could have told me this information, too," Hans suggested wryly. "It cost me a lot of money to find that little tidbit."

"No, I did not know about the name change," Juaniata insisted. "But, when we were in Nicaragua together, he sometimes said he should never go back to America. He said he wanted to go AWOL, change his name to Juan Perez, and live in Nicaragua forever. *That way*, he always teased, *Uncle Sam would never find him*. He was very worried, too, about his mother. He said she was a refined lady in a high society, and she would not accept someone like me into her family so easily."

"Yet, you married anyway?"

"Daniel and I loved one another," she insisted. "But, when the United States pulled their troops out of Nicaragua, I told him to go with them. I did not want him to go to prison, to become a deserter to his country. Eventually, I wore him down, and he left with his company, but I know that his heart was not in it. He cried the day he left, we all cried, even Charity. She was only a few months old, but she knew that something was wrong that day."

"Did you have his address? Did you write? Did he write to you?"

"Yes. But, Nicaragua was caught up in civil war. My parents and two sisters had already been killed. My brother, Rafael, had moved to Costa Rica several years earlier. To San José . I waited for Daniel to write, but no one was getting any letters through. The only mail coming in was carried by foot over the Costa Rican border by rebels. My brother sent word that the Sandinistas were wiping out villages in their path to take over Managua, and our village was in their path. He begged us to come to Costa Rica, promising he would take care of us. I could not risk Charity's life, nor the life of the child growing within me. I left my forwarding address with three of my neighbors, telling Daniel where we had gone, and how to find us."

"So, you don't know if Daniel came for you, or not."

"Two years later, I met one of the women who had stayed behind. She was living in San José. She told me that the Sandinistas ransacked our village, and she barely escaped with her life. In all those two years she was there, Daniel did not come for us."

"What did you do then? Is that when you wrote to him?"

"I wrote to Daniel the day he left. I wrote to him every single week for two years!" she snapped, her temper flaring. "You think I did not write?"

"Forgive me, Mamá. I need to know everything, otherwise how can I help you?" Hans apologized.

She seemed to reconsider her anger. Finally, she nodded and continued. "I wrote to Daniel every week from Costa Rica. But, in the seventies and eighties, Costa Rica was not that efficient with the postal service. I thought my letters were getting lost in the mail, or sometimes the mail was opened and read, and if the government didn't like what you said, the letters were thrown away. In 1981, around the Christmas season, I received several of my letters back in one week. They were marked, *REFUSED. RETURN TO SENDER.* They were some of the first letters I ever sent to Daniel. I had sent them to his parents' address because the United States government was not well-liked by middle America after they withdrew their troops from Nicaragua. Our people were being slaughtered by the Sandinistas, and the USA turned their backs on them. I was also afraid if my letters were addressed to Daniel at an army base in Missouri, the postal workers in Nicaragua could cause trouble for me and the children." Tears welled up in her brown-black eyes with the harsh memories.

Hans gave her a clean handkerchief. "And you never found out who sent the letters back?"

"No, my son. But, don't you see?" Juaniata dabbed at her eyes. "If Daniel changed his name to Juan Perez, it can only mean that he did not want his mother to find him. He had already served Uncle Sam, and was out of the army by the end of 1980."

"Or it can mean that he wanted no one to find him, and didn't think you would ever look for him under Juan Perez," Hans suggested.

"Mamá-mia! You are just like my Charity! Blind to what stares you in the face! If he did not get our letters, and he is hiding from his family, maybe he is still looking for us! Maybe he changed his name to Juan Perez so that he could more easily gain entrance into the Middle American countries."

"For Charity's sake, I want nothing more than to believe that," said Hans. "But, you need to be realistic, Mamá, and face what may be more likely . . . Daniel may not have wanted anyone to find him."

Juaniata went off into a Spanish tirade over his foolishness. He let her rant for a little while, and when she started slowing down, he said, "¿Traigamos el tópico retrocede a Charity, debe nosotros?"

Stopping mid-sentence, Juaniata blushed crimson. "Forgive me, my son. I forget that you understand my language," she apologized. "Yes, we will change the topic back to Charity, for it will take cunning and determination to soften her heart."

"Meaning she is still furious with me?" Hans asked, even though he knew the answer to this question.

Nodding, Juaniata said, "That first morning, after you told her Daniel was still alive, Charity seemed to feel better about this situation, but as the morning wore on, her anger returned. Now, I am giving her scriptures about forgiveness. She is a good girl, my Charity. She will soon let God help her work through her anger."

"Perhaps you should remind her that by searching for her father, I have only the noblest of intentions and the purest of love in my heart. And, ask her to read Moroni 7:47," Hans suggested.

Chapter Nineteen

"Where is he?" Charity demanded, sweeping her long, silky black hair off her shoulder.

"Hans is gone," said Juaniata. "We spoke only for a few moments, then he said he had to go out of town for a while."

"And why have you got our wedding invitations?" Fear enveloped Charity, choking her, making her light-headed. She had just come from the bedroom, dressed for the day, and ready to start a light breakfast.

"Using the list you gave him last week, Hans addressed all of the them to his and your family and friends, and said that you should address however many of the remaining ones you want that may not have been included on the list. They are all stamped and sealed, and the home address at your new condo is on them. Look."

Juaniata handed a large box of wedding invitations to Charity.

"What am I supposed to do with these?" she asked, placing them on the counter top in the kitchen. "Hans does not love me. How can he still want to marry me?"

"Hans asked, very much like a true gentleman, if you would first pray about your decision to marry, then read Moroni 7:47. And then, if you please, he asked that you decide if you still want to marry him. Hans will leave the decision entirely in your hands. He said, 'Tell

Charity that if she still loves me, she will mail these invitations. If she does not mail them, it will be the answer to my question and I will step out of her life." Patting Charity's hand, Juaniata added, "The post office closes at five this evening. I must go down to my shop, for I have much to do there."

"How am I supposed to get to the post office?" Charity asked.

"Oh!" Fishing a set of keys out of her pocket, Juaniata placed them beside the box of cards on the kitchen counter, and answered. "Hans followed me in his car this morning, and took a taxi from here to the airport."

"He's leaving town?" Dismay and bewilderment slumped Charity's shoulders, and she pulled her robe tighter around her and went over to the sofa, where she sank upon it, her knees shaking. "Now? But, why?"

When she saw the look on her mother's face, she had her answer even before Juaniata said, "The search for Daniel goes on."

Raw anger swept through her, but Charity tried to control her feelings. She did not want to get into another argument with Juaniata. Bewildered by this information, she asked, "Mamá, how can you condone what Hans is doing?"

"Hans and I have talked at length about Daniel, very early this morning. I am convinced that your assessment of your father is incorrect, Cari." Juaniata gave a proud tilt to her head, and stood more erect. "In your mind, you have made Daniel out to be a horrible man, but he is not. You did not know him like I did. If he had known where we were, he would have come for us. Of this, I am convinced."

"It's been twenty-six years since you knew Daniel. If he loved you so much, why did he send your letters back?"

"We do not know that *he* sent them." Juaniata pulled from her purse one of the returned letters she had received, and gave it to Charity. "Look at the writing. Neat, block letters, all capitals. Compare that writing to Daniel's," she insisted, giving Charity a faded piece of frail parchment that she slid from a plastic sleeve.

Charity unfolded the delicate parchment and saw a shaded, pale pink heart drawn upon it. Inside the heart, written in black ink, Charity read:

My One and Only Juaniata

You are the beat in my heart
Whenever we are apart
I know we'll always be one
Our love has just now begun

Darling, you've no need to fear
My heart will always be near
The oceans and seas, they cannot
Diminish the love we have got.

No one can keep us apart
You are the joy in my heart
Soon I will come for your love
With help from Father above

Wait for me, darling of mine
I will return in due time

Keep your love burning for me
You are my soul's destiny

All my love,
Daniel
June 23rd, 1980

"When did Daniel give this to you, Mamá?" Charity asked, refusing to allow her tears to surface.

"The day his military unit left Nicaragua," Juaniata responded.

"You never showed it to me!" accused Charity. "Never!" Why her mother had kept this beautiful poem from her, Charity did not understand.

Dark eyes glistening, Juaniata explained, "Some things between a man and a woman are not meant to be shared with anyone else, Charity. I only show you now so that you can compare the writing on this poem from Daniel to the letters that were returned."

Charity compared the bold capital letters upon the returned envelopes that read

REFUSED — RETURN TO SENDER

to the capital letters of Daniel's poem. She only had the O, D, S, T and N with which to make the comparison, but it was clear that Daniel's letter formation was much more involved and created with a sweeping flair, his freehand was not as crisp and plain as found on the refusal letters, and his handwriting was much more slanted, not so straight up and down.

After perusing the two types of penmanship, Charity insisted, "Someone sent these letters back, Mamá. Perhaps it was the new woman in Daniel's life."

Juaniata, apparently frustrated with Charity's response, slipped the letters and parchment back inside her purse, then went around the kitchen counter where she started banging dishes and pans as she unloaded the dishwasher, muttering a string of Spanish just loud enough that Charity knew she was angry, but soft enough that Charity could not hear the words clearly.

"I am going to call this Colton Wright and find out what he knows about Daniel that Hans has not shared with me," Charity announced, standing up and walking toward her bedroom door.

"Only because you refused to let him tell you everything," said Juaniata. "Hans told me all that he knows this morning aboard his boat. And he gave me copies of all the documents Colton has sent to him." She removed a stack of papers that had been folded in half and shoved into her purse, and placed them beside the box of invitations and the car keys on the kitchen counter top.

Charity turned and walked back toward the counter, sitting herself upon a barstool while watching her mother put away the clean dishes. The stack of papers beckoned her to read them, but stubbornly, Charity refused. "Then tell me, Mamá. Where is Daniel?" she demanded.

After listening to all the details surrounding her father's life, and his ability to maintain his distance from his own mother and sister, Charity concluded that Hans was no closer to finding Daniel than before he started this absurd quest of his. "And you think Daniel changed his name to Juan because he did not want his mother and sister to find him?" she asked, convinced that the story of her father's disappearance made him seem even more guilty of abandonment.

"Charity," her mother pleaded. "You must remove this anger from your heart regarding your father. If you do not, I fear this animosity will destroy the special person that you are. Do you not remember that Nephi taught us not to have malice, nor to contend one with another? He taught that none of these iniquities come from the Lord, and *whoso doeth them shall perish*."

Reciting the passage from 2 Nephi 26:32 and 33 in her heart, Charity knew that her mother not only spoke truly to her, but she spoke out of the compassion and love only a parent can have for their child. Charity felt duly chastened, and cried, "I am sorry, Mamá. Fear jumps in my way. Can you possibly know what it is like to feel that your father abandoned you, all your whole life? And to hope that he died when you were an infant because it would be less painful in your heart if he had no choice in whether or not to return for you? I know that you've suffered, too. I have watched you cry yourself to sleep at night, not knowing that I was still awake."

Juaniata came around the counter and took Charity into her arms, cradling her against her chest as Charity wept. "We will find him," promised Juaniata. "And when we do, he will have a reason for us that we can understand. You will see. Hans and I prayed together this morning, and I have a good feeling in my heart, now. You must forgive Hans for trying to help us find Daniel, for he is only doing what the Lord has asked him to do."

"I want to believe that, Mamá. Truly I do," Charity sobbed. "But, Hans has a way of trying to buy himself into or out of whatever situation that comes along. It is difficult for me to accept that Hans could initiate this search out of his love for me. It seems more likely that he has gone after Daniel's trail only because he can."

"You must not speak of Hans this way, Cari," Juaniata said, stroking Charity's hair and holding her gently. "Hans asked me to tell you that he has only the noblest intention and the purest of love in his heart. He wanted me to remind you to live your life as though the Savior stood beside you, and for this counsel, I consider Hans a wise and faithful steward."

"Why didn't you tell him to stop looking?" Charity asked, drying her eyes on a tissue. "Why must he continue hurting me?"

"Do you remember all the prayer that you put into whether or not you should work at Cocos Island?" Juaniata asked.

Nodding, Charity recalled the days of fasting, scripture study and prayer that preceded her decision. "Yes. I would have to miss three Sundays of every four at church, and give up my primary nursery class. It was a terrible decision, yet the Lord told me in my heart that I could best help Perry and our family by taking the job."

"For Hans, it is the same. He, too, has had to make a terrible decision, whether to hurt your feelings by doing what the Lord asked, or deny the Lord's request in order to keep you happy. If you were in his shoes, what would you have done?"

Charity shook her head. "You're saying that Hans is following the Savior's plan in trying to find my father?"

Juaniata smiled and held her daughter apart from her so that they could look into one another's eyes. "Yes, Charity. And if you will fast and pray about this, have faith in Christ and not waver, He will tell you in your heart and in your mind, so that you, too, will understand why Hans is searching so diligently to find your father."

Sniffling, Charity smiled through her tears. "I shall try, Mamá. I shall try."

"Good. Now, tell me. Will you mail your wedding invitations?"

Charity looked at the box sitting on the counter. "I will pray about them," she suggested, "with all my heart and soul. It will be of no consequence if they are mailed one day late. The postal service in America is much faster than Costa Rica."

Calculating, Juaniata said, "Yes. If you mail them on Tuesday, your guests will receive them by Friday at the latest. That gives them eight days' notice. It will be enough."

"Except our Costa Rican friends," said Charity, "and Uncle Rafael's family."

Juaniata smiled conspiratorially. "I announced the engagement and your wedding date to them, weeks ago. They will not be disappointed if they do not receive their invitations more than a day or two ahead. Besides, very few could afford to attend the wedding anyway."

Charity gave her mother another hug, then stood up. "I will begin fasting now. Please, Mamá, do not let Perry disturb me when he comes in tonight."

Neither of us will bother you until you tell us that you have ended your fast," agreed Juaniata. "Now, I must go to the store. Perry is at the medical center. You will have the day to yourself. If you want to go to the temple grounds, or anywhere else, Hans' keys are beside the box of invitations."

They kissed each other's cheeks and said goodbye.

Charity spent the remainder of the day in prayer and fasting, reading from Moroni 7, and several other passages from the scriptures to enlighten her mind and uplift her. Several times, she knelt and talked to her Father in Heaven, asking for guidance.

Later that night, after her mother and brother were sleeping, Charity went out to the kitchen counter and compared all the hand-addressed invitations with the master list she and Hans had made together, and found that he had not forgotten a single person. There were over seven hundred stamped envelopes, and they were all nested in a sturdy cardboard box. Touched by Hans' diligence in preparing the invitations, Charity remembered the day they had made the list. She couldn't believe how many people he knew from all around the country. She was surprised to see two invitations she hadn't expected:

To Mrs. Anna Blake
412 Lincoln Court
Chicago Heights, Chicago

To Mr. and Mrs. Robert Cragonne and Family
412 Lincoln Court
Chicago Heights, Chicago

She recognized the names of Daniel's mother, Anna, and his sister, Angela's husband, Robert, and their family. Hans intended to invite Charity's aunt and grandmother, whom she'd never even met.

The fact that Angela and Anna had been searching for Daniel for twenty-four years and had never found him spoke volumes in terms of what dead ends Hans had faced in his search for Charity's father.

Now that her grandmother had a name, Charity longed to put a face to that name. She'd never known her grandparents on the Perez side of her family, for they died in the Nicaraguan uprising.

Juaniata had left a stack of papers on the counter that had a detailed list sitting on top, revealing everything Hans had uncovered about Daniel Blake and his family up to that moment. She looked down the list, noting that Hans had written names, birth dates, birth places, current addresses and telephone numbers of every person Colton Wright had contacted so far. The list was impressive and encompassed twelve pages. Charity noted there were at least six hundred men named Juan Perez, with phone numbers and addresses, and by whose names an age was written in, and the notation, "too old" or "too young" beside most of them.

It appeared from the list that Colton Wright and Hans were down to less than a dozen names. In Hans' hand under a long list of California entries, she found the notation, "I'll search these three." The three names were circled.

Charity suspected that she now knew where Hans had gone, and that solved one of the puzzles facing her. The fact that Hans hadn't bothered to say goodbye, but had gone through her mother, still irritated Charity, but then she hadn't left him any room to wriggle back into her life when they last saw each other, so she could only blame herself.

Aching for Hans, for his nearness, his gentle touch, Charity was painfully aware of how terrible her temper could be, and how much she had let the image of her father, the fear of facing her father, consume her. She persuaded herself that she had to put her fears aside, and work toward the common good of her family.

The Lord had answered Charity's prayers, but His responses stung, and she felt duly chastened. Trying to stand in the way of Hans completing his errand from the Lord was tantamount to her single-handedly trying to prevent a school of hammerheads and white-tip sharks from living around Cocos Island. Impossible. She had been fighting against a God-given challenge, and against a man who thrived on challenges.

The hardest thing for anyone to admit is that they're wrong. Charity was no exception. She was dead wrong in thinking she could throw a tantrum and Hans would give up on something the Lord told him to do.

Charity had expected Hans to be less than the man he was, and her internal punishment for so doing was severe. Now, Charity wondered how Hans could ever forgive her, but as she thumbed through the invitations on the counter top she realized that Hans already had. He had shown her that he had the pure love of Christ in his heart, while she had shown him how bitter her heart had become over the issue of her father.

Seeking the solitude of her bedroom, Charity knelt beside the bed and began to pray again, this time asking forgiveness, and promising a more Christ-like attitude in her life. By dawn, her knees were aching, but her heart was filled with the sweet spirit of the Lord.

She took a quick shower, dressed in her favorite sun-dress and sandals, left a note for her mother, then grabbed the box of invitations from the kitchen counter, as well as the car keys and stack of papers, and headed for the car.

The moment the post office opened, Charity walked inside and placed the box on the counter top, first person of the day to be served by a postal worker.

"Someone's getting married?" he asked as he offloaded her huge box of invitations.

"Yes," she said happily. "I am."

For the rest of the day, Charity went shopping for blankets and pillows, bed linens, towels, kitchen towels, and dishes. She stopped by the photo studio and picked up the photos that they'd had made earlier, and gasped as one of the photos of Hans took her breath away. The frames they'd chosen were exquisitely beautiful, and she wanted to hang the large photo of them together in the living room, along with some smaller prints they'd ordered. But, the photo of Hans, she would keep by her side of the bed.

Seeing the photo of Hans made it crystal clear to Charity that she needed to talk to Hans, wherever he was, and put an end to their disagreement. She put all her purchases in the back of the car and pulled the cell phone out of her purse. The battery was dead. Refusing to return to her mother's condo to make this phone call, Charity drove out to Shelter View Condominiums, where she and Hans would live after they married.

After unloading all the packages from the SUV, which took several trips, Charity unpackaged everything, washed the linens and towels in their new washing machine, and took all the packaging materials back down to the garbage bins near the garage door.

Then, while she waited for the first load to dry, she went to the kitchen counter and picked up the phone. Having memorized Hans' cell phone number, she dialed it immediately and waited for Hans to answer.

Just hearing his deep voice say, "Hans Clark here," Charity smiled. She inhaled sweetly, savoring the moment.

"Charity?" she heard Hans ask. "Is that you?"

"Yes," she said. "Hans, I'm sorry I snapped at you. I—"

"I'm sorry, too, Sweetheart. I should have discussed it with you sooner, so that you wouldn't have found out the way you did."

In those first two words, *I'm sorry*, Charity learned a lesson that would stay with her forever. Governments may fall, kingdoms may be overthrown, terrorists may strike anywhere at anytime, but two people who truly love can overcome any obstacle that comes between them just by exercising those two little words.

"I'm sorry," she blubbered for the second time. Suddenly, tears of joy filled Charity's heart and she started crying in earnest.

Hans, apparently overwhelmed, gasped, "Sweetheart, what is it? What have I done wrong now?"

"Nothing," she sobbed. "I'm just so very happy!" Then, she burst out laughing and crying at the same time.

After a little while, Hans said, "Are you all right now?"

"Yes. But, I'm so sorry you're rich, Hans, because when I get discouraged, I have a tendency to go shopping. I hope you won't be angry, but I bought bed linens and towels and dishes for the kitchen."

"The wedding guests usually provide most of that, Charity," he reminded.

Charity giggled, "I know, but these will match perfectly to our decor. Besides, you said most people get toasters and blenders and glasses. I didn't get any of those things."

Hans laughed, "You can buy whatever you want for the condo. If we get something for a gift that we can't use, we'll leave it in storage until we're invited to someone else's wedding."

"Or, we could exchange it," she said. "Do you think that's in poor taste?"

"Absolutely not," he encouraged. "Most people expect exchanges. I mean, no one can use fifteen toasters, right?"

Smiling, Charity said, "I picked up the photos we had taken. Oh, you're going to love them! When will you be home?"

"Probably tomorrow. I've been to see Juan Perez in Los Angeles, it took me all day yesterday and half of today to track him down."

"But, he's not Daniel?" she guessed.

"No, he's not. Now, I'm headed over to Long Beach to check up on another one."

"I think I'll stay at our condo tonight," she said. "Will you mind?"

"Why would I mind?" he asked. "It's your condo, too."

"Wait until you see how I'm decorating it," Charity told him. "You'll be so surprised."

"Thank you for calling me," Hans said. "I've been half blind with worry, Sweetheart."

"I'm all right, really," she insisted. "But, I do have a terrible temper, I'm afraid you'll have to learn when to tread softly."

"You're not upset anymore about my searching for your father?" he questioned.

"Yes, it still upsets me very much." Charity saw no reason to lie to him. "But, the Lord has softened my heart, and I have to trust that He knows what's best for me."

"You have no idea how much I needed to hear you say that," Hans confessed. "Colton Wright telephoned today, and his secretary has added another two dozen names to the list of possibilities. It looks like we won't find Daniel anytime soon."

"Even if you never find him," Charity comforted, "it's okay, Hans. I can't live the rest of my life worrying that you will or that you won't. Whatever the Lord wants, I'm going to be okay with it."

"That means more to me than I can tell you. But, Charity, I have this feeling that we're getting close to finding him. I can't begin to tell you why, it's just one of those haunting, undeniable feelings."

"I hope you do, Hans. For your peace of mind, as well as mine. I've decided that if we find Daniel and the worst case scenario exists in our discovery—"

"Such as?" Hans asked, interrupting her.

Charity paused, then explained, "If he's remarried and has other children, I'm going to tell him and his family exactly how it feels to have your father abandon you. When I'm finished with him, he's going to wish he'd been packing a stun gun."

"I hope it won't come to that, Sweetheart. I hope we'll find reasons behind his actions that go beyond our understanding."

"Me, too," she admitted. "But, it will take some hefty explaining before Daniel Blake will ever convince me that he did not abandon his family."

Chapter Twenty

Hans opened the condo door with his key. He had arrived at the San Diego airport on the midnight express, and rather than wake anyone up, he had walked as far as the Bay Club Marina, where he showered and cleaned up aboard *Charity's Bridge*, then taken a taxi to the condo. Now it was dawn, and he couldn't wait any longer to see his fiancée. Hans paid the taxi driver and came up the elevators to let himself into the living room.

A soft, muted light came filtering through the dining room curtains, and Hans tiptoed over to them and opened them, letting the first rays of the eastern sun dance through the palms on the deck. Looking around the room, Hans saw that Charity had hung their wedding photo in the center of a group of photographs they'd had taken a few weeks ago, along the wall behind the sofa.

The furniture had been polished to a beautiful sheen, and he noticed plump pillows and potted plants with lamps that added to the mystery and drama of the room. In the kitchen, he found a stack of tea towels and dish cloths folded neatly on the counter top, as though Charity could not decide which drawer to put them in, and he noticed a key hanger had been mounted onto the far right kitchen cupboard side, along with a decorative mail holder. Hans was pleased to see the keys he'd left for Charity hanging on the key holder.

A bouquet of silk flowers that looked remarkably like fresh cut blossoms sat poised dramatically upon the new dining room table in an ivory vase. Stepping past the table, Hans saw two wall lamps hanging against the hall wall, opposite the archway and on either side of the main bathroom door.

He went first to the right, and looked at the beautiful furnishings of the third bedroom, where Charity had made the bed with a quilted comforter in varying shades of blue and yellow. Bright Moshi pillows that contrasted the quilt were stacked at the head.

In the den, he found the desk they'd ordered, as well as the computer, set up along the back wall, with just enough room behind it for the comfortable office chair with plush cushions. Along a side wall a matching bookcase stood waiting for a load of books. Against the other wall was another bookshelf, with matching, built-in file cabinets taking up the lower half of the shelves.

Turning back toward the master bedroom, Hans tapped lightly on the bedroom door, hoping with all his heart that Charity was still asleep.

He heard her murmur something, and he knocked a little louder.

"Hans?"came a worried voice. "Is that you?"

"It's me," he said. "Are you decent?"

"Yes."

Hans didn't wait for her to say *come in*, he opened the door and saw his lovely bride-to-be laying in the middle of the bed, a rich bedcover pulled up to her neck. He slipped off his shoes, and stretched out beside Charity, on top of the comforter, and slipped his arm under her shoulders, pulling her to him. "I couldn't wait to see you," he apologized. "I hope you'll forgive me for barging in like this, and waking you."

"I've only been asleep a couple of hours," she confessed. "It took me all night to get everything exactly how I wanted it, and I still couldn't decide on some things in the kitchen."

"Like where to put the towels and dish cloths?"

"Exactly," she nodded, snuggling close to him. "I missed you so!"

"Do you think we could spend the day together?" he asked. "The past four days have been terrible without you."

"For me, too."

Unable to restrain himself any longer, Hans' lips sought hers, and she willingly let him linger there for quite a while. Just when Hans felt that he should get off the bed and leave the room, putting some distance between their passion before it got out of control, he heard the doorbell ring.

Withdrawing, relieved and feeling emotionally ragged, Hans slipped from the bed and stood up. "Who do you suppose would be calling this early?"

He left the bedroom, giving Charity the privacy she would need to get out of bed and put on her robe. Stepping quickly to the condo door, he looked through the peephole and got a jolt! Shocked completely, he unlocked the door and opened it.

The woman who greeted him was dressed in a cream and taffeta dress that hit her slender legs at mid-calf. She wore a long pair of silk gloves and camel-colored heels, and carried a matching leather handbag. Her blonde hair was blended with streaks of natural silver, and done up in a coif at the crown of her head. Her emerald eyes still had a lot of fire left in them for her age.

"Anna," he gasped. "How—"

"Your private investigator, Mr. Wright, gave me this address," Anna Blake answered. "I have come to speak with my granddaughter."

"Yes, of course. Come in."

"This will be your apartment when you marry?" she asked.

"Yes, it will. Charity's been decorating it."

"Does she know about me?" Anna asked.

Hans pursed his lips together. "She knows that you're her grandmother."

"I presume you have some explanation as to why you are here in her apartment this early in the morning. From the invitation, I assumed you were planning on a temple wedding, which isn't for another," she glanced at her watch, which evidently had a calendar in it, "ten days."

"She's safe with me," Hans explained. "I only just arrived. We were going to spend the day together."

"Will you get her for me, Mr. Clark, or must I wait all day?" said Anna, giving Hans a sly smile.

"Yes, of course. Why don't you sit down?" Hans suggested, then he turned and went back to the bedroom, where he knocked on the door.

❦ ❦ ❦

"I'm decent," Charity told Hans as she opened the bedroom door. "Who's here?"

"Whoa! You're a quick-change artist, Sweetheart. I hadn't realized."

She had already removed her nightgown, slipped into a bright yellow sun-dress, and brushed out her hair. Noticing Hans staring at her bare, copper-skinned legs and feet, she said a second time, "Who is here?"

His smile and the desire in his eyes made her suddenly relieved that they had been interrupted.

"It's your grandmother," Hans said.

"How did she find me?"

"She said she got the address from Colton Wright."

"What does she want?"

"She wants to see you."

"Not without you, she won't," insisted Charity, taking his hand.

Hans gave her a kiss on the forehead. "All right, steel yourself, Sweetheart, because she's a real class cut."

"Whatever that means," teased Charity, leading him out into the living room.

As they approached, Anna stood momentarily and said, "So, you are my granddaughter?"

"I am Daniel Blake's daughter," said Charity, feeling that her sundress in comparison to Mrs. Blake's finely-tailored suit set the two women completely at opposite ends of the social spectrum.

"I am well aware of that, child," said Anna, and her voice seemed to soften a little.

"Sit down," suggested Charity, sitting opposite her grandmother on the love seat, Hans at her side. She squeezed his hand, and hoped he knew that she did not want him to let go of her.

"What can I do for you?" said Charity after Anna had sat down and stared at her for several long moments.

"I wanted to see you for myself," said Anna. "Daniel suggested that I owe you and your mother and brother an apology."

"You know where my father is?" Charity asked, forcing her tears to remain hidden for now.

"At Diamond Valley," said Anna. "I spoke with him last night."

"You've made up?"

"As much as two stubborn fools can, I suppose," she said.

"Does he want to see me?" Charity didn't dare to hope that such a possibility even existed, but she had to ask.

Suddenly, Anna's green eyes filled with moisture, and she dabbed at them with a handkerchief she held in a gloved hand. "Yes, of course."

"Is he coming to San Diego?"

"You must go to him, I'm afraid," said Anna. "He is as strong-willed as his mother. It is not a character trait for which I am proud, child."

"How will I find him?" Charity asked.

"Mr. Clark has his address. Isn't that correct?" Anna turned to look at Hans.

"Yes, I have it. But, frankly, I'm astounded to learn he's at Diamond Valley." Hans confessed. "I had almost decided not to check him out. If that's your father, Charity, he's now an almond farmer."

"You must go quickly," said Anna, dismissing Hans' words with a wave of her hand. "Much time has been wasted, but I will accept full responsibility for your long separation."

"Why?" asked Charity. "What did you do?"

"It was I who persuaded Daniel to wait until his father could go with him to bring you and your mother back from Nicaragua. It was a busy season in your grandfather's business, Daniel had just been released from the military, and I was not certain that he even knew what was best for him. In my rash attempt to dissuade him, I crippled whatever relationship I had garnered with my son. I was proven wrong. Daniel should have gone to Nicaragua immediately upon his release from military duty, and not waited for his father's health to improve, as I insisted it would. I have carried the burden of my guilt for almost your entire life, child. I deprived you of your father, and there is nothing that I can say or do now to make amends. I only ask that you search your soul, and try to find some particle of forgiveness within you, for I am truly sorry."

"Daniel wanted to come for us, but you persuaded him not to?" Charity asked, bewildered by this information.

Anna nodded, and a tear slipped silently down her cheek.

"Why?" Charity insisted.

"I was a fool," admitted Anna. "I cannot expect you to understand . . . or even to forgive me."

"But, why didn't he come find us after my grandfather died?" Charity persisted.

"You must ask Daniel these questions. I do not know everything that he did after his father died." Anna stood. "I will see my way out. I must still visit your mother and your brother. Thank you, Charity, for listening to me."

"Thank you for coming," Charity said, feeling a sudden, desperate urge to fling her body across the door and prevent her grandmother from leaving. It was irrational and Charity knew it, but when Anna walked out that door, she knew she might never see her again.

Following Anna to the door, Charity said, "Abuela? Um . . I mean Grandmother?"

Anna turned back to face her. "You may use Spanish, if you like, child. I am honored to hear you call me Grandmother in any language."

Charity could hold herself back no longer. She threw her arms around her grandmother and cried against her shoulder. Anna wept also, and they stood there several minutes before either one could speak. Finally, Charity knew she had pressed beyond the limits of common decency and she released Anna. "Will you come to my wedding, Abuela?"

"Yes, I will," said Anna. "I would not miss it for anything in the world."

Anna put her hand upon the doorknob and opened it. They did not say goodbye, it was the one word that Charity could not bring herself to say.

When the door closed, leaving Charity and Hans alone, she went quietly into his strong arms and wept with him. "I cannot believe it," she said. "That was my grandmother."

"More importantly," said Hans, "she's spoken with your father, and he wants to see you."

"We must tell Mamá," Charity said, turning to head for the phone.

Hans took her hand, preventing her from doing so.

"I think we should stay calm, have breakfast, wait a little while. We must give your grandmother time to make amends with Mamá and Perry for herself."

"But, how will she know?"

"Believe me, Sweetheart, if she can find Shelter View, she can find Greenbriar. And Colton Wright would have given her both addresses."

Charity hardly dared to believe him, but she knew the surprise Mamá would feel when Anna appeared at her door would be far greater than whatever Charity could say to her. She nodded at Hans' wisdom and insight, and stepped back into his arms, grateful that he had come over to wake her that morning.

❦ ❦ ❦

Driving to Diamond Valley seemed to take forever, but it would have taken much longer if they'd tried to take Interstate Fifteen northbound any earlier than ten in the morning. From the freeway, they took state road number seventy-nine, toward Winchester.

While Hans drove, Charity sat beside him, and chatted amicably with her mother, Juaniata, and brother, Perry, in the back seat. They talked about nothing, really, for words alone . . . whether about the apartment, or the shop, or the weather . . . were inconsequential to all of them. Tension built up steadily as the SUV ambled along.

Diamond Valley Lake sat between Winchester and state road R3, just south of Hemet, and Juan Perez's almond farm sat on the southern edge of the lake. The winding dirt road that led to it kicked up a cloud of dust, as the summer had been extremely dry this year in Southern California. September rain had not arrived, either, and it seemed they were destined for a drought fall, as well.

The SUV passed through the center of an almond grove, where a thousand drupaceous, green-leafed trees stood in orderly formation, like guards at attention, surrounding a central house that resembled an Australian ranch, with a central-peaked roof that surrounded a bannister-free porch all around the square structure.

A well stood off to the west side of the house, and a garden of beautiful roses and plumeria trees, often called frangipani, surrounded a quiet patio to the east of it.

Since Hans had telephoned earlier that morning to make an appointment with Juan Perez, without giving him specifics, they now found Juan Perez standing on the front porch, waiting for them.

Charity prayed with all her heart and soul that this meeting would go well. Her mother's and brother's silence in the back seat told her that they, too, were praying.

Hans set the brake and turned in his seat to face all three of them. "Let me go up, first," he said. "We don't want to shock him into a heart attack. And don't be too disappointed if he doesn't recognize you, Charity. He hasn't seen you since you were an infant."

As though she needed this reminder. "I'm going with you," she said, her stubborn will refusing to wait any longer.

He shook his head and sighed. "All right. Anyone else want to assert their authority and go with us?"

Both Perry and Juaniata shook their heads.

"I will wait," said Juaniata. "I must see his reaction from a distance. I will know if he is pleased or not."

"But, it is him?" Hans asked her.

Charity looked toward the man on the porch. He wasn't more than a hundred feet from them. He had blonde hair that he wore almost shoulder length, and a straw cowboy hat on top of his head. She couldn't see the color of his eyes, but she was surprised to see that the shape of his chin was almost identical to her own. Brushing at his jean-clad leg, he put a booted foot on the first step down and headed toward them.

"Yes," wept Juaniata softly. "It is my Daniel. I would know him anywhere."

"Mamá?" Charity asked.

"Go! Quickly, Charity. Do not let him see me until I am sure that he will want to see me."

Charity opened her door and obeyed her mother immediately. Hans came around from the driver's side and took her hand. She looked up at him and his smile gave her strength.

"Shall we?" he asked.

Nodding, Charity took a step forward. Daniel had stopped at the bottom step, and seemed to be waiting for them to approach.

It was difficult to tell who was doing the leading, Charity or Hans. In her heart, she felt only conflict. Here was the man who had stolen her dreams from her, leaving her with a bitterness that was difficult to swallow. Yet, her grandmother had said that he wanted to see her. Why was he holding his ground? Maybe he wasn't as thrilled as Charity had hoped.

Within seconds they were standing face to face, and Daniel tipped his hat back slightly. When he did, Charity looked deep into his emerald eyes, startled to see how much they resembled her own . . . and Anna's.

"Are you the man who called me?" Daniel asked.

His voice was huskier than Charity had imagined, his smile more genuine, yet his eyes knew sadness and heartache. Of that, she was positive.

"Yes, Mr. Perez. I'm Hans Clark, and this is my fiancée, Charity Perez Blake."

Daniel blinked. He stared. He studied her face and her eyes. Suddenly, he scooped her into his arms and wept like a young child. "Charity! My sweet Charity! How can this be?" Pulling back, he kept his hands upon her shoulders, holding her at arm's length, as though he was afraid that if he let go of her, she would disappear.

"Papá?" she asked. "It is really you?" She knew his answer before he said the words.

"How can this be?" he asked, taking her hand and leading her over to the east side of his house, to an aging garden with roses and plumeria. "Look, Charity. For twenty-six years, I have mourned your loss."

Upon the ground, embedded into the hand-set cobblestones, was a brass engraving that read:

Juaniata Perez	*Charity Perez*
Beloved wife	*Precious Daughter*
1963–1980	*1980–1980*

The wear upon the cobblestone path between the house and the memorial told Charity that Daniel had walked it often, perhaps daily, and sat upon the bench looking upon the monument to his wife and his daughter. Suddenly, all the pieces fell together. Tears welled up in Charity's eyes. "Papá, you thought we were dead?"

"I went to Nicaragua shortly before my father died," Daniel explained. "The village where I once lived with you and your mother had been bombed three weeks earlier. The few who survived told me everyone else was killed. I searched for you for weeks, but the survivors had burned all the dead bodies in a big trench. I could not even find your bones," he wept, his arm about her shoulder.

"Papá," pleaded Charity, stopping him from continuing. "Mamá is in the car." It was all that Charity could say. Her father had to know that his beloved Juaniata was still alive. There would be time, later on, for explanations.

Before she could tell him about Perry, her father was dashing toward the car, forgetting about Charity and Hans. She watched in amazement as Mamá got out of the SUV the moment she saw Daniel headed toward her. They raced to each other. Daniel grabbed Juaniata around the waist and held her tightly, twirling her round and round until they both fell over, laughing and crying and holding each other, kissing and hugging, and saying, "Daniel!" "Juaniata, my love! I thought you were dead!"

Hans led Charity over to them, but she wished that her parents' reunion could have had a little more privacy. When Perry stepped from the car, his tall frame every bit as tall as Daniel's, Juaniata stopped Daniel and pointed to Perry. "Daniel, this is your son, Daniel Perez Blake. We call him Perry."

"I have a son?" gasped Daniel, jumping to his feet and wrapping Perry in a bear hug.

Hans assisted Juaniata up from the grass.

"Yes, Papá," said Perry. "I was born seven months after you left. Charity is only eleven months older than me."

"I have a son!" Daniel roared with pride. "Look at him! This is my son!"

"You will have another son in ten days," said Juaniata as she stood and held Hans' hand. "Hans Clark will marry your daughter in the San Diego Temple."

"You are in love with my daughter?" Daniel asked with a hint of skepticism in his voice.

"Here we go again," said Hans, winking at Charity as he nodded in agreement.

"Papá," Charity confided, "Hans is a good man. It is Hans who helped us find you."

"Is he a good man, Charity?" asked Daniel. "Kind and thoughtful?"

"Yes, Papá. He is."

"You have approved of their marriage, my love?" Daniel asked Juaniata.

"I have," she agreed. "You will learn to love him like we do."

Charity saw the smile these words brought to Hans' face.

"What great miracle the Lord has brought to me," Daniel said. "Let us pray."

He knelt upon the ground, and his family knelt around him. Daniel offered the sweetest prayer Charity had every heard. He wept with them, as he thanked God for each one of his family members, and lastly for Hans' inspiration in finding him.

When he had finished, they stood and hugged all around. "Come on into the house," said Daniel, one arm around Juaniata, the other hand holding onto Perry's hand. "Juaniata, let's prepare a feast to celebrate this special day."

It didn't take long. While they sat in the living room holding hands, Charity thrilled in listening to Juaniata and Daniel teasing one another in the kitchen.

Soon, they were seated on the porch, eating tacos, burritos and refried beans with rice. The afternoon sun soon dipped its way out of the valley called Diamond Lake, and the mosquitoes drove them back indoors.

"Why did you not remarry, Papá?" asked Perry as they visited in the living room. "If you thought Mamá and Charity were dead?"

"I must confess," said Daniel. "I had you both sealed to me in the temple."

Charity laughed. "I suppose we'll have to correct that sealing."

"Yes, of course," said Daniel. "May we do that on your wedding day?"

"I would be honored to be sealed to you on my wedding day," said Charity.

"This is still so very odd," Daniel confessed. "I had a dream last night that my mother came to visit me. She said she had found my family, and promised she would see that we were reunited today."

"A dream?" said Hans. "I thought she told us that she actually visited him?"

Since Hans' question was directed at Charity, she answered, "Yes. She said that she visited you last night, and we just assumed that she had come straight from Diamond Valley to see us."

"You saw her this morning?" Daniel asked.

"Yes," Juaniata affirmed. "Anna came to see Perry and me after she left Hans and Charity."

"Strange," said Daniel. "Very strange." He gave them an anxious expression. "After my dream, I thought perhaps it was God's way of telling me that I should forgive my mother in person, instead of in my dreams. I telephoned my sister this morning, but her housekeeper said they weren't at home."

"Don't worry, Papá," insisted Charity. "Grandmother said she would come to my wedding. You will see her in ten days time at the temple."

"I don't think so," said Daniel. "My sister's housekeeper told me my mother died four days ago. Yesterday was her funeral."

Juaniata fainted immediately, but Daniel caught her before she hit the floor, and carried her into one of the bedrooms to rest. Perry slipped outside, leaving Hans and Charity alone.

Chapter Twenty-One

"I don't understand," Charity said for the fifteenth time. "How can my grandmother be in our condo, and in her coffin at the same time?"

Hans cradled his fiancée against his side as they sat together on Daniel's big leather sofa at the almond farm in Diamond Valley. She had her back to him, her legs up on the sofa, resting her back against his chest.

"I told you," he soothed. "Our family that goes before us across the veil, they watch over us closely. They are our cheering section and they are heavily invested in what happens to us. Sometimes, it's necessary for one of them to show up and help us out. I believe that's what Anna was doing. She knew that I had dismissed Diamond Valley before I made any effort to come here. I had already considered that no man with a degree in engineering would ever want to become an almond farmer. Before Anna arrived, I had decided to give the almond farmer back to Colton Wright and tell him to look this Juan Perez up last, if at all. I could not imagine that a man like Daniel would want anything to do with raising almonds. I felt this visit would be a waste of my time."

Hans spent the better part of the next hour teaching Charity the principle of miracles and the ministering of angels. He told Charity about his own special experiences of witnessing a miracle while sailing aboard *Bridger's Child* off the Washington Coast two summers ago, about both Kayla's and Ed's miracles at the *Bar M Ranch* and in the Rocky Mountains, and finished by quoting from Moroni 7:29—30, "... *have miracles ceased? Behold, I say unto you, Nay; neither have angels ceased to minister unto the children of men. For behold, they are subject unto Him, to minister according to the word of His command, showing themselves unto them of strong faith and a firm mind in every form of godliness.*"

"So you're saying that you think I have strong faith, and all that other stuff?" she asked.

"You must," he admitted. "Besides, I think this was an exceptional circumstance. I'm not sure Anna wanted to return home to God until she had resolved the problems she had with your father, and apologized to you and Perry and Mamá."

"Why didn't we know?" Charity asked. "Why couldn't we sense that Anna had come from beyond the veil?"

"It wasn't expedient for us to know at that time," explained Hans. "Remember, Sweetheart, the Lord is still in control. He gives us just as much as we need to live by faith. He doesn't pour His complete knowledge into us all at once. We receive some form of inspiration every day of our lives. Sometimes, the Lord chooses to present a portion of His Gospel in a miraculous fashion. We're very fortunate to have been given this rare gift, for we can both stand as witnesses to the eternal truth that our ancestors do watch over us from beyond the grave."

Perry had gone out to the memorial to Juaniata and Charity that Daniel had built in his garden east of the house, to meditate. When Juaniata had fainted, Daniel had carried her to a bedroom, to let her rest. Now, he joined them from the hall.

"Is Mamá all right?" asked Charity, sitting up straight, leaving the cradle of Han' arms.

Hans was keenly disappointed that she had moved, for he enjoyed their nearness after the past few days of trial and hardship.

"She is sleeping," said Daniel. "We have talked and are agreed. Although we are still married, we will not consider ourselves married until we are sealed in the temple. This way, we will have our own honeymoon to celebrate."

"Wonderful!" said Charity. "Papá, everything has happened so differently from what I expected. Please, tell me what drove you and my grandmother apart."

Daniel looked at the floor. Hans could tell by his expression that his past was filled with regret and stubborn pride.

"When I arrived back in the United States, after leaving you and your mother in Nicaragua, I hardly made enough money to survive on, and I asked my parents to loan me the money to bring you and Juaniata to America with me."

He ran a hand through his shoulder-length hair. "Your grandmother was furious when she learned I had married beneath my station. In my opinion, marrying your mother had been above my station, but I wasn't going to fight over differences of opinion. My father was ill, he had been sick a long time with heart problems. So I started saving every penny I could, and writing to your mother at her Nicaraguan address. I had no idea that she had gone to Costa Rica. When I left, her parents and two sisters were still alive. Rafael had been in San José for three years by then, and we'd only met at the wedding."

His hands trembled slightly, but Charity seemed not to have noticed. Her eyes were transfixed upon her father's bright green eyes.

Continuing, Daniel said, "Mother asked me to wait until Father felt a little better. 'Perhaps in the spring,' she said. 'He'll go with you then, and help you bring your wife and daughter home.' When my father, who had some surgery while I was in the military, needed my help with his business, it was my mother who arranged it. In our family, if you needed anything from Father, you went to Mother, and she acted as the liaison between us. My mother promised me that by spring Father's health would be improved, and that he had agreed to go with me to Nicaragua then. I had not been able to save enough money to bring both of you back yet, and I was devastated. My mother convinced me that soon, Father and I would bring my family back to Chicago. But, I could see that his heart was failing. He could hardly walk up a flight of stairs without fainting, and I didn't talk to him about Juaniata because I didn't want to be the one who pushed him into his grave. I begged my mother to loan me the rest of the money I needed to go get you that August. She refused, and said that I was cold-hearted if I could not see that my father needed me here. Again, she promised that by spring, when Father was better, I could come for you then."

Shaking his head, Daniel shuddered. "It was a terrible time. I went to see my father one morning in early September, and told him how desperately I needed to borrow some money and go to Nicaragua to get you and my wife. Mother had not even asked him for money. She had lied to me, hoping that I would forget all about you and my Juaniata. Father was furious with her. He loaned me the money, and I left immediately, but I was three weeks too late. The village had been bombed, and the few survivors who were left told me that you and your mother had died. I searched like a man possessed of an evil spirit. I could not sleep or eat. I lost thirty pounds that month. Finally, when I realized that you were both gone, I went back to Chicago. My father had taken a turn for the worse, and he was in the hospital when I arrived. I went immediately to see him. I didn't tell him of my failure in Nicaragua. He was too ill, and he died the next day. I learned at the reading of his will that Father named me as his executor. Everything my father had was to be split three ways. So, I sold everything, except my mother's house. The house I did not include in the dispersal of funds. I left the house to my mother, wanting no part of it. Mother was furious with me because I sold the business. We had a terrible quarrel. That day I told her about you and Juaniata dying. I yelled at her, told her that if she had loaned me the money when I first begged her, you would still be alive. I blamed her for your deaths. She screamed back at me, told me that I was responsible for my father's death because I had burdened him with my problems. We parted ways, and I never saw her again. I changed my name, so that she would never be able to find me.

"My sister, Angela, was my only regret. Although I did look in on my sister those first few years afterward, she did not know it. I attended the school games where she was a cheerleader. I went through the Los Angeles Temple the same day Angela married in the Chicago Temple. I've always taken the Chicago Times, so I could learn of her children and husband. But, I refused to let them know where I was, or what I was doing. About twelve years ago, I settled here. I needed something to do with my life. I needed to return to a semblance of normality. Besides, my mother would never expect me to become a farmer. It would be too far below my station."

"Oh, Papá," moaned Charity as she stepped across the space from them and sat beside him on the sofa. "Papá, there was no way to know that we were alive. And Uncle Rafael moved twice after we started living with him."

"No," said Daniel slowly. "I didn't even consider looking for you at Rafael's place. I doubted that he knew about Juaniata's death, or yours. Who would have told him? His parents and all his family were dead. And I didn't want to be the one to tell him that they were all gone. All of them."

"Do you know who returned Mamá's letters?"

"It is my mother's handwriting on the envelopes," Daniel answered. "I can only imagine what she must have been thinking. Perhaps it was one more way of making sure that Juaniata would not want me, should I return to her."

"Oh, Papá," Charity rubbed his shoulder. "All these years, I thought that you did not want us anymore." Tears slipped down her cheeks.

"There was never anything further from the truth, Charity," he said. He kissed her forehead and stood up. "Now, I have a son out in the garden who needs a father's guidance. Will you forgive me if I go to him?"

"Of course not," said Charity. "Perry has needed his father for a long, long time."

"Besides," said Daniel. "I think your fiancé might get jealous if I monopolize you too much."

"No, that's fine," said Hans quickly. "I can wait. Charity and I will have an eternity to catch up."

"You are a good man," said Daniel, reaching for Hans' hand.

Hans stood up and shook it vigorously. "My wife tells me that she could not have found another man in all the world who would be better for our sweet Charity. I must thank you for making the effort to find me."

"You're welcome," said Hans, "but in actuality, I think your mother brought us together."

Daniel gave a wan smile. "Perhaps you are right," he said. "Excuse me. My son awaits."

Hans took Charity's hand and pulled her up into his arms. "Are you still upset that I went looking for your father?" he asked.

She gave him an endearing smile, and he felt his heart thump madly inside his chest. "Not at all," she answered demurely.

"Charity," Hans said, pulling her close to him, "do you remember the time we went diving at Manuelita island, and you shared my rebreather with me?"

"Yes." Her green eyes twinkled, and a quirky smile played around the corners of her mouth.

Hans was learning to expect this teasing expression and love it. "Did you not feel anything for me that day?"

She shook her head in denial, but when her smile broadened, deepening her dimples, he knew that she wasn't telling all the truth.

"Not even a little twinge in your heart?" he asked.

Charity licked her lips, shook her head and waited for a response.

"You're teasing," he accused.

"Now, Hans, would I ever do that?" she bantered.

He lowered his head and kissed her sensual lips with his, sweeping over them playfully, until he knew he was pushing her beyond what he should.

Suddenly, he heard a familiar woman's voice yell, "Mamá-mia! Can I not trust you two alone for ten minutes? Papá, come and see what your children are doing! You two must wait ten more days for all this kissing!"

Daniel came into the living room, Perry following him quickly.

"What is it?" Daniel asked.

Charity giggled, her forehead against Hans' chest, her color flushed. "Sorry," she whispered to Hans, as she stood on tiptoe to kiss him on the cheek in a more respectable manner. "You're going to have to put up with both my parents now!"

Daniel roared, "That's it! There will not be any of that in this house! Not even after you're married!"

At first Hans thought he was serious, but when Perry started laughing, then Juaniata, Hans knew that he'd been tricked.

Daniel bellowed with laughter and slapped his knee.

Mamá-mia! thought Hans, bemused. *Mamá-mia, indeed!*

Epilogue:

Juaniata recalled looking lovingly over the altar at her husband, son and daughter, as they were sealed to her for time and all eternity. This was the perfect answer to the prayers she had offered thousands of times upon her humble bed back in Costa Rica.

She always knew the Lord would answer her prayers, and although He certainly took His time, she couldn't have been more thrilled with the outcome.

If she thought the sealing room had been crowded, she was ill-prepared for the massive invasion at the reception held at Josh and Kayla's expansive home and gardens that overlooked Tecolote Canyon near San Diego. She had no idea so many people had such a special interest in her new son and his wife. It seemed that hundreds of people had tried to line Hans Clark up with someone they knew, at one time or another. Many of them called Hans *Dr. Clark*, which seemed to surprise Hans as much as it did Juaniata. Many were delighted that Hans had finally taken a wife. After all, a handsome, eligible bachelor like Hans had to have had his share of opportunities to marry.

That someone had finally struck his fancy seemed to astound everyone, and there were people from all around the globe shaking

Hans' and Charity's hands in the reception line, congratulating Charity on her fine catch.

Juaniata knew better. The Lord had brought Hans to Cocos Island for Charity, it wasn't the other way around. Although, she had to admit, Charity had certainly "caught" Hans once he met her. Hook, line and sinker.

So far, Juaniata had met all the Clark and Sparkleman Clans: Abbot, who was just back in Seattle from an honorable mission, and his fiancée, Bekah Stevens, who would be marrying in the Seattle Temple next month; Ed, on crutches, and Alyssa babying him; Tom Sparkleman, a man with quite a cowboy inflection to his manner; Will and Melanie Sparkleman, and their two children, from somewhere near the Green River in Utah. She'd also met the lovely Native American, Morning Sun, and her son, Matthew, and about eight ranch hands who were glad to move the black Angus herd to winter pasture a little early, in order to attend the reception of the newlyweds.

In addition, there were military men by the hordes, thick as locusts in the summer. The Admiral, full of pomp and ceremony, stood in line with them, next to Hans, and beside his lovely wife, Sarah. Even more amazing, the Admiral knew the first and last names of every man in uniform, and something about them with which he could inquire after their welfare.

Hans had arranged for most of her Costa Rican ward members to attend, including Juaniata's brother, Rafael Perez, and his family, providing plane fare and accommodations along Hotel Row in San Diego. He'd also flown in a popular South American band to play the tango-style music of Charity's native land, which added to the joviality of the reception.

Professors and scholars from all around the country came to see who finally stole Hans' heart. Juaniata was pleased to find they were not disappointed.

As Juaniata squeezed Daniel's hand, she felt a divine sensation of gratefulness that she was now sealed to him for time and all eternity. Her children were now sealed to them, as well. And, if Juaniata had her way, she would be having another child one day in the future. She and Daniel had discussed the possibility. Juaniata had not yet started through her change of life and was still quite healthy. Since Daniel had been denied the opportunity to raise his first two children, they were both praying that the Lord would bless them with at least one more child. Juaniata was ready for whatever possibilities the Lord wanted to give her, for it seemed to her that with the Lord, nothing was impossible.

Looking up the line at Charity, with her ebony hair pulled into an elegant twist, and her pearl and diamond veil crowning the top of her head, and her lovely white satin dress, Juaniata's chest swelled proudly. The dress Juaniata had designed was beyond beautiful, and Charity's graceful curves made it come alive. She could not have been prouder of her family, nor more pleased with the Lord's answer to her prayers.

At least thirty women had asked for the dress designer's name, and Juaniata could see that she would have a thriving business now that word had been released to the Admiral's and Joshua's friends that she was a dress designer with her own shop, opening up just in time for the holidays.

Daniel had put his almond farm on the market, and would join his wife in the city. He wanted nothing more than to help her make her way in the world. His own needs and wants he put aside, he said, for he now had what he had always wanted . . . his wife and his family, together at last.

As a brief lull in the line gave Charity a chance to breathe, Juaniata glanced over at her daughter and watched Hans wink at his new bride. The resultant smile on Charity's face lit up Juaniata's eyes. It was a look that only a woman in love can give, and her mother's heart filled to overflowing.

When Daniel squeezed her hand, Juaniata turned her eyes back to his, loving his hand in hers, their shoulders touching. Then, he winked at her, much the same as Hans had just done to Charity.

A smile of absolute joy spread across Juaniata's face, filling her heart with such happiness she thought she would burst with it. The scriptures are true, she decided, for *charity*, the true love of Christ, *never faileth*.

Other Books by Sherry Ann Miller

Oregon Flame:

Oregon Flame opens with a punch, has a white-nuckled, page-turning power, and delivers the miraculous impact for which Sherry Ann has earned her reputation.

Nicole Travis could easily fall for Wade Reilly's fiery charm . . . if only she could trust him. But, how can Nicole ever believe Wade's sincerity? He took advantage of her brother, and destroyed her relationship with her fiancé.

Granite Publishing—ISBN# 1-59936-005-5

Fourth novella in Granite's *Love Notes Collection*, hailed nationally as "Romance You Can Trust."

The Gift Series

You're going to love all five novels in Sherry Ann Miller's popular **Gift Series**, which take you on the individual sojourns of Kayla Dawn Allen and the five men who have influenced her life for good: the Sparkleman boys, Ed, Abbot and Tom, who grew up with Kayla on the *Bar M Ranch*; and the seafaring Clark twins, Joshua (who loves Kayla more than life itself) and Hans (who is always one step behind in finding his soul-mate). Each novel will plunge you into a miraculous, spine-tingling journey about life, love, heartache and triumphant joy. If you've a thirst for suck-you-in adventure, drama, action and romance, you'll want to read all five novels in Sherry Ann's award-winning **Gift Series:**

One Last Gift

Lovely Kayla is rescued from her own scientific

disposition, her misguided infatuation with Ed Sparkleman, and even more desperate and dangerous elements in ***One Last Gift.*** Kayla's remarkable journey from her sailboat in San Diego to her childhood home high in the Uinta Mountains, finds her facing one obstacle after another, until she finally discovers God's mighty miracles are all around her. At the miraculous and satisfying conclusion, you will be left with the question, "What about Ed?"

Granite Publishing—ISBN# 1-930980-01-9

An Angel's Gift

Ed Sparkleman meets his match when Alyssa drops in on the *Bar M Ranch* (literally!) and disrupts his life forever. As ranch foreman, Ed is responsible for keeping his men in order, but with Alyssa around, all the ranch hands begin to act oddly out of character . . . especially Ed. Is Alyssa truly ***An Angel's Gift*** sent straight to him from heaven? If so, what about his brother, Abbot?

Granite Publishing—ISBN# 1-930980-98-1

The Tyee's Gift

Set in the picturesque Pacific Northwest, adventure meets Abbot Sparkleman when he discovers the greatest archaeological site of the century and falls in love with the beautiful and mysterious Bekah. ***The Tyee's Gift*** will bring tears of laughter, joy and heartache while Abbot learns where much is given, much is required.

Granite Publishing—ISBN# 1932280758

Charity's Gift

Fourth book in the ***Gift Series,*** the compelling book you're reading right now!

The Refiner's Gift

The fifth and final novel in the ***Gift Series*** is now in progress, and answers the worrisome question, "What about Tom?" who was accused of a vicious crime in ***One Last Gift***, six years ago. Tom Sparkleman has not yet escaped the consequences of that crime. The miracle that awaits him in ***The Refiner's Gift*** will astound everyone. The Refiner's Gift is currently in progress.

Note: The ***Gift Series*** can be read out of sequence without losing continuity.

The Warwick Saga

Historical fiction at its very best! Story is complete in two books.

Search for the Bark Warwick

Beginning with the stowaway who interrupts and changes John's life forever, and concluding with John's desperate search for his captive son, this historical novel, based loosely on a true story, is a stirring tale of surprise, compassion, love and tenacious devotion to family. The story of a genuine hero in 1630's England, ***Search for the Bark Warwick*** will keep you on the edge of your seat, and leave you begging for more.

Granite Publishing—ISBN# 1-932280-33-2

Search for the Warwick II

Proving once and for all why she is known as the writer of miracles, Sherry Ann Miller's absorbing sequel, ***Search for the Warwick II***, concludes the search for John Dunton's son who is enslaved in 1630's Algeria, where a generous reward has been offered for John's capture. Now, John must not only find Thomas, he must avoid recapture while he and his devoted crew attempt to outsail and outmaneuver a horde of evil pirates. Nothing else matters to John or his men . . . not even their own lives.

Granite Publishing—ISBN# 1-932280-95-2

Gardenia Sunrise

A stand-alone novel and not part of any series, ***Gardenia Sunrise*** is the emotional journey of Brandje Fulton, who flees to her villa on the west coast of France, hoping to prepare herself emotionally and spiritually to meet God after she learns that she has cancer. Her plans are altered when a hot-headed American arrives for his annual holiday at the villa, unaware that his reservation has been canceled. Brandje's remarkable story is a heart-thumping, inspirational romance of the finest kind.

Granite Publishing—ISBN# 1-930980-33-7

UPCOMING BOOKS:

Scottish Legend:

Coming soon! Sherry Ann's new novella, ***Scottish Legend***, will whisk you from San Francisco to Great Britain and back again, taking your breath away in a fast-paced, action-packed tale of danger, intrigue and edge-of-your-heart romance. When FBI undercover agent, Jacey Munroe, meets legendary Scottish Lord, Rob McCormick, she is disguised as Katie Chester, the spoiled, wealthy daughter of a man standing trial in America for treason and murder. Rob, however, suspects there is more to this beautiful woman than meets the eye. Jacey diligently prevents Rob from learning the truth about her at every encounter, which not only angers him, it boggles his understanding of women. To complicate matters, Jacey and Rob are drawn to each other like a flame toward oxygen . . . a situation Jacey cannot allow. Falling in love with someone you are deceiving while working undercover is not permitted in the FBI, regardless of what your heart tells you.

From the book:

Just as abruptly as his kiss began, Rob pushed her away from him, wiping his mouth with his hand. "Ye act like a woman of means on rare occasions," he challenged. "Other times, ye seem too real, too tender to have been raised in luxury. 'Tis almost as if ye are a complete and separate entity from whom ye claim."

***

Jacey quelled her temper, but she was certain some of it showed through when she hissed, "... I've been shot, shot at, abducted, kidnaped, my pilot was poisoned in order to crash my airplane, I had to smash up a BMW protecting your life, I went sailing off a bridge and was dumped into the River Tweed, and I nearly drowned for you."

"But, that's your job, Agent Munroe," Katie whimpered.

***

Don't miss Sherry Ann Miller's upcoming, exciting novella, ***Scottish Legend.*** If you want to be notified when ***Scottish Legend*** is released to your favorite booksellers, send an e-mail to Sherry Ann, putting the title in the subject line: sherry@sherryannmiller.com

---

OTHER BOOKS IN PROGRESS:

Sariah's Back Door, a compelling time-travel mystery romance.

Victoria's Lullaby, a balance of light-hearted drama in a time-travel comedy romance.

Changing of the Guard, is Sherry Ann Miller's first non-fiction book.

Sherry writes: "***The Changing of the Guard*** is a collection of experiences I've had from beyond the veil while researching my kindred dead, and at other times as allowed by the Lord. It answers my own questions from my youth about what's on the other side. As it turns out, that question should have been, 'Who's on the other side?' "

Thank You, Mr. President, a fictional biography.

Sherry Ann Miller writes: "Years before his demise, I asked my father to write his autobiography because he had so many fantastic and incredible experiences. He answered, 'No one would believe all the stories I could tell. People would say my life was nothing but pure fiction.' With that thought in mind, this book gives a brief glimpse of Pop's life from a fictional perspective. Writing Dad's book in this manner will leave readers asking, 'Is this part true? Or did Sherry Ann make this up?' Because I admit there is fiction mixed in with the facts of my father's life, only Pop and I will know the truth. I believe this is how my dad would want his story told, if he were here to tell it himself. My siblings and I didn't joke that Dad was the 'old gaffer'[1] without justification."

---

[1]Gaff, a transitive verb, originating in 1933, meaning to deceive or trick. Gaffer, someone who gaffs.

Readers' Comments

Participate in the Readers' Comments section of my novels and receive a free, autographed copy of the book in which your comments appear. Many readers have received a free book from me, and you can, too! Simply e-mail me at sherry@sherryannmiller.com putting the title of the book in the subject line, and your comments in the body. If your comments are selected for inclusion in one of my upcoming releases, you"ll get your own autographed copy of that book, **ABSOLUTELY FREE!**

Permission to use your comments must be included, as well as your full name, and current e-mail and postal mail addresses. Thanks!

"I just wanted to write to say how much I enjoyed **The Tyee's Gift**. I stayed up until 3:30 this morning to finish it . . . My favorite book you have written is **Gardenia Sunrise**. I've read it over and over."

– Noelle Platt

"I have just finished reading **The Tyee's Gift** and I enjoyed it very much. I had already read the first two books in the series and each time was very happy to know that there was another one coming. And then when I bought this one (I have all three now) I was thrilled to know that there are two more to come. You have quickly become one of my favorite LDS authors! Thank you so much for making miracles a major part of your stories I love reading about them. And thank you for sharing your testimony. It serves to strengthen mine.

"I am also looking forward to reading ***Search for the Bark Warwick*** and ***Search for the Warwick II***. I know that I will enjoy them every bit as much as the others. It sounds like I will need to expand my collection.

"Thank you again for sharing your talents in such a delightful way."

– Sylvia B. Anderson

"I wanted to send along my thoughts and feelings about ***One Last Gift*** and ***An Angel's Gift***. I read both of them really fast, ignoring almost everything but work. The stories were both wonderful . . . I felt such a strong spirit within the stories that I had a hard time forgetting and moving on to another book after finishing them. Yes, I do believe in miracles and I am so glad for them in my life and in my heart. Thank you for sharing your strength and your spirit as you write your stories."

– Robyn Cox

"Thank you so much for your **Warwick Series**! How did you learn to fish with your fingers for bait? Have you done this yourself? I could just picture it! Your characters are so real, it's as though they became my friends! While reading your books . . . I felt for John as he searched and risked everything to save his son. I liked the way you wrapped things up in the end."

– Lora McLaughlin

"I bought ***Search for Bark Warwick*** and ***Search for the Warwick II*** on the same day and 3 days later I had finished reading both of them. I just could not put them down and I even had to make myself turn off the light at night so I could get some sleep. The story was so intriguing and I kept wondering what was going to happen next. I hope that you do a 3rd book on their life in the Americas."

– Ellen Daugharty

"I loved ***An Angel's Gift!*** It is one of my favorites. I could not put it down, it was good from beginning to end. I have told so many people about it. Keep up the good work. I can't wait for the next one!!"

– Marzzieh I.

About the author:

When Sherry Ann Miller is not hobbling around the beach near her Port Ludlow, Washington home or sailing off into the sunset aboard her 36' sailing vessel, *Shoosey-Q*, she can be found in her library, researching and writing family histories, or writing her popular, award-winning novels.

By writing miracles that foster hope and belief in a caring and loving Father in Heaven, Sherry Ann hopes to teach her readers ". . . with God, nothing shall be impossible" (Luke 1:37). She confesses, "It is only natural to include miracles in my stories because I have lived from miracle to miracle all my life . . . from the moment of my birth to the present day."

For more information about Sherry Ann Miller and her award-winning novels, please go to her website: www.sherryannmiller.com . Sherry loves to hear from her readers. Please email her at sherry@sherryannmiller.com.